T0363390

GREEK
Paradise
ESCAPE

JENNIFER FAYE

MILLS & BOON

GREEK PARADISE EDSCAPE © 2024 by Harlequin Books S.A.

GREEK HEIR TO CLAIM HER HEART
© 2022 by Jennifer F. Stroka
Australian Copyright 2022
New Zealand Copyright 2022

First Published 2022
Second Australian Paperback Edition 2024
ISBN 978 1 038 91979 3

IT STARTED WITH A ROYAL KISS
© 2022 by Jennifer F. Stroka
Australian Copyright 2022
New Zealand Copyright 2022

First Published 2022
First Australian Paperback Edition 2024
ISBN 978 1 038 91979 3

SECOND CHANCE WITH THE BRIDESMAID
© 2022 by Jennifer F. Stroka
Australian Copyright 2022
New Zealand Copyright 2022

First Published 2022
First Australian Paperback Edition 2024
ISBN 978 1 038 91979 3

Except for use in any review, the reproduction or utilisation of this work in whole
or in part in any form by any electronic, mechanical or other means, now known
or hereafter invented, including xerography, photocopying and recording, or in any
information storage or retrieval system, is forbidden without the permission
of the publisher.

This book is sold subject to the condition that it shall not, by way of trade or
otherwise, be lent, resold, hired out or otherwise circulated without the prior
consent of the publisher in any form of binding or cover other than that in which
it is published and without a similar condition including this condition being
imposed on the subsequent purchaser.

All rights reserved including the right of reproduction in whole or in part in any
form. This edition is published in arrangement with Harlequin Books S.A. Cover
art used by arrangement with Harlequin Books S.A. All rights reserved.

This is a work of fiction. Names, characters, places, and incidents are either the
product of the author's imagination or are used fictitiously, and any resemblance
to actual persons, living or dead, business establishments, events, or locales is
entirely coincidental.

Published by
Mills & Boon
An imprint of Harlequin Enterprises (Australia) Pty Limited
(ABN 47 001 180 918), a subsidiary of HarperCollins
Publishers Australia Pty Limited (ABN 36 009 913 517)
Level 19, 201 Elizabeth Street
SYDNEY NSW 2000
AUSTRALIA

MIX
Paper | Supporting
responsible forestry
FSC
www.fsc.org   FSC® C001695

® and ™ (apart from those relating to FSC®) are trademarks of Harlequin
Enterprises (Australia) Pty Limited or its corporate affiliates. Trademarks indicated
with ® are registered in Australia, New Zealand and in other countries.
Contact admin_legal@Harlequin.ca for details.

Printed and bound in Australia by McPherson's Printing Group

CONTENTS

Books by Jennifer Faye

Greek Paradise Escape

Greek Heir to Claim Her Heart
It Started with a Royal Kiss

Wedding Bells at Lake Como

Bound by a Ring and a Secret
Falling for Her Convenient Groom

The Bartolini Legacy

The CEO, the Puppy and Me
The Italian's Unexpected Heir

Her Christmas Pregnancy Surprise
Fairytale Christmas with the Millionaire

Visit the Author Profile page
at millsandboon.com.au for more titles.

Greek Heir To Claim Her Heart

Award-winning author **Jennifer Faye** pens fun, heartwarming contemporary romances with rugged cowboys, sexy billionaires and enchanting royalty. Internationally published, with books translated into nine languages, she is a two-time winner of the *RT Book Reviews* Reviewers' Choice Award. She has also won the CataRomance Reviewers' Choice Award, been named a Top Pick author and been nominated for numerous other awards.

Dear Reader,

This book was created during the pandemic, a time when the only escape was an armchair vacation. For me, it meant this trip could be as glamorous and fantastical as my imagination would allow. And who wouldn't want to visit a sunny private Greek island for a Valentine's ball, no less?

Well, now that you ask, my hero, that's who. Security expert and CEO Atlas Othonos doesn't want to visit Ludus Island and its luxury resort... even though he now owns it. Because dealing with the island means coming to terms with his painful past, and that's the last thing he wants. Atlas is determined to sell the resort to the first buyer.

Hermione Kappas has gone from a state of homelessness to being the manager of one of the world's finest resorts. In the process, the employees have become her makeshift family. But when the owner unexpectedly dies, the resort's future is at stake.

One stormy night, Atlas's and Hermione's lives collide and a friendship is born. But in the light of day, everything changes when identities are revealed. Atlas is there to destroy Hermione's world, but she's not going down without a fight.

Happy reading,

Jennifer

**Praise for
Jennifer Faye**

"A fantastic romantic read that is a joy to read from
start to finish, *The CEO, the Puppy and Me* is
another winner by the immensely talented
Jennifer Faye."

—*Goodreads*

CHAPTER ONE

CHANGES WERE AFOOT.

Changes that didn't bode well for the immediate future.

Hermione Kappas wanted to be optimistic, but at the moment she was too tired. She was the general manager of the exclusive Ludus Resort. As she'd settled into her position this past year, she thought at last her life would be peaceful and predictable—two things she hadn't had growing up. And they had been for a while, but as quick as the flip of a coin everything had once more changed.

On this particular Monday evening, darkness had come early. She yawned as she gathered her things. She hated working this late. Thankfully it was a rare occurrence.

On her way to her car, she paused in the resort's spacious lobby. "How are things going, Titus?"

The nighttime desk clerk looked up. His gaze rose over the rim of his reading glasses. His older face, trimmed with a gray mustache, lit up with a friendly smile. "It's another quiet evening, just the way I like them." He removed his glasses. Concern reflected in his eyes. "You've been working late a lot recently."

She nodded. "I have been. I hope this evening is the end of it."

She'd been coordinating all of the requested information for the independent auditors. Now that the resort's owner had unexpected died, the resort's future was uncertain. And an audit was being conducted.

She hadn't been privy to the details of the will—only the part about her having the authority to keep the resort in operation until the estate was finalized, whatever that meant. She just did as instructed by the resort's legal team.

Titus nodded in understanding. "I'll miss chatting with you each evening, but I'm sure you're anxious to have life return to normal. Be careful out there. It's an ugly night."

"I will. Good night."

She paused at the front door and stared out at the pouring rain. With it being winter, she longed for just a little snow. In the northern part of Greece where she'd grown up, there was snow in February but down here in the south, the snow was replaced by periodic rain.

So be it. It wasn't like she'd melt. She pushed open the door. Once she stepped outside, the wind immediately caught her unzipped jacket. She grabbed the flaps and held them closed. When she reached the edge of the portico, she ran across the garden area to the nearby parking lot.

The rain fell in large drops, flattening her bangs and soaking her clothes. She hurled herself into the car. Wet and disheveled, Hermione sat in the driver's seat. As she wiped the wetness from her face, the raindrops pounded on the roof.

Hermione loosened her hair from the French twist at the back of her head and finger-combed her long hair. She leaned her head back against the seat and closed her eyes, letting the constant rap-a-tap-tap of the rain lull her into a state of relaxation. After being hunched over her desk since early that morning, her body ached.

With a sigh, she started the car and set off for the ferry that would transport her to the mainland. She couldn't wait to get home. There were some leftovers in the fridge so she wouldn't even have to prepare dinner. She could even eat in bed. The tempting thought had her pressing harder on the accelerator.

Just then there was a brilliant flash of lightning. It lit up the entire sky as though it were daytime again. A crack of thunder rumbled through the car. Then as though the heavens had opened up, the rain came down even harder and faster. The car slowed to a crawl. She increased the speed of the wipers as she squinted, trying to see the roadway.

A chill of apprehension raced down her spine, leaving a trail of goosebumps in its wake. In the glow of the dashboard lights, her knuckles shone as she clutched the steering with both hands. As the wipers failed to keep up with the deluge of rain, she leaned forward, trying to see better.

A blur of white light blinded her. This time it wasn't lightning. It was a constant light and getting brighter. Headlights? Was there a vehicle headed toward her?

Her foot tramped the brake.

The weather was foul.

Just like his mood.

Atlas Othonos braked as a branch crashed onto the roadway in front of him. Luckily the road from the ferry to the Ludus Resort was deserted. He carefully wheeled around the debris and continued on his way. The strong winds pushed against the small car as though trying to shove him off the road.

Why hadn't he checked the weather forecast before deciding it was a good idea to pick up his brand-new car today of all days? He groaned in frustration. Weren't Greek islands supposed to be sunny and warm year-round?

The truth of the matter was that he didn't want to be on this small island—even though by some ironic twist of fate, it was all his. He owned an island—an exclusive island—the playground for the rich and famous. And he didn't want it. He didn't want any part of it. The sooner he could rid himself of it, the better.

His estranged mother, Thea as he called her, had died nearly two months ago. Not having seen her since he was young, he refused to acknowledge any feeling about her passing. Was that wrong? Perhaps.

Since it took Thea's attorneys a while to track him down in the States, the funeral was over before he knew what had happened. It was for the best. But the fact that she'd left everything in her will to him was not for the best. Not at all.

He'd dragged his heels as long as he could. The attorneys warned him the longer he took to sell the resort, the greater the chance of the business running into trouble. The only catch to selling the place was that he needed to oversee the estate.

The more he thought about it, the faster he drove. He'd worked so hard to avoid any of this, and in the end, he was to spend the next two weeks on the island going through his mother's personal finances and belongings. The thought twisted his gut up into a tight knot.

Atlas squinted, trying to make out the road. With the rain coming down in sheets, it was hard for him to see.

A flash of lightning or was that of headlights? Definitely headlights. They were headed straight toward him. They weren't slowing down. And they weren't moving over.

His body tensed.

He swerved.

His foot stomped the brakes. The tires slid forward over the wet pavement. He cut the steering wheel hard to the right. The car wouldn't respond. There was too much water on the road. His heart lodged in his throat. The car kept careening forward.

His body stiffened for the impact.

His car slid off the roadway and went down a small embankment. It finally slowed to a stop. With the windshield wipers rapidly swishing back and forth, he stared out into the darkness. He didn't spot the other car. Where were they?

He put the car in reverse. He pressed on the accelerator. The engine revved but the car didn't budge. Not about to give up, he tried to drive forward. But once again, the car refused to move.

A groan emanated from the back of his throat. He was stuck. He wasn't going to get his new car out of this mess without some help.

Tap-tap.

He glanced to the side to find the outline of a person holding a flashlight as they rapped on his driver's-side window. So he hadn't imagined the other car—a car that had been headed straight for him.

He rolled down the window.

"Are you all right?" a female voice called out over the noise of the wind and rain.

He squinted at her flashlight. She lowered the beam. "I'm okay. But my car needs help. Can you call for a tow?"

She straightened and checked her phone. "There's no cell service."

They were on their own on this dark stormy night. As though to confirm his thoughts, the whole sky lit up. A crack of thunder shook the ground.

Atlas's gaze moved to the crop of tall trees surrounding them. This was not a good place to be during an electrical storm. They needed out of there as quickly as possible.

There was another brilliant bolt of lightning followed by a crack of thunder. This storm was sitting right over them.

As though reading his thoughts, she said, "Come on. My car is over there."

He hesitated. "I can't just leave my car."

"Sure, you can. It's not going anywhere—at least not tonight. Are you a guest at the Ludus Resort?"

"Yes."

"Good. Let's go." She turned, and in her rush up the embankment she slipped in the mud. She landed on all fours.

"Are you all right?"

Before he could exit the car, she got to her feet and acknowledged that she was fine. By now she was soaked and muddy from her effort to help him.

With great reluctance, he grabbed his travel bags from the passenger seat and got out of the car. It was raining so hard that he was instantly soaked. As he carefully climbed the embankment, he could feel the rainwater seeping into his shoes. His back teeth ground together. Could this evening get any worse?

Once inside the car, he said, "You should learn to drive more carefully."

She hooked her seat belt. "What are you talking about?"

"You were driving in the middle of the road."

"I was not." Her restrained voice failed to mask her indignation. "Perhaps you were driving too fast for the road conditions—"

"I was not." Was he? He had been distracted. And perhaps he was taking his bad mood out on her.

He sat quietly while she slowly and carefully turned her car around. When she finally had the car straightened on the road, she barely pressed the accelerator. They were never going to reach the resort tonight if she didn't pick up the speed.

With a huff, he sat there stiffly. He stared straight ahead at the rain pounding the windshield. When they finally reached the resort, he'd insist they get someone out there to tow his car. He just hoped it wasn't damaged.

While she gripped the steering wheel with both hands, they rode on in silence. At last, the glow of lights hovered in the distance. Seconds later they came upon lampposts lining the road that led to the resort.

They parked beneath a fully lit portico. He glanced over at the woman as she undid her seat belt. Her long hair hung well past her shoulders. Even though it was wet, it had loose waves.

And when she glanced at him, he was immediately drawn in by her eyes, but she turned away before he was able to fully appreciate her beauty. She didn't say a word as she got out of the car.

He rushed to do the same. The large glass doors swept open, bidding them entrance to a marble floor that gleamed. In the center of the spacious lobby was a water fountain with lights that played off the droplets of water. It was surrounded by groups of light aqua upholstered chairs.

He glanced down at his wet clothes and shoes that were making a mess of the floor. He couldn't wait to go to his suite and get cleaned up. Except there was no one at the reception desk. He found a bell at the end of the counter. He banged his palm down on it, over and over again. He hoped the rest of the resort's service was better.

The woman covered his hand with her own. The touch jolted him from his thoughts. It felt as if an electric current had arced between them before racing up his arm and making his whole body tingle. His gaze met hers. It was then that he noticed the color of her eyes, brown with gold flecks. And right now, agitation radiated from them.

"Stop." She kept her voice low but firm.

He glanced down to where her hand rested on his. Her touch was warm and soft. As though realizing they were still touching, she swiftly moved her hand.

A door off to the side of the counter area opened. An older man rushed out. He struggled to place his black-rimmed glasses on his face. When his gaze collided with Atlas's glare, his eyes widened. And then the man took in Atlas's appearance. By the horrified expression of the desk clerk, he must look quite the mess. But it was his car he was worried about right now.

Before the clerk could utter a word, Atlas said, "There's been an accident."

The clerk's gaze moved from Atlas to the woman and then back again. "Is anyone hurt?"

"My new car. It's stuck out there in the mud. Someone has to remove it from the side of the road. And then I need to check in."

"Yes, sir. I can call for a tow and get you registered." The man hesitated as though not sure what to do first.

"Call them," Atlas said in his get-it-done-now voice.

That seemed to stir the man into action. A phone call later, the clerk wordlessly hung up. "No one answered."

"Surely there has to be someone working at this hour." He started to wonder how there could be a five-star resort in a place that was so far removed from a major city that they didn't have twenty-four-hour road service.

"I'm afraid not, sir. But I assure you it'll be a priority in the morning."

The morning? That wasn't good enough. The clerk had no idea how valuable his car was, but he would know soon.

Atlas opened his mouth to explain when the woman intervened. "That will be good, Titus. Perhaps we should get the gentleman checked in."

"Oh." Titus appeared startled out of a stupor of uncertainty. "Yes, I can do that." The man visibly swallowed. "Do you have a reservation?"

"I do."

The clerk typed something into the computer. "Last name?"

"Othonos."

"First name?"

"Atlas."

He waited, wondering if the man recognized the name. Moments passed. "There you are." The man's fingers moved rapidly over the keyboard. "You have one of our finest suites—the jungle suite."

"Sounds intriguing." Atlas glanced over to find the woman had moved toward the doors. Was she leaving? Atlas called out to her. "Surely you aren't thinking of going back out there."

"I need to go home."

"The ferry just left. It's the last trip tonight," Titus said.

The woman approached them. Her shoulders drooped. "What am I supposed to do now?"

"You could get a room for the night," Atlas suggested.

"That's not possible. The resort is fully booked." Titus sent the woman a hesitant look. "I'm sorry—"

"It's okay. I understand." A flicker of emotion reflected in her eyes, but she blinked it away before he was able to discern it.

Atlas told himself he should be happy that he'd inherited a profitable business, but he didn't think anything about his inheritance was going to make him happy—not until he signed the sales agreement. And that wasn't happening fast enough.

But in the meantime, he felt bad because if this woman hadn't stopped to help him—if she hadn't given him a ride to the resort—she would be on her way home. And now there wasn't even an available room for her to spend the night.

He turned his head, taking in the spacious lobby. There wasn't even a comfortable couch to stretch out on.

The last thing he needed was to feel bad because this woman had to sleep in her car. She'd done him a good deed, and so he'd do her one in return. "You can stay with me."

"I don't even know you."

He stepped up to her and extended his hand. "Hi. My name's Atlas Othonos. I'm the CEO of Atlas Securities. I can give you references. There's my assistant and—" He stopped himself from mentioning that his mother had owned this resort. It was a subject he wasn't prepared to delve into that night.

She eyed him up as though trying to make her mind up about him. "Thanks. But no thanks." She turned to the desk clerk. "Could you have a cot and linens sent to my office?"

Titus nodded. "Of course." And then the clerk turned to him. "If I could have your keys, sir, I'll see that your car is taken care of."

Atlas hesitated before handing over the car keys. "Thank you." He turned back to the woman. "You aren't planning to spend the night like that, are you?"

Her muddy clothes clung to her, and there were goosebumps

lining her arms. Her face and lips were pale. A sense of responsibility passed over him.

She glanced down at her disheveled clothes. "I'll be fine."

As the air conditioner kicked in, she started to shiver and his concern grew. "No, you won't. Not like that. You need a hot shower and some dry clothes. If you won't stay in my suite, at least stay long enough to get a shower and warm up." A flicker of interest shone in her eyes. "Let's go."

Even though she was shivering, she shook her head.

"If this is about us being strangers, I'll wait here in the lobby while you use my shower."

Her eyes widened with surprise. "You'd really do that?"

"I would."

"But you're wet too."

"Not as wet or cold as you."

"There are actually two bedrooms in your suite, so you wouldn't have to wait your turn."

His thoughts suddenly took a steamy turn. "I hadn't planned to share my shower, but if you're offering—"

"I'm not!" Her cheeks took on a rosy hue. "That isn't what I meant."

The rumble of laughter started low in his chest and burst forth. His amusement resulted in her fine brows knitting together in a frown.

He subdued his amusement. "I'm sorry. It's been a really long day. If there are two bedrooms, it's all the more reason for you to warm up. I promise to be a perfect gentleman."

"I don't know."

"I'll just have a seat over here until you come back." He started toward one of the chairs in the lobby.

"Wait." When he turned back to her, she said, "You need a shower and dry clothes too. Let's go."

He thought of asking if she was sure but then thought better of it. He quietly let her lead the way. A hot shower would feel really good. The truth was he was exhausted and had absolutely

no interest in sitting around the lobby. He'd been up extra early
that morning to head to the airport. Maybe some sleep would
make him less irritable.

"Here we are." The woman stopped next to an oversize wood
door.

He opened it and gestured for her to go first. His gaze followed her into the room. She was unique, and he liked all things
unique from cars to women.

CHAPTER TWO

TONIGHT HAD CERTAINLY taken an unusual turn.

Hermione stood in the suite not quite sure what to say to her undeniably handsome host. Maybe it was her being cold that had her tongue-tied. She rubbed her upper arms, hoping to chase away the chill that had taken hold of her.

Her gaze caressed his chiseled jawline before moving to linger on his kissable lips. Her attention swept up past his straight but prominent nose and came to rest on his light blue eyes framed with dark lashes and brows. He was drop-dead gorgeous. If he were a Greek god, she could imagine him being Zeus with his many lovers.

Why was a sexy man like him checking into the resort alone? It didn't happen often at the Ludus. Most often the resort hosted couples and families. It wasn't known as a singles spot.

Atlas ran his hand over his clean-shaven jaw. "Do I have something on my face?"

Heat flared in her cheeks. "Um, no. Sorry. You just remind me of someone."

"You already know who I am but I don't believe you introduced yourself." And then he sent her a dazzling smile that made her insides melt into a pool of desire.

"Hi. I... I'm Hermione Kappas." Good grief. Now he had

her stuttering. And she realized she was once again staring at him. She quickly averted her gaze.

"It's nice to meet you." He held his hand out to her. She hesitated. What was it about him that had her feeling off-kilter?

She refused to let him know that his presence got to her. She placed her hand within his. His long, lean fingers engulfed her hand. His touch was warm, and it sent an electrical current up her arm that made her heart pitter-patter. As he gave her hand a gentle shake, she came to a conclusion—this man was dangerous to her common sense. She should get away from him as fast as her mud-covered heels would carry her. And yet her feet refused to cooperate.

He released her hand. "Thank you for the help tonight."

"Glad I was there to help."

Just then her stomach decided to rumble its complaint about its lack of nourishment. Lunch had been many hours ago. And she thought she'd be home by now.

"I...ah...should go get that shower." Her gaze moved between the two bedroom doors. "Do you have a preference of which room you want?"

He shook his head. "Help yourself." As she started to walk away, he said, "Wait. You need some dry clothes."

He was right but she'd make do. She'd already imposed on him enough. But when she turned to tell him so, he was pulling clothes out of a bag.

"These will be big on you but at least they're dry." He tossed some drawstring shorts and a T-shirt at her.

She hesitated. The thought of warm, dry clothes was too much to resist. "Thank you."

She knew she should feel grateful for him going out of his way for her and leave it at that, but she had to question why he was trying so hard to be nice to her. Maybe it was just that she'd been on her own since she was seventeen when her mother had died. She'd learned the hard way that the only person you could count on was yourself.

The last man she'd trusted was her ex-boyfriend, Otis. Things had been good in the beginning. Then he'd moved in and she'd started to think they had a future together. What was the saying? Love makes you blind. That must have been what happened to her because in the end, she'd seen his true colors and she didn't like what she saw. That's when she'd kicked him out.

But she wasn't about to get involved with Mr. Tall and Sexy. However, it didn't mean she wasn't curious about the man. She wanted to know everything about him from where he came from to what he was doing on the island. And she was curious about one other thing... Her gaze strayed to his hands. No rings. Interesting.

He looked as though he wanted to say something more when his phone buzzed. "Sorry. I need to get this."

"No problem. I'm just going to go get that shower."

With his phone pressed to his ear, he moved toward his room. She turned and headed in the other direction.

She stepped inside her bedroom and closed the door behind her. Even though she'd previously been in this suite, it felt so different to be here as a semi-guest. She looked around, seeing her surroundings differently. She admired the beauty of the room and anticipated the luxurious comfort awaiting her. As a resort employee, staying in a guest suite was frowned upon.

But what did she have to worry about? It was only a shower and she was the boss...for now. Until the will was resolved, she could do as she pleased and there was no one to reprimand her. A smile pulled at her lips.

As she moved to the bathroom, she noticed that it was practically the size of her entire flat. No expense had been spared when this resort was built. And updates were completed on a regular basis.

She stepped farther into the room and admired the enormous white soaking tub. It beckoned to her. She really shouldn't give in. But she was already here, so why not indulge?

As she filled the deep white tub with warm sudsy water, she

unwrapped a purple bath bomb and smiled as she dropped it in the tub.

She quickly undressed. An inspection of her stained and torn clothes had her placing them in the garbage. Then she stepped into the warm and inviting tub. As she soaked, her thoughts drifted to Atlas. She was quite certain he wasn't soaking in a tub, though that didn't stop her mind from conjuring up the very steamy image. Her heart beat faster. Oh, what an image!

His broad shoulders had hinted at a muscular physique. Not even his tailored suit could hide the fact that he worked out, probably daily. And boy did it pay off. Not that she was interested. Not even a little. Okay, maybe just a little.

But she had her career to think about now. And with the future of the Ludus up in the air, she had to be prepared to fight for the livelihoods of her employees. She just hoped it didn't come to that drastic measure.

CHAPTER THREE

SHE WAS UNFORGETTABLY BEAUTIFUL.

And an indulgence he couldn't afford right now.

Atlas wasn't at the Ludus Resort for a holiday. He was here to conduct business—at least that's the way he'd come to regard his mother's estate. Because to consider what it truly meant would mean scratching back scabs on old wounds. It would mean dragging to the surface emotions he'd worked for years to bury.

Now with room service ordered, he'd showered and changed into a fresh button-up and jeans. He rolled up his sleeves as he stepped out of his bedroom into the living room. He glanced around the suite, taking in the details from the palms and trees that soared up to the second-story ceiling with fake cockatoos and parakeets in the trees to the forest green wallpaper. He couldn't help but wonder how the other rooms were decorated. Or what Thea's private apartment was like—not that he wanted to spend time there. He wanted nothing to do with her things.

He turned his thought to his security business. For him, working was like breathing. His business was the reason he got out of bed in the morning.

Whereas people were unreliable, his business never let him down. It was there for him each day, and it rewarded him for all of his efforts. As it was, if he didn't work another day in his life, he would never want for a thing in his life.

But at this late hour, business was concluded in Europe. He grabbed his phone to check his messages and answered a couple of emails that he'd received while he'd been in transit to the island.

He decided to send a text message to his old friend, Krystof.

Have arrived. This resort has a lot of promise. Will send pictures soon.

He slipped the phone back in his pocket. No sooner had he done that than it vibrated. He withdrew it to find a response.

Looking forward to them. Can't wait to see in person.

Come now. We can see it together.

Can't. Playing cards in Monaco.

Krystof was always moving from one challenge or game of chance to the next. He was a nomad much like himself. But he was the one person Atlas knew and trusted that had the funds to buy this place.

Come as soon as possible.

I'll check my calendar. Maybe next week.

See you then.

Atlas returned the phone to his pocket. By next week, he planned to be finished with this part of his life. The sooner, the better.

He sat down on the hunter green leather couch, finding it surprisingly comfortable. In his vast experience of traveling from one place to another, he'd found most hotel furniture looked nice but ended up being terribly uncomfortable. Not so with the Ludus Resort.

Was it Thea who'd put all of the thought into this resort with its themed suites and furniture that not only looked good but felt good too? Not that he cared what Thea did. Just as she'd never cared what he did.

Knock-knock.

He welcomed the interruption. Thinking about Thea only angered him. Why she'd left this island to him seemed like some sort of cruel joke.

When he opened the door, he found a server wearing a black-and-white uniform pushing a white linen-covered cart with two covered dishes, and yellow and purple flowers in the center. Once the food was placed on the dining table next to the window overlooking the stormy evening, the cart was removed.

Atlas turned to find Hermione had emerged from her room. Her long hair was wet and hanging down her back. His clothes engulfed her petite frame. Even so, she looked adorable.

"Would you care to join me at the table?" He gestured to an empty chair.

She hesitated. "I don't want to intrude any further."

"You won't be. And I ordered enough for two. What do you say? Will you join me?"

She hesitated as though considering her options. "I did miss dinner."

"All the more reason for you to join me." He pulled out a chair for her before taking a seat himself.

She lifted the lid from her plate. "Breakfast food?"

He nodded. "I travel a lot, and I've found this food appetizing at any hour. I wasn't sure what you'd like, so it's a little bit of everything. But if you want something else, I'll call down to the kitchen. They are open twenty-four hours a day, but you already know that."

"This is fine. Thank you."

They ate quietly as though each were lost in their own thoughts—thoughts of the accident, thoughts of how their lives had collided and thoughts of what tomorrow would bring each of them. He turned his gaze to the window and stared out at the turbulent night as lightning etched against the dark sky.

If not for the storm, he would have missed meeting Hermione. She was different from the other women who'd passed through his life. Hermione wasn't chatty. She hadn't told him her whole life's story in the first five minutes of their meeting.

Instead, he found her to be a mystery of silent looks. Her eyes let him know there was a lot going on in her mind, but whatever her thoughts were, she was keeping them to herself. The quieter she became, the more he wanted to know what was going on behind her captivating brown eyes.

"Was your meal good?" he asked.

She nodded. "It was."

And then she looked at him like she was trying to read his thoughts. She wasn't the first one to look at him that way. But he liked to think of himself as unreadable.

"Will anyone be joining you?" she asked.

He couldn't help but wonder where this conversation was headed. He thought of his invitation for Krystof to join him here on the island, but he knew that wasn't what she meant. But she didn't appear to be trying to hit on him. So what was her angle?

Curiosity got the best of him. "No."

"No wife? Or girlfriend?"

She surprised him with her very pointed questions. "Just me."

It wasn't that he didn't have relationships—if that's what you wanted to call them—it's that he wasn't any good at them. At least that's what he'd been told as the women exited his life.

Maybe he didn't try hard enough to make any of the relationships work. Or maybe they saw what his mother had seen in him—he wasn't worthy of love. Either way, he focused all of his energy on his business. It hadn't let him down.

Hermione nodded as though he was giving all of the right

answers. "This just doesn't seem like the sort of destination for a single man."

He sat up straighter. "Why not?"

She shrugged. "The resort doesn't exactly have much of a nightlife or an abundance of single women."

His gaze moved to her hands. No rings. He ignored the excitement that raced through his blood. He hadn't intended to have a holiday fling, but now he was reconsidering his options.

"What about you?" If she could ask personal questions, so could he. "Are you single?"

She hesitated. "I am."

He smiled. "See. I didn't even have to look around and yet I found the most beautiful single woman on the island."

That's all it took to bring a rosy hue to her cheeks. And it made her even more attractive. Oh, yes, a holiday fling was becoming more appealing by the moment.

"You probably say that to all of the women." She reached for her water glass and took a sip.

"Trust me. I don't throw around compliments lightly." It was true. He used them sparingly and only when he truly meant them.

As his phone vibrated in his pocket, it reminded him that he had his hands full while he was on the island. He had to stay on top of his security business while cleaning out Thea's apartment and retrieving all of the documents in her personal safe. In addition, he had to make sure the property was ready to hit the market. And he planned to have it all done in less than two weeks.

In order to meet his aggressive timetable, he had to stay focused on his mission. But maybe Hermione could help him in a different way. "How much do you know about the island? I mean you must know most everything, right?"

She shrugged. "What are you curious about?"

"This is my first visit here." *And my last.* "As you probably know, this resort doesn't have a website. And there really aren't many pictures of it online."

"That's because the island has a privacy policy. It gives the rich and famous a chance to unwind and enjoy themselves without the risk of ending up in a tabloid."

"But doesn't it make it hard to lure in new visitors?"

"Not really." She frowned at him. "You make it sound like you're a journalist." And then her eyes narrowed in on him. "Listen, if you're here to write some exposé—"

"I'm not a journalist." When she continued to stare at him with suspicion reflected in her eyes, he said, "I swear. I'm not."

"You sure sound like one."

How was he supposed to convince her that he wasn't a journalist? "Do you really think a journalist could afford to stay here?"

She paused as though giving the idea consideration. "Your publisher could pick up the tab."

He inwardly groaned. She wasn't going to give him any slack. And then he had an idea. "Wait here." He moved to his room and quickly returned. He sat down and handed her a card. "This is my business card."

She read it. "You install security systems like they sell on television?"

He couldn't help but laugh at her underwhelmed expression. It'd been a long time since someone didn't recognize him or his company. "Not exactly. Atlas Securities develops and installs very sophisticated systems."

She yawned. "I'm sorry."

He found himself smiling at her bored expression. She was definitely unique. The more he got to know her, the more he liked her. "It's okay. My business doesn't excite everyone."

"No, it's not that. It's just been a really long day. I had to finish a special project and it wiped me out."

"What sort of project?"

She shook her head. "You don't want to hear about that tonight or I'll put us both to sleep." She yawned again. "We should call it a night."

"Agreed." He set aside his napkin and got to his feet. "Are you sure I can't convince you to stay in the guest room?"

She shook her head and then walked away. At the door, she turned back. "Thank you for the shower and food." And then color bloomed in her cheeks. "And the clothes."

When she started out the door, he asked, "Will I see you again?"

"It's a big resort. Probably not." And then she was gone.

He was sorry to see their evening end so soon. They were beginning to be friends and he liked that idea. Having a friend on the island might make his job here less painful. Maybe tomorrow he'd seek her out—to help him find his way around the island. Yes, that sounded like a fine idea.

CHAPTER FOUR

HAD LAST NIGHT been some sort of dream?

When Hermione opened her eyes the next morning, she glanced around, finding herself in her office, wearing clothes that most definitely weren't her own. Last night had been no dream.

She wasn't ready to move. Not yet. She closed her eyes, and her mind filled with the image of the handsome man she'd met last night. At first he'd been rather testy, but then he'd offered her a hot bath, food and the clothes off his back. Okay, maybe they weren't off his back, but it had been a kind gesture. She lifted the T-shirt to her nose and inhaled the faint spicy scent that clung to the soft material. Mmm… She inhaled again, deeper this time.

The alarm on her phone went off. She reached for it on the floor and checked the time. As her gaze focused on the numbers, she groaned. She needed to get moving.

The first thing she did was call one of the resort's boutiques and request they send over an outfit. Next she located some sample toiletries in her bottom desk drawer. She took them to the ladies' room where she styled her hair into her usual French twist. She liked its sleek professional look and the way it kept

her long hair out of her way as she leaned over her desk to review reports.

After rushing through her morning routine, she returned to
the office and called the car garage about Atlas's...er... Mr.
Othonos's vehicle. They promised to immediately see to tow-
ing and detailing it.

Knock-knock.

She swung open the office door to find a young woman
with a rack of clothes. Hermione didn't recognize her. Her gaze
moved to the name tag: Iona. She must be one of the new hires.
Now wasn't exactly the right moment for an introduction.

She quickly sorted through the selections. The clothes that
had been chosen for her were of bright, cheerful colors, everything Hermione wasn't feeling right now. She picked the least
vibrant shade, a peachy-pink-colored outfit. She thanked the
young woman and sent the rest of the clothes back to the boutique.

Her gaze moved to the price tag on the outfit. She stifled
a moan. The clothes cost as much as her monthly rent, but
what choice did she have? Her navy-blue business suit had been
stained, and there had been a tear across the knee from when
she'd fallen. She'd left it in the trash back at Atlas's suite.

When she was ready to face the world—ready to face Atlas—
she headed for the door. She moved quickly through the quiet
hallways. The closer she got to Atlas's suite, the faster her pulse
raced. Last night, she told herself she wasn't going to see him
again, but...well...she did have his clothes. And she really
should thank him again for all he'd done for her last night.

When she stopped in front of his door, her palms grew
clammy. Before she lost her nerve, she knocked.

When Atlas opened the door, his gaze met hers. She felt as
though she could drown in his mesmerizing blue eyes. Her heart
thump-thumped in her chest. And when he smiled, she noticed
how his eyes twinkled. She subdued a dreamy sigh.

She forced herself to look away. If she didn't get the words out quickly, she feared she'd forget her reason for being at his door.

"Here are your clothes." She handed them to him. "Thank you for last night—"

Someone cleared their throat.

Oh, no! He isn't alone.

She glanced past him and into the room. Hermione's heart sunk down to the white canvas shoes she'd been supplied by the boutique. There before her stood Adara Galanis, the resort's concierge and her friend. When their gazes met, Adara's eyes momentarily widened in surprise.

Atlas stepped back and bid her entrance to the suite. Hermione didn't know what to say as she stepped forward. Heat engulfed her cheeks as he closed the door behind her. How was she supposed to explain any of this?

Atlas cleared his throat. "This is Hermione. She came to my rescue last night and ended up stranded on the island."

Adara's startled gaze moved between her and Atlas. "I heard about the accident and as the concierge, I wanted to personally offer my services. If there's anything I can do—"

"Yes, you can make sure my car is detailed and inspected," Atlas said.

"I've already taken care of your car," Hermione said. "It was the first thing I did this morning."

Adara sent her a concerned look. "Hermione, are you okay?"

"Perfectly fine. Not a scratch on me." She tried to sound calm and in control, but being this close to Atlas made her insides shiver with nervous energy. "His car was the only one involved in the accident."

His gaze moved between the two women. "You two know each other?"

"Of course," Adara said. "Hermione is the resort manager. She didn't tell you?"

His gaze narrowed on Hermione. "No. She failed to mention it last night."

At first she'd kept her position from him because he'd been agitated about his car. And later it was just easier to keep things casual. The muscles around Hermione's chest tightened like a vise.

"I can explain," she said.

Atlas shook his head. "I don't have time for explanations. I'm expecting a very important business call." He turned to walk away. "Just go."

"Wait. Give me a moment to explain." Hermione moved to block his exit.

His gaze caught hers. The anger reflected in his eyes stopped her in her tracks. He walked around her and strode into his room. The door closed behind him with a resounding thud.

The breath trapped in her lungs. She had totally messed this up.

First, there had been the downpour followed by his accident. And now she'd made a huge miscalculation by not admitting last night that she ran the entire resort. A little voice in her head said to just walk away. It didn't matter if he liked her or not. They would never see each other again. But there was this other part of her that had started to like him.

Resort manager.

He was still surprised to learn Hermione was in charge of the resort. He couldn't help but notice how she'd purposely left out that detail last night. He couldn't help but wonder why.

Had she recognized him? Had his mother shown her a press release of him? Surely not. Thea's life hadn't had room for him.

The questions mounted one right after the other. He raked his fingers through his hair as he tried to discern what sort of angle Hermione was working. Usually he was able to see a con from afar but with her, he hadn't sensed a thing.

Whatever. He had work to do—contracts to review, emails to

answer and that phone call that still hadn't come. All in all, he didn't have time to play games. In his spacious bedroom, he sat down at the large desk facing the wall of windows overlooking the beach, but he didn't take the time to appreciate the beauty of the scenery. Instead, he opened his laptop and set to work.

As his fingers moved over the keyboard, his thoughts repeatedly drifted back to Hermione. He replayed their meeting in his mind. Perhaps he hadn't made the best first impression. He wasn't usually this agitated.

Perhaps Hermione hadn't announced her position because he hadn't made her feel comfortable enough to reveal her true identity. And there was the fact that he hadn't admitted who he was either.

Knock-knock.

When he didn't immediately respond, Hermione called out, "Mr. Othonos, can we speak?"

He pressed Send on an email to his assistant in the London office. "I'll be out."

Her heels clicked over the marble floor as she retreated. He didn't rush out to speak to her. He wasn't used to being summoned. He was the one who did the summoning. And so he answered one more email.

Then he quietly joined her in the living room. He glanced around, finding that they were now alone. As though she sensed his presence, she turned. Their gazes met and held for a second too long. In that moment, he forgot about his irritation with her.

Her dark hair was pulled back in a much too severe style. He imagined unpinning her hair and letting it flow down over her shoulders. Definitely better. His fingers tingled with the temptation to comb through her long silky locks.

And then there was her beautiful face with dimples in her cheeks. High cheekbones led to a pert little nose, but it was her brown eyes that drew him in. His pulse spiked. And when a smile pulled ever so slightly at her lips, he realized that he'd let himself get distracted for much too long.

He glanced just past her left shoulder and out the window at the gray sky. He cleared his throat. And then proving to himself that he had control over his reaction to her nearness, his gaze met hers again. "Why weren't you honest about who you were last night?"

Emotions flickered in her eyes, but in a blink, they were hidden behind a wall of diplomacy. "I'm sorry if you feel I was in some way dishonest with you."

Her restrained manner and resistance to admit her error only succeeded in further agitating him. "I didn't ask for an apology. I want an explanation."

"You were dealing with enough last night with your car going off the road—by the way it will be delivered a little later this morning."

"I hope they're careful." He frowned at her. "You know none of this would be necessary if you had stayed on your side of the road last night?"

She opened her mouth to argue with him but wordlessly closed it. In the light of day, she couldn't deny that she forced him off the road.

He expected to feel some sort of satisfaction at her acknowledgment of fault, but he didn't. Okay, it wasn't exactly an acknowledgment. It was more like a lack of denial. Either way, he'd been in the right and her in the wrong.

She blinked and then two lines formed between her fine brows. "I can assure you the garage does exceptional work."

"You don't understand. That car is unique. There's not another one out there like it." When she still looked confused, he said, "It's a kit car with every upgrade you can imagine. I just picked it up. I'm planning to have it shipped back to London."

She looked at him like he'd just spoken a foreign language. She obviously wasn't a sports car aficionado. "I thought you would be happy to have it back as quickly as possible."

He raked his fingers through his hair. She was right. He

wasn't usually this on edge. It was being here in this place—Thea's place. He didn't want to be here.

"Of course," he said. "Thank you for seeing to it. This place just unnerves me."

The words had crossed his lips before he'd realized that he'd said too much. His pulse raced. It was though the earth had shifted beneath his feet. A moment ago he'd been Atlas Othonos, founder and CEO of Atlas Securities, and soon he would be known on the island as Thea's son. It was a title he hadn't worn since he was a little boy. It was a title he never thought he'd have again.

Hermione's gaze searched his. "I don't understand."

"Thea is, er, was my mother."

Her eyes widened. "We heard the island had been inherited, but we weren't even sure Thea's son was still alive."

"Why wouldn't I be alive?" His voice came out harsher than he'd intended.

Had his mother told everyone he was dead? The thought sickened him. It was one thing not to want to be a part of his life but quite another to want him dead. Could his mother have been that cruel?

"I'm sorry," Hermione said. "It's just none of us have ever seen you around the resort."

How did he explain this? And then he decided he didn't have to explain any of it. It was none of her business.

"My mother and I weren't close." That was as much as he was willing to admit. It wasn't anything Hermione couldn't surmise on her own. "But I would appreciate if you kept this information to yourself."

"You don't want anyone to know that you now own the resort?" Hermione asked.

"No, I don't. At least not yet."

"But you'll want to get to know the staff right away—"

"No, I won't."

Her diplomatic expression slid from her face. In its place was a look of surprise. "Why not?" Her eyes widened as though she realized she'd just vocalized her thoughts. "I mean is there a better time for you to tour the resort?"

"I don't need to see it. I'm selling it." He pressed his lips together.

He hadn't intended to tell anyone about his plans yet, but there was something about Hermione that had him acting out of character. Now he braced himself for a barrage of reasons that selling the resort was a bad idea.

"What? But why?" Her gaze searched his.

"I can't keep it." Still she sent him an expectant stare so he added, "My life isn't here. It's in London." It wasn't the whole truth but it was enough of it.

Concern reflected in her eyes. "But what about the resort? Will it be kept the same?"

Once again he raked his fingers through his hair. She wanted answers from him that he didn't have. "I don't know. That will be up to the new owners."

"But you haven't even seen the resort yet. You might change your mind about selling it."

He shook his head. "The sale is going to happen. The only question is when. Now if you don't mind, I have work to do."

He walked her to the door. He could tell the wheels of her mind were turning. This conversation might be over for the moment, but he had no doubt she would broach the subject in the near future. And his answer would be the same—the resort was for sale.

CHAPTER FIVE

THIS MORNING WAS not going well.

That was one of the biggest understatements of her life.

Hermione wondered what else could go wrong. Her steps were quick as she hurried down the spacious hallway. She forced a smile to her face as she greeted everyone she passed. It wasn't her staff's fault that she'd had the most unfortunate run-in with the resort's heir. Or the fact that he was the most stubborn, annoying man to ever walk the earth. Okay, maybe that was a bit over the top, but he really got under her skin.

How could Atlas not even slow down and consider keeping the island? Who wouldn't want their very own island? Wasn't that what dreams were made of?

But, no. He didn't even want to hear about how profitable the resort was, or how it basically ran itself, so his immediate intervention wasn't needed…or wanted.

Now what was she supposed to do? Start looking for a new position elsewhere? The thought left a sour feeling in the pit of her stomach.

The Ludus Resort was more than her place of employment. It was her makeshift home. Without having any relatives of her own, she'd adopted the resort employees or rather they'd adopted her. She wasn't quite sure of which way it'd happened.

But the point was she would be lost without this great big, loving group of people.

She glanced at her smartwatch. She had almost two thousand steps already. It was the pacing she'd done in Atlas's suite. And now it was five minutes before the start of the workday. She'd meant to get to her office much sooner, but the run-in with Atlas had taken longer than she'd anticipated. Not that her pleading had done a thing to sway his decision about the fate of the resort.

Her assistant, Rhea, glanced up from her desk as Hermione walked through the doorway. "Good morning."

So far there was nothing good about it. Still, it wasn't Rhea's fault. Hermione forced another smile to her lips. "Morning."

Rhea's gaze followed her as she crossed the outer office to her doorway, but her assistant didn't say another word.

With the door closed, Hermione's thoughts returned to Atlas. She'd always wondered what had happened between Thea and her son. Her friend was always light on the details of their estrangement, but Hermione was starting to figure things out. And she didn't like what she saw.

In fact, she was really worried. She sank down on her desk chair. Whereas the Ludus was steeped in traditions from the employees' monthly luncheon to the annual regatta, Atlas didn't seem to care for tradition.

She blew out a frustrated sigh. More changes were coming to the Ludus. And she would predict that they weren't going to be good for her or the staff. Even worse, she didn't know how to stop Atlas. How did you stop an heir from doing what they wanted with their inheritance?

"Hermione?" Rhea's voice interrupted her troubling thoughts.

She glanced up. "What did you say?"

Rhea hesitantly stepped in her office. "I asked if everything is all right."

"Uh, yeah. Perfect." Everything was so not perfect. It was anything but perfect.

"That outfit is pretty. Is it new?"

Hermione glanced down and wanted to say that it was just something she'd pulled out of the back of her closet, but she couldn't bring herself to lie. It just wasn't who she was. Instead, she nodded.

Rhea smiled. "I was tempted to buy it."

She was so busted. "I… I just decided to splurge."

Rhea's eyes sparkled with amusement. "What's his name?"

"What?" Heat immediately rushed to her cheeks. "It's not like that. There is no he. Surely you don't think I had a one-nighter with a guest." She pressed her lips together to keep from rattling on and digging a hole deeper for herself.

"It's okay. Relax. I heard about the accident."

"You did?"

She smiled and nodded. "Titus let me know you had a rough night."

The heat in her cheeks increased until the roots of her hair felt as though they might instantaneously ignite. "It's not like you're thinking."

"I'm thinking that you got stranded on the island and there weren't any available rooms so you slept in your office."

"Oh." Hermione was caught off guard. It took her frenzied mind a moment to catch up with reality. "It is exactly what you were thinking."

Rhea stepped out to her desk and soon returned with a pair of scissors in hand. She approached Hermione. "Stand up and turn around."

"What?" She really needed some caffeine because she was having problems following Rhea's words. "Why?"

She continued to smile at her. "Trust me."

And so Hermione did as she was told. There was a distinct snip and then Rhea adjusted the neckline on Hermione's top.

"Okay. You can turn around."

When she did Rhea was standing there holding a tag. Oops. She'd been in such a rush that morning that she'd forgotten to remove it. She inwardly groaned. She wondered how many people had seen the tags hanging off her clothes.

Atlas! He would have seen her blunder. The heat rushed back to her cheeks. The best thing she could do was just keep her distance from him. It was obvious she didn't think clearly around him and in turn she rubbed him the wrong way.

"Thank you."

"Anytime. You would have done the same for me."

Hermione nodded. Friends watched out for each other. "Now I'm going to go hide in my office all morning. If anyone wants me, I'm not here."

Rhea arched a brow. "Seriously?"

Hermione sighed. "No. But it is tempting."

Rhea closed the door on her way out, giving Hermione a chance to gather herself. Perhaps she took more comfort in her morning routine than she'd realized because she felt utterly rattled and out of sorts.

She moved to her coffee maker and brewed a cup. She was never more grateful than now that it only took a couple of minutes to create a steaming cup of coffee. She added some sweetener and creamer and gave it a stir before carrying it to her desk.

It was there that she settled into her work, and soon she was caught up in reviewing department budgets and approving large disbursements. For a moment, she forgot about everything, including the man with the sky-blue eyes.

She didn't know how much time had passed when there was a knock at the door. She glanced up to find Adara standing there. "Do you have moment?"

Hermione waved her in. "What's up?"

"I just wanted to tell you how sorry I am about this morning. I didn't mean to make things awkward for you."

If she was upset with anyone, it was herself. "Don't worry about it. And just for the record, I didn't spend the night with him." She explained how she'd used the shower and then slept in the office. "Thank goodness I didn't. He's Thea's son."

Adara's eyes widened as her mouth gaped. "He is?"

She nodded. "It came out after you left. He was upset that I hadn't told him I was the manager."

Adara settled on the arm of the chair across from Hermione's desk. "Why didn't you?"

"Because he was really upset last night, and I didn't want to make things worse."

"And how are things with you two now?"

Hermione leaned back in her chair. "Not good. He's selling the resort."

Her eyes widened. "He is?"

She nodded. "I offered to give him a tour but he declined. He said he had work to do."

"So he's in his suite working instead of enjoying all of the resort's amenities?"

"I guess so. I haven't checked on him."

"Don't you think you should? I mean if he sells this place, everything is going to change. You need to show him that he's making a big mistake."

Hermione shook her head. "You didn't hear him. He's very determined. And he's angry with me because he thinks I ran his precious car off the road last night."

"Oh, no. That's not good. Did you apologize?"

"No." Her response came out harsher than she'd intended. "I didn't do anything wrong. The road was flooded. He must have overcorrected and gone off the road. Anyway, I had the garage tow his car today. They're cleaning it up and having it delivered this morning."

Adara nodded. "So then he had nothing to be upset about. You should try again and show him that the Ludus is special."

Hermione resisted the urge to roll her eyes. "I don't think anything will convince him of that. Certainly not me saying it. It's like he arrived on the island all set to hate the place and anyone associated with it."

"Then give him things to like about the Ludus—like the employees." Adara smiled brightly. "We're a great group, if I do say so myself. Once he meets us, he'll have to like us."

At last Hermione smiled. "You think that highly of this group?"

"I do. I really do." Adara pondered the idea for a moment. "You know the best way to immerse him in the atmosphere is to bring him to lunch today."

"Today?" She shook her head. "I don't think he'd be interested in a covered dish lunch. He doesn't strike me as the social type."

"We'll see about that." Adara stood. "You get him to the lunchroom and I'll spread the word that we need to melt his frosty exterior. After all, he's Thea's son. Surely he has a heart in there somewhere." She made a quick exit.

"I wouldn't count it," Hermione muttered under her breath.

The last thing she wanted was to deal with that man again. He was like a grumpy old man. Only he wasn't old; in fact, he didn't appear to be much older than her. And maybe he did have a reason to be grumpy. After all, if she'd just picked up a new car, she'd probably be upset if it went off the road and got stuck in mud.

And then there was the death of his mother. Close or not, that had to hit him hard. At the very least, it had to make him feel his mortality. It was one of the many things she'd felt when she lost her own mother.

She sighed. Had she really just talked herself into giving him another chance? It would appear so. She just wondered how he felt about home cooking because that's what they served for their monthly employee luncheon.

His phone rang nonstop all morning.

Atlas frowned as he stared blindly at his laptop. The voice of his vice president sounded over Atlas's speakerphone. He knew he shouldn't have come to the island. He'd only been gone one night and there were already problems. He should be back in London so he could go to the office and straighten out this mess in person.

But on a good note, by midmorning a resort employee had returned his keys. His car was now safely tucked away in the resort's private garage. Atlas had immediately given it a thorough personal inspection as well as a short test drive. Thankfully no damage had been done.

"What do you want to do?" The VP's voice drew Atlas from his meandering thoughts.

He gave his company's problem some serious thought. "I want the head of our installation department to fly to the embassy, and I want him to do what needs to be done to fix this problem. And I want him on a plane today."

"Yes, sir. I'll see to it."

"Make sure you do. Because as of now, this is your highest priority. No. This is your only priority. The embassy is counting on us to get this right or we can forget about any future national security contracts."

"I'm on it."

"On second thought, I want you on the plane too. I need someone on the ground who can smooth things out." He'd do it himself, but that would mean dragging out the mess with Thea's estate even longer.

There was a distinct pause on the other end of the line. "Yes, sir."

"Keep me updated."

Ding-dong.

"What was that, sir?"

"That is an interruption I don't need right now. See that this problem is corrected." And then Atlas ended the call.

Ding-dong.

Someone was certainly impatient. He couldn't imagine who it might be. He swung the door open and was surprised to find Hermione had returned so quickly. For a second, his voice failed him. Had they set up a meeting and he'd forgotten about it? No. Not possible.

"Can I help you?" he asked.

She sent him another tentative smile that didn't go all the way to her eyes. Then as a happy couple strolled by, Hermione waited until they'd moved further down the hallway before speaking. "Can we talk?"

He opened the door farther and stepped aside. "Come in." After she'd stepped inside, he said, "I don't have much time. You'll have to make it quick."

"Have you been in this suite all morning?"

"Yes. I have work to do."

"So why come to the island?" She looked at him expectantly.

His body stiffened. So much for them starting over. "You know why I'm here, to deal with my mother's things."

"You could have just had someone box up her things and ship them to you."

She was right. Why hadn't he done that? Why hadn't the thought even crossed his mind? When he'd received news of her death via his office, his first thought was to come here. But by the time he'd heard the news, the funeral was over. He was left figuring out why he suddenly felt so much more alone on this great big planet.

His brain said he shouldn't feel anything about Thea's passing. After all, it wasn't like they were a part of each other's lives. And that had all been her decision. She's the one who walked away and left him behind.

And yet there was this hollow spot in his chest that felt as though something was now missing. He refused to explore that feeling further. He was here to do a job, nothing more.

He cleared his throat. "Is there a reason you're here, Ms. Kappas?"

"It's Hermione. And yes, there is a reason. Have you eaten lunch yet?"

Was it that late, already? He consulted his Rolex. Yes, it was that late. "No, I haven't."

"Then come with me." She started for the door without even waiting for his response.

He started after her, prepared to set her straight. "Listen, I don't have time to go to lunch with you." He was out the door, trying to catch up with her. "I have work to do."

She paused in the hallway to glance back at him. "And you have to eat in order to do your work." She gestured behind him. "Don't forget to close the door."

He glanced over his shoulder to find she had him so distracted that he had walked out the door without a thought to closing it. He retraced his steps and did just that. Then he took long, rapid steps to catch up to her.

"I don't think you understand," he said. "I run a huge international security company. I have things that need my attention." Just then his stomach growled as though in protest to him trying to skip out on another meal.

She glanced over at him and arched a brow. "You need to take care of you. And besides, I think you'll enjoy this lunch."

He sighed. "Couldn't we just order room service?"

She shook her head. "This is better than room service. Trust me."

That was the problem. He didn't trust her. He didn't even know her. Still, he walked with her. Maybe he'd order some food to take back to his room.

They appeared to be heading away from the lobby and common areas, which he found odd. Why wouldn't the restaurants be in highly trafficked areas? Perhaps it was something the new owner should correct.

Hermione swiped her employee card to open a set of heavy steel doors. He caught the placard on the door that said: No Entrance. Employees Only.

"Where are we going?" He glanced around the brightly lit

hallway, taking in the buzz of voices mingled with the hum of machines.

"You'll soon see. We're almost there."

Maybe he had been a little too focused on his work, but that was how he'd built his company to be one of the biggest and best in the world. The only problem with being the biggest and best was that there was nowhere to go from there. It was though his drive was starting to wane and he found himself looking for a new challenge. He just didn't know what that would be. Nor did he have time to figure it out—not with the embassy problem to sort out.

Just as he was about to tell Hermione that he didn't have time for this expedition, she stopped in front of a door. She turned to him with a smile. "We're here."

Here? He glanced around. This wasn't a restaurant.

Hermione opened the door and stepped inside. He followed her because he'd come this far, he might as well see what this was all about.

The first thing he noticed were the delicious aromas. They smacked him in the face and sent him spiraling back in time to when he was a little boy. He recalled how much his mother used to love to cook. Their kitchen used to be filled with the most delicious aromas of fresh herbs, clove and allspice. He hadn't thought of that in a long time.

Another memory came flooding back of his mother saving him leftovers from his favorite meals. She would say growing boys needed extra helpings. His father didn't agree. And so she would hide the food and let Atlas eat it when his father was at work. He'd felt so special, so loved—

He gave himself a mental shake, pushing away the unwanted memory. Because the only thing that mattered was that Thea had left him.

His gaze scanned the room as he tried to figure out why they were here. The room was filled with tables and people—lots of people. Most were dressed in work uniforms from maid outfits to cooking staff and some in janitorial coveralls.

Atlas stopped and turned to Hermione, feeling as though he'd somehow been set up. "What are we doing here?"

"I thought you'd want to meet the employees. They are excited to meet you." And without giving him a chance to say that it was the last thing he wanted to do, she turned to the people. A hush had come over the crowd as they stared at him as though trying to decide what to make of him. "Hi, everyone. I'd like you to meet Thea's son, Atlas. He is the new owner of the resort and I hope you'll give him a big, warm welcome."

Suddenly people surged forward with their hands outstretched. Some wore smiles while others sent him hesitant looks. They all wanted one thing from him—the knowledge that their lives weren't about to change. This was exactly what he'd been hoping to avoid. They wanted a promise he couldn't give them. And so he artfully darted around the subject of the future of the resort. Instead, he found himself focusing on the here and now—which meant promising them that he would tour the resort.

It felt as though he'd just fallen into a trap—a trap set by the beautiful manager. He'd most definitely underestimated her. He glanced around for Hermione, but she'd disappeared into the sea of Ludus employees.

It would appear this was some sort of special employee luncheon. He missed the part about why they were holding such a luncheon, but he was handed a plate. Food was heaped on it, so much so that it took both of his hands to hold it.

Now he felt obligated to view the resort because one thing he wasn't was a liar. And he had Hermione to thank for this latest development. So if he could miss work to tour the grounds, so could she. Although the thought of spending more time with the crafty manager didn't sound so bad; in fact she intrigued him.

It was working.

Or perhaps it was a bit of wishful thinking.

Hermione couldn't decide if Atlas was putting on a good show for the employees or if he was starting to let down his guard with them. She hadn't spoken to him throughout lunch. It wasn't that she was avoiding him, it was that he was constantly surrounded by employees greeting him.

But now that lunch was over, the crowd was thinning. Atlas approached her. It was impossible to tell what effect the luncheon had on him. His poker face gave nothing away.

He leaned in close to her ear. "That little trick wasn't very nice of you."

"Would you have agreed to come if I'd have told you we were eating with the employees?"

"No. Because it won't change my mind about the sale."

She resisted the urge to sigh. She'd never met such a stubborn man. Maybe Adara could reason with him because she was done with him. "Well, I need to get back to my office—"

"Not so fast. Thanks to your plotting, I've now promised the employees that I'd tour the resort and I've chosen you to be my guide."

"Me." This had to be a joke. He didn't even like her.

The corners of his mouth lifted in a devious smile. "Where shall we start?"

Her phone buzzed, distracting her. She withdrew her phone from her pocket and checked the screen. "Something has come up. I must go."

"Not so fast. If I'm going to miss work for this tour, so are you."

She shook her head. "You don't understand. The royal jewels have arrived. I must go sign for them."

"What are royal jewels doing at the resort?"

"I don't have time to explain now. Do you remember how to get back to your suite?"

"I can manage. But I'm coming with you."

So all it took were some famous jewels to spark his interest in the resort. If she'd have known, she'd have mentioned their pending arrival for the upcoming Valentine's Day Ball much sooner. The holiday was not quite two weeks away. She couldn't help but wonder if Atlas would be attending.

Perhaps there was more to this resort than he'd originally thought.

There was definitely more to its general manager than he'd first suspected.

She wasn't above pulling out all of the stops if she felt something was important, not only to herself but to those around her. He respected her determination, but it wasn't enough to change his mind. Nothing would convince him to keep this island.

Still, he was curious to learn why royal jewels had been delivered to the resort. It could possibly be a selling point. He was quite certain most resorts didn't play host to royal gems. Perhaps he'd been too quick to dismiss the idea of touring the resort.

His security expertise might come in handy. He liked the thought of doing some manual labor instead of answering the unending list of emails awaiting his attention. And it would give him a chance to know the general manager a little better—from a business standpoint of course.

"Do you really expect me to believe these jewels are royal?" It had to be some sort of PR campaign to draw in more guests.

As they made their way along the hallway, she glanced at him. "You really don't know much about your mother, do you?"

He'd made a point not to know anything about her. If Thea could so easily forget him, he could forget her. "What is that supposed to mean?"

Hermione shook her head. "The jewels are real, and they are from the royal family of Rydiania."

He vaguely recalled hearing of the country, but he couldn't place where he'd heard the name. "Why would they send the resort jewels?"

"The prince visits every year."

So they'd worked out some sort of arrangement with this

prince. Interesting. "I want to know why this prince would agree to such an arrangement."

Hermione stopped walking and turned to him. She waited for a family to pass, and then she lowered her voice. "Which part would that be—the part where the prince is your step cousin? Or the part where your mother married a former king?"

He didn't recall his mouth opening but it must have happened, because a little bit later when his mind came out if its stupor, he pressed his lips together. This couldn't be right. Thea had married royalty? No. Really? None of this was making sense to him.

Hermione continued walking. "Your stepfather, Georgios, had already abdicated the throne by the time he'd met your mother. In fact, they met right here on this island. She was a maid and he was a lonely, sad man, who missed his family as they'd disowned him. In that way, Georgios and your mother felt as though they had something in common—"

"I didn't disown my mother. If that's what she told you, it was a lie." His words were quick and sharp.

"No. I'm sorry. That isn't what I meant. I shouldn't be telling you any of this. It isn't my story to tell."

He sighed in frustration. "It's me who should be sorry. I didn't mean to snap. This is just a lot to take in."

Sympathy reflected in her eyes. "I can't even imagine what you're going through. When my mother died, our circumstances were different. We were very close. I'd been able to say goodbye."

"I'm sorry for your loss."

She resumed walking. "Thank you. It was quite a while ago. Although there are times when something happens and she's the first one I want to tell. And then the loss comes washing back over me. We were as close as a teenager can be to their mother."

"I didn't know my mother when I was a teenager. She took off when I was five. And my father and I were anything but close." It wasn't until he'd spoken the words that he realized he'd never admitted any of this before. But there was just something about Hermione that made it easy for him to open up. Perhaps too easy.

It was best to focus on business. He didn't want to dredge up any more memories of himself at five years old, crying into his pillow for his mother—a mother that would never come back for him—at least not for many years.

He cleared his throat, hoping when he spoke his voice didn't betray the raw emotions raging within him. "Having the jewels here, it's quite a liability for the resort to take on, perhaps too much. What if something were to happen to these royal jewels? It'd put the resort in quite a difficult position."

She stopped walking and turned to him. "It's what your mother wanted."

He opened his mouth and then closed it. He had a sinking feeling this wasn't the first or the last time Thea's memory or wishes would be an issue. "But she's not here now and I am."

Hermione's eyes narrowed. "What are you saying?"

He wasn't going to delve back into the subject of his relationship with Thea. The fact was this island and the resort were now his responsibility. And until it was sold, he had to do what he thought was best for the business.

He met her gaze straight on. "I'm saying that I'm not comfortable with this arrangement with a prince I've never heard of."

"And yet you're the one that didn't want to get too involved with the resort or its employees, remember?" Her eyes glinted with agitation. "This resort is my responsibility—at least until the resort is sold."

He didn't want to make an enemy of her. He'd already heard the employees sing her praises. They would go to battle for her. And all of that would hamper any hope of a sale.

He needed to divert this conversation. "We should get moving. They'll be waiting for you."

She gave him an intense stare. "I know you have your reasons not to like this place, but I love it and its people. You

would too if you let down your guard. Regardless, I will fight
to maintain our ways."

"Change is inevitable, whether it's coming from me or someone else. Now let's not be late."

She was nothing if not observant. He'd prefer if she didn't
read so much in him. It made him feel exposed and vulnerable.
It was a position he wasn't used to being in. And one he hoped
not to be in again.

CHAPTER SIX

SHE DIDN'T THINK she could do it.

There weren't many things that defeated her, but Atlas's stubborn disposition about retaining ownership of the resort might be one of those things.

Hermione grew quiet as they approached the large glass doors of the Ludus Gallery. She was still processing the fact that the rift between Atlas and his mother went so much deeper than she'd ever imagined. While her heart went out to him, she still had an obligation to her employees. No matter what, she couldn't give up on changing his mind about keeping the resort.

Perhaps he needed to remember the good parts of his relationship with Thea. Were there good parts? She thought of Thea—kind, generous and caring Thea—yes, there had to be good parts. Maybe he'd forgotten them. Maybe he didn't want to remember them. But Hermione knew that until her dying day, Thea had loved her son.

Something awful had gone wrong. Hermione couldn't fathom what it might have been. Atlas might try and tell himself that it didn't matter after all of this time, but it did matter to him. If it didn't matter, he wouldn't be here.

She wanted to help him find some peace. She told herself that she would be doing it in memory of her dear friend, who had given her a hand up when she'd needed it most. It was her chance to pay back Thea's kindness.

She stopped next to the thick frosted glass doors before she reached for the oversize brass handle. Atlas grasped it. He opened the door for her. She thanked him as she stepped inside the gallery.

"This part is currently open to the resort guests," she explained. "But if you'll follow me to the back area, it's where we're preparing for the Valentine's Day reveal."

There were a few people here and there, admiring the latest watercolor acquisitions. Hermione glanced over at the six-piece collection of seascapes. Though they were all of the same scene, each displayed a different time of day, from a morning scene to an evening sunset. Each was so detailed that she could stand there for an hour or two and still not catch all of the minute details.

"Do you do these special exhibitions on a regular basis?" Atlas's voice drew her from her thoughts.

"While the resort owns the pieces on display out here, the ones in back are the ones on loan from other museums or countries." She stopped and turned to him, hiding her excitement that he was finally showing some interest in the resort. "We try to always have something special either on display in the back room or in the planning stage."

She used a key to open the door to the sealed-off section. She held the door for Atlas. He was intently inspecting the door, which she found surprising when there was so much else to see back here.

"Is everything all right?" she asked.

"I was just surprised that there isn't higher security for this section."

"We haven't had any problems with it so far."

"That's what everyone says before they're robbed."

She frowned at him. In a low voice she asked, "Are you saying we're going to be robbed?"

"No. I was just thinking that your security needs to be up-graded."

She glanced around, hoping they weren't overheard. "Perhaps you should think about those matters a little quieter."

"We can discuss my ideas for the new system later."

She didn't speak for a moment, not trusting what would come out of her mouth. "I don't think that's necessary. This system was just installed last year."

"And as you pointed out, this is now my resort."

She wondered when he would play that card. "The jewels are this way. I can't wait to see the Ruby Heart. I've seen pictures, but that is never the same as seeing it in person."

She didn't think of herself as the jewelry type. There was only one piece of jewelry that she cared about—her mother's locket. But it was lost to her forever. Still, there was just something exciting about viewing jewels that have been worn by queens and princesses.

An armed guard stood in front of the room where the Ruby Heart was to be displayed. He nodded at them.

"Is it in the display case yet?" she asked.

"They're waiting for you before they unpack it."

"Understood." She started past him.

The guard stepped in front of Atlas, impeding his entrance. "You can't go in there. Only approved employees."

"I'm with Hermione."

"There are no exceptions."

"Are you serious?" Atlas's voice grew deep with agitation.

"Absolutely."

"It's okay," Hermione said. "He owns the resort."

"It doesn't matter if he's the president. If he hasn't had a full background check and been added to my list, he can't go inside."

Her gaze moved to Atlas. "I'm sorry. We can get this straightened out later. The security firm doesn't work for the resort."

"It's okay. Do what you need to do. I'll be fine here."

She wasn't so sure he would be fine. He looked more like a

caged animal as he started to pace. But people were waiting for her, so she moved into the secure room. While the rest of the gallery had white walls to make it feel airy and spacious, this section was done with black walls and ceiling.

Spotlights were used to highlight the specific items on display. Nothing was to distract from the features of the show. And it worked. It drew people's gazes where they needed to go. But the spotlights hadn't been set up yet as the star of the show had just now arrived.

A couple of royal guards stood with the locked box. She knew the procedure. She had to produce two forms of identification and have her fingerprints scanned. Then she signed the digital receipt. Once all of that was complete, one of the guards entered the security code that released the digital lock.

The Ruby Heart was revealed in all of its sparkling grandeur, and Hermione was left speechless. She didn't know a gem could look that impressive. She felt bad that Atlas wasn't able to see it. But if he stayed until Valentine's Day, he could see it once it was secure in its display case.

"Did I miss anything?" Atlas's voice came from behind her.

Hermione spun around. "What are you doing back here? How did you get past the guard?"

He held up his phone. "Remember, I own a security company. I have connections around the world. I called up the owner of this security firm, and I was immediately added to the list."

"You were?" She blinked. "But it normally takes weeks for the background checks."

"I have top security clearance in a number of places, including Greece. I have to for my work." He moved closer and stared at the gem. "So this is the beauty that's causing all of the problems?"

"Isn't it beautiful?" She was still in awe over it.

"It's not bad."

"Not bad? Are you serious? It's one of the biggest rubies in the world."

"I'm just giving you a hard time. I think it is quite impressive."

"And look, there's a brass plaque with it." She moved closer to read it aloud. "'The legend of the Ruby Heart. If destined lovers gaze upon the Ruby Heart at the same time, their lives will be forever entwined.'"

Heat warmed her cheeks. She suddenly regretted reading the legend. Not that they were lovers—far from it.

"Whatever works," he said.

"What does that mean?"

"It's clearly a gimmick. A lure to draw in an audience." His gaze moved to her. "Surely you don't believe it, do you?"

Did she believe the legend? Of course not. Did she want to believe it? Maybe. Was it so wrong to believe in eternal love?

"No." She wasn't about to tell him how she truly felt. After signing for the other royal jewels, she turned to Atlas. "We should get moving and let these men take care of things."

"Now that I know there are priceless gems on the grounds, I'm definitely having my people upgrade the security. You can never be too safe."

"That won't be necessary."

"Sure, it is."

She pressed her hands to her hips. "Are you saying the current security isn't good enough?"

"I'm saying it could be better."

What she heard was that the security system that she'd painstakingly researched and ultimately chosen wasn't any good. Was he right? Had she made a costly mistake?

She stopped herself. He was doing the same thing to her that Otis used to do—make her doubt herself. The current security was more than sufficient.

She opened her mouth to tell him that, but then she realized this might be a way for Atlas to invest himself in the resort. And though it took swallowing a bit of her pride, she chose to put the future of the Ludus first. "It sounds like you have a plan. Let me know what you'll need from me."

"I will." He grabbed his phone and started texting someone.

She could only imagine he was contacting his office. For a man anxious to keep his distance from this resort, he was getting more involved by the minute. But she resisted pointing this out to him. She didn't want to scare him off. In fact, she was looking forward to him staying around much longer.

This place could definitely use his expertise.

The next day, Atlas had gone over the resort's blueprints and made arrangements to fly in his best crew. A resort this size was going to take a lot of work, but it was doable. And then when the place was sold, it would be a selling point. In his book that was a win-win.

But he'd gotten so caught up in the security aspect of the resort that he still hadn't toured the place. And the tour would let him scope out the best type of security for the different areas.

At least that's what he told himself when he went to track down Hermione and collect on the tour she still owed him.

He had just opened his suite door when he spotted her walking down the hallway. "Do you have a moment?"

"Sure." She followed him into the suite. "What do you need?"

"I believe you owe me a tour of the resort. After all, we wouldn't want me to lie to the employees, right?"

She opened her mouth as though to disagree with him, but then she wordlessly pressed her lips together. He noticed her pink shimmery lip gloss and her lush lips. They were so tempting. So very tempting. He wondered what it'd be like to kiss her. Would one kiss be enough? And then realizing where his thoughts had strayed, he raised his gaze.

He couldn't help but wonder if she knew what he was thinking. He hoped not because it wasn't like him to let pleasure get in the way of business. And right now, this was his most important business. Because the sooner he wrapped things up here, the sooner he could leave the past in the past.

"I don't have a lot of time. Where do you want to start?" she asked.

"Wherever you choose will be fine."

She reached for her phone. "Let me update my assistant."

He knew showing him around was the last thing she wanted to do. But then again, she'd been the one to get them into this situation. He checked his phone while he waited for her. Just then a message popped up from Krystof.

We need to talk.

Agreed. If you don't want the island I need to find another buyer ASAP.

Commence your search for another buyer.

That wasn't the news he wanted to hear. A sale to Krystof would be fast and painless. But trying to line up another buyer wouldn't be so simple.

You still planning to visit?

I'm not sure.

A frown pulled at Atlas's mouth as he slipped the phone back in his pocket. He moved to the floor-to-ceiling windows. Now that the rain had moved on, he noticed the lush green foliage. So this was after all a beautiful sunny Mediterranean island. Buyers would fight to own it. Wouldn't they? There might even be a bidding war. Or was he being overly optimistic?

"Sorry about that." Hermione slipped her phone back in her purse. "Shall we go?"

They entered the spacious hallway with plush red carpeting

that silenced people's footsteps. Hermione led the way. She hadn't stated their destination and he hadn't thought to ask. All the while, he was taking in his surroundings from the expensive and notable artwork on the walls to the crystal chandeliers.

"Are all of the rooms normally booked?" He hated the fact that he knew so very little about this property. He had a lot to learn and quickly.

"Yes. The reservations fill in well in advance."

"Really?" His voice came out quite loudly in the quiet hallway.

"This is an exclusive resort that offers privacy and pampering. Our clients return regularly."

"It can't be that great."

Hermione arched a fine brow. "You'll soon see."

A couple of employees passed by them. They smiled and silently nodded in greeting. This appeared to be the time of the day when the resort was abuzz with employee activity as suites were cleaned.

An older woman pushed her cleaning supply cart toward them with a big, friendly smile on her face. When she reached them, she paused. "Hermione, I'm so sorry I missed the luncheon. We're shorthanded this week so I picked up a few extra rooms. You know, if everyone pitches in it makes it easier for everyone."

"Thank you, Irene," Hermione said. "Your efforts are greatly appreciated."

Irene turned her attention to Atlas. The smile slipped from her face as she stared at him. He wanted to ask what she was doing, but he already knew—she was looking to see if he had any resemblance to his mother. He didn't.

"You must be Thea's son." As his back teeth ground together, she continued, "We're happy to have you here. My condolences on the unexpected passing of your mother. She was the kindest woman. You were lucky to have her for a mother. I always thought she died from a broken heart. I just wanted to say how sorry I am for your loss. I'll let you two get on with things. I have another room to clean."

The woman's well-meaning words tore at his scarred heart. The Thea these people knew was not the same person he had known. He knew he should thank the lady, but the words bunched up in the back of his throat.

As they continued walking, Hermione asked, "Are you okay?"

He nodded. No, he wasn't, but he refused to let on to Hermione.

He swallowed the lump in his throat. "The people are friendly here."

"Yes, they are. It's a really great place to visit and work."

"If the resort is so great, why haven't I heard of it?"

"We have no need for the media..." Her voice trailed off as though she were lost in thought. "We have a mailing list that goes out regularly to our select clientele. And from there our guests use word of mouth to spread the news to other visitors."

It was inconceivable to him that in this day and age a resort could be amazing enough to generate sufficient business by guests returning regularly and recommending it to their family and friends. After all, it was just a giant hotel. Right?

Okay, so maybe the suites were on the lavish side, but there was no way they could do that for the rest of the resort. After all, there had to be limitations. No place was that incredible. He didn't believe it.

He glanced at Hermione as they walked through the resort. "How long have you worked here?"

"Since I was eighteen. In some ways, I feel as though I grew up here."

He noticed that she didn't feel the need to elaborate. He wondered in what ways, but he didn't ask. If she were to confide in him, she would expect him to do the same in return. And he'd already said more than he'd intended.

Atlas rubbed the back of his neck as memories of his youth

came rushing back to him. They hadn't had much money growing up. Whatever they had his father spent on expanding his auto business.

Atlas hadn't always enjoyed his current state of creature comforts, including a small fleet of unique sports cars. He knew what it was like to do without. His father had withheld money as a way of controlling him. It was only when Atlas had finished university and went into business for himself that he became wealthy. But it never stopped him from getting his hands dirty if the need arose.

If he were to keep the island, he would change things. He would make the island less exclusive and open to everyone. It wouldn't be as lavish as it was now, but it would still be a fun destination. But it wasn't like he was entertaining thoughts of keeping the island. No way. He wanted the sale to go through as quickly as possible.

"Are you staying for the Valentine's party next weekend?"

"I don't think so." The idea most definitely didn't appeal to him. He didn't do hearts, flowers and romance. "Even if I am still here, I won't be attending."

"You won't want to miss it. The party will be spectacular."

"I'll be too busy." He averted his gaze.

He hadn't planned to share any of this with Hermione, but he was quickly finding it was very easy to talk to her. He'd have to be cautious around her or he'd be opening up about all of his secrets. And he didn't want to do that.

CHAPTER SEVEN

SHE WAS DOING FINE...

If fine included the imminent possibility of losing her job.

But it was the resort employees that Hermione worried about the most. Some of them had worked at the Ludus longer than she'd been alive—talk about devotion to their occupation.

She knew what it was to get bounced around in life and having to reinvent herself time after time. Even though she'd grown quite comfortable working here, she could reinvent herself again as a hotel manager or something else, but she didn't want to do it.

She chanced a glance at the heir to the Ludus Resort. As her gaze touched upon his handsome face, her heart raced. He was busy taking in his surroundings, giving her a chance to study him. He wasn't smiling. There was a firm set to his jaw. What was he thinking? Was he calculating the resort's monetary value?

It was as though the happiness had been sucked out of Atlas. She felt bad for him, which most people would find odd since he was the one who was about to upend her life. What had happened to him?

Buzz-buzz.

She lifted her phone to find an urgent message from Nestor,

the resort's event coordinator. It was regarding the special effects for the Valentine's party. "I'm afraid the tour will have to wait. There are some urgent disbursements that require my signature."

"Perhaps I could come with you." His gaze met hers, sending her heart rate into triple digits.

She wanted to tell him no. She needed some space so her pulse could slow to a steady pace. But when she opened her mouth, she said, "It won't take long."

"Even better."

She messaged Nestor that she'd meet him at her office. And so they set off for the administrative suite. Hers was the largest office, as well as having the prime spot in the corner. When she passed by her PA's desk with Atlas hot on her heels, Rhea arched her dark brows as unspoken questions reflected in her eyes.

Hermione paused and made introductions.

Rhea was her usual sweet and charming self. And to Hermione's surprise Atlas soaked up Rhea's pleasantries and returned them. It was though he'd transformed into another person on the way here. Because if that wasn't the case, it meant he didn't enjoy her company. The last thought nagged at her.

After a minute or two, Hermione moved into her office. She wasn't sure if Atlas was going to follow her or stay in the outer office chatting with Rhea. But then he joined her and closed the door behind him. He made himself comfortable on a chair facing her desk while she took a seat behind the desk. As she logged onto the computer system, she found herself glancing over the top of her monitor and noticing that he'd retrieved his phone and appeared to be scrolling through messages.

She got to work, but she kept finding her attention drawn to Atlas. When he'd glance up and catch her staring, heat would flood her cheeks.

Knock-knock.

"Come in." Hermione pressed Send on an email.

Nestor stepped into the office. His tan face lit up with a

warm smile. She noticed how he was starting to take on some gray at his temples even though he was in his early forties with a young family.

She introduced Atlas and the men shook hands.

"How's the party coming?" she asked.

Nestor's face lit up. "It's on track to be our biggest and best. I think the guests will be impressed."

That was the kind of news she liked to hear. "What would we do without you?"

He continued to smile. "Hopefully you'll never have to find out."

Hermione resisted giving Atlas a sideways glance. "Do you have the disbursements and backup?"

He nodded and handed them over.

These were sizable payments. She tied in each number, initialed where required and then signed the bottom of the requisition.

After Nestor left, she continued to work. A half hour later Hermione was finally done. She pushed her chair back and stood. "I'm all set to go."

Atlas glanced up from staring at his phone with a confused look on his face as though he'd been totally lost in his thoughts and had no idea what she was talking about. "Sorry. What?"

"I didn't mean to interrupt you." She wondered what had him so preoccupied.

"No problem." He got to his feet and opened the door to the outer office.

"Do you still want to tour the resort?"

His dark brows furrowed together. "Why wouldn't I?"

"It just seems like you have something else on your mind."

"My mind is on seeing the resort. I have a promise to keep."

She had a feeling there was something he wasn't telling her. Well, she knew there was a lot he wasn't telling her, seeing how they were virtually strangers. A niggle of worry ate at her.

Thea had once encouraged Hermione to follow her dreams

wherever they would lead her. In fact, she'd pushed for Hermione to finish her higher education and even paid for it. She owed Thea a huge debt of gratitude.

Thea had been so nice. She would speak with all of the staff just like they were family. She'd inquire about the staff's children, grandchildren and pets. Thea was very down-to-earth, so much like her husband.

But Atlas was nothing like his mother. Where Thea was open and welcoming, Atlas was closed off and distant. Where Thea had a fair complexion and was short in stature, Atlas was dark and tall. The only glimmer of Thea that she could spot in Atlas were his eyes. He had his mother's sky-blue eyes.

"Where are we going?" His voice drew her back to the present.

"I thought we would start with a visit to the spa."

"The spa? Do I look like the spa type?"

"Honestly, I don't know what type you are as I just met you last night, but you wanted to see the resort and the spa is a huge part of the resort. It's near the lobby."

"That seems like an odd place for a spa."

"Why? It's not like people wonder around in their robes. Trust me, the spa is a world unto its own." She walked a little farther in silence and then came to a stop in front of two large wooden doors with oversize brass handles. "Here we are."

He remained quiet as they stepped inside. The young woman behind the desk practically drooled at the sight of Atlas. The woman's obvious infatuation with him aggravated Hermione. She told herself it was the woman's obvious lack of professionalism that bothered her and nothing else. She would have a discreet word with the woman's supervisor later.

After Hermione had stated the purpose of their visit, the young woman said, "I'll send someone out to give you a tour."

Once the woman walked away, Atlas turned to Hermione. "I thought that's what you were going to do."

She shook her head. "I can't."

"Why not?" His tone carried a note of displeasure.

"Because I… I'm not that familiar with the spa." The surprise that flashed in his eyes made her feel embarrassed.

Did he think she wasn't good at her job because she didn't know the intimate routine of the spa? Because she was very good at her job. She had department heads and supervisors that saw to the little details. And when there was a problem they couldn't resolve, she stepped in.

Suddenly she felt as though she didn't measure up in Atlas's eyes, and that bothered her. She'd worked very hard in her life to get this far. She was proud of how she'd gone from having nothing after her mother died to being able to put a roof over her head and now she was in charge of one of the world's most glamorous resorts. But she supposed none of that would impress Atlas. Wait. Did she want to impress him?

Part of her screamed out that yes, she did. But she quickly silenced that little voice. She didn't need his approval or any other thing, except her job.

"But you work here," he said.

"As the general manager." Why was he making a big deal of this? She lowered her voice. "Staff doesn't make use of the spa. It's reserved for guests only."

He frowned at her response. "That's a silly rule."

At that moment, a young woman in bright aqua scrubs approached them. "Mr. Othonos?"

"Yes." Atlas turned to the woman.

"We're ready for you."

"Good. Right now, we—" he gestured to himself and Hermione "—are going to have massages."

"I can wait here," Hermione said softly.

"Nonsense. You are my guest. I insist."

"You mean you won't get a massage unless I do?" She'd never faced such a predicament.

A smile spread across his handsome face. "That's exactly what I mean."

Adara's words echoed in her mind about making him comfortable here. But a spa treatment? Really? And during work hours? This was totally unheard-of.

"If it makes you feel better, as owner of the resort, I'm giving you the afternoon off and free access to the spa." His gaze dared her to challenge him.

It didn't make her feel better. She hated how he picked when he wanted to play the owner card. If he wanted to be involved in the resort's policies and management, he needed to fully commit himself. Otherwise, he needed to leave things to her.

Both Atlas and the attendant looked at her expectantly. She knew to back out now would cause even more tension with Atlas. Maybe it was best to indulge him this once.

"Fine. But I don't have long."

He sent her a satisfied grin. He seemed to like challenges and especially winning them. She tucked that bit of information away. She might need it in the future.

And so they took a tour of the sprawling two-story spa followed by chocolate massages. Hermione opted for a hand massage with a mani-pedi with *Kiss Me Pink* polish. Atlas agreed to a full-body massage. She could only hope it left him in a much better disposition.

Things needed to change.

Atlas didn't like the resort's atmosphere of haves and the have-nots. It reminded him too much of his childhood. His father had it all, and he had to beg for what little he got.

His father was big about the haves and have-nots. His father, being a small business owner, believed he was part of the "haves." He'd preached to Atlas that if he wanted to be someone in this world, he had to be rich like him—rich being a relative term. Back then his father made Atlas beg for new clothes or shoes when the old ones no longer fit.

These days Atlas tried not to waste his time thinking about his father—a father who said Atlas would never amount to anything just like his worthless mother. Atlas wondered what his father would think if he knew how much Atlas was worth now. He could buy his father's auto dealership many times over. And the fact that his mother had gone on to own and run this impressive resort would really get to his father.

But money hadn't changed Atlas. He hadn't become rich because of his father; he'd become successful in spite of his father. All he'd ever wanted to do was help people. And that's how he'd gotten started in the security business. He wanted to give people a sense of security—something he never had growing up. A state-of-the-art security system wasn't quite the same as the safety of a loving family, but it was as close as he could get.

And then he reminded himself that it wasn't his job to approve or disapprove of things at the resort. That particular responsibility would belong to the new owner. He just didn't know who that would be at this point.

He hadn't given up hope on changing Krystof's mind. But this was too important not to seek out other potential buyers.

As they passed by a poster advertising the grand Valentine's Day Ball, Atlas started to get an idea. He pulled out his phone and texted his real estate agent.

I want to invite potential buyers to a party at the Ludus Resort.

People like parties. When?

Valentine's Day. But there's a problem.

What sort of problem?

The resort is booked solid. Guests would have to stay on the mainland.

Not good. Let me think about it. Talk soon.

He slipped his phone back into his pocket. He was pretty proud of himself for coming up with a potential way for buyers to see the resort at its finest and with the royal jewels on display.

But his next thought was that if they worked out the logistics, he'd be obligated to attend the Valentine's ball. It was the sort of scene he worked hard to avoid. But if he focused on business, perhaps it wouldn't be so bad.

His gaze moved to Hermione. She would be at the ball. Suddenly he imagined her in a glittering dress with her long hair down around her slender shoulders. He imagined taking her in his arms and holding her close. The image was so tempting. Maybe a main course of business with a side of pleasure wouldn't be so bad after all. He didn't allow himself to think of what dessert might be.

"What did you think?" Hermione's voice drew him from his thoughts.

Having lost track of their conversation, he asked, "Think about what?"

Hermione's brows scrunched together. "The spa."

"Oh. It was nice."

"If you would like, I can arrange for you to spend more time there."

He shook his head. "I'm afraid the rest of the tour will have to wait for another time. It's getting late, and I have some urgent calls to return."

"I understand. I, too, have work awaiting me. I'll see you tomorrow."

"Yes."

And then she was gone. Suddenly he felt very alone. It was as though she were all bright and sunny and now with her gone, a long, dark shadow had fallen over him.

Which was utterly ridiculous because he was used to being on his own. It'd been that way since he was a child. He didn't need someone in his life—someone to share his time. His business was all he needed.

He used to be able to sell that line to himself, but lately it wasn't ringing as true. For a second, he thought of going after Hermione and asking her to have an early dinner with him.

Buzz-buzz.

He glanced at his phone. It was a call from the embassy where he'd sent his men to resolve a problem with their system. With a sigh, he took the call and started walking in the opposite direction from Hermione.

CHAPTER EIGHT

HE WAS GETTING DISTRACTED.

And that wasn't good.

Thursday morning, Atlas had set up his temporary office in his suite. The problem at the embassy was more elusive than originally imagined. He'd done his best to help troubleshoot from afar. It was very frustrating not to be there.

That's why his very next phone call had been to his real estate agent. The sooner the resort was sold, the sooner he could get back to his life.

"So far there hasn't been a lot of interest in the island, but it's still early in the search," the agent said. "The lack of publicity has buyers hesitant."

"But the place is booked solid."

"That's definitely a selling point, but when it comes down to your island resort, well, it's remote and doesn't have a reputation with world travelers. The big hotel chains are going to go with a known location over something that isn't easy to reach. And I have to be honest with you. A lot of the properties are changing hands right now, so your resort is going to have competition."

He raked his fingers through his hair. "So what you're saying is that you can't sell the resort?"

"No. What I'm saying is that we need to build a portfolio,

starting with the resort's history. I did an internet search but couldn't find much. Do you know the history?"

"Uh, some of it." He thought about his mother's marriage to a former king. But he wasn't ready to share that information. "I'll find out more."

"Good. And I'll arrange for one of our best photographers to come out and take photos. The images will be used for prospective buyers as well as growing a social media presence. Does this place even have a website?"

He hesitated. She wasn't going to like his answer. "No."

She clucked her tongue. "That's not good. I'll hire a designer and be in touch."

"When will the photographer arrive?" He didn't want to drag out his stay.

"I'd have to check on his schedule, but I'd say in a week or two—"

"Two weeks?" He once again raked his fingers through his hair as he stood and started to pace.

"I could try and find someone with an earlier opening on their calendar, but I couldn't vouch for their talent."

They couldn't be that bad, right? "Good. Do that."

He promised to forward her the required information. After he disconnected the call, he couldn't concentrate on business matters. He was frustrated that getting rid of his mother's island and resort was proving to be so difficult.

He needed to see Hermione. Maybe the resort had a professional photographer who could speed things up. At least that was the excuse he told himself when he went in search of her.

When he arrived at her office, her PA informed him that Hermione was dealing with a problem in the resort's gallery. He didn't have to request directions; he recalled how to get there.

He made his way across the resort. When he found Hermione, she was in the back of the gallery signing paperwork.

"Another delivery?" he asked.

Her gaze lifted to meet his. "As a matter of fact, yes." She gestured to the large canvas behind her. "It's called *Clash of Hearts*."

He gazed at the artwork with its hot pink and silver hearts entangled together. The conjoined hearts were repeated in varying sizes all over the canvas. "It's different."

She smiled. "You're not a modern-art fan?"

He shrugged. "Art is okay."

"So it's the hearts you have a problem with?"

This was not a subject he wanted to delve into. He cleared his throat. "I need your assistance."

"I'm sorry. I really don't have time. We're a bit shorthanded right now."

"Is that why you're here signing for a painting?"

"Yes. The woman who oversees the gallery went out on maternity leave." Hermione pulled out her phone. "I'll message Adara. She can help you with whatever you need."

"No. It has to be you."

She drew in a deep breath as though subduing her frustration. "Why me?"

"Because you knew my mother."

Her brows drew together. "Yes, I did. We were good friends." She hesitated. "What do you need help with?"

"A couple of things. First, does the resort have a professional photographer on retainer?"

She shook her head. "We've never needed or wanted one."

Of course they didn't. That would have made things easier for him.

The silence dragged on before he spoke again. This was something he'd given a lot of thought. "I want to know if you'd assist me on going through Thea's things."

"Oh." She was quiet as she absorbed this information.

"I need the help and with you being her friend, I thought you might know what she'd want done with her things." Not giving her a chance to back out, he said, "What can I do to convince you to help me? Name your price." That was how badly he didn't want to face his mother's things alone.

This was his fourth day on the island, and he hadn't even stepped foot in Thea's apartment much less started sorting her items. He knew if he didn't get help that he'd keep making excuses to avoid it.

He could see the wheels in Hermione's mind turning. She was going to turn him down, and he couldn't really blame her. This wasn't her mess to clean up. And she'd already taken time out of her busy schedule to make sure he enjoyed his stay.

"If I help—" her voice drew his full attention "—will you make sure the resort's staff is retained by the new owner for at least six months?"

And there she went again, impressing him with her generosity. Most people would have asked for something for themselves, but Hermione thought of others instead of herself.

"Done." He was unable to deny such a selfless request, even though it would hamper any sale negotiations.

"And the employees won't lose the seniority and benefits they've so rightly earned." Her voice was firm.

"Done and done. Anything else?"

She shook her head. "If you help them out, I will help you, but it will have to be in the evenings. I still have a day job."

He held his hand out to her. "It's a deal."

She looked at his hand before her gaze rose to meet his. And then she placed her hand in his and gave it a firm shake. For an instant, he considered tightening his grip and drawing her to him. He had this growing urge to kiss her—to feel her lush lips pressed to his. He wondered how she'd react.

As he continued to stare into her eyes, he felt his heart pound. What was it about this woman that had such an effect over him?

And then he realized he was making too much of things. After all, he was already out of sorts with being here on his mother's island with the dread of having to go through her personal items hanging over him. As well as learning how happy she'd been here—without him.

It was a lot to deal with at once. It was no wonder his mind was so quick to find a diversion. And that's what this infatuation with Hermione was—a break from reality. He withdrew his hand, already missing the softness of her touch.

His mouth grew dry. He swallowed hard. "Why don't we continue the tour of the resort?"

She frowned at him. "Right now?"

"Is there a problem?"

She hesitated as though she were thinking up an excuse to get out of it. "No. Of course not. Let's go."

And off they went on a walking tour of the resort, from the play area for the children and those who were young at heart with their ballroom and art room to the casino, which looked as though it belonged in Monte Carlo with its gold, flashy slot machines and table games to the gold-trimmed ornate ceiling and enormous crystal chandeliers. The staff was all dressed up in pressed white dress shirts, wine-colored vests, gold neckties and black pants.

Atlas started to get an idea. "Would there happen to be a high rollers room?"

Hermione arched a brow. "You like to play cards?"

"No. I'm not asking for myself."

She led him outside the casino. They walked a little way and then turned a corner. There stood one of the largest bouncers he'd ever seen. The man was taller than Atlas as well as wider.

Hermione stopped at the end of the hallway. "The private room is there. I believe there's a poker game in progress. You'll need to wait until it ends to go in."

"That won't be necessary." This might be just what he needed to lure Krystof to the island. "What's the buy-in?"

"It's high."

"How high?"

"A hundred."

"Thousand?" When she nodded, he said, "Interesting."

"Would you like a seat at the table?"

"No. I don't gamble on games of chance, but I do know someone who would be very interested."

They continued walking until they came to the indoor pool area that had not one or two but four long slides with skylights overhead. The area was filled with smiling people and rambunctious children. He had to admit that the resort did a fine job of offering entertainment for most everyone.

Next to the pool area was a food court with cuisine from around the world. They decided to have a late lunch there. Hermione opted for fish tacos while he chose a gyro with lettuce and tomato topped with *tzatziki* sauce and a side of *sfougata* cheese balls.

"What do you think of the resort?" Hermione asked after finishing her two tacos.

"I think it's like a small city with a lot to offer the guests."

"And you haven't even seen the outside."

"I still can't believe Thea owned all of this." There was a part of him that wanted to know more about her. "Was she happy here?"

"Very much so. She loved her husband dearly, and this island was her whole world."

He shouldn't have asked. He didn't want to hear about Thea's perfect life—a life that didn't include him. What was it about him that made her reject him? Was he that unlovable?

"I don't understand why Thea left this place to me." He was still asking himself why she'd done it.

"I'm not. She never stopped loving you."

He wanted to believe Hermione, but his mother's actions or rather her lack of action where he was concerned told him all he needed to know about his mother's feelings toward him. There was something inherently wrong with him that his own mother rejected him.

"My mother and I had a lot of unresolved issues."

"Is that why it took you so long to come to the island?"

"I was away in the States when I was notified of Thea's passing." As he said the words there was a twinge of pain, but he refused to acknowledge it. "I should have dropped what I was doing to deal with the solicitors but…"

"But what?"

He was about to brush off her inquiry when his gaze met hers and he saw the genuine concern reflected in her eyes. "But my mother and I hadn't been close since I was a little kid. I… I didn't, well, I didn't realize what all was involved with her will."

"You didn't know that she owned an island much less a hugely profitable resort?"

"I had absolutely no idea about any of this. When I knew her, my mother didn't have much—certainly not when she walked away from my father." Atlas rested his elbows on the table and gazed at Hermione. "But you knew someone different."

She smiled, but it didn't quite reach her eyes. She missed his mother; that much was obvious. "We all knew and liked her. Thea was very involved in the resort."

His back teeth ground together. Thea had been very involved with what mattered to her—the resort—not him. He'd already been dismissed by not just his mother but his father as well. His father was all about his auto business and stroking his own ego. If you didn't look up to his father and regard him highly, he didn't have time for you—even if you were his own flesh and blood.

Atlas preferred to be on his own because then no one could hurt him. It also gave him the ability to come and go as he pleased, never staying in one place for too long. Never getting too attached to anything or anyone.

"Atlas, what is it?" The concerned tone of Hermione's voice drew him from his thoughts.

He shook his head. "Nothing."

"You know you can talk to me. I'm an okay listener."

He couldn't help but smile. "Just okay?"

She smiled and shrugged. "A great listener sounds like brag-ging, and if I said I was a terrible listener you wouldn't say a word. So I went with the middle of the road description."

He laughed at her explanation. Hermione was exactly what he needed right now. She was like a ray of sunshine on a cloudy day. And what they were about to do was going to be so hard. Thankfully Hermione would be there to hopefully take the edge off the painful task.

Hermione nodded. "What would you like to see next? I can take you to our indoor golf driving range or our tennis courts."

He shook his head. "As tempting as that sounds, I have some-thing else in mind."

"What would that be?"

"I… I'd like to see my mother's apartment."

"Certainly. Let's go."

Hermione quietly led the way from the food court. All the while he took in the decor of the building. A lot of it was old, but it was all elegant and well cared for. It was like being in an older home that had been loved and preserved through the years.

Atlas couldn't help but think that there was still room for up-dates. He was certain the buyer would want to do a total remodel to bring the place up-to-date with the rest of their global prop-erties. Of course that would mean the resort would lose some of its unique charm, but there were always trade-offs to keep things modern. It's what he told clients when his team had to make adjustments to properties for their security equipment.

Speaking of security equipment, not only the gallery but the entire resort could use a complete overhaul. He was a bit sur-prised they hadn't hired his company in the first place. They were the best in the business. Or did his mother purposely not hire him? It was another prick to his heart.

After stopping by her office to pick up the key card to Thea's apartment, Hermione led them to the back of the resort. She stopped next to two steel doors with a sign that read: Authorized

Personnel Only. She inserted a master key card in a reader. The lock on the double doors clicked as they released.

"I thought we were going to my mother's apartment," he said in confusion.

She held the door open for him. "This is the way to the private entrance."

Interesting. They entered a service hallway. So this was the inner workings of the resort. Signs in the hallways clearly marked each entrance to the massive kitchens, to the laundry and to the janitorial services.

"Do you want to go to the apartment alone?" she asked.

Atlas didn't speak, not that he was being rude but rather his vocal cords were frozen. Instead, he shook his head. The last thing he wanted right now was to be alone.

His body filled with dread. The closer they got, the faster his heart pounded. If he was smart, he'd turn around and request that everything in the apartment be disposed of. But he knew it wouldn't be that easy. There would be legal papers and whatnot in the apartment that he, as the heir to his mother's estate, would need to sort out.

At the end of the lengthy hallway was a private elevator. This time he slid the key card that Hermione had given him into the reader. The silver doors silently slid open.

"Are you sure you want to do this?" she asked.

"I have to." His voice was monotone as he refused to let Hermione see just how much this bothered him. He had gotten through worse—like when Thea left him alone with his neglectful father.

On wooden legs, Atlas stepped into the small elevator car. There were no buttons to press as it had only one stop, Thea's apartment. The seconds it took to ride to the third floor were silent as he prepared himself to deal with his mother's things.

The door slid open, and he stared out at the large foyer. It was all done up in white with a large painting of the colorful sunset reflected over the sea to add a splash of color to the room. She certainly did love art.

The glass door leading to the apartment was propped open as though it were always open to visitors. He wondered what his mother would say if she knew he was about to enter her private space.

"Atlas?" When he glanced at Hermione, she asked, "Are you going to step out of the elevator?"

He swallowed hard and then took a step forward. "I never thought I'd be doing this."

All he could surmise about Thea's motives was that since she didn't have any other children, he had become her heir by default. Still, another prick to his scarred heart.

"I'm sorry it's come as such a shock. I have some idea what you're going through."

"Because you lost your mother too?"

She nodded. "When I was seventeen. She had a brain aneurysm. One moment she was fine, the next her head hurt so bad she went to the hospital. I didn't know what was going on at first. Who thinks they'll die from a headache?"

He reached out and took her hand in his. His thumbs gently stroked the back of her hand. He didn't say anything. He didn't know what to say. He felt helpless.

"They…they, um, rushed her to surgery. I never prayed so hard in my life. But…but it had ruptured by the time they got in there. She hung on for a little bit but…"

Her words failed her. She held up a finger as she gathered herself. "When it came time to discuss when to turn off life support, I'd never felt so alone in my life."

Atlas drew her to him. Her cheek came to rest on his chest as his hand slowly and gently rubbed her back. Her arms wrapped around him as though he were an anchor to the present, who kept her from getting swept away in the painful memories of the past. He'd never been someone's anchor before. He liked the feeling of being needed—being able to comfort her in some small way.

She drew in an unsteady breath and then pulled away. "After she died, I lost everything."

For a moment, this wasn't about him. Hermione's loss was so much greater than his. "I'm sorry. That must have been awful."

"It was. My mother was my best friend. I miss her all of the time. I'm sorry you didn't have that closeness with your mother."

He shook his head. "She walked away from me when I was very young."

"I bet she wishes she hadn't done it."

He shrugged. "She came back once years later, but the damage was done by then. I wanted nothing to do with her."

"She never gave up on you."

His gaze swung to her. "Why would you say that?"

"Because she left all of this to you."

He shrugged it off. "That's only because she didn't have any other children."

"Maybe. But I don't think that's the reason. I think she wanted you to have this place because it brought her such happiness." When he shook his head, refusing to accept what Hermione was saying, she continued. "If she didn't want you to have it, she could have donated it to a worthy cause."

That was true. Maybe Hermione had something there, but in order to accept Hermione's theory, it would mean he'd have to accept the fact that his mother still cared about him. And he wasn't ready to do that. He wasn't ready to forgive and forget.

"Let's see what we have to deal with." He stepped past her and entered the apartment.

The living room was huge. Size-wise it put his penthouse in London to shame. He stepped forward, finding a wall of windows that gave an unobstructed view of the beach. The view was priceless.

"It's beautiful, isn't it?" Hermione stepped up next to him.

"You've seen this view before?"

"I have. Your mother liked to host parties for the staff. She called us her family. After your stepfather died, she felt very alone up here. She spent more and more time working with the staff."

"She didn't have to be alone," he muttered under his breath. He refused to feel sorry for her. She'd made her choices—she'd walked away with barely a glance back.

"I think I see some rays of sunshine poking through the clouds," Hermione said. "We can go out on the deck."

She led him to the door that opened onto a partially covered deck. They quietly stared out at the sea for a couple of minutes. The sea breeze had warmed up a bit. It was like being on top of the world up here. But he wasn't here to vacation or enjoy the view. He was here to pack up his mother's belongings and dispose of them—just like she'd disposed of him.

"I better get to work." He held the door for Hermione.

Once back inside the living room with its white-and-aquamarine decor, he looked around, taking in all of the artwork from statues to wall hangings. He had no doubt the art in the apartment alone would be worth a fortune. This was going to be more involved than he'd originally thought. Did he auction it all off? Or donate it to the Ludus Gallery?

There were so many decisions to make. What would Thea want? Why hadn't she left detailed instructions? Why did he even care about what she'd want?

His head started to throb. He needed to think about something else—anything else. He turned to Hermione. "How did you come to work here?"

"Your stepfather was the one who hired me after my mother died. I was so happy to no longer be living on the streets that I was willing to do what was asked of me, and that was good enough for him. I started at the front desk and under your mother's guidance I worked my way up to the administrative offices. Then they offered to pay me to go back to school."

"It's impressive. Not everyone could have come through what

you did and remained standing. The more I learn about you, the more you amaze me."

He stared into her eyes, seeing the pain those memories brought to her. And then he felt guilty for feeling sorry for himself. From the way he saw it, Hermione had it so much worse than him because she'd not only lost a mother who had loved her, but she'd been homeless. He couldn't imagine how horrific that must have been for her.

"I'm so sorry," he said.

"For what?"

"For acting like I had it rough because my mother rejected me."

Hermione's gaze narrowed in on him. "Don't do that."

"Do what?"

"Feel sorry for me. I'm fine." Her voice took on a hard edge. "I'm taking care of myself. And I haven't done too bad. I don't need you or anyone else feeling sorry for me. Got it?"

He didn't blame her for being defensive. It's probably what got her through those long, cold nights on the street. Sympathy welled up in him.

He held up his hands in surrender. "Got it."

"Now, what is your plan for this place?"

He told her how he wanted everything in the apartment inventoried. And then he would take the list and split it into trash, donations, and at Hermione's insistence there would be a keep category. He didn't want to fight with her so he went along with it, but he already knew there wouldn't be anything he was keeping.

And then they agreed to meet back at the apartment as five o'clock. He realized the sooner he finished his time on the island, the sooner he'd have to say goodbye to Hermione. The thought sat heavy in his chest.

CHAPTER NINE

IT HAD BEEN a rough evening.

At least it had been for Atlas.

In that moment, Hermione did what she'd just yelled at him for—she'd felt sorry for him. But it was different. Really it was.

Going through a parent's belongings no matter how good or bad the relation, it was never easy. It was like an emotional jack-in-the-box. And you just never knew when you opened something what emotions were going to be attached to that particular item.

He'd started working in one of the guest rooms while she set to work in the living room. She'd had the forethought to have Rhea track down some colored stickers to mark items after they were inventoried on their computers. They worked non-stop for a few hours.

When they decided to call it quits for the night, she decided to take him to a late dinner at the Under the Sea restaurant. But when she found it was booked solid, she did something she rarely did—she exerted her executive privilege. Minutes later there was a text message that the best table in the restaurant had just opened up.

"Can't we just order room service?" Atlas asked when she'd prodded him to dress for dinner.

"No. We can't. You came here to see the resort. Consider this part of your tour. Now hurry. We can't be late."

"Why?"

She sighed. "Because I had to pull some strings to get this reservation. With the resort fully booked, reservations are at a premium."

"Which restaurant are we eating at?"

"You'll see." And then she smiled. "Trust me, you'll like it."

Twenty minutes later, she exited her office dressed in a little black dress. After being caught without a change of clothes the night of the storm, she'd decided to keep some outfits in her office. The dress wasn't too fancy. And it wasn't boring either. It was cut to fit her curves as though it were specially made for her.

And then there were the black heels. They were...well, they were stunning. It's the reason she'd splurged on them. And they fit her perfectly. She rarely had an occasion to wear them. But dinner at Under the Sea seemed like the perfect occasion.

Rhea had already gone home for the evening when Atlas had arrived to escort Hermione to dinner. He had relented and changed clothes. He now wore a dark suit with a light purple dress shirt and a vibrant purple tie. It was different and yet it looked quite attractive on him. When her gaze rose and met his, her heart fluttered. It was getting hard to remember that this was a business dinner and not a date.

"You look beautiful." It was though his deep voice caressed her.

Heat swirled in her chest. It rushed up her neck and set her cheeks ablaze. "Thank you. You clean up really well too."

He held his arm out to her. She couldn't remember the last time a man had done that for her. Otis never had. He thought chivalry was a waste of time.

She should resist Atlas's offer and keep a boundary between them because he was far too sexy and he made her pulse race. But she threw caution to the wind as she slipped her hand in the crook of his arm. She noticed the firm muscle beneath her fingertips. Her heart thump-thumped as they set off for the evening.

As they stood in the elevator, he said, "I didn't realize there was a lower level. What's down here?"

"We're going to Under the Sea."

"We're going to look at fish? But I thought we were eating."

She smiled at his frown. "I promise you will eat soon."

The doors swung open into a darkened room. It was more like a wide hallway that had glass walls and ceiling. The glow of the fish tank cast a blue glow over the room. And on each table was an LED candle. There were only a couple dozen tables lining each side of the room.

"This is amazing," Atlas said, gazing all around, taking in the hundreds of fish in all variety of colors. "Did you see that?"

"See what?"

"I think it was a small shark. But I don't see it now."

They were shown to their table, which sat midway down the dining room. It gave them an amazing view of it all. He lifted his head to watch the fish as they swam overhead.

"No wonder you wanted to bring me here," he said in awe, as though he'd totally forgotten what they'd been doing just an hour or so ago in his mother's apartment. "You must eat here often."

"Actually, I've never eaten here."

He glanced across the table at her. "But why not? Don't you like fish?"

"No, it's not that. I think this is amazing." Then she lowered her voice. "Remember I work here."

"Oh. Sorry. Sometimes I forget that employees aren't able to enjoy the amenities. You know, someone really needs to change that rule."

"You mean someone like the owner." She looked expectantly at him.

"Oh, you want me to change the company policy?"

"Well, you do own the resort."

He shook his head. "I don't think you want me changing things."

She arched a brow. "Why not?"

"Because you seem to like everything exactly the way it is. You take comfort in the routine of it all."

She wasn't so sure she liked him trying to figure her out. And even worse, he was right.

"Maybe I do," she said defensively. "But that's because I know what it's like not to know where I was going to sleep at night or where my next meal was coming from." She hadn't intended to admit all of that, but Atlas had a way of burrowing under her skin and she found herself uttering things she preferred to keep to herself.

"I'm sorry." He had the decency to look sheepish. "I never should have said any of that. I was just trying to point out how different we are."

Perhaps she'd overreacted. "And maybe I'm a bit defensive. My ex had criticism down to a fine art by the end of our relationship. I guess I still haven't developed a thick skin."

"Don't. You're perfect just the way you are."

Her cheeks grew warm. "You don't have to say that."

"I meant it." He smiled at her. "I'm so happy I found you—I mean because you've been so helpful."

But the way he looked into her eyes she couldn't help but wonder if he meant something else. Because she was starting to develop feelings for him and she knew that wasn't good. Not good at all.

Once he'd accomplished his business on the island he'd be gone. And she'd be left with nothing but a broken heart. She wouldn't put herself through that again. She just had to keep reminding herself that this candlelit dinner was business. But it sure didn't feel like it.

Dinner was delicious.

The atmosphere was out of this world.

But it was the company that was priceless.

Atlas hadn't thought he would smile again after sorting through Thea's belongings. At the apartment, he'd been reminded of how alone he'd been after his mother had left him.

But now inside this giant aquarium-like room, he was no longer alone. He had Hermione—as a friend, or course. Though they'd only known each other a short time, he didn't know how he'd get through any of this without her.

After their dinner dishes were cleared, he reached across the table and placed his hand over hers. In the candlelight, he stared into her eyes. "Thank you."

"For what? Bringing you here? I'm sure you'd have eventually made it here on your own."

"Not the restaurant—though I am glad you refused to do room service—but rather I meant helping me through this process." As she smiled at him, he gave her hand a squeeze. His gaze dipped to her lips, causing his heart to beat faster. Then realizing what he was doing, he lifted his gaze to meet hers once more. "It means a lot. And I won't forget it. If you ever need anything, all you have to do is phone me."

She withdrew her hand and glanced away.

What had he said wrong? He could speak programming language fluently, but he didn't have a clue how to speak on a personal level to a woman. And he didn't want to mess up this thing they had—this working relationship. Because it wasn't anything more—it couldn't be. He didn't do long-term anything. He liked his freedom—at least that's what he'd been telling himself for years.

"Would you like dessert?" he asked.

She shook her head. "I'm ready to call it a night."

"Not yet." His eyes pleaded with her. "Maybe we could go back to my suite for some coffee. You could tell me more about the resort." When he sensed she was going to reject his invitation, he said, "Please."

She hesitated. "Just a few minutes. I have to get home."

"I understand."

She stood and pushed in her chair. Her gaze never met his. He felt as though he needed to apologize for something, but he just couldn't figure out what it would be.

They quietly made their way back to his suite. Each was lost in their thoughts. Only this time he didn't have a clue what she was thinking.

Inside the suite there was a lamp lit on a side table. It sent a soft glow throughout the living room. They both sat on the couch. Hermione left a great distance between them. For Atlas, it felt as though she were trying to get away from him. And for the life of him, he couldn't figure out what had happened. Whatever he'd said or done, he wanted to take it back. He longed to return things to the way they'd been before the dinner—light and easy.

"I'm sorry if I said or did something wrong at dinner," he said.

"It's okay."

"No, it's not. I don't even know what I did to upset you." He raked his fingers through his hair. "Here's the thing. I'm not very good with speaking to women, you know, on a personal level."

Her gaze met his. "You seem to do just fine with me."

"Really? Because I'm thinking that if I was better at it, you wouldn't be so anxious to get away from me." He leaned back on the couch. The events of the day weighed heavily on him. "Maybe I shouldn't have drawn you into my nightmare. It wasn't fair of me."

"I don't mind helping you." When he sent her a skeptical look, she said, "I mean it."

"Then what happened between us? Things were going so well, until they weren't." And then he wondered if it was this growing attraction between them that had made things awkward.

"Do you really care what I think?"

"Of course I do."

"Why?"

She wanted him to dissect his feelings and put them into words? His chest tightened. He wasn't good with mushy stuff. But as he gazed into her eyes, he realized that's exactly what she expected. His hands grew clammy.

He cleared his throat. "Because you're my one friend on this island."

She smiled at him. It was the kind of smile that lit up her eyes and made the gold flecks in them twinkle. "Stop overthinking things." Her voice was soft and sultry. "We're good."

He sat upright, rubbing his palms on his pants. He was so anxious to move beyond this awkward moment. "We are?"

She nodded as she continued to smile. "We are."

Maybe there was something to this mushy stuff. When he spoke, his voice came out deeper than he'd intended. "Because when this is all over and I go home, I'm going to miss you."

"You are?"

With his gaze still holding hers, he nodded. "Definitely."

"I'll, ah, miss you too."

His gaze lowered to her lush lips. His heart pounded. As though drawn to her by a force that was beyond his control, he leaned toward her. Surely she had to feel it too. Right? It couldn't just be him.

His eyes closed as his lips pressed to hers. He willed her to kiss him back. Surely he hadn't misread things between them. Had he?

And then her hands reached out, cupping his face. Her touch was feathery soft, as though she was afraid he might disappear in a puff of smoke. Her lips slowly moved over his as she took the lead.

Thoughts of his mother's estate slipped from his mind. Worries over selling the island were swept away. Anxiety about the security of the royal jewels eased. In this moment, his thoughts were only of Hermione and how right this kiss felt.

He wanted this moment to go on and on. Because a kiss was normally just a kiss, a prelude to something more. However, with Hermione, it was all by itself an earthmoving event. His lips gently brushed over hers. He didn't want to scare her off. He wanted to hold her in his arms as long as possible.

As he drew her closer, their kiss intensified. His whole body came alive with the rush of adrenaline. He'd never been so consumed with a kiss.

Hermione was unique in so many wonderful and amazing ways. As her lips moved beneath his, he wondered how he'd been so lucky to meet her.

The reality of their circumstances slipped away. The only thing that mattered right now was him and her. And this kiss that was like a soothing balm on his tattered and torn heart.

He didn't want this moment to end. His hand reached up and gently caressed the smooth skin of her cheek. His fingers slid down to her neck where he felt her rapid pulse. She wanted him as much as she wanted him.

Buzz-buzz.

He didn't want his phone to ruin this moment. He didn't want anything to come between them. It vibrated in his pocket, distracting him from Hermione's tantalizing kiss.

She pulled away. His eyes opened to find her staring at him. He couldn't read her thoughts. Was she happy about the kiss? Or was she angry that he'd overstepped?

She glanced away. "You better answer that. It's probably important. And it's getting late. I'll see you in the morning."

Buzz-buzz.

"But I don't want to answer it. I want us to talk."

She shook her head as she stood. "We've definitely said more than enough for tonight. Good night."

And then she was out the door in a flash. Once more he was left with questions where she was concerned.

Buzz-buzz.

Why wouldn't his phone stop ringing? Surely it must have

switched to voice mail by now. He yanked it from his pocket to turn it off, but then he caught sight of the caller ID. It was an important client from London.

Normally, he'd drop everything to answer it. But these weren't normal times. It was his policy to meet problems head-on instead of letting them fester. But this problem wasn't with his client. It was with Hermione.

He'd made a mistake by kissing her. He should have known better, but he'd let himself get caught up in the evening—he'd let himself imagine their dinner had been something more than it was. And now he'd blurred the lines of their relationship.

He needed to focus on business. It didn't confuse him or hurt him. It was a constant that he could always count on. And so when his phone rang again, he answered it.

"Atlas, what's going on?" Krystof practically shouted into the phone.

It was best to find out what he knew before admitting to anything. "What are you talking about?"

"Don't give me that. You left me this urgent message that we had to talk right away. What's wrong?"

"Everything." He raked his fingers through his hair. "And nothing."

It wasn't the reason he'd left the voice mail. But so much had changed since then, and he needed a friend to speak to. Krystof was a very old friend, someone he could confide in.

"What are you talking about?"

Atlas blew out a deep breath. Suddenly, he wasn't so sure he was ready to discuss Hermione with anyone.

"Nothing. It's just been a long day."

"It's a woman."

"What? No." He suddenly felt self-conscious about this avalanche of emotions for Hermione.

"I'm right. I knew it. What's her name?"

"There's no woman," he snapped. "I mean not really. Anyway, that isn't the reason I called. I think the resort has more to offer you than you think."

"I'm listening."

Atlas went on to tell him all about the casino and the high rollers room. "So how soon can you get here? You'll love it."

"Says the man anxiously trying to unload the island. Sorry. I still can't get there any sooner than next week, and this place better be as good as you say it is."

They wrapped up the phone call with Atlas promising Krystof that he would fall in love with the island.

But as Atlas opened his laptop to go back to work, his thoughts turned to Hermione and their kiss. Had it been a mistake? If it was, it was a delicious one.

CHAPTER TEN

WHY HAD SHE done that?

Why had she kissed him back?

Hermione knew the answer, but she didn't want to admit it to herself or anyone else. The truth was she couldn't quit thinking about that kiss and replaying it over and over in her mind. She was drawn to Atlas in a way that she'd never been drawn to a man in her life—not even her ex. And that scared her.

Even to crack open the door to her heart a little and let Atlas in frightened her. Because every time she opened herself up to care about someone, she lost them. They either disappeared from her life or they ended up not being who she thought they were—except for her Ludus friends. They were always there for her.

And worse yet, Atlas was out to ruin the world she'd immersed herself in here at the Ludus. Sure, he might have promised to protect the employees' jobs for six months, but that protection wouldn't include her.

She understood that the new owner would have a different style and require different management. The thought not only saddened her but scared her. Without Adara, Rhea, Titus and the rest of the Ludus team, she would be all alone again.

And so that night at her apartment instead of sleeping, she

worked on her résumé. It needed a lot of updating. And then she went online and set up an account on a professional networking site. She worked late into the night.

Friday morning, she almost slept through her alarm. She rushed through the shower and dressed. She had to get to work early. The employees' future employment hinged on her holding up her end of the bargain. And she refused to give Atlas any reason to void their agreement.

There had to be a way to rewind things. Yes, if they could just pretend the kiss hadn't happened they would be totally fine. They could work together until he left. As anxious as he was to finish cleaning out his mother's apartment, he'd most likely be gone by Valentine's.

Knowing she had to get a move on before a large chunk of the morning slipped by, she jumped in her car and headed for the island. She told herself to focus on her work and not the soul-stirring, heart-fluttering, best ever kiss. Definitely not that.

When she entered the resort, she immediately turned toward her office. But as she deposited her purse on her desk, she realized she wasn't going to get any work done until she told Atlas what was on her mind.

When she went to his suite, Atlas didn't answer the door. She messaged him and he told her to come on in. He was out on the balcony.

Her stomach knotted up with nervous tension. Maybe this wasn't such a good idea. But it was too late to change her mind. She used her master key card and let herself inside.

Atlas glanced up from his laptop when he heard her step onto the sunny balcony. "Good morning."

"Morning." Hermione didn't smile. "We need to talk."

"Have a seat?" Atlas gestured to the chair next to him.

She opted to sit across the table from him. Coffee was offered and she declined. Hermione's empty stomach churned. She told herself it was nervousness over what she had to say, and it had absolutely nothing to do with her close proximity to the man whose kisses made her go weak in the knees.

"We need to talk about last night," she said.

"Agreed."

His quick, agreeable response surprised her. "It shouldn't have happened. It...it was a mistake."

His gaze searched hers. "Is that what you really think?"

She glanced down at her hands. "I do."

She couldn't let herself fall for him. He was the enemy of sorts—the man who would steal away the life she'd come to cherish, from the monthly luncheons to the friendly greetings in the hallways. Even some of the guests had become friends.

Her ex may have stolen her money as well as her mother's locket, but Atlas was preparing to steal something so much more valuable—the family she'd worked so hard to create. She couldn't bear the thought of having to start over again.

Buzz-buzz.

Hermione glanced at her phone. There was a message from Adara.

Urgent. Need to talk.

What's wrong?

Adara wasn't one to panic. She was really good at taking things in stride. It's what made her so good at her job of concierge.

Where are you?

I'm meeting with Atlas in his suite.

I'll be right there.

"What's wrong?" Atlas asked.

"It's Adara. She says something urgent came up. She's on her way here." She followed him inside the suite.

Knock-knock.

Atlas opened the door. "Come in."

Adara strode into the suite in her navy-and-white skirt suit and high heels. It wasn't so much her actions or the smile she briefly forced on her face but rather the worry reflected in her eyes that had Hermione on alert.

Adara's worried gaze met hers. "It's Nestor. His wife just called. He's in the hospital."

Hermione knew Adara lived near Nestor's family, and she'd become good friends with his wife. "Oh, no. What happened?"

"A heart attack." Adara's voice was filled with emotion. "They're taking him into surgery. His wife said it was touch and go for a while."

"How awful." Her heart went out to Nestor and his family. He was always so reliable and generous. People naturally smiled when they were around him. He put people at ease, and that really helped him do his job of event coordinator.

Adara nodded. "I just can't believe this happened to him."

"His wife wanted us to know he'll be off work for quite a while."

"Tell them not to worry. His job will be waiting for him when he's ready to return."

Adara nodded. "I will. And I don't want to be crude at this moment, but this complicates matters."

Atlas rubbed his fingers over his freshly shaven jaw. "What's complicated?"

Adara's gaze flickered to him and then back to Hermione. "Nestor is supposed to be planning a Valentine's wedding as well as the Valentine's ball. And his assistant just went out on maternity leave."

Hermione inwardly groaned. What was it with this week? Things just kept getting worse.

Her gaze moved to Atlas to see how he was taking the news.

If the frown lines marring his handsome face were any indication, he wasn't taking the information very well. He moved to the glass wall and stared off at the sea.

"I can coordinate the party," Hermione said. "But I can't organize the wedding."

Handling the management of the resort in addition to planning an extravagant party wouldn't leave her any spare time, but this wasn't about her. It was about helping a coworker at his most vulnerable time.

Atlas turned to them. "Would you even know where to begin?"

She straightened her shoulders. "I can figure it out."

He shook his head. "This is a big event. Have you ever planned a party of that size or grandeur?"

Translated to mean that the party was too important to let an amateur handle. He had no faith in her abilities. No wonder he was anxious to sell the place. He was worried she'd destroy the resort.

"No, I haven't but it doesn't mean I can't do it. Nestor was good at keeping notes." She turned to Adara. "Do you know where his company laptop is?"

"As far as I know, he was never without it. It's probably at his house. I can pick it up for you."

"Thank you. It's the key to everything." Upon seeing the doubt reflected in their eyes, Hermione said, "Everyone stop worrying. I can handle it. Most of the plans should already be in place. The trick is the follow-through. You know, making sure everything arrives on time and is put in its place."

"You really think you're up to this?" Adara asked. "It's a lot with everything else you're doing."

"I do." She ignored the flutter of nerves in her stomach. "But what about the wedding?"

"I'll take care of it," Adara said.

"You can't do that. You also have your hands full," Hermione said.

"Listen to who's talking." Adara crossed her arms and arched her brows in challenge. "If you're going to pick up some slack, so am I."

Hermione knew how stubborn her friend could be. "You're not going to change your mind, are you?"

Adara shook her head. "You know me better than that."

Hermione breathed a little easier. "Okay, now that we have the two big items on his calendar taken care of, I'll have to see what else he has going on."

"And I'll talk to Rhea about setting up a schedule to make sure there's food for Nestor's family," Adara said. "If that's all right with you."

Hermione nodded. "Yes. That's a great idea."

"We could hire a professional party planner," Atlas said. "It'll cost extra at this late date, but it'll be worth it. That's what we'll do. I'll put my assistant on it."

If she had been worried about how she'd stay out of his arms going forward, she didn't have to worry any longer. Anything she'd thought had been started between them had been officially doused with his outright disbelief in her abilities.

Hermione glared at him, but he refused to back down.

"Then I'm no longer needed here." Hermione lifted her chin ever so slightly and strode away.

"Hermione, wait," Atlas called out. "I didn't mean it that way."

He'd meant every word he'd said. Of that she was certain. At every turn, he was questioning her and her choices. The backs of her eyes stung. She blinked repeatedly, refusing to let on that his words had hurt her. She would not give him that power.

Her steps came quickly. The truth was she wanted to be as far from Atlas as she could get. The man utterly frustrated her. One minute he's kissing her like he never wanted to stop—like she was the most beautiful woman in the world.

The next moment he's insulting her abilities. No wonder she

hadn't been in a relationship in a long time. Men were utterly exasperating—most especially Atlas.

She walked out the door. She gave it a firm yank but with its gentle close feature, she wasn't given the satisfaction of it slamming closed.

What had he done?

He'd totally messed up everything.

Atlas had watched the storm clouds gather in Hermione's eyes and he hadn't done anything to calm the waters. The reasons—the good reasons—had all been there in his head. But had he used the right words? No.

It seemed that whenever he was in close proximity to Hermione that his mind and mouth had a glitchy disconnect. There were so many things he wanted to say to her, but for one reason or another he'd kept them to himself.

But he couldn't let things stay like this. He couldn't stand the thought of Hermione being upset with him and jumping to the wrong conclusions. He had to fix things or at least try.

After apologizing to Adara, he rushed to the hallway, finding no sign of her. Would she go back to her office? Or would she walk out the front door and keep on going?

Stop. He was getting ahead of himself. After all, she was an employee of the resort. Her address was on record. He could easily track her down if he was so inclined.

Who was he kidding? He was most definitely inclined. He just wasn't sure it was a good idea. After the kiss last night, he knew the volatile attraction ran both ways. He also knew Hermione was in denial of their chemistry. Whether they wanted to admit it or not, it existed.

If he was to go after her now and things got heated—if their attraction spiraled out of control, she'd never forgive him. He wouldn't forgive himself. Things needed to cool off, and then they could talk like rational adults.

After calming down, hopefully she'd see the merits of his

plan. She was overextending herself. At the same time, it impressed him the way she was worried about those around her and asked for nothing for herself. There weren't many people that were so selfless.

He returned to his suite where Adara was checking messages on her phone. She glanced up when he entered the room. She slipped her phone in her pocket.

"I didn't handle that very well," he said.

"Did you have a chance to speak to her?"

He shook his head. "I didn't catch up with her."

He sunk down into the chair. "When I came to Ludus I knew it wasn't going to be fun, but I didn't expect things to keep getting worse at every turn."

Adara paused as though not sure she should say what was on her mind. When her phone buzzed, she checked it and then returned it to her pocket.

"It's okay," he said. "Just say it."

"I think you should let Hermione decide how much she can handle. She'll ask for help before she does anything to damage the resort. She loves this place. It's her home—her family. And we won't let her fail. We'll help her every step of the way."

It sounded nice, but he wasn't sure it was based in reality. "Even though it would be above and beyond everyone's duties?"

"Even then. This group pulls together to help each other."

His business didn't run on such employee devotion. This resort was so different from anything he knew. It was a good thing he was selling it because he knew his management style would clash with the established routine.

"The guests will be unhappy if the party goes awry." When Adara sent him a surprised look, he said, "I've heard them talking in the hallways. This place is abuzz with excitement."

"And you should know that Nestor does have a couple of other staff members. I'm sure they'll pitch in so the party isn't overwhelming for Hermione. And like I said, if more help is required the resort is full of people who would lend a hand."

This whole thing made him uneasy. There was a resort full of famous and influential people who were waiting for a splashy and impressive party. If the party was a failure, it would really hurt the resort's reputation and hamper any potential sale.

He rubbed his jaw. "Even if I could find Hermione, I don't think she'd be willing to hear me out."

Adara sent him a smile. "I think you underestimate yourself. But you have given me an idea."

He braced himself. "Do I even want to know what it is?"

"Don't worry about it. Just go talk to Hermione."

"I don't know where she went."

Adara held up her phone. "But I do. She texted me and mentioned she was stopping by Thea's apartment."

"Really?" Even though Hermione was upset with him, she was still holding up her end of their agreement. He didn't know it was possible, but she impressed him even more.

"Now I have to go." Adara started for the door but then paused to say, "Good luck."

He was going to need it. Hermione had never been this upset with him. And he had no idea how to make it up to her. But that wouldn't stop him from trying.

CHAPTER ELEVEN

SOME PEOPLE WOULD say she was foolish.

Other people would say she was smart.

Hermione really didn't care what people thought of her—well, that wasn't quite true. She cared what Atlas thought. The truth was she cared too much.

She should be in her office right now, but she was too worked up to sit still. She needed some physical activity. She needed to work off some of her frustration.

Hermione carried a stack of books from the bookcase in Thea's living room to the coffee table. There she opened each one, turned it over and shook it to make sure there were no loose papers tucked inside. And then she placed them in a cardboard box to donate as Atlas had instructed.

Though it nearly killed Hermione to admit it, Atlas was right. She couldn't do everything—even if she wanted to. Delegating was the only way she could get through the next week leading up to Valentine's.

She'd had Rhea on speakerphone going over a couple of urgent matters, including the double-booking of the Cypress Room. Once that was sorted, she asked Rhea to temporarily take on some more responsibilities. Her assistant understood that this was a difficult time for the resort and enthusiastically offered to pitch in.

Rhea's kindness and generosity brought tears to Hermione's eyes. Thank goodness they were on the phone. Hermione wasn't usually overly emotional. She blamed the tears on Atlas.

When she disconnected the call, she continued to mull over the scene with Atlas. If she didn't care for Atlas, would his lack of faith in her abilities hurt so much? Unwilling to answer that question, she told herself it was a pride thing. However, deep down she knew it was more than that. She wanted him to be different from her ex, who was always handy with a backhanded compliment. She wanted Atlas to see her as an equal—someone he could share more than a passing moment with—

The breath caught in her lungs. What was she thinking? She was not falling for Atlas. Absolutely not.

"Hermione?" Atlas's voice carried from the elevator into the living room.

She hesitated to answer. If she remained quiet, would he go away? No. Atlas was way too determined when he wanted something. And she would not let him think she was afraid to face him.

"In here." She would just treat him like any other coworker.

The sound of his approaching footsteps echoed in the foyer. And then he was there, filling up the doorway with his broad shoulders. "Can we talk?"

"Now isn't a good time. I'm a little busy." She continued opening books, shaking them and placing them in the box.

It was the same way she'd act with any other coworker. But any other person wouldn't make her heart race just by their presence.

Just ignore it. He'll be gone soon.

"This is important."

She stopped working. Hesitantly her gaze met his. "So is this. I have my end of a bargain to keep. And the sooner I finish, the sooner we'll no longer have to deal with each other."

He sighed. "Hermione, you took what I said out of context—"

"I don't think so." She resumed her task.

Buzz-buzz.

Her gaze moved to her phone, resting on the cherrywood end table. It wasn't her phone. That meant it had to be Atlas's, and she'd never been so grateful for an interruption. His phone went off again. She willed him to answer it.

"I need to get this, but we're not done talking."

She didn't say anything, but she was thinking plenty. None of her testy thoughts would make this situation any easier.

He stepped into the foyer to take the call. He didn't say much. Most of the conversation appeared to be one-sided. Then he stepped back in the study. "I have to go take care of something, but I'll be back."

"Don't rush on my account."

He hesitated as though he were going to say something, but then he'd thought better of it. He walked away, and at last she could take a full breath.

She had to quit letting him get to her. After all, it wasn't like they were a couple or anything. She needed to work faster because once Nestor's laptop was delivered to the resort, she would need to focus most of her energies on the Valentine's ball.

She continued her task with renewed determination. After quickly moving through a dozen or so books, her phone rang. She had no intention of answering it, especially if it was Atlas. But curiosity had her checking the caller ID.

When she saw Adara's name on the screen, she couldn't help but wonder what she would need. Perhaps the laptop had already arrived. She was anxious to see exactly what party details needed to be completed. It would be a lot as no detail was overlooked or extravagance forsaken when it came to a Ludus event. They were the definition of lavish.

She pressed the phone to her ear. "Hello."

"Hermione, I'm so sorry to bother you, but there's a problem at the dock. It's something about a special shipment for the party, and they're insisting on your signature."

Hermione inwardly groaned. This was the last interruption she needed at the moment. Her gaze moved around the study. It wasn't like the work wouldn't be here when she got back.

"Okay. I'm on my way."

Adara gave her the instructions and then hung up. It all seemed easy enough. And with it being an unusually warm, sunny day, it'd be a good day for a walk. It would be a chance for her to clear her mind and figure out how to deal with Atlas in a calm, reasonable manner.

A strange place for a meeting.

Atlas sat aboard the resort's luxury yacht—*The Sea Jewel*. Adara had phoned him and asked him to meet her there. She'd sounded anxious or worried; he wasn't quite sure which but something was definitely not right with her.

He was starting to worry about the resort. Without his mother at the helm, would the service decline? Hermione seemed good at her job, but she was getting spread too thin.

The problem was that she was too fiercely independent for her own good, and that could spell trouble for the resort. And he wouldn't be of much help. He didn't know a thing about running a resort, but he did know how to manage people. Still, his style of management and hers were two very different things.

Should he step in and assume control of the resort? It was the very last thing he wanted to do. He'd only come here to settle his mother's personal affairs and now he felt as though he was being drawn in more deeply with every passing hour.

The captain escorted Atlas to the interior of the boat. It was spacious and appeared to have every amenity a person could want, from long comfy white couches to captain chairs along with a large bar and a giant screen television.

Atlas sat down on the couch but unable to sit still for long, he started pacing. He was forever staring out the long bank of windows, hoping someone would arrive soon.

Tired of waiting, he reached for his phone. There must have been some sort of mix-up. He would call Adara and find out what was going on. His finger hovered over the screen when he detected movement on the dock. *At last.*

He slipped the phone back in his pocket. He headed for the deck to greet Adara and get down to business. But when he stepped outside, he was greeted by Hermione.

When her gaze met his, her eyes widened. "What are you doing here?"

"That's just what I was going to ask you."

"I was told I needed to sign for a shipment, but when I got to the dock, I was guided onboard the yacht." Her brows drew together. "I don't understand. Why are you here?"

"I was told to meet Adara here, but I haven't seen her."

Hermione crossed her arms. "What's going on? I don't have time to play games."

He had a suspicion who might be behind this setup. "Who called you?"

"Adara." Hermione's brows rose as her eyes lit up. "Let me guess. She called you too?"

"Yes. It looks like she set us up."

As though in confirmation, the engine started. The boat started to move away from the dock.

"Hey!" Hermione called out. "Wait."

Atlas shook his head. "They can't hear you."

"What are we going to do?"

"Apparently we're going for a ride." It was certainly one way to obtain Hermione's undivided attention. He just didn't know if this cruise would be long enough for him to convince her to forgive him.

"But…but that's kidnapping." Hermione frowned. "I have work to do. I don't have time to go sailing." She turned to him. "Are you just going to stand there?"

"I was actually thinking of sitting down and enjoying the view." And he did just that.

"You can't be happy about this."

"I will definitely have a word with Adara when we get back." He would thank her for this terrific idea, but next time he wanted to be clued in on her plans ahead of time. Then he was going to give her a well-deserved raise.

Hermione huffed. "You could tell the captain to turn around right now."

Perhaps a change of subject would help. "I didn't know the resort owned a yacht."

"They own many boats but not all are this fancy. This one is brand-new. Your mother ordered it just before she...well, uh, it was just delivered." She looked flustered as she avoided his gaze.

"What you're saying is that we're the first ones to ride in it?"

She shrugged. "I don't know for sure, but I think so. It'll come in handy come June."

"What's in June?"

"The Royal Regatta."

He was intrigued. And the more Hermione talked about the resort the less stiff her posture became. "What does it entail?"

She sat down. "It's a boat race around the island."

He joined her. "And who participates in this race?"

"A lot of people—even the prince of Rydiania. It's his country that cosponsors the race."

"The same country that loaned the resort the Ruby Heart and the other jewels?" When she nodded, he asked, "Why would a foreign country lend the resort what must be priceless gems? I thought Thea's husband had been thrown out of the family and exiled to this island."

"That's not quite how it went down. Even though Georgios had been exiled from his homeland of Rydiania, he was free to travel the world—to make his home wherever he pleased. However, his family preferred that it was a long way from Rydiania."

The more Hermione talked, the more her voice took on its normal bubbly lilt. Her arms now rested at her sides. And the frown lines had smoothed from her face.

"And he picked this island of all places to live?" Atlas didn't want her to stop talking about the island and its history because when she was unveiling the past for him, she wasn't thinking about how angry she was with him.

"Georgios said it was love at first sight. He knew once he stepped on the island that he was home. But he quickly grew lonely, and that's when he got the idea to invest his savings into building the Ludus Resort. He said he never regretted that decision."

"If I had a private island," Atlas said, "I don't know if I'd want to share it."

"But you do have an island. Remember? This is all yours."

"It doesn't feel like it."

"What does it feel like?"

"Some sort of messed-up dream and soon I'll wake up."

"But this is no dream. It's your future—if you want it to be."

He didn't want to think about that now. He'd rather enjoy this truce he'd somehow struck with Hermione. "I'm still confused. If this king was cast out of the family—"

"He wasn't cast out. He abdicated the throne. He said he wasn't meant to be a king. He believed his brother could do a better job."

"Still, he was exiled from the country, so why would they lend their jewels?"

Hermione smiled. "Well, that's another story. The current king and queen of Rydiania have three children. The oldest being Prince Istvan. He had known Georgios when he was very young. You might say those two hit it off. When Georgios was exiled, the prince was deeply upset. The king and queen forbade him from contacting his uncle. But you know how kids can be when they're forbidden to do something."

He thought back over his own troubled youth. "It makes the temptation even greater."

"Exactly. When the prince was old enough to travel without his parents or chaperones, he sought out his uncle. To hear it told, and to have witnessed them together, it's like the two had never been parted all of those years."

"And so all was forgiven with Georgios?" He was hoping there would be a happy ending. He needed to know all families weren't messy and broken like his.

"No. I'm afraid not. Georgios said it was enough to have the prince back in his life, but every now and then when he didn't think anyone was looking, he would get this faraway look in his eyes and then a sadness would come over him."

"So much for a happy ending."

"Oh, I think for the most part Georgios was happy. It was just when he thought of his brother that he realized what he'd lost. And as for the royal jewels, they belong to Prince Istvan. He inherited them from his grandmother. He loved your mother and visited often after his uncle passed on. He knew how much your mother loved Valentine's and thought the jewels might cheer her up."

And yet another person Thea had won over. It would appear he and his father were the only two she didn't care for. The thought weighed heavy on him. Was he too much like his father?

"Now that you know the backstory on the jewels, it's time to turn this boat around. I can't believe Adara would do this." She reached for her phone.

"Don't do that. It's a beautiful day." He stood and moved out to the deck. "Why not enjoy some of it?"

"Atlas, we can't just run off for the day. We have things to do." She followed him.

The sea breeze combed through his hair and rushed past his face, offsetting the warmth of the sun. But Atlas didn't pay much attention. He was drawn to the emerging landscape.

"This is beautiful." He stared back at the rocky shoreline with its lush green foliage. "Is that a waterfall off in the distance?"

"Yes. It's one of them. If you want you could explore the island."

He shook his head. "I have too much work to do."

"You should see it during the summer when the orchids and wildflowers are in bloom. It's a cascade of color."

He opened his mouth to say that he couldn't wait to see it but then wordlessly pressed his lips back together. He wouldn't be here come summertime. By then Ludus Island would be in this rearview mirror...where it belonged.

He swallowed. "So the only thing on the entire island is the resort?"

She nodded. "This all belonged to Georgios. He liked having the ability to keep the paparazzi at a distance so he and his guests could enjoy the island's beauty."

"Do you offer sightseeing boat rides for the guests?"

"No, we don't. But now that you mention it, perhaps we could work on putting together something. Maybe a lunch and dinner cruise."

"I'm glad we have this moment together."

She arched a brow. "Don't go thinking any of this erases what happened earlier."

"Will you at least let me explain?"

She didn't say anything at first, then she sighed. "Fine. It's not like I have anyplace I can go. And I don't plan to swim back to shore."

"Back at the suite, the things I said didn't come out right."

"It sounded pretty clear to me. You don't trust me to organize the Valentine's ball. All I'm good for is to clean your mother's apartment."

"Whoa. Where did that come from?"

"Isn't that what you're thinking? That I'm not cut out to run this resort?"

He shook his head. "I never thought such a thing. Who put

these thoughts in your head?" When she didn't respond, he said softly, "Hermione, talk to me. What's going on?"

"My ex, Otis, was always planting doubts in my mind. Just little things here and there when I went back to school. At first I didn't pay much attention. It wasn't until Adara pointed out how his little comments over time had eaten away at my self-confidence until I doubted myself about almost everything that I realized he was jealous of my career."

Anger balled up in his gut over what that jerk had done to her. Who did such a thing to such a smart, accomplished and caring person like Hermione?

And then he recalled all of his questions and suggestions for the resort. He'd also insisted on upgrading the resort's security over her objection. And finally he'd questioned her ability to take over the Valentine's party on top of all her other responsibilities. Not because he didn't think she could do it but rather because he cared if she took on too much work.

He cared.

The revelation echoed in his mind. It'd been so long since he'd allowed himself to get close enough to a person to truly care about them. In the process, he'd totally messed up everything.

His gaze met hers. "Hermione, I'm not like your ex."

Disbelief reflected in her eyes. "It doesn't matter—"

"It does matter." His voice was soft but firm. "I know I haven't handled any of this correctly." He needed her to truly hear him. That would only happen if he put himself out there and revealed things he'd never shared with anyone. "Coming to this island—Thea's home—is the hardest thing I've ever done." His voice grew gravelly with emotion. He cleared his throat. "And then to find out how much she cared for all of you…it was hard."

Pity reflected in Hermione's eyes. "I'm so sorry. I should have been more sensitive."

"Don't pity me. I'm fine." He didn't feel fine. He felt beaten and scarred. "I've been caring for myself since I was a kid. I'll get through this."

"You don't have to get through this alone. You could let people in."

He shook his head. The thought of setting himself up to be abandoned like his mother had done or rejected like his father had ultimately done made his protective wall come back up.

"I... I can't talk about this." He strode back inside the yacht.

Hermione followed him. "Running from your past isn't working. Once you face it, it won't have any control over you."

"That's not what I'm doing. I only mentioned it because I'm trying to explain the reason I said and did certain things when I arrived. Instead of telling you what I intended to do, I should have asked for your input. Like the security system we're supposed to work on tomorrow. Do you feel it's too much for the resort?"

Her eyes momentarily widened. "We haven't had problems in the past but what you said got me to thinking. If the resort is to grow, it's feasible to update the security. Just don't go too overboard. We're still just a small island resort."

"Thank you for your input. I'll do my best to run my ideas for the resort past you. My input wasn't meant to demean your capabilities. They were about me and my need to prove myself... that Thea was wrong to leave me—to forget me."

"But she didn't. She loved you—"

"No." His voice came out harshly. He made an effort to soften his tone when he spoke again. "Don't say that. People who love you don't abandon you."

He was losing track of this conversation. Why did he keep revealing more and more of himself? This conversation was supposed to be about Hermione, not him.

He sighed. "I'm saying this all wrong."

Her gaze narrowed in on him. "What exactly are you saying?"

"I'm saying I think you're capable of anything you set your

mind to, but I didn't want you to take on too much. As it is, I think you should stop working on Thea's apartment so you can focus on the party. Just promise me one thing."

"What's that?"

"If it's too much or you need help that you'll tell me."

"I'll tell you. But don't worry, I've got this. This is going to be the best party ever." And that's when she leaned into him, wrapping her arms around him as she hugged him.

His heart immediately started to hammer against his ribs. His body froze. He was afraid to move or breathe for fear that she'd pull away. Because having her so close was the most amazing feeling that caused a warm spot in his chest.

When at last she pulled away, he said, "Hermione, I—"

She pressed her fingertips to his lips. "Maybe we've done enough talking."

What? There were still things he wanted to say. But when she moved her fingers from his lips, those words escaped him. What exactly did she have in mind? As though in answer, she pressed her mouth to his. He liked the way she thought.

It wasn't a slow and gentle kiss. No, this was a kiss full of need and longing. Her hand slid up over his shoulder and around his neck until her fingertips raked through his hair. It was the most exhilarating feeling. Desire pumped through his veins.

The right and wrong of their intimacy was long forgotten. A driving need to feel her next to him pulsed through his veins. He wanted to explore all of her. He wanted to make her moan with pleasure.

He scooped her up in his arms. He carried her to the spacious chaise longue and gently laid her down. He joined her. His fingertips swept the loose strands of hair behind her ear.

"Does this mean I'm forgiven?" he murmured.

"Obviously I haven't been doing something right if you have to ask that question. Maybe I should try again." Her eyes twinkled with merriment.

A slow smile pulled at his lips. "Yes, I think we need some definite clarification."

She reached out to him. The backs of her fingers caressed his jawline as desire burned in her eyes. A bolt of need shot through his body.

He'd never had an afternoon tryst. Afternoons had always been for doing business. But with Hermione in his arms business was the last thing on his mind.

CHAPTER TWELVE

HER FEET DIDN'T touch the ground.

At least that's the way it felt.

Hermione's steps were light and quick as she made her way back to the office. She'd never felt this happy—this alive—this, ugh, she ran out of adjectives. Her brain was abuzz with images of being held in Atlas's arms as they'd made love. She had no idea he could be so gentle and loving.

There was so much more to him than she'd ever imagined. She could talk to him—really talk to him. And she felt safe when she confided in him that he wouldn't tell anyone else or use it against her—like Otis had done.

The thought of her ex weighed down her steps. Coming back down to earth, she recalled how excited and certain she'd been of Otis in the beginning. And look how wrong she'd been.

Was she wrong about Atlas too? After all, he still hadn't said he was going to change his mind about selling the resort. But with every passing day, she could see that he was getting more comfortable on Ludus Island. Soon he would realize that it was his destination.

The last thought buoyed her heart once more. It was like his presence on the island was his destiny. He just needed a little more time to figure things out.

Adara headed down the hallway toward her. "I was looking for you."

"Like you didn't know where I was since you're the one who had us whisked away on the yacht." Hermione knew she should be upset with her, but it was so hard when all she wanted to do was smile.

Adara acted as though she hadn't heard her. "I just talked to Nestor's wife and the surgery was a success. Now all he has to do is recover."

"That's the best news I've heard all day. If they need anything, let me know." Hermione was so happy for Nestor and his family. But she wasn't quite done with Adara. "You know I should be really mad at you for pulling that stunt with the boat."

Adara smiled. "But you're not because it worked. You two made up...didn't you?"

"I'm not going to tell you." Hermione resumed walking toward her office. "I can't believe you set us up—set me up. I thought we were friends."

Adara's smile faltered. "We are friends. I... I thought I was helping, but now you've got me worried that it went all wrong."

Hermione chanced a glance at her friend. "You should be worried. That was a very awkward situation."

"Oh." Her shoulders dropped. "So it didn't go well. I'm sorry. I won't do it again. I was just trying to help."

"Actually, it went very well." Hermione smiled.

Adara's eyes widened. "It did?"

"Yes, but you still shouldn't have done it."

"It just felt like you both needed a push, no, make that a shove in the right direction. I've seen the way you two look at each other when you think the other isn't looking. And you've both got it bad."

Her heart did a leap of joy. Atlas was checking her out. "We talked. And we worked some things out."

"Is that what we're calling it these days?" Adara grinned.

Heat flared in Hermione's cheeks. "We aren't discussing that.

And I really do have to get back to work. I wasn't expecting to take a boat ride in the middle of the workday."

"So does mean you two are officially a couple now?"

"I… I don't know." They hadn't gotten that far, but she'd like to think they were. There's no way he'd confided in her and then made love to her without feeling anything. But as for labels for their relationship, it was all too new.

"Just be careful around the Ruby Heart. I just saw it—alone, thank goodness—because there's some legend if lovers view it together that their lives will forever be entwined."

Hermione was starting to wonder if there was something to that legend. She wasn't ready to reveal that she'd viewed it with Atlas. "Do you believe it?"

Adara shrugged. "I've heard of stranger things. Why? Are you planning to visit the ruby with Atlas?"

"Stop trying to matchmake."

"But you're totally into him, aren't you?" Adara sent her a hopeful look.

Hermione hesitated. It was as though once she spoke the words it would make not only them but this whole thing with Atlas real. But she knew how silly that was because nothing could have been more real than the love they'd made on the yacht.

With her heart hammering with excitement mixed with a little fear, she said, "Yes." It was barely more than a whisper. She swallowed hard. If she was going to do this, she had to believe in it—in them. "Yes," she said with more force. "How could I not be? Have you looked at him?"

Adara nodded. "He's hot. Does he have a brother?"

"I'm afraid not. He's one of a kind."

Adara sighed. "I guess it's good that I'm happy with my life just the way it is."

Hermione wondered if her friend was as happy with her single status as she'd like others to believe. But considering that Hermione was about to put her tattered heart back out on the line for a man that didn't even live here, much less in the same country, well, she might not be the best person to give relationship advice.

When Monday rolled around, she still couldn't stop smiling.

Hermione felt like she was walking on air ever since Friday when they'd returned from that very special boat ride. She and Atlas had come to a new understanding. They hadn't made love again—not that she hadn't thought of it—but they'd shared meals and updates on their day.

It was as though a wall had come down and they were able to really communicate. She did notice that he didn't mention their relationship or what happened on the boat, but she also knew he was under a lot of stress with having to clean out Thea's apartment.

And though he hadn't spoken of their future or the resort's future, she told herself they still had time. She couldn't rush things—even though that's exactly what she wanted to do.

With each passing day, he was getting more involved in the resort. She shouldn't have doubted that the island would work its charms on him. At this moment, he was off meeting with his security team as they began installing a new state-of-the-art security system. He wasn't one to pass off tasks to others; he was overseeing this installation personally.

But now with the party at the end of the week, she had to focus fully on the preparations. Thankfully Nestor had everything well organized. Her main tasks were to make sure the ballroom had been cleaned from top to bottom and then verify everything had been delivered.

"How's it going?" Atlas stood in the doorway of the event coordinator's office.

She looked up from where she sat behind Nestor's desk. "I just finished a phone call to make sure the ice sculpture would be here on time."

"And what did you learn?"

"It will be here early and stored in our walk-in freezer. Nestor made this job very easy for me."

Atlas lounged against the doorjamb. "Don't go jinxing yourself. You still have a lot to do before everything is set to go."

"I know." She stood up and moved toward him. "But I think a positive attitude is half the battle."

He nodded in agreement. "It's nice to see you in such a good mood." His voice took on a serious tone. "But I have something to ask you."

"Uh-oh." Her mind raced. "If this is about Thea's apartment, don't worry. I'll get back to it after the party. I never meant to pull out of our agreement."

He shook his head. "That isn't it. I have a special guest flying in for the party, and I need to know if there is anywhere for him to stay?"

"No. I'm sorry. The resort is fully booked. The Valentine's ball is always a big draw." She gave the idea some thought. "There's the spare room in your suite."

"I thought of that, but I'm not sure that's the right impression I want to give him of the resort. And I don't know if he'll be traveling alone."

"What about putting them in Thea's apartment?"

Once again Atlas shook his head. Then he sighed. "But I could move there and give him the suite."

She knew he'd had a very complicated relationship with his mother. She also knew he was happier when he spent the least amount of time in Thea's apartment. This couldn't be easy for him. This guest must be very important to him.

And then she thought of an idea. "Or you could stay on the mainland at my flat."

He sent her a barely there smile. "Thank you for the offer. But I need to spend more time sorting Thea's things. If I'm staying there, I won't be able to procrastinate nearly as much."

She nodded. "I understand. I'll have your things moved—"

"Don't worry. I have it under control."

When he didn't move on, she asked, "Did you need something else?"

"I just noticed that with the nicer weather more people are gravitating outdoors." He opened his mouth as though he wanted to say more but then wordlessly closed it.

"When the weather warms up, it's even busier. And the regatta draws a huge crowd."

"Interesting. It'd probably be an even larger crowd if the resort wasn't for select clientele."

"You mean rich people."

"Yes. I'm just not sure why my mother hadn't changed it. I don't recall her being all about status. But then again, I was just a little kid when I knew her. What did I know back then?"

"I'm only guessing, but something tells me your mother kept the resort the same because it's the way her late husband liked it. And it really is nice the way it is. Give it a chance. It'll grow on you."

"I don't know." *Buzz-buzz*. He glanced at his phone. "I've got to get this. We'll talk more later."

And then he was gone. She didn't know what to think about what he'd suggested. Why would she change things when she loved them as is? Was it possible the island hadn't worked its charms on Atlas like she'd hoped? And if so, where did that leave her?

CHAPTER THIRTEEN

HE DIDN'T KNOW how to act around her.

Atlas could see that their lovemaking had changed things for Hermione. She no longer looked at him like he was the enemy— out to destroy the traditions of the Ludus.

But had things changed for him? He didn't think so. He was still moving ahead with the sale of the resort. But when it came to Hermione, all he wanted to do was to pull her into his arms and hold her close. Still, he resisted the idea because when he left the island, he didn't want to hurt her.

And since she hadn't mentioned their lovemaking, neither had he. He wouldn't know what to say—hey, it was amazing but a mistake. He couldn't say that to her, especially after knowing how her ex had treated her.

Instead, he'd kept a respectable distance from her. It wasn't helping because he noticed that she looked at him differently now, like she was caressing him with her gaze. And the way she spoke was of a softer tone, not to mention her agreeable attitude.

He wasn't much better. When he'd sought her out earlier, he'd almost asked her to go strolling on the beach with him. He couldn't imagine anything better than her hand in his with a gentle sea breeze as the sun warmed their faces.

But then he wondered what sort of idea that would give her. It was the sort of thing couples did. Was that what he wanted?

No. He was terrible with any sort of relationship; just ask any of the women who'd passed through his life.

The only thing he knew to do was to throw himself into upgrading the resort's security. Once that was completed, he would spend all of his time working on Thea's apartment because he couldn't stay here forever.

It was late by the time he and his team finished working for the day. He fully expected Hermione to have gone home by then, but when he strolled by her office, she was so immersed in her work that she didn't notice him at her doorway until he knocked.

"Hey, it's time to call it a night." He stepped into the office, automatically pulling the door shut behind him.

"I still have so much to do." Her gaze moved over the various stacks of papers and files on her desk.

He glanced around her desk, noticing that it wasn't as neat and tidy as it'd been when he'd first arrived.

"And it will wait until tomorrow." He couldn't believe he had just uttered those words.

He was a certified workaholic. But the more time he spent on this island, the more he was finding an interest in things other than work such as spending as many meals with Hermione as their busy schedules allowed.

She sighed. "Maybe you're right." She began shutting down her computer. "It has been a long day."

"Do you have a moment before you go home?" He'd missed spending time with her and hoped she wouldn't rush off.

"Sure. What do you need?"

"I have something I want to show you." He'd found a photo album full of Ludus employees, and he'd thought Hermione would know what to do with it.

After she gathered her things, she said, "Let's go."

"Right this way." He opened the door for her.

As they walked, she asked, "Did you eat?"

He cleared his throat. "I had something with the guys." And then he worried she'd waited for him. "Did you eat?"

She nodded. "I wasn't sure how late you'd be."

"There was a lot to do, and there were a couple of problems with the installation. In order to have it all up and running by the unveiling of the Ruby Heart on Valentine's, we had to work late." He rubbed the back of his neck.

For a while, they walked in a peaceful quietness. He couldn't help but wonder if this was what it was like for couples after a long day. Did they quietly enjoy each other's presence without having to speak?

He chanced a glance at Hermione as they took the private elevator to Thea's apartment. Her face was drawn with exhaustion and he had an urge to step in and take over the party planning, but he knew that was the last thing Hermione would want. She had promised to say something if it was too much. He had to trust her.

Once in the apartment, he gestured to the couch. "Why don't you come sit down?"

He took a seat next to her. "How's the party prep coming?"

"Good. The ballroom was cleaned until it gleamed. Tables have been set up. Tomorrow we'll start decorating."

"Is there anything I can do?"

She shook her head. "I've got this."

"I do have a question for you. My friend Krystof Mikos arrives tomorrow, and he's very interested in getting a seat at the high-stakes poker game. Is that possible?"

"Sure it is. I'll have Adara make the arrangements." She wrote a note and then paused. "The buy-in won't be a problem for your friend, will it?"

"Not at all." Krystof had more money than a small country, but he didn't act like it.

"Are you sure you wouldn't like to try your hand at cards?"

He shook his head again. "I only take chances on sure things."

"You mean your business?"

"Yes."

"And what about us?" Her gaze searched his. "Are we a sure thing?"

At last she'd broached the ominous subject weighing over them. The word yes teetered on the tip of his tongue, surprising him with his willingness to involve himself in a relationship. He bit back the answer. It was a moment of delusion—a moment when he wanted to believe that happily-ever-after truly existed.

It was Hermione's fault. She made him want to believe in fairy tales and happy endings. The last thing he should do was get anywhere near her.

The memories of their lovemaking were always there, lurking at the edge of his thoughts. And getting close to her would be too tempting. He'd want to pull her close and continue where they'd left off.

But that would be wrong. He couldn't offer her anything but a good time. And Hermione didn't strike him as the type to have a casual relationship. When she cared about people, she put her whole heart on the line.

"Listen, I've been meaning to talk to you but there just wasn't a chance earlier." He struggled to find the right words.

"I wanted to talk to you too. I don't want to rush things."

"Rush things?"

"With us. I've done that before. I led with my heart instead of my head, and it didn't go well."

He didn't like being grouped with her jerk of an ex. "I'm not your ex."

"I know that. It wasn't what I meant." The pained look in her eyes said her ex had hurt her worse than she was letting on. "Otis was handsome and said all of the right words. And he happened into my life just when I needed someone."

"Sounds like you cared a lot about him." An uneasy feeling snaked its way through him.

"I did. At least in the beginning. I thought—well, I hoped he'd fill the hole that my mother's death had left in my heart.

The emptiness. The loneliness. It was just so much. When Otis came along, he flirted with me and flattered me. I thought it was meant to be."

The uneasy feeling swelled within him. "You were happy?"

She nodded. "For a time."

"And then what happened?"

"He lost his job. When he had problems finding another one, he grew jealous of my education and my career. Somewhere along the way he stopped looking for work. He sponged off me and then took my money to the bar where he bought rounds of drinks for his friends."

"That must have been rough."

She shrugged. "It wasn't the best, but I thought it was a bad spell and we'd work through it so I put up with it for a time. But even I have my limits. I kicked him out. He stole all of my money and the few pieces of my mother's jewelry before he skipped town."

"That's horrible." Anger replaced the jealousy that had coiled up in his gut. "Who does such a thing?"

She shook her head. "It doesn't matter. It's over. I just wish I could get my mother's heart-shaped locket back. I tried every pawnshop I could find but none had it."

He hoped he never met this Otis guy. It wouldn't be good for either one of them. Though it would make Atlas feel a bit better to knock some sense into the guy.

"What did the locket look like?" he asked.

"I have a picture of it." She pulled out her phone. Her finger rapidly moved over the screen. And then she held up a photo of her wearing the locket.

He took the phone from her and enlarged the photo. It was a heart locket with an intricate engraved design. And in the center was a ruby.

Who would steal the necklace of a dead woman from her daughter? Atlas's gut knotted. Otis was lower than low.

"May I take a copy of this?" he asked.

"Why would you want to do that?"

"I have some friends who are good at tracking down things. I was thinking they could have a look and see if they can find it for you."

"You don't have to go to that trouble."

"But I'd like to. I'm not sure it's possible to find the locket, but I'd at least like to try."

She shrugged. "Go ahead. But I don't think you'll find it. Trust me, I've tried. For all I know, he threw it in the sea."

Atlas reached out to her, taking her hand in his own. "I'm so sorry you had to go through all of that. You deserve so much better. You deserve someone who loves and cherishes you."

Her eyes shimmered with unshed tears. "You really think so?"

"I do."

"No one has ever said that to me."

When a tear splashed onto her cheek, he moved closer and swiped it away with his thumb. "You should have someone who tells you that you're the most beautiful woman in the world." Their gazes met and held. His heart pounded. "You should be told you have the most alluring eyes that look upon the world with kindness and compassion. And most of all you have the biggest heart."

Another tear splashed onto her cheek. This time she swiped it away. "You don't have to say all of that. It isn't why I told you about Otis."

"I know I didn't have to. I wanted to." It was the truth. He meant every word. "The fact that it's taken me this long to say is my fault."

And then he didn't take the time to weigh the right or the wrong of it. He let himself do what felt right. He leaned toward Hermione, intending to place a kiss upon her cheek. But she turned just as he neared her and his kiss fell upon her lips— her soft, luscious lips.

He should pull away, but he didn't want to. He'd been thinking about her sweet kisses all day. They were addictive.

And then her mouth began to move beneath his. A moan swelled deep down in his throat, and he made no attempt to suppress it. In that moment, he didn't care if Hermione knew how much he wanted her.

There was just something about her that had him acting so out of character—acting like someone he didn't quite know. With Hermione, he wasn't shut down and cold. She made him open up and feel things. With her, he wanted to take chances and put himself out there.

He thought of the Ruby Heart's legend. Was it possible there was a bit of truth to it? As quickly as the thought came to him, he dismissed it. This thing between Hermione and him wasn't forever. He didn't do commitments.

The next thing he knew, Hermione was pushing him back on the couch. And then her soft curves pressed against him. She started a string of kisses along his jaw that eventually trailed down his neck. His heart beat wildly. How had he become so lucky to have her in his life? And she wasn't looking for a commitment. It would be the perfect holiday fling.

CHAPTER FOURTEEN

SHE AWOKE WITH a smile.

Her hand reached out, finding an empty spot next to her.

Hermione's eyes sprang open. She rolled over and then her gaze searched the room, finding that Atlas was gone. It took her a moment to realize where she was—a guest room in Thea's apartment. They'd moved to the bed sometime during the night—a night in which they hadn't gotten much sleep. Heat rushed to Hermione's cheeks at the memory.

The sun hadn't even risen yet. She couldn't believe she hadn't heard him get up. She yawned and stretched before settling back against the soft pillow, not quite ready to get out of bed and face the day. Atlas must have a lot to do if he was out of bed so early.

She reached for her phone and sent him a text.

Good morning <3

When an immediate response wasn't forthcoming, she scrambled out of bed and headed for the shower. There was no time to waste with Valentine's Day just a few days away.

She was thankful for having had the forethought to bring extra clothes to her office. The very last thing she wanted to do was walk around in yesterday's clothes. That would be a big announcement to everyone that she hadn't gone home last night. And it wouldn't take her friends long to figure out with whom she'd spent the evening. Heat flared in her cheeks as the memories of spending the night in Atlas's arms replayed in her mind.

She took the back way to her office and sneaked inside to switch clothes. Luckily it was so early that even Rhea hadn't arrived yet. Hermione took the opportunity to delegate some tasks to her staff as well as make a minor adjustment to the Valentine's menu.

By the time Hermione completed her emails, the resort was in full swing.

She grabbed her digital notebook so she could start checking off items. As she rushed back to the ballroom, she nearly ran into Adara. "Sorry. It's a busy morning."

"Good morning. Should I ask how things are going?"

She wasn't sure if Adara meant with the party preparations or between her and Atlas. She opted to go the safe route. "The preparations are on schedule. I just feel like the party needs something else."

"Something as in? The menu? The decorations?"

"That's just it. I don't know. It's just this feeling I have that won't leave me."

Adara sent her a smile. "I'm sure it'll come to you. And how are things with you and Atlas?"

Her body tensed. Their relationship was all so new to the both of them. She wasn't ready to dissect it. She wanted to leave it be for a little longer.

"Things are…are good." She swallowed hard. "Oh, yes, I was supposed to let you know that Atlas's friend, Krystof, has arrived. Atlas is showing him around the resort, but this evening Krystof will require a seat at the high-stakes poker game."

Adara's brows rose. "Does he know that it's a hundred-thousand-dollar buy-in?"

"Atlas said money wasn't an issue."

Adara nodded. "Okay, then. I'll make sure he's on the list."

Hermione gave her Krystof's full name. She didn't know much else about him. The truth of the matter was she'd been too distracted with Atlas as they explored this new facet of their private life to talk about much else. But if Atlas was inviting his friends to the island, that had to mean he was thinking of keeping it.

Adara finished adding the information to her digital notebook. "I'm glad everything is going well with you and Atlas. Let me know if you need anything. I think between the two of us, we might convince him to stay on the island."

Hermione smiled. "I was just thinking the same thing."

"I should be going. I have a meeting with a nervous bride-to-be. If I ever decide to change professions, please remind me that wedding planning is not for me."

Hermione laughed. "It's going that well?"

Adara nodded. "But we'll get through it. And how about you? Are you excited about attending the Valentine's ball?"

Hermione vehemently shook her head. "I'm not going. At least not as a guest."

Adara's eyes reflected her surprise. "But you have to after all the work you put into the preparations. And I know Atlas will be disappointed if you're not there."

Hermione again shook her head. "I can't." She failed to mention that she didn't have a dress for the ball. And she had absolutely no time to shop for one. Plus there was the tiny matter that Atlas hadn't asked her to be his date. "But I'll be working in the background."

Adara studied her for a moment. "Isn't there some way to change your mind?"

"It's for the best. Besides I'd never find anything to wear at this late date." Completely uncomfortable with the conversation, she said, "Can we talk later? I really have to get to the ballroom."

"Don't dismiss the idea of attending the ball. We'll talk more later."

And then Adara was gone. Hermione continued on her way. She knew Adara meant well, but she wasn't going to the ball. She'd have to be content with planning it. Still, why hadn't Atlas mentioned it?

The day had not gone as planned.

This morning's meeting with the photographer for the real estate agent had been agonizingly slow and beyond frustrating. Atlas wasn't good with playing the patient tour guide as the photographer took his time getting the perfect shot.

But the day wasn't a total loss. Krystof had arrived. And Atlas had him on the go most of the day. There was so much to see and do at the resort. It was concluded with a late dinner at Under the Sea. To Atlas, the restaurant felt as though it were part of a great big aquarium. He thought of it as the highlight of the resort.

As soon as the thought crossed his mind, he realized it wasn't true. Hermione was the true highlight of the resort. She kept the place humming along smoothly. And even when they hit some rough water, such as the problem with the Valentine's ball, she did what was needed to keep things going.

She was a true leader—a great leader. And if he were to keep the resort, she'd definitely remain the manager and get a large raise.

"What are you smiling about?" Krystof studied him.

He was smiling? He swallowed and assumed a neutral expression. "What do you think of the restaurant?"

"I don't think it's what had you smiling."

He wasn't going to have this conversation with Krystof. He'd make too much of what was going on with him and Hermione. "I was able to get you a seat at the card table tonight."

"Good. I've been looking forward to seeing what the island has to offer."

"I think you'll be impressed." At least Atlas hoped so. "And then we can revisit the idea of you buying this island paradise."

Krystof rested his elbows on the table and leaned forward. "Paradise? Aren't you layering it on a little thick?"

Atlas shook his head. "I don't think so. You can settle down here and soak up some sun when you're not trying your hand with lady luck."

"I don't know. I'm not one to stay in one place for long."

"Trust me. This place is awesome."

"If it's so great, why aren't you keeping it?"

"I probably would if it wasn't a constant reminder of Thea."

Guilt reflected in Krystof's eyes. "Sorry. For a moment, I forgot."

Krystof knew that Thea had abandoned Atlas as a young boy. It was kind of hard to hide when she was never around for any of the school events, but Atlas never went into details.

"Just give the island a chance. It's all I'm asking. And if you want to pass, I'll understand. I have a real estate agent working on a listing. One way or another, this island will cease to be my problem."

"Unless you find a reason to stay."

"Not going to happen." Hermione's face flashed into his mind. "I can't stay."

When they finished their meal, Atlas showed Krystof to the casino and the high rollers room. And then he passed by Hermione's office as well as the event planner's office. She wasn't in either place. A sensation of disappointment settled over him— was it possible he missed her? He wasn't used to missing people. He used to pride himself on not needing anyone.

But he had things he wanted to tell her. And he wanted to hear about her day. There was also that matter of clarifying things between them. Atlas expelled an exasperated sigh. Instead of clarifying things with her last night, he'd succeeded in making things more complicated.

The one thing he had accomplished was he'd sent the picture of Hermione's mother's locket to have a private investigator put out feelers with a reward for its recovery. And he'd had one of the finest jewelers in Athens start working on a replica. He paid extra to have it completed as soon as possible because he'd wanted to give it to Hermione before he left the island. And his departure hopefully wouldn't be too far off—not if he could get Krystof to buy the island.

He took the private elevator to Thea's, er, his apartment and was surprised to find the lights on. "Hermione? Are you here?"

"Back here." Her voice came from one of the bedrooms.

He strolled back the hallway and came to a stop at the doorway of his room—the room where they'd made love last night. But Hermione wasn't alone. There was another older woman standing there next to a table.

He was confused. "What's going on?"

"I have a surprise for you."

"For me? But it's not my birthday."

"Aren't you even curious what it is?"

He hesitated. "What is it?"

"A chocolate massage."

Though the idea was quite tempting, he shook his head. "I don't think so." Then his gaze met the older lady's. "Sorry. No offense."

Hermione approached him. "Look at you. You're all tense. This will do you good. Trust me." She clasped her hands together as she pleaded with her big brown eyes. "Please."

He was quickly learning that he had no defense when she looked at him that way. "Okay. But you have to join me."

She shook her head. "I can't."

He reached out for her hand, drawing her close. In a low voice that melted her insides, he asked, "Is there a way I can change your mind?"

She hesitated. "I have plans."

He arched a brow. "Should I be insulted? Or jealous?"

"Neither." She laughed. "It's not that kind of plan. Adara asked me if I'd meet her this evening."

"To do what?"

"I'm not sure."

After she left, he felt as though the air had been sucked out of the room. There was just something about being around Hermione that filled him with a warmth. The thought of returning to his flat in London no longer appealed to him. He just wanted to be near Hermione. But he refused to acknowledge what that meant.

What did Adara want?

Hermione was surprised by her friend's invitation. She'd been unusually mysterious about their plans for the evening. The only thing she'd said in the text was that she really needed some help.

Hermione had no time to spare, but she'd make an exception for her best friend. She just couldn't stay late. With only four days until Valentine's, she had so much to do. Her stomach shivered with nerves. She may run the resort, but it was very different work from planning a lavish party.

What if she hadn't ordered enough champagne? What if they didn't schedule enough servers? This list of worries went on and on.

The party had to be spectacular. She needed Atlas to see the resort at its very best. She knew the place and its people were growing on him. A successful party would be the final touch to convince him to step into his inheritance.

Maybe she'd made a mistake by not taking time from her hectic schedule to hunt for a party dress and asking him to the dance. After all, who said the woman had to wait around for the man to extend the invitation. But it was too late now to worry about it.

She would be content to hear the after-party stories and see the photos. But the best part would be if Atlas was happy with the event.

Hermione paused outside Adara's office and knocked.

"Come in."

Hermione opened the door. "Hi. What's going on?"

"I need a little help."

Hermione's gaze took in two glamorous dresses. "These are amazing." She stepped closer to the dresses. "How can I help?"

"I'm having problems deciding on a dress. I was hoping you could help me settle on one for the ball."

Surely she hadn't heard her correctly. "You want me to pick out a dress for you?"

"You sound horrified at the thought."

"No. It's just that I don't know how much help I'll be. I don't wear fancy clothes like these. I'm more of the business casual type."

"They are just material sewn together."

Hermione moved closer to the red and white dresses to have a better look. "Silky, shimmery, sexy material sewn together in the most amazing vintage styles."

Adara laughed. "I take it you like them?"

"Who wouldn't like them? I don't know how you'll pick just one."

"How about you try them on?"

Hermione pressed her hand to her chest. "Me?" When Adara nodded, she asked, "But shouldn't you see how they fit you?"

"I need to see how they look on a person and not on a hanger. It'll help narrow things down for me. Go ahead. I know you want to."

Hermione sent her a hesitant look. "Are you sure?"

"Positive."

She tried on the white one first. She didn't have enough curves to fill it out properly. And it hung much too long for her. She insisted Adara try it on. It fit her perfectly.

While Adara wore the white one and tried to decide if she liked it, Hermione tried on the red gown. It fit her so much better. Since the office lacked a mirror, they took photos of each other in the dresses. In addition, there were sparkly, stunning heels to wear with the dresses.

"You need to wear the red dress to the ball," Adara said.

"I told you I'm not going."

"I remember your excuse being that you didn't have a dress. And now you do."

"What? No. These are your dresses."

"Not if I give you one. Besides, the red one looks far better on you."

Hermione shook her head. "You're just saying that so I'll go."

"I mean it."

"If I did go and I'm not saying I will, I'd have to pay you for the dress and shoes."

"Fine. Now we have to work on getting you a date." Adara's eyes twinkled as she smiled. "You should ask Atlas to go with you."

Hermione's mouth opened to refuse, but she couldn't think of a reason not to ask him. Wordlessly she closed her mouth.

"See," Adara said. "You like the idea."

Hermione knew Adara was once again matchmaking and she should stop her, but she didn't want to. Instead, she decided it was time to turn things on Adara. "I'll ask Atlas if you ask someone to go with you."

Adara's mouth gaped. It took her a moment to gather herself. "Who would I ask?"

"I'm sure you can find someone." Hermione snapped her fingers as the answer came to her. "Atlas's friend is here. Ask him?"

"He…he probably has a wife or a girlfriend."

"He doesn't. I asked."

Adara looked flustered. "He probably doesn't like dances."

"You won't know until you ask him." When Adara frowned at her, Hermione laughed. "Now you know how it feels. So will you ask him?"

"If that's what it takes to get you to the ball with Atlas, then yes."

With a bottle of wine and a pizza delivered for dinner, it was quite an evening. They talked. They laughed. And they had a great girls' night. She'd miss it dearly if the resort was sold.

Anxious to stop by Atlas's apartment on her way home and tell Atlas about her evening, she told Adara good-night. She might even work up the courage to ask him to the ball. She wondered what his answer would be.

But when she got there, she found his bedroom door open and him draped across the bed as though he'd been meaning to get back up but never made it. She grabbed a throw blanket and tossed it over him before tiptoeing away. Her question would have to wait until another time.

CHAPTER FIFTEEN

Tomorrow was Valentine's Day.

And it was all coming together.

Friday morning, Hermione stood in the center of the ballroom taking in the amazing scene. When they'd started the prep work at the beginning of the week, the room had literally just been four plain walls with a ceiling and floor. There hadn't been anything else in the room. But the last few days had been a blur as this humongous room was brought to life. It was magnificent.

Love Under the Stars. She loved the theme. She wished she could take credit for it, but it was Nestor's idea.

Buzz-buzz.

She glanced at her phone. It was a message from Adara.

Did you ask Atlas yet?

No. Did you ask Krystof?

No.

Ticktock.

Back at you.

Hermione resisted the urge to roll her eyes. Then she turned her thoughts back to the party preparation. She still felt as though something was missing. She gazed around at the positive words displayed in neon lights on the one wall and then onto the wall of glass that opened onto a patio that led to the beach, and finally to another wall with a giant mural of the night sky with a crescent moon and the various astrological signs. As beautiful as it all was, she was certain they were missing something.

She turned to where the refreshments were to be displayed. The chocolate fountain was already assembled. No. It wasn't that. It was...

Ugh! It was right on the edge of her thoughts but when she closed her eyes to focus, there was Atlas's very handsome face. His image was always there, distracting her from her work. When she opened her eyes, he was standing in front of her looking so handsome in a light blue houndstooth button-up with his shirttail untucked and wearing a pair of dark jeans with his boat shoes. He looked totally dreamy.

She blinked, making sure she hadn't imagined him. But he was still there smiling at her, making her heart go rap-a-tap-tap. "Hi. Did you need something?"

He sent her a sexy smile that made her swoon. "I came to see if you needed a hand. I know this is a lot of work. I've cleared my schedule. All I need you to do is to tell me what needs to be done."

She glanced around, trying to figure out a task for him. But she couldn't think of anything that wasn't already being done.

Then she turned to him. "You could tell me what's missing."

His brows drew together. "Missing?"

She nodded. "I have this feeling I can't shake that something is missing."

He glanced around. "You have all of the food sorted, right?"

She nodded. "And the chocolate fountain is all set to go."

"That sounds good to me."

"Are you serious?" She pressed her hands to her hips. "This is the event of the year. It has to be perfect."

He stepped in front of her. "It will be."

She arched a brow. "How do you know?"

"Because you'll be there, and that's all I need to make my evening perfect."

Her heart rapidly thump-thumped. Heat swirled in her chest and rushed up her neck, warming her cheeks. What was she supposed to say to that? She opened her mouth, but her mind and mouth were at a disconnect. She wordlessly pressed her lips together.

He stepped closer to her. His gaze met hers as he reached for her. "Would you like a demonstration of what makes a perfect evening?"

She stepped out of his reach. "Atlas, stop." But secretly she didn't want him to stop. She wanted to sneak off with him and spend the rest of the day in his arms. "There's work to be done."

One of the workers approached them. "Hermione, where should the champagne fountain go?"

She swallowed hard, trying to hide the fact that Atlas had totally undermined her train of thought. She turned to the young man. "Um, what did you say?" After the man repeated the question, she instructed him to place it on the opposite end of the buffet from the chocolate fountain. Then she turned to Atlas, who wore an amused smile. "You're not funny. I have a job to do. You can't distract me."

"But it's so fun."

This was the moment she should ask Atlas to the ball. Her stomach shivered with nerves. If he escorted her, it would take their relationship public. It would solidify things between them. But if he turned her down...did that mean he wasn't as into her as she was into him?

She swallowed hard. "Atlas—"

"Hermione, we have a question." Two women approached her with inquiries about the buffet table. Once more asking Atlas to the ball would have to wait, but she was running out of time. She'd ask him soon, she promised herself.

A few minutes later she returned to Atlas's side. "Sorry about that."

"No problem. After all, you're the star of this production."

"That's it." She just had a light bulb moment. A big smile pulled at her lips.

"What's it?" Confusion reflected in his eyes.

"Stars. That's what's missing. A few years back there was a big wedding and they'd used crystal stars. There were hundreds of them everywhere. We can suspend them from the ceiling and use white twinkle lights to make them sparkle." She was so pleased with herself.

"Do you think you have time for all of that?"

She nodded. "But I have to hurry. I think the stars were put in the storage room. It's so big though that it's going to take me some time to find them."

"Why not send someone else?" Atlas asked.

She glanced around the enormous ballroom. It was abuzz with activity. There were people rushing here and there. People either had their arms full or they were putting something together.

"Everyone is busy. I'll just go. It'll be faster and easier."

Atlas frowned. "Two people can find them quicker than one. I'm coming with you."

Hermione shrugged. "Suit yourself."

Moments later they were in the maintenance elevator that would take them to the lower level. Hermione had to admit that she'd never liked it down here. The first thing she did was prop the heavy metal door open. No way was she getting trapped down here.

She glanced over her shoulder at Atlas. Okay, so maybe getting stuck wouldn't be the worst. After all, they'd have to find some way to pass the time, right? A smile pulled at her lips.

The overhead lights weren't that effective, certainly not to read the labels on the boxes. They located flashlights in the janitor's closet, and then they split up searching the storage room. She took the left side while he went to the right. Row after row of shelving units were lined with cardboard boxes.

Hermione flashed the light on the boxes that were well labeled. However, there wasn't any rhyme or reason to their placement on the shelf. This was going to take them some time—time she didn't have. They had to hurry.

What was happening to him?

He hardly recognized himself anymore.

Atlas had left his team to finish the security system in the gallery on their own so he could help Hermione. That wasn't like him. His business always came first...at least it used to.

In the evenings, he'd been cleaning out Thea's very large apartment, but it was slow work. So much so that he'd had to extend his stay for another week. His mother, to his utter surprise, was the sentimental type—except perhaps when it came to her only child. However, her apartment was filled with all sorts of photos and mementos.

His first reaction had been to toss it all in the nearest dumpster, but he knew the things would mean something to the Ludus staff, who had been thoughtful enough to give the items to Thea. And so he started returning the gifts one at a time.

In the process, he'd gotten to know more of the staff. They were good people with a willingness to give him the benefit of a doubt, even though he'd never visited the resort while Thea was alive. For the most part, they didn't bother him with probing questions. But there were a few of the older employees who greeted him with a raised brow. Even that hadn't been so bad because he understood their confusion. It appeared Thea didn't say much about him beyond her close circle of friends.

Even though he had other tasks requiring his attention, he couldn't abandon Hermione. He knew she was nervous about the party. He was certain with all of the attention she'd given the event that it would be a huge success. So much so that he'd arranged for the real estate photographer to come back and snap some more photos.

They really didn't have time to waste meandering around this dusty storage room. There were so many boxes that he was fairly certain they weren't going to find the stars. Still he flashed his light on box after box. St. Patrick's Day. New Year's. The names of the boxes were everything but what he needed. They were searching for the Jericho wedding.

Other than holidays, he'd found the Wilson wedding, the Smith wedding and about a dozen other weddings, just not the right one. Where was it? And how long was Hermione going to persist in this search?

He sighed as he kept checking one box label after the next. Bored of this monotonous task, his mind rewound to his conversation with Krystof about the ball. Atlas had a policy about avoiding weddings and dances at all costs, but this was different. He'd seen how excited Hermione was about the ball. How could he not be there to support her?

He wondered what she'd say if he asked her out for Valentine's? The truth of the matter was that he didn't have any idea of her plans. And he wouldn't know until he asked her—

"Atlas! I found them." The excitement rang out in Hermione's voice.

A high-pitched metallic squeak filled the silence. What was she up to now? As he headed to her location, he noticed that she'd found a ladder on wheels. She'd wheeled it over and was already halfway to the top by the time he got there.

As he looked up at her, he noticed she was on the ladder in high heels. "Hermione, you shouldn't be up there. Let me do it."

"Why? You don't think a woman can climb a ladder?" She took the last step to the top little platform.

"No. I think you wore the wrong shoes to be climbing around the storage room."

"It's okay. I'm up here now." She reached for the first box.

"Be careful."

She glanced down at him and smiled. "Are you worried about me?"

Was he? He supposed so. But he wrote it off as general concern, like he'd have for anyone. But with each passing day he was finding that Hermione wasn't just anyone—she was someone special.

"Just pay attention to what you're doing." His voice came out a little gruffer than normal.

"Yes, sir." She smiled down at him again.

He held the ladder, even though the wheel lock was secure. It was the only thing he could do as Hermione pulled box after box and piled them in front of her on the little platform.

"Let me carry them down," he said.

"I've got it." She hooked an arm around the first box and started to back down the ladder.

He stood there with his body tensed and ready to spring into action. But she took one careful step after the next. He was about to take his first easy breath when she was one step from the bottom. Then the tip of her heel caught on a rung. He reached out to her, pulling her and box safely to him.

Her head came to rest on his chest. Nothing had ever felt so right in his life. It was like they were two halves of a whole. She'd shown him that even though his heart was tattered and scarred it was still capable of more emotion than he'd ever dared feel before.

Since their lives collided during the rainstorm, his life had been irrevocably changed. He knew deep down he was never going to be the same man. Hermione had changed him for the better.

Once she regained her balance, she glanced up at him and sent him a sheepish smile. "Oops."

She looked so cute in that moment that he couldn't resist taking the box from her and letting it fall to the floor with a thump. Then he wrapped both arms around her and drew her snugly to his chest.

"What is going to happen to you when I'm not around to catch you?" He stared deep into her eyes, feeling as though he could see his future in them.

The gold flecks in her brown eyes twinkled. "I guess you'll have to stick around just in case I need you."

"And what do you need now?" His voice grew deep and gravelly with desire.

Her arms snaked around his neck as she drew him closer. And then her lips were pressed to his. Oh, yes, that's exactly what he needed too.

Hermione pulled away far too soon. "That should hold you over until later."

"Later? But I want more now."

A soft laugh filled the air. "We have work to do. How about you carry down the rest of the boxes. There are a few more on the shelf. And I'll go find a cart to move these to the ballroom."

She turned and walked away. He was left with the awful thought that one day much too soon, he'd be saying goodbye to her and those delicious kisses. The thought twisted his gut up in a knot.

But what was the alternative? Stay here on Thea's island, living in Thea's resort, in Thea's apartment? No. That was impossible. It wouldn't work. With the constant reminder of the woman who'd rejected him and yet fully embraced the Ludus staff, he would become bitter and it would destroy anything he had with Hermione.

There was another alternative: ask Hermione to leave the island with him. It wasn't ideal because he knew how much she loved it here. But it was an idea that he wasn't so quick to let go of, if it meant a chance to see where things would go with Hermione.

CHAPTER SIXTEEN

IT WAS VALENTINE'S.

The day she'd anxiously awaited.

And yet Hermione was totally bummed. Now that all of the party plans were ready to go, she realized she still hadn't asked Atlas to the dance. She reached for her phone to text him, but she hesitated. This was something she should do in person.

Her memory strayed back to their kiss in the storage room. The memory made her heart thump-thump. That kiss was forever etched upon her mind. It wasn't so much his lips touching hers, it was more the way he looked at her. It was though he too sensed there was something serious growing between them. And it was just the beginning.

Hermione had hit the ground running that morning with no makeup and a messy bun. She headed to the ballroom for the final preparations. Everything must be perfect for tonight.

Speaker system test. *Check.*

Musical acts and comedian. *Check.*

Food and refreshments. *Check.*

Ice sculpture. *Check.*

Twinkle lights and stars. *Check.*

She scanned her checklist one last time. Everything on it had been checked, double-checked and in some cases triple-checked. They were all set for tonight. Her stomach shivered with nerves.

She'd told herself that it'd be okay.

She'd told herself she could deal with it.

But she'd only been lying to herself.

She checked the time. Six o'clock. The party was set to start at seven. Atlas had been sweet to offer her his apartment for her to shower and change into her new red dress instead of having to commute back and forth from her place.

When she stepped into the apartment, Atlas was there. But he wasn't alone. There was another man with him. She recognized him as Atlas's friend Krystof. They both turned to her with a serious expression on their faces.

"Hi. Sorry." Hermione wasn't sure if she should stay or go. "I didn't mean to interrupt."

"Hermione, join us," Atlas said.

The men stood. Introductions were made. She noticed that Atlas didn't introduce her as his girlfriend—in fact, no titles were used. But that was okay. She didn't need a title. They knew what they had growing between them.

"I'm sorry for monopolizing so much of Atlas's time," Krystof said.

Her gaze moved between the two men. She hadn't known they'd spent that much time together, but she was happy that Atlas had a friend here at the resort. It would help him feel more at home.

"Not a problem," Hermione said. "I hope you're enjoying your time on the island."

"So far we've scaled the climbing wall twice, enjoyed the wave pool and visited the spa," Krystof said. "I don't like to sit still. I can only imagine what all we'd have to do if it were summer and the beach was open."

"You'll definitely have to come back in June. We have our annual regatta. Do you have a boat?"

"As a matter of fact, I do."

"Then you should consider entering. The prince of Rydiania enters every year."

"I'm sure you'd enjoy it," Atlas said.

Krystof's eyes widened. "You've attended?"

"Uh, no," Atlas said, "but I've heard a lot about it. Sounds like a good time."

"I'll keep it in mind. But right now, there's a Valentine's ball to attend." Krystof turned to Hermione. "Atlas tells me you've put together a fabulous party—the best in the resort's history."

Heat rushed up her neck and settled in her cheeks. "I don't know if it'll be the best, but I hope everyone will have a wonderful time."

"I'm sure they will." Krystof held out his hand to her. "It was nice to meet you." They shook hands. "But now I have to go because I have a date."

"A date?" Atlas sounded surprised before he smiled and shook his head. "Why am I not surprised?"

So Adara had held up her end of the agreement.

Hermione felt the pressure mounting for her to ask Atlas to the ball. But not in front of Krystof.

Atlas walked Krystof to the elevator. "I'll see you at the party."

"See you there."

Atlas closed the glass door and turned to her. "Looks like you have an admirer."

"Hardly. He was just being nice to me because he's your friend."

"I think you underestimate your beauty. It starts on the inside and glows out, putting people at ease. You're like a ray of sunshine on a cloudy day."

Her gaze strayed to the wall of windows. "But it's dark out now."

He smiled and shook his head. "You know what I mean."

"I do. Thank you for the kind words."

She filled him in on the final details for the party. And he let her know that the new security system was up and running. The conversation was very comfortable, very ordinary as though it were customary for them to fill each other in on their days.

Hermione knew it was now or never if she was going to ask him to the ball. Her heart pounded as her hands grew clammy.

"Will you go to the ball with me?" they asked in unison.

Hermione's mouth gaped as Atlas smiled at her. Had that really happened?

When she gathered herself, she pressed her lips together and swallowed. "Did we just ask each other to the ball?"

"I believe we did."

"Does that mean it's a date?" She needed him to confirm they were having an official date that evening—that they were going to let everyone know they were a couple.

"Yes, it does. Now you better get ready. You don't want to be late for your own party."

Buzz-buzz.

Atlas reached for his phone.

Tonight her very own Prince Charming would be her escort. A smile pulled at her lips. This was going to be the best night ever. And she couldn't help wondering if the Ruby Heart had something to do with it.

Atlas's voice interrupted her musing. "It's Krystof. Something came up and he needs to see me. But I can put him off—"

"No. Go. It must be important. We'll meet up at the ball."

"But this is supposed to be a date."

"It still will be. Now go see what he wants."

"Okay. I'll see you later."

And yet he continued to stand there, looking torn between staying with her and going to his friend. The fact he valued her that much wasn't lost on her. Her heart swelled with…with happiness. She wasn't ready to admit to a deeper feeling—not yet.

CHAPTER SEVENTEEN

HE WANTED TO LINGER.

He longed to be the first to see Hermione all dressed up for the ball.

And yet Atlas had been called away because Krystof said he'd made a decision about buying the island. He'd seen enough and was ready to negotiate. If it were for any other reason, Atlas would have willingly skipped out on the meeting. But he needed to close this chapter of his life—move beyond Thea's long shadow.

First, he needed to change clothes. He'd already showered for the second time that day. He changed into his tux. He'd had it sent via special messenger to the resort. He never anticipated needing it when he'd packed for this trip—it seemed so long ago.

The elevator chimed, alerting him to the fact that they had company. He went to meet their guest.

Adara stepped out of the elevator in a white shimmery gown. "Oh. Hi." She smiled at him. "How are things?"

"Good. How's the wedding coming?"

"It was absolutely lovely. Now that it's over, I had a few minutes to slip away and help Hermione get ready for the party."

He was out of excuses to linger around the apartment. And yet he was still hesitant to leave. This wasn't like him. He used to be the type who didn't let anything stand between him and a meeting.

Business used to be the thing he could count on in his life. It was the one constant. His professional endeavors were what got him out of bed in the morning, what drove him all day long and were the last thing he thought of before he fell asleep at night.

But now, it was Hermione that he rushed out of bed to see in the morning. Her engaging company was what kept him going through this whole trying experience. And it was her image that was the last thing on his mind as he fell asleep at night.

And yet his time at the resort was running out. He just couldn't stay here. And he was torn about asking her to leave with him. He'd witnessed how she fit in here at the resort. Her work fulfilled her, and the people were more than just friends. This was her home and the people were her family. To rip her away from this after all she'd gone through after losing her mother would be so very wrong.

Feeling as though the world were weighing on his shoulders, he left the apartment. As he walked through the resort, memories of his time with Hermione lurked around each corner. When he'd come to the island, he'd never anticipated making memories here. Was he ready to give them up so quickly?

He shoved aside his tormenting thoughts. Right now, he had some negotiating to do with his old friend. Krystof greeted him at the door. Over a couple of bourbons, they haggled back and forth. Coming to a sales agreement was harder than Atlas thought it would be. He said upfront that the Ludus employees would need to retain their jobs for at least six months—including Hermione. Krystof agreed. But Atlas still wasn't ready to shake on it.

Krystof leaned back in his chair and studied him. "You don't want to sell the island, do you?"

"Of course I do," he said with more force than was necessary. "Why else would we be meeting?"

Krystof crossed his arms. "I get the feeling your heart is no longer in it. And if I had to guess, it has something to do with that beautiful manager."

"It does not." *Liar.*

"I don't believe you. You have it bad for her." His friend's eyes lit up as he smiled at him—like he had all of the answers to life. "You're in love."

"I am not." Atlas shot out of his chair and began to pace. His back teeth ground together as his body tensed. He didn't know who he was most upset with at the moment. His friend for having fun pointing out the obvious to him. Or himself for letting things get so out of hand with Hermione.

It would never work between them. He wasn't handsome like Krystof. He didn't have a way with words like his car salesman father, and he didn't have a selfless heart like Hermione.

He was...well, he was unlovable.

It's what he'd been telling himself since he was a kid and his mother left. He'd blamed himself. There was something about him that drove her away, and it kept his father from caring about him. And when Hermione got to know him better, she'd find out she couldn't love him either. He had to put an end to all of this now.

His gaze moved to Krystof. "Do you want to buy the island or not?"

His friend arched a brow. "And you don't care what I do with this place after six months?"

Atlas shook his head because he didn't trust his voice. The truth was that he was more invested in this island than he was willing to admit. But if he were to stay—if he were to keep it—he feared the ghosts of the past would destroy him.

Krystof stood and held out his hand to him. Atlas gripped it. When they shook, Krystof said, "It's a deal."

Atlas hadn't realized how much time had passed. If they didn't leave now, they'd be late for the ball. And he didn't want to miss this party—the party that Hermione had worked so hard to put together.

With Krystof next to him, Atlas led the way to the ballroom. Though the party had just started, the room was abuzz with people in black tuxes and glittery dresses. Atlas smiled. He was so happy to see that Hermione's party was off to a successful start.

Neon lights in red and white lit up the wall with inspiring words of hope and love. He glanced toward the grand patio. It was lit up with white candles. While inside, red roses adorned all of the tables as well as bowls of heart-shaped candies with printed messages such as *Be Mine* and *Kiss Me*. But it was the crystal stars and twinkle lights suspended from the ceiling that made the whole room appear magical.

But where was Hermione? His gaze searched the room for her. It was so hard to see with so many people in attendance. She had to be here. But where?

He made his excuses to Krystof, who appeared to be looking around for his date. They'd been so caught up in making a deal for the resort that Atlas hadn't even thought to ask him about his mystery date. It must be the reason for his interest in the resort.

Atlas moved about the room, searching for the woman who made this whole evening possible. And still he couldn't find her. He had a feeling with a room of this size, he might be walking around it all night and still miss her.

He moved to the stage where a world-famous K-pop band was playing dance music. He stood off to the side in order to look out over the crowd. Still, no sign of her.

But then his gaze strayed across to Krystof. And not surprisingly, he wasn't alone. The surprise was the identity of the woman he was dancing with—Adara. Both were smiling and appeared to be having a good time.

He'd be having a good time too if he could find Hermione. He was about to backtrack to the apartment to see if she'd changed her mind about attending the party when in through the entrance came Hermione. His gaze latched on to her and stayed with her.

Her long hair hung past her shoulders in loose curls. On top of her head were curls secured with sparkly pins. But it was the smile on her face that drew him to her. He longed for her to smile like that at him.

He hurried off the stage and headed toward her. He just hoped she didn't get away before he made it through the crowd. With a lot of *pardon me* and *excuse me*, he made it to the entrance.

And there was Hermione in an off-the-shoulder red gown. The fitted bodice was studded with crystals that sparkled. The material gathered at her slim waist and then fell loosely down over her hips and stopped at her heels, which also sparkled with crystals. She was…breathtaking.

She stepped up to him. "Atlas, is everything all right?"

He swallowed hard. "Uh, yes…everything is perfect. You… you are perfect."

Color flooded her cheeks. "I don't know about that."

"I do. I've never seen someone so beautiful." As the color in her cheeks intensified, he rushed on to add, "And this party is amazing. Everyone is having a great time."

"Really?" Her eyes lit up with excitement. "You think so?"

"I do." He held his arm out to her. "Will you dance with me?"

A bright smile lifted her lips. "I'd love to."

He had a feeling his feet were going to be sore by the end of the night because he intended on claiming every dance with her. With their time together drawing to a close, he wanted to make more of those happy memories—memories he would carry close to his heart.

As they danced to a slower tune, he drew her in close. He breathed in the delicate floral scent of her perfume. He would never breathe in that scent without thinking of her. How was he ever going to tell her that the sale of the island was in the works?

CHAPTER EIGHTEEN

THE EVENING FLEW BY.

Atlas couldn't remember being so happy. They'd spent the entire evening together. They were making more of those memories that would keep him warm on those long lonely nights ahead of him.

He needed to tell her about the pending sale of the island, but he hadn't found the right moment. And with nine o'clock approaching, the guests had made their way onto the beach to watch the fireworks that would be set off offshore.

And then the countdown began...

"Ten—nine—eight—"

Atlas joined in the countdown. And he couldn't be happier to have Hermione by his side.

"Seven—six—five—"

Though everything had been a disaster when he'd first arrived on the island, they'd taken a surprising turn for the best. And it was all thanks to Hermione. She'd made his visit an enjoyable event.

"Four—three—two—"

Too bad it was coming to an end. Whereas Valentine's was meant to reaffirm one's love and commitment, this thing between Hermione and him, well, it was an ending. And, oh, how he was going to miss her. More than he'd ever imagined possible.

"One!"

A loud boom thundered around them signaling the beginning of the fireworks. A softer *whoosh* could be heard as the fireworks were launched. A cascade of white and red lights glittered in the black velvet sky.

Another *whoosh* was heard, and a sparkling pink heart filled the sky.

Hermione turned to him. "Isn't it spectacular?"

He stared into her eyes and was immediately drawn in by her boundless happiness. It filled his scarred heart and filled in the cracks and crevices—making him feel whole.

Hermione leaned into him. He reached out to her. And the next thing he knew, they were in each other's arms. His lips claimed hers with a need to remember everything about her. He didn't ever want to forget her or this moment.

Even though he wasn't leaving for another week, he already missed Hermione. He pulled her closer, feeling her soft curves pressed to him. A moan swelled in the back of his throat.

There would never ever be anyone like Hermione. She was sweet and funny at the same time that she was fiercely independent and stubborn. It was an intoxicating combination. And he longed to hold her in his arms forever and ever because he was in love with her. The thought startled him.

He pulled back. Hermione didn't seem to notice that the world seemed to have shifted. Maybe it was just him. Because loving Hermione meant loving this island, and he couldn't do that. This was Thea's island, not his. Never his.

He couldn't let himself get drawn into a fantasy where Hermione was concerned. His business was waiting on him to hit the road and land other big deals. That's what he could count on—his business.

He glanced over and noticed that Krystof was still talking to Adara. "Krystof and Adara seem to have hit it off."

Hermione arched a brow. "Is he the one you were thinking of selling the island to?"

"I still am. That's the reason I invited him here."

Frown lines etched her eyes and mouth. "I thought you changed your mind."

"You want me to keep this island?" When she nodded, he said, "You don't know what you're asking of me."

"But isn't that what we've been working toward? You've even gotten to know the staff."

"Hermione, you're asking too much of me. Krystof will do a much better job managing the island than I've done."

"No, he won't. He doesn't have a connection to the island like you do."

She was right. No matter how much he wanted to deny it, he was forever linked to this island via Thea. But not in a good way. Thea chose this life and this island over him. How was he ever supposed to reconcile himself to that fact?

He shook his head. "I'm sorry. I can't do it. This sale is going to happen."

Her eyes grew dark as though a wall had just come down between them. "And that's it? No conversation? No negotiation?"

"This is the way it has to be." It was killing him to say these things. He wanted another option. And even though he knew it was selfish, he said, "Come with me. I can show you the world."

She was quiet for a moment as though giving his suggestion serious consideration. "When we're done seeing the world, I want to come home. I want to come back to Ludus."

He shook his head. "I can't."

Disappointment flashed in her eyes. "Then this is goodbye."

Hermione turned to leave but he reached out to her. His hand caught hers. "Don't go. Not like this."

She turned back to him. Her eyes shimmered with unshed tears. "Do you want me to wait so you can leave first? Because once you sign the sales agreement you'll be leaving and we'll never see each other again. My life is here. My friends are here." She gazed deep into his eyes. "Have you ever stayed in one place long enough to make close friends—friends who have your back and you have theirs?"

The truth was that he'd been moving around since he finished university. Though he had a flat in London, he was forever on the road making deals. With technology he didn't have to be in one place to do his job.

"I have a home in London." His tone was firm. "Everything I care about is there."

"Except me." The pain reflected in her eyes dug at him. "Goodbye, Atlas."

He stood still as she walked away.

He desperately wanted to go after her—to tell her that he'd changed his mind. But he couldn't do that. This island would slowly but surely eat away his soul. Thea's memory lurked in the paint colors, the wall hangings—she was everywhere—reminding him that the people you loved the most were the ones that hurt you the most.

Right now, he was the one doing the hurting. And he hated himself for it. But it was better now than later. Because the longer this went on, the more Hermione would invest herself in him, in them, and he would eventually let her down. It was in his genes.

He wanted to rewind life to that rainy night when their lives had collided. He wanted things to go back to the way they used to be—easy and fun. And then he wanted to slow time so he could savor their moments together. But none of that was possible. He was left with his few precious memories.

CHAPTER NINETEEN

HE'D MADE THE biggest mistake of his life.

Buzz-buzz.

And he had no interest in hearing from anyone.

Bleary-eyed, Atlas stumbled through Sunday morning. He'd barely slept the night before. He kept replaying the scene at the party over and over in his mind. The kiss had been perfect. Hermione had been perfect. And he—well, was broken.

The more he told himself that he'd done what was best for Hermione, the more his heart told him it wasn't true. The reason he'd been fighting his love for her was much more serious. He'd been protecting himself from being rejected yet again.

He loved the lilt of her voice. He loved the way her eyes lit up when she laughed. He loved how she stood up for herself— believed in herself. And most of all, he loved how she cared for others—putting their needs ahead of her own. And sadly he knew he couldn't give her what would make her happy. He couldn't stop moving around and settle here on this island.

He knew Hermione would find someone else to love her— someone who would make her happy—someone who would share her vision for the future. The thought of her with someone else made his stomach churn.

Buzz-buzz.

What was it with his phone that day? Did everyone think he constantly worked? Even on Sunday. Well, he used to be that way, but since he'd been on the island, Hermione had shown him what it was like to have balance in life. It was something he intended to carry on after he left here.

Ring. Ring. Ring.

His gaze moved to the landline phone, but he made no motion to answer it. Obviously whoever wanted him was getting impatient. He should care, really he should, but he didn't. The business and the rush of closing a new deal no longer had a pull over him without Hermione in his life.

He was supposed to meet Krystof to sign the papers this morning. There was no point in putting off the inevitable. Once they were signed, he wouldn't be plagued by the what-ifs that had bothered him all night.

He showered without bothering to shave. He dressed but in jeans and a dress shirt that he didn't bother to tuck in. He didn't feel the compulsion to worry about his casual appearance. It was what it was.

Ding-dong. Ding-dong.

He thought of ignoring the private elevator too, but the fact that he needed it to go to a meeting made that impossible. With a resigned sigh, he headed for the intercom and pressed the button to allow whoever it was up to the apartment. A moment later the elevator door slid open, and Adara stood there with her fine brows knitted together in a frown.

"I've been trying to reach you," she said.

"We weren't supposed to meet, were we?"

"No." She crossed her arms. "But we need to talk."

"I'm not really in a chatty mood—"

"This is important." Her firm tone brooked no argument.

He gestured for her to step into the living room. "Give me a second." He strode over to the bar and retrieved a water. "Can I get you anything?"

She perched on the edge of the couch. "No. Thank you."

He sat down on the chair and turned to her. "What do you need?"

"Krystof's counsel has arrived. There's some question as to the ownership of the resort. They want to know if you have a copy of the will."

"Uh...no. I didn't think I'd need it. My attorney assured me that all of the paperwork had been properly filed."

"I believe you. I just think the gentlemen in the meeting room would feel better if they could see verification."

He didn't want to do it. He didn't want to have to deal with Thea's will...again. "I guess the sale will have to be delayed."

"Maybe not."

He arched a brow. "What do you have in mind?"

"Thea, Hermione and I had become very close over the years. She told us if there were any problems that she'd placed a copy of her will in her safe."

"She told you that?"

"Yes. It was after your stepfather passed on. She wanted to make sure the resort went on as it always had and the employees didn't lose their jobs."

He shook his head in disbelief. "If it means ending this sooner rather than later, I'll go check her safe."

And with that he walked away. In the hallway his strides were long and quick. He'd had it with Thea pulling his strings from beyond the grave. He just wanted his life back the way it was supposed to be—where he was in control. It couldn't happen soon enough. Because being here—being without Hermione—was killing him.

By the time he reached Thea's bedroom and removed the large painting from the wall to reveal the wall safe, he was in a perfectly awful mood. He pulled up the code to the safe from the note he'd made on his phone.

The first time he moved the tumbler too rashly and it didn't work. He took a deep breath and blew it out. And then with a steadier hand, he tried once more. This time the safe opened.

He hadn't explored the safe yet. The truth was that he'd been putting it off. He'd been ignoring Thea's entire bedroom. It was just too personal.

The safe was filled with jewelry boxes. None of that interested him. He scanned the safe, looking for the will. As soon as he got it, he was out of there. He was half inclined to tell Adara to do what she wanted with the rest of Thea's belongings since they'd been friends.

On the top shelf of the safe were some papers. He pulled them out. One by one he glanced at them, looking for the will. And then he happened upon an envelope with his name handwritten on it.

He froze. Why would this be in the safe? And then he realized it must be a copy of the will. Since he was the sole heir, it would make sense to have his name on it. Though the envelope did seem a bit slim for such a document.

He opened the envelope, expecting to find some sort of legal document. Instead, what he found was blue stationery with Thea's handwriting.

My dear Atlas,
If you're reading this it means my worst fear has happened. I have died without us reconciling. And for that I am so deeply sorry.

First, I love you. I've always loved you. You are a piece of me—the best part of me.

But I am human, and I made huge mistakes—mistakes I wish I could undo. I never meant to leave you. I swear. I left because I didn't have any other choice. Your father and I couldn't live together any longer. I'll spare you the details but please believe me when I say it was bad, very bad.

Atlas stopped reading. He wasn't going to let Thea rewrite the past. No way. He was there. He knew what happened.

He tossed the letter aside. He continued his search for the

will. That was the reason he was here—the only reason. He wasn't going to give Thea's words any power over him.

He reached back inside the safe and pulled out another stack of stuff. This time there was a book of some sort. Surely the will wouldn't be in there, but curiosity got the best of him and he lifted the other papers off the big bound book. He opened it to find a baby photo of himself.

A voice in his head said to close it and move on, but apparently his body wasn't listening to his mind because the next thing he knew, he was turning the page. Again there were pictures of him as a little boy. Why would she still have these after all of this time?

He turned page after page, finding photos he'd never seen before. His father wasn't big on family photos. But some of these photos were of him and Thea. She was smiling as she cheered him on to blow out candles on his birthday cake. There were others of them at the park.

Page by page, he aged in the photos until they suddenly stopped. And then there were media releases about his company—about him. She'd followed his career from his small start-up company to becoming one of the largest security firms in the world. She had press clippings in here that he'd never seen before.

And then something splashed onto the page. Luckily there was a clear plastic sheath over the clippings so he could wipe away the moisture without it damaging anything. And then there was a drip on his hand. He lifted his fingertips to his cheek and realized the moisture was coming from him.

He swiped at his cheeks as he continued flipping through the pages. Thea had followed his life right up until she'd died. Why would she do that if she didn't care about him?

He set aside the scrapbook and reached for Thea's letter once more. He continued reading as she explained that his father had physically thrown her out. With his father being much older than Thea, he'd had a lot of power over her. He'd threatened that if she ever tried to see Atlas again that both she and Atlas would pay for it. At the time she'd been too poor to fight him in court as he owned a car dealership and had many resources and lots of influential connections in the community.

It wasn't until she met Georgios and fell in love that she was able to fight his father. She went back for Atlas but by then he had been swayed by his father into thinking that she'd willingly abandoned him. He'd wanted nothing to do with her.

She went on to explain that she didn't know what to do. She didn't want to make things worse for him so she left. But she never stopped loving him.

She left him this island because it's where she healed and flourished. She'd hope it would bring him happiness and love. He rubbed his eyes and read the letter again.

All of this time, he'd thought his mother hadn't loved him. And maybe she hadn't handled the situation the way he would have liked, but she did the best she could. No one was perfect, most especially not him.

And that was the reason he'd been holding himself back from picturing a future with Hermione. But the truth was that he couldn't imagine his future without her.

If he left the island now, would he be following in his mother's footsteps? Would he be walking away from the chance to give love and be loved? Shouldn't a lesson be learned from what happened with him and his mother? Sometimes people weren't given second chances—sometimes you had to seize the moment.

Atlas set aside the letter. He had to find Hermione. And he had to find her right now. No, he needed to pause in order to form a plan—proof that he loved her.

CHAPTER TWENTY

A WEEK OFF from work.

Monday morning, Hermione looked around her modest flat and couldn't find a thing she felt like doing. And yet she couldn't go back to the Ludus—not yet. She had a lot of unused time off, and now was the time to use some of it.

In a week, Atlas should have his business wrapped up at the resort. She pushed the painful thought of him to the back of her mind. She supposed she should be happy he hadn't fired her.

How had she ever let herself get caught up in the legend of the Ruby Heart? She blamed it for letting herself fall hard for Atlas and believing that he could change. She had been so foolish.

She needed to stay busy. Her gaze moved around the bedroom. Her bed was already made up without a wrinkle. Everything was in its place. And it all felt so empty.

She told herself it had nothing to do with Atlas—nothing to do with the fact that he'd soon be flying back to London, nothing to do with the fact that she would never again lay eyes on him.

She retraced her steps to the living room. Her heart ached as she pictured his handsome face. She reached for an old faded throw pillow on the couch and hugged it to her chest. Then just as quickly she tossed aside the pillow. She was not going to sit around feeling sorry for herself. She was fine before Atlas and she'd be fine after him.

She moved to the two houseplants she'd bought yesterday at the market. She'd given them names. One was Spike and the other Ivy. Not original names, but she liked them.

She gave them each a drink of water and placed them on the windowsill to soak up some sunshine. She glanced around for something else to do—something that needed her attention. Perhaps she should adopt a dog. Then again, when she went back to work, she wouldn't be home much. Perhaps a cat would be better. She liked the idea. It would be nice to have someone to come home to. Then Atlas's image once more appeared in her mind. She exhaled a deep sigh. How could she have read things so wrong between them?

Knock-knock.

It was probably her neighbor, Mrs. Persopoulos. She was very sweet. And Hermione tried to help her out by carrying her groceries up the stairs or helping to clean her tiny apartment when she was available.

Hermione moved across the flat in just a few steps. She forced a smile to her face as she opened the door, only to find it wasn't Mrs. Persopoulos. There was a delivery person holding a bouquet of red roses.

"Ms. Kappas?"

"Yes."

"These are for you." He held the arrangement out to her.

She automatically accepted them. "Thank you."

Her heart raced. No one had ever sent her flowers—certainly not her ex. Could these be from Atlas? No. Of course not. Why would he send her flowers?

She rushed to her small table and placed the vase of flowers atop it. There was a note attached. She pulled the card from the envelope.

I'm sorry!
Atlas

They were from him. Her breath caught in her throat. What did that mean? He was sorry for what? Hurting her? Walking away?

The questions continued to roll around in her mind. Hope began to swell in her chest. She knew that was dangerous. She didn't want to get her heart broken. But wasn't it already broken?

Because she loved Atlas, even if he didn't love her in return.

She leaned over and inhaled the flowers' delicate scent. She had to know what this was all about; she reached for her phone. Her hand had a slight tremor as she dialed Atlas's phone.

It rang once. Twice. Three times.

Knock-knock.

She rushed to the door and swung it open. There stood another delivery person. "Ms. Kappas?"

"Yes." This was beginning to take on a sense of déjà vu.

He held out a small brown-paper-wrapped package. She thanked him and closed the door. She moved to the couch and sat down. What was it this time? She assumed it was also from Atlas. Why was he showering her with gifts?

She tore off the paper to find a box of specialty chocolates and an envelope. She opened it, finding a gift certificate for a chocolate massage at the resort's spa. And a note in Atlas's handwriting.

I know how much you love chocolate. I hope you will enjoy these and maybe you will find it in your heart to forgive me. Please. Perhaps a chocolate massage will help. I know I enjoyed the one you planned for me. You are so thoughtful—so kind. And I miss you!

Hermione read the message again. And again. What was he trying to tell her? Had he changed his mind about keeping the island—about their relationship?

Knock-knock.

CHAPTER TWENTY-ONE

HE WAS TAKING a chance.

This was a risk he'd never taken in his life.

In the past, when a woman was tired of his workaholic and nomadic ways, she walked away. He never followed—never asked for a second chance. And yet with Hermione, he was willing to risk it all—his pride and most of all…his heart—if it meant a chance for him to win her back.

He'd done a lot of soul-searching over the past two days since she'd left, and he knew his life just wasn't the same without her in it. But would he be able to convince her to give him a second chance?

His heart thump-thumped as he knocked on her door. He braced himself for the possibility of having the door slammed in his face. He wouldn't blame her. He'd made an utter mess of things.

Each second dragged on. And then he heard footsteps and the door swung open. Hermione looked adorable in her blue jeans and pink cotton top. Her long hair was swept back in a ponytail. And there wasn't a trace of makeup on her face—not that she needed any. She had a natural beauty about her. But he did notice the shadows beneath her eyes.

"Atlas, what are you doing here?"

"I'm hoping you'll come somewhere with me."

"I... I don't know." She worried her bottom lip. "Where?"

He noticed she didn't invite him inside. "Back to the beginning."

"What beginning?"

"Ours." His gaze searched hers. "Please."

There was a moment of silence as though she were deciding what she should do. All the while, he willed her to agree. He wanted so badly to make things right between them.

"Okay." Her voice was so soft that for a moment he thought he'd imagined it. "Let me grab my stuff."

A moment later she had on a light jacket, white tennis shoes and a gray purse slung over her shoulder. He led her downstairs and outside to his one-of-a-kind black sports car. As he zipped along the streets, she peppered him with questions but he held her off.

He wanted to do this right.

And so he distracted her with talk of the warm weather and trivial matters. The fact they were communicating on any level he took as a positive sign. Soon they arrived at the dock. A short ferry ride and they were on Ludus Island. He navigated the car along the winding road until they came to the spot of the accident. He pulled to the side of the road and turned off the engine.

"What are we doing here?" Hermione asked.

He got out but when he rounded the front of the car to open the door for her, she was already exiting the vehicle. "I thought we should go back to the beginning of you and me."

"You meant it literally." She gazed around.

"Signs of the accident have all been washed away with the flooding rains, but one thing wasn't, the initial feelings I had for you. They've only grown since I've gotten to know you."

She eyed him suspiciously. "The only thing you felt for me that night was anger."

He shook his head. "I'm sorry I was so grouchy in the beginning, but you didn't let it run you off. You stood your ground and made me see sense during one of the darkest times of my life. You're the strongest woman I know. And I'm so much better off by knowing you."

Her eyes shimmered with unshed tears. She blinked repeatedly. "You really think I'm strong?"

Once more he nodded. "So much stronger than me because you were willing to admit that what we had wasn't just a holiday fling—it was so much more. But I was afraid to put my heart on the line—afraid I wasn't worthy of your love."

She reached out to him, cupping his cheek with her hand. "How could you think that? You are amazing and sweet. Any woman would be lucky to have you in their life."

He leaned down and pressed his lips to hers. The kiss was short. He didn't want to get distracted. He needed to get this all out there. He needed to fix what he had broken.

Summoning all of his strength and determination, he pulled away from her sweet kiss. Her eyes fluttered open and stared at him with confusion reflected in her eyes.

Her heart raced.

Hermione could hardly believe she was here with Atlas and that he was kissing her. Hope and excitement swelled within her, but she refused to let it take over. She had to know that Atlas was fully invested in their relationship. She had to hear him say the words.

She loved him, but she wasn't going to make this easy for him. She wasn't going to assume what he meant by this grand gesture. If he was going to be in this for the long haul with her, he had to be willing to put himself out there—the whole way.

"Why did you bring me here?" she asked.

"I told you, so we could start over. Come back to the resort."

"You mean to continue running the place until the new management can take over?"

He shook his head. "There isn't going to be any new management."

She was confused. "There isn't?"

"Krystof and my mother helped me see that this place, this island—and you are my future. That is if you still want me."

Oh, boy, did she ever. It would be like a dream come true. Wait. Had she heard correctly? "Your mother?"

He nodded and explained about the letter and the scrapbook. "I just wish she'd have reached out again and that I would have been mature enough to hear her out." His gaze searched hers. "I don't want to repeat my mother's mistake and walk away from someone I love. Will you give me another chance?"

A tear splashed on her cheek. "You love me?"

He held up a finger for her to wait a moment. Then he reached in his suit jacket and pulled out a black velvet box. Her heart leaped into her throat.

"Go ahead," he said. "It's for you."

Another gift? The gifts were really sweet. He was trying really hard to get this right. She accepted the box and opened it. Inside was a locket. The breath hitched in her lungs. She knew this locket. She looked closer. It looked so much like her mother's missing locket.

"It's not the original," Atlas said. "I had a duplicate made until we can recover the original."

No one had ever done something so thoughtful for her. She lifted her gaze to his. "Thank you for being so sweet."

"Open it."

She swiped at her cheeks and then she did as he asked. Inside were two little heart-shaped pieces of paper with the words *I love you* written on them.

Her gaze lifted to his. "You do?"

He nodded. "With all of my heart."

And then she had the most incredible realization. "It's true."

"What's true?"

"The legend of the Ruby Heart."

"Is it?" His gaze challenged her. "Will you come back to the resort with me?"

She smiled and nodded. "I love you too." But then she realized that she now had other responsibilities. "But can Spike and Ivy come with me?"

"Spike and Ivy?" He shrugged. "Bring whoever you want. My home is your home."

"Good. Because I've kept those houseplants alive for two days now and I'd hate for anything to happen to them."

He laughed and shook his head. "Maybe we should think about getting you a dog."

"Or a cat."

"Or one of each." He pulled her close. "I've always been a bit of a nomad, but I can't wait to set down roots with you. And Spike and Ivy."

"Before we do that, how about we do some more of this?" She lifted up on her tiptoes and pressed her lips to his.

EPILOGUE

Four months later... Ludus Island

EVERYTHING WAS LOOKING UP.

The resort was bustling with sunseekers.

And Hermione had never been happier in her life.

Right now, she was gearing up for the resort's biggest event of the year—the Royal Regatta. It was due to kick off tomorrow, and Hermione was a nervous wreck. Everything had to go perfectly with Prince Istvan of Rydiania in attendance.

Additional staff had been hired to make this year's regatta bigger and better than ever. Nestor was back at work, seeing to all of the event's details. While Atlas was splitting his time between his security business and running the resort. He was very busy, but Hermione had never seen him happier. And that filled her heart with joy.

Hermione stood outside on the veranda taking in the view of smiling guests enjoying the beach. June was her favorite time of the year. There was an energy that flowed through the resort—

"Excuse me, Miss Kappas. Where do you want me to set up?"

Hermione turned to their latest hire. She searched her memory for the young woman's name. It took Hermione a second to recall it. "Good morning, Indigo. We're so happy to have you as part of the Ludus family. I've had a large umbrella set up for you on the beach. Just let us know what else you need—"

"Good morning, Hermione." The deep male voice had a distinct foreign accent.

Hermione would know that sexy voice anywhere. She immediately turned and then curtsied. "Your Royal Highness."

He smiled. "Hermione, I told you curtsying isn't necessary."

"But it feels wrong not to. After all, you're a prince."

"Don't remind me. I have those guys to constantly remind me." He gestured over his shoulder to the small army of dark suited men with sunglasses and earpieces. His gaze moved to Indigo. His smile broadened. "And who might you be?"

Hermione noticed how the young woman's eyes widened. When Indigo appeared to be shocked into silence, Hermione intervened. "This is Indigo. She's a talented artist."

"Is that so?" The prince's gaze studied the woman. "A beautiful artist."

If Hermione didn't know better, she'd think the prince was drawn to Indigo. But he was normally smooth and flirtatious with all of the pretty ladies. This meeting was no different. Or was it? "Perhaps she could do a sketch for you."

"I'd like that." He was still staring at Indigo, who was now blushing. "But it'll have to wait. I have some business to attend to." He turned his attention to Hermione. "I wanted to say hello and find out how things are going now that Thea's son owns the island."

"Things are going well." She smiled as she thought of Atlas. "Very well. I'll have to introduce you to him."

"I'd like that. Now I must be going." He gave Hermione's hand a butterfly kiss. And then he did the same for Indigo. "I look forward to our next meeting."

After he was gone, Indigo still hadn't spoken a word. Hermione couldn't blame her. The prince was quite charming. And then there was that sexy accent.

"You can go set up," Hermione said, jarring the woman out of her stupor.

"I... I can't believe I didn't say a word to him."

Hermione smiled. "It's fine. I'm sure he's used to it."

Once Indigo moved on, Hermione checked her email on her digital tablet. She should be in her office working, but the sunshine and sea breeze had called to her. She'd have to go inside soon, but she just needed a minute or two more of fresh air.

"Here you are." Atlas stepped up next to her. "Are you busy?"

"I'm never too busy for you." She lifted up on her tiptoes, pressing her lips to his. When she pulled away, she asked, "What do you need?"

"More of those kisses." He smiled at her.

"I'm afraid you'll have to wait until later."

He sighed. "In that case, I need you to come see something."

"Please tell me nothing's wrong. The prince just arrived. Oh, and he wants to meet you."

He arched a brow. "Should I be jealous that you're buddies with a prince?"

"No. I already have my prince." She gave him another quick kiss. "Now what's going on? Is it the security system?" She followed him inside to the elevator. "We assured the prince that everything was now state of the art."

"It's not the security system." He pressed the down button.

"We're going to the Under the Sea restaurant?"

Atlas turned to her. He cupped her face in his hands. "Stop worrying. I promise you everything is going to be perfect."

"But you said I had to see something."

"I didn't say it was something bad. Did I?"

"But—"

He leaned over and pressed his lips to hers. Immediately her stress started to dissipate. She leaned into him and returned the kiss. She would never ever get tired of kissing him.

The elevator dinged as the door slid open. With great reluctance, she pulled away from Atlas. But he in turn took her hand in his.

"Come on." He led her past the waiting area.

The restaurant was only open for dinner service so with this being noon, it should be empty. But when they stepped into the dining room, there was a table in the middle of the room. There was a few candles and a huge bouquet of red roses.

Hermione turned to Atlas. "I don't understand."

He smiled. "I have a surprise for you." He drew her closer to the table that was set for lunch—a champagne lunch. He picked up a black velvet box. He held it out to her. "This is for you."

She smiled. "You have to quit spoiling me."

"But I enjoy it. I love making you smile."

She opened the box. Inside was a locket, exactly like the one she was wearing. "You got me another locket?"

"No. I got you the real locket—your mother's locket."

"You found it!" Tears rushed to her eyes as her finger traced over it. "I never thought I'd see it again." Her watery gaze moved to his. "Thank you."

"Open it."

This definitely felt like déjà vu. But she did what he said. Inside, resting on top of the photos of her parents, were two little pieces of paper.

On the left it said: *Will you...*

The right read: *...marry me?*

She read it twice, just to make sure she'd read it correctly. When she looked at Atlas, she found him on bended knee. He held out a smaller black velvet box with a big beautiful emerald cut diamond ring.

"Hermione, I fell for you from the first time I saw you. I didn't need a ruby to tell me how special you are. I just had no idea how much you would change my life for the better, and now I can't imagine my life without you in it. Will you marry me?"

By now the tears of joy had rolled onto her cheeks. Her heart went pitter-patter with love. "Yes. Yes, I'll marry you."

He straightened, slipped the ring on her finger and then pulled her into his arms, claiming her lips with his own. She had found the love of her life. How had she gotten so lucky?

* * * * *

It Started With A Royal Kiss

Award-winning author **Jennifer Faye** pens fun, heartwarming contemporary romances with rugged cowboys, sexy billionaires and enchanting royalty. Internationally published, with books translated into nine languages, she is a two-time winner of the *RT Book Reviews* Reviewers' Choice Award. She has also won the CataRomance Reviewers' Choice Award, been named a Top Pick author and been nominated for numerous other awards.

Books by Jennifer Faye

Greek Paradise Escape

Greek Heir to Claim Her Heart

Wedding Bells at Lake Como

Bound by a Ring and a Secret
Falling for Her Convenient Groom

The Bartolini Legacy

The Prince and the Wedding Planner
The CEO, the Puppy and Me
The Italian's Unexpected Heir

Her Christmas Pregnancy Surprise
Fairytale Christmas with the Millionaire

Visit the Author Profile page
at millsandboon.com.au for
more titles.

Dear Reader,

Sometimes thoughts are instilled in our minds from an early age and it can be difficult to overcome those beliefs in order to find our own truth. Such is the case for both my hero and heroine.

Artist Indigo Castellanos's life has faced much turmoil. And now, in order to provide for her ailing mother, she's taken a position at the Ludus Resort, where she runs into Prince Istvan. Her father had warned her not to trust a Rydianian royal. But he never mentioned how the prince could be so charming and persistent.

Prince Istvan of Rydiania is on Ludus Island for the royal regatta. He's convinced his destiny is preordained. And then he latches on to the idea of hiring Indigo to paint his formal portrait. Her fresh approach will be a visual reminder of the change he intends to bring to the kingdom.

Under normal circumstances, this job would be a dream come true—if only this prince's family hadn't ruined her father's life. However, Indigo can't afford to turn down Prince Istvan's generous offer. But when he discovers her true identity, will it ruin any chance of happiness for them?

Happy reading!

Jennifer

Praise for
Jennifer Faye

"A fantastic romantic read that is a joy to read from start to finish, *The CEO, the Puppy and Me* is another winner by the immensely talented Jennifer Faye."

—*Goodreads*

CHAPTER ONE

A PRINCE.

A genuine, sexy-as-all-get-out royal prince.

Indigo Castellanos swallowed hard. She couldn't believe she'd come face-to-face with Prince Istvan of Rydiania. She didn't want to be impressed—not at all—but she couldn't deny being a little bit awed by his mesmerizing blue eyes and tanned face. Just the memory of his shirtless body sent her traitorous heart racing.

She never in a million years thought they'd actually meet. When she'd taken this artist position at the Ludus Resort, she'd known the prince had ties to the private island. Still, it was a large resort—big enough to avoid certain people. Sure, the royal regatta was going on, but she'd mistakenly thought the prince would be too busy to attend. And if he did make an appearance, he wouldn't meander around the resort like some commoner.

And then, when she did meet him, she hadn't said a word. If staring into his bottomless eyes hadn't been bad enough, she'd been stunned into silence by his muscled chest and trim waist.

She gave herself a mental shake. None of that mattered. Not at all.

Nothing changed the fact that the prince came from the same family that had cast her father out of his homeland. But she didn't have time to think of that now. Besides, she didn't expect to see the prince again.

She perched on a stool beneath a great big red umbrella. Her bare, painted toes wiggled in the warm sand. She was so thankful for this job. It helped her care for her ailing mother. And she would do anything for her mother.

"Is she sitting in the right position?"

The woman's voice drew Indigo from her thoughts. She focused on the mother and young daughter in front of her. The girl was seated on a stool. "Um, yes. Why?"

"Because you were frowning." The mother didn't look happy.

"So sorry. Your daughter is just perfect." Indigo forced a reassuring smile to her lips. "The glare off the water is making it hard to see."

Indigo shifted her position on the stool. She couldn't afford to have her clients think she wasn't happy or they wouldn't continue to bring their children and family members to have her draw caricatures of them. And without the clients there would be no job—without a job, she wouldn't be able to pay the mounting medical bills.

She forced herself to concentrate on her work. Her art was what had gotten her through the tough times in her life, from her father's sudden death to her mother's collapse. Whereas some people lived charmed lives—Prince Istvan's handsome image came to mind—other people were not so fortunate. She didn't let the challenges stop her from striving for something better—from believing if she just kept trying, good things were awaiting her.

Minutes later, she finished the young girl's caricature and gently unclipped the paper from her easel. She handed it over to the mother, who didn't smile as she examined Indigo's work. She then held it out to her nine-year-old daughter and asked her opinion. The girl's eyes widened as a big smile puffed up her cheeks. And that was all Indigo needed to make her day. After all, it was as her father used to say: *it's the small things in life where you find the greatest reward.*

"Wait until I show my friends."

"Now what do you say?" the mother prompted.

The girl turned her attention to Indigo. "Thank you."

"You're welcome." In that moment, it didn't matter that Indigo was doing fun sketches instead of grand works of art. The only thing that mattered was that she'd brought some happiness to this girl's life.

"May I see it?" a male voice asked.

Indigo turned her head, and once again, she was caught off guard by the handsome prince. Her heart started to pitter-patter as she stared at him. What were the chances of them accidentally running into each other again?

"Oh." The mother's hand flew to her chest. "Your Highness." The woman did a deep curtsy.

The young girl's eyes filled with confusion as her gaze moved between her mother and Prince Istvan. Then her mother gestured for her to do the same thing. While the girl did a semi curtsy, Indigo sat by and took in the scene.

Was the prince here to see the mother? Did they have some sort of business together? Because there was absolutely no way he was there to see her. Not a chance. The royals and the Castellanos no longer intermingled—by royal decree. The reminder set Indigo's back teeth grinding together.

The prince turned in her direction. His eyes widened in surprise. Was it because he wasn't expecting to run into her again so soon? Or was it that she wasn't falling all over herself in front of him doing a curtsy? She refused to bow to him.

She should say something, but her mouth had gone dry. Words lodged in the back of her throat. And her heart was beating out of control. What was wrong with her?

The prince turned his attention back to the drawing. "It's fabulous. And who would the pretty young woman in the drawing be?"

"That's me," the girl said proudly.

The prince made a big deal of holding the sketch up next to the young girl, and then his dark brows drew together as his gaze moved between her and the drawing. "So it is. You're lucky to have such a lovely sketch." He returned the paper to the girl. "Enjoy your day."

The mother and daughter curtsied again. Then the mother reached in her bright orange-and-white beach bag. She withdrew her phone. With the consent of the prince, she took a selfie with him. Though the prince smiled for the picture, Indigo noticed how the smile did not go the whole way to his blue eyes.

After the woman repeatedly thanked him, she turned to Indigo. "How much do I owe you?"

"Nothing," Indigo said. "It's a courtesy of the resort."

"Oh." She dropped her phone in her bag. "Thank you." And then her attention returned to the prince. She curtsied again.

Indigo wondered if she'd looked that ridiculous the other day when she'd first met the prince. She hoped not. But she had been totally caught off guard.

She expected him to move on, but he didn't. His attention turned to her. "And so we meet again."

She swallowed hard. "Your Highness."

Quite honestly, she didn't know what to say to him. He certainly didn't want to hear anything she had to say about him or his family—about how they were cold and uncaring about whom they hurt in the name of the crown. No, it was best not to go there. She didn't think her boss would approve of her vocalizing her true feelings about the prince's family.

She glanced down at the blank page in front of her. She could feel the prince's gaze upon her. What was he thinking? Did he recognize her?

Impossible. She'd only been a very young child when her family had fled Rydiania. Back then she'd been scared and confused. She'd had no idea why they were leaving their home and everything they'd ever known to move to Greece—a land that she'd never visited, filled with people she did not know.

"Shall I sit here?" The prince's deep voice drew her from her troubled thoughts.

"If you like." In an effort not to stare at his tanned chest, she barely glanced at him. Though it was a huge temptation. Very tempting indeed. Instead she fussed over the blank sheet of paper on her easel, pretending to straighten it.

What did he want? Surely he wasn't going to take the time to flirt with her when she had no standing in his regal world. So if he wasn't there to flirt with her, why was he lingering?

Curiosity got the best of her. "Is there something I can do for you?"

He smiled at her, but the happiness didn't show in his eyes. It was though there was something nagging at him that he didn't want to share with her. She wondered what could weigh so heavily on a prince's mind.

"I would like you to draw me."

Her gaze lifted just in time to witness him crossing his arms over that perfectly sculpted chest. *Oh, my!* The breath stilled in her chest as she continued to drink in the sight of his tanned and toned body. She wondered if he spent all his free time in the gym. Because there was no way anyone looked as good as him without working at it.

Her attention slipped down over the corded muscles of his arms and landed on his six-pack abs. It wasn't until her gaze reached the waistband of his blue-and-white board shorts that she realized she shouldn't be staring.

"Will that be a problem?" His voice drew her attention back to his face.

This time when she stared into his eyes, she noticed a hint of amusement twinkling in his eyes. She'd been totally busted staring at him. Heat started in her chest and worked its way up her neck. What was she doing, checking out the enemy?

Just keep it together. You need to keep this job.

Her little pep talk calmed her down just a bit. She drew in a deep breath and slowly released it. "Surely you have better things to do—erm, more important things than to have me sketch you."

She couldn't believe she was brushing off an opportunity to sketch a prince. If her friends could see her now they'd probably rush her to the hospital, certain she'd lost her grip on reality. But Istvan wasn't just any prince.

"I'm right where I want to be. Go ahead. Draw me."

Indigo hesitated. If he was anyone else but a member of the Rydianian royal family, she'd have jumped at the opportunity.

She'd grown up hearing stories of how the royal family wasn't to be trusted—that they put the crown above all else, including love of family. Her father was never the same after the former king, Georgios, and those in service to him were cast out of the kingdom. How could they do something so heartless?

"Is there a problem?" The prince's gaze studied her.

Unless she wanted to reveal the truth and put her new position at the Ludus Resort in jeopardy, she'd best get on with her job. She just had to pretend he was like any other guest at the resort, but she feared she wasn't that good of an actress.

She swallowed hard. "I don't think my sketch would do you justice."

He arched a brow. "Are you refusing to draw me?"

She thought about it. How many times had this prince been denied something he wanted? She doubted it ever happened. Oh, how she'd like to be the first to do it. But even she wasn't that reckless.

"No." She grabbed her black brush pen. Then her gaze rose to meet his. "I just want you to understand that it won't be a conservative, traditional portrait."

"I understand. And I don't want it to be. Just pretend I'm any other patron." He settled himself on the stool while his security staff fanned out around him.

He was most definitely not just any other person—not even

close. And yet he didn't have a clue who she was or how his family had destroyed hers. She thought of telling him, but what would that accomplish?

As she lifted her hand to the page, she noticed its slight tremor. She told herself she could do this. After all, the sooner she finished the sketch, the sooner the prince would move on. And so she pressed the brush pen to the paper and set to work.

It was impossible to do her job without looking at him. Her fingers tingled with the temptation to reach out to the dark, loose curls scattered over the top of his head. The sides and back of his head were clipped short. His tanned face had an aristocratic look, with a straight nose that wasn't too big nor too small. Dark brows highlighted his intense blue eyes with dark lashes. And a close-trimmed mustache and goatee framed his kissable lips.

In order to do her job, she had to take in every tiny detail of the person in front of her and translate them onto paper. And normally that wasn't hard for her. But sketching the prince was going to be the biggest challenge of her career as her heart raced and her fingers refused to cooperate.

She glanced around at the finely dressed men with hulking biceps and dark sunglasses. They were facing away from Istvan and Indigo, as though they were giving them some privacy while protecting them from the rest of the world.

"Don't worry about them," Prince Istvan said as though he could read her thoughts. "They're here to make sure there are no unwanted disturbances."

Indigo kept moving the black brush pen over the page. On second thought, the prince was really a pleasure to sketch with his strong jawline and firm chin. And then there was the dimple in his left cheek. Under any other circumstances, she'd readily admit that he was the most handsome man she'd ever sketched. But she refused to acknowledge such a thing—not about a member of the Rydianian royal family.

Prince Istvan might not have had anything to do with her

father's dismissal from his lifelong service to the royal family or his subsequent banishment from the country, but that didn't mean Istvan wasn't one of them—raised to be like the uncaring, unfeeling royals who had destroyed her family.

"Does it take you long to do a sketch?" His smooth, rich voice interrupted her thoughts.

"No."

"How long does it usually take?"

She wasn't sure what to make of him going out of his way to make small talk. "Five to ten minutes. It all depends on how much detail work I do."

"That's amazing. It would take me twice as long to draw a stick figure." He sent her a friendly smile that made his baby blues twinkle.

She ignored the way her stomach dipped as she returned her focus to the drawing. Why did he have to be the prince from Rydiania? Why couldn't he just be a random guest at the resort?

She smothered a sigh and focused on her work. She took pleasure in the fact that she didn't have to do a true sketch of the prince. Her job was to exaggerate certain characteristics. She chose to elongate his chin and emphasize his perfectly straight white front teeth. His hair was perfectly styled, as though not a strand would dare defy the prince. She would fix that by drawing his hair a bit longer and messier. And then she took some creative liberty and added a crown that was falling off to the side of his head. A little smile pulled at the corner of her lips. It definitely wasn't the image of a proper prince.

The man on the page was more approachable. He didn't take himself too seriously. And this prince wouldn't endorse the demise of innocent and loyal subjects. If only fiction was reality.

With the outline complete, she started to fill in the sketch with a bit of color. When she first took this job at the resort, she'd considered just doing black-and-white sketches, but she was partial to colors. And it didn't take her much more time.

When she focused on the prince's blue eyes, she had a problem combining the blues to get that intense color. Maybe she should have just done a plain light blue color like she would have done for any other person. But it was though his eyes held a challenge for her. How could she resist?

When she glanced at him, it was though he could see straight through her. She wondered what he thought when he looked at her. But then again, he was a royal, so he probably didn't even see her—not really. He most likely saw nothing more than someone who was there to serve him.

Indigo switched up color after color. Her hand moved rapidly over the paper. He became distracted with his phone. With his attention elsewhere, it was easier for her to finish her task.

"I see you've decided to get a caricature done," a female voice said.

Indigo paused to glance over her shoulder to find her boss approaching them. Hermione wore a warm smile. Indigo wondered if Hermione had a secret crush on the prince. It wouldn't be hard to imagine her with him.

But then again, Hermione was now sporting a large, sparkly diamond ring. And her fiancé was almost as handsome as the prince. Hermione and the prince made chitchat while Indigo continued to add more details to the sketch. At one point, she leaned back to take in the partial image. Her discerning gaze swept down over the page. She surprised herself. There wasn't one negative aspect of the sketch. How could that be?

No imperfection that had been exaggerated. No big front teeth sticking out. No bulbous nose. No pointy chin. Nothing but his hotness exaggerated on the page into a cute caricature. And the crown she'd added to make him look like a carefree prince—well, even that didn't look like a negative. In fact, it just upped his cute factor.

As Hermione moved on, Indigo was still puzzling over the image that lacked any of her normal exaggerations. Was this really how she saw him? Like some fun, easygoing and kind royal?

Obviously not. He was heir to the throne. He would do things just as they had been done before—stepping on loved ones and family for the good of the crown.

CHAPTER TWO

DID HE HAVE better things to do with his time? Yes.

Did he really care about the mounting messages on his phone? No.

Prince Istvan lifted his head and stared at the top of the young woman's head as she worked behind the easel. He shifted to the side to get a better view of her. Her long hair was pulled back into a ponytail that fell over her shoulder. His fingers tingled with the urge to comb their way through the dark, silky strands.

His gaze strayed to her gold name tag. Indigo. Such a pretty name for someone so strikingly beautiful.

His attention returned to her face. Lines formed between her fine brows as she concentrated on her work. A pert little nose led to heart-shaped lips that were just begging to be kissed. It was such a tempting idea.

Just then she glanced up. Their gazes caught and held, causing a warm sensation in his chest. Did she know he had been fantasizing about pulling her into his embrace? Without a word, her attention returned to the easel.

There was something about her that made him feel like they somehow knew each other, but as he searched his memory, he was certain if their paths had crossed he would have remembered her. She had an unforgettable natural beauty about her, from her big brown eyes with flecks of gold that made them twinkle to her pert nose and lush lips that tempted and teased.

But he didn't have time to be distracted. He had problems awaiting him back home. His father was reaching a point where his health was forcing him to step down from the throne. Istvan was expected to take on more and more royal duties in preparation for the transfer of power.

The problem was, the more responsibilities he took on, the more unhappy he became. It wasn't the work he didn't like— it was the lack of time he had to devote to his pet projects. He had taken under his wing the Arts for Children, Homes for All and his biggest project, We Care—a foundation to support sick children and their families. All such worthy causes, and all needed more attention than he could possibly give each of them once he ascended to the throne.

But with his name attached to the charities, more people stepped up to help. More people were willing to give of their time, energy and money. If he were to walk away now, the future of the foundations would be in jeopardy because they weren't designated as royal charities. To fall under the royal designation, each charity had to meet stringent criteria—including being established for a minimum of fifty years. His projects were still in their infancy. And quite honestly, he didn't want to walk away. It was good work—important work. The foundations put him in direct contact with the people of the kingdom in a way he never would have been if he'd secluded himself in the palace. How was he supposed to rule over people when he didn't know what was important to them?

He was quickly coming to the realization that his family was becoming antiquated. It was a sobering thought he didn't dare share with anyone.

What was wrong with him? He should feel like he was on top of the world, but as the day of his crowning approached, the more he felt himself withdrawing from his family.

He couldn't help but wonder if this was how his uncle felt

before he'd abdicated the throne—not that Istvan was planning to do the same thing. He'd been young when it happened, but he clearly recalled the turmoil it'd caused his family. There couldn't be a repeat.

His phone started to ring. He withdrew it from his pocket. The caller ID said it was his eldest sister, Gisella. He could already guess what was on his sister's mind—royal business. She might not be the heir to the throne, but that didn't keep her from assuming an important place in the family business.

He could only imagine she was calling to admonish him for missing some meeting. He always heard the disapproving tone in her voice when he was away from the palace.

It wasn't like this trip had been spontaneous. It had been on his calendar for a year. He had the speed boat race tomorrow. And he intended to win. He wasn't going to let anyone ruin these few days of relaxation. He'd be back at the palace soon enough.

And so he pressed the ignore button on his phone. Whatever it was, it could wait.

"If you have somewhere else to be, I can finish this without you." The sweet, melodic voice drew him from his thoughts.

Istvan blinked and stared at the artist. "Excuse me. What did you say?"

"That I can finish this drawing without you and have it delivered."

"That won't be necessary." He forced a smile, reassuring her that everything was all right.

She looked at him for a moment longer but didn't say anything. It was impossible to tell what she was thinking behind those big brown eyes.

A few minutes later, the young woman released the white paper from the clips on the board. She grasped the paper and approached him. "Here you go."

He took the paper from her. He didn't know what he expected. Under normal circumstances, an artist would be very reserved in their work since he was, after all, a prince. So he supposed he expected something similar from Indigo.

But when he held the sketch out in front of him, he realized she'd treated him just like she had her other clients. In fact, for a moment he didn't recognize himself. Instead of smiling, he was frowning in the sketch. Was that how she saw him?

But the seriousness of the frown was offset by a crown that was sliding down the side of his head as his eyes were upturned, trying to figure out what was going on. He noticed the details from his eyes and lashes to the pucker lines in his rather large bottom lip.

Had she really been that observant? She was able to translate his thoughts to paper. Because he'd been thinking of how unhappy he was with the restraints the crown would place upon his life. But a casual observer would never pick up on it. This woman was keenly observant.

"This is remarkable," he said.

Her fine brows momentarily lifted, as though she were truly surprised by his praise. "I'm glad you like it."

"I think it's amazing that you can do all this in just a matter of minutes. I wish I could do something like this."

"Have you ever tried?"

He shook his head. "No. But I'm sure any attempt I'd make would be a disaster."

"You'll never know until you give it a try."

Art had never been an important part of his upbringing. His lessons had consisted of the basics in grammar and math, but the emphasis had been on history, specifically the history of Rydiania, government and civics. There was no room in his busy schedule for sports or arts.

He wondered what he'd missed by not exploring the arts. Was he an undiscovered grand pianist? He immediately dismissed the idea. There was nothing wrong with the piano, but he had never been curious about it or drawn to it.

Perhaps he would have been good at playing the guitar—

maybe he would have been the lead guitar player in a rock band. He struggled not to smile as he imagined his parents' horrified expressions if he'd wanted to go in that direction.

Indigo pursed her lips as her brows drew together. "You find the suggestion funny?"

Oh, no. He hadn't hidden his thoughts as well as he'd thought. "No. It's not that. I was thinking of my parents' reaction if I told them I was giving up the throne to pursue something in the arts field."

"Oh." Her lush lips smoothed out, and her brows parted. "I'm guessing they would absolutely hate the idea."

His brows rose. "You sound as though you know them."

She shook her head. "No. Not at all. I… I was just guessing about their response."

He nodded in understanding. Just then the head of his security detail stepped up and whispered in his ear. His sister was eager to reach him and not happy that he wasn't answering his phone.

Istvan cleared his throat. "I must go now. But I want to thank you for this…interesting drawing. I've never had one like it. How much do I owe you?"

Color bloomed in her cheeks. "Nothing. It's courtesy of the resort."

"But surely I can tip you."

She shook her head. "I am paid well."

"I see." He hesitated. This never happened to him. Most people asked many things of him. Some requests he could accomplish, but there were many other requests that were far beyond his power. But this beautiful woman wanted nothing from him. He was intrigued.

"Sir, we must go," his head of security reminded him.

Even here on his uncle's island, far removed from his kingdom, his life was still not his own. "Yes. I'm coming." He turned back to Indigo. "I must leave, but I just want to thank you for this drawing. It's truly unique."

Her cheeks pinkened. "You're welcome."

And with that he walked away. He was tempted to glance over his shoulder at the woman who treated him like any other human instead of the crown prince. Was she really that immune to his charms? Or was there something more? Some other reason she kept a wall up between them?

Buzz. Buzz.

He didn't have time to consider the answers to his mounting questions. Royal duty took precedence over everything. His jaw tightened as he reached for his phone.

He didn't have to check the caller ID to know who was at the other end of the phone call. Princess Gisella.

"Hello." He struggled to keep the irritation out of his voice.

"It's about time. I've been trying to reach you. You should have known it was important, because I do not like making phone calls."

"I was preoccupied." He knew she was expecting an apology for not jumping when she'd called, but he was tired of feeling like their roles were reversed—tired of Gisella always proving she was the most loyal to the crown. "What do you need?"

"You. Back here at once."

He restrained a sigh. This was not their first conversation about his whereabouts or her utter displeasure with him for visiting their uncle's island. "I'll return after the weekend. I have a race to participate in."

"You shouldn't be racing. It's dangerous. You can't take frivolous chances with your life. You're the crown prince. If something happened…"

"You'd step in and be an amazing queen."

"Don't say that. It's like tempting fate."

Laughter erupted from his throat. "Gisella, you do worry too much."

"Someone has to. You certainly don't."

"I'll be safe."

"Make sure you are. What about the visit from the Spanish

delegation? The festival is this weekend, and you must make an appearance."

"I'm sure you can charm them."

Gisella sighed. "I can't always fill in for you. You are, after all, the crown prince."

"Maybe you should be. You enjoy all that pomp and circumstance."

"Istvan!" Gisella's voice took on a warning tone, telling him that he was going too far.

"Relax. I'm just giving you a hard time."

There was a strained pause. "See that you are here early. There's a cabinet meeting on Monday morning, and you are to attend with the king. And you have yet to sit for your portrait. It is needed not only for the palace, but it is also to be added to the currency."

And he had been dragging his feet. He didn't know how he felt about his face being on Rydiania's currency. Sure, it was only one denomination, while his father appeared on the rest. But still, it felt as though it were sealing his fate—hemming him into a life exactly like his parents'. The thought of being locked up in the palace for the rest of his life made him feel claustrophobic.

He'd much rather stay here on this sunny island with its colorful, fruity drinks and the most alluring artist. It was far more appealing than being cooped up with the royal painter for hours.

Suddenly a thought came to him. Perhaps sitting for the portrait didn't have to be as miserable as he'd been imagining. Perhaps it could be pleasurable.

Indigo's image came to mind. He wondered if she had any experience with personal portraits. He didn't know the answer, but it was something he planned to look into as soon as possible.

CHAPTER THREE

HIS VIVID BLUE eyes haunted her.

Later that afternoon, Indigo clipped a fresh paper to the easel. She couldn't stop thinking of the prince. He was not what she'd been expecting. Not at all.

Somehow she'd imagined him as a spoiled brat. He was not that. She'd expected him to be totally full of himself. He hadn't been. And she'd expected him to take himself too seriously— to the point where he wouldn't have been able to appreciate the sketch she'd done of him. And yet he'd genuinely seemed to like the silly sketch. What did that mean?

It would be so much easier to dislike the prince if he had some obvious negative qualities. But right now she was struggling to find something legitimate to dislike about him—other than his lineage.

As she bent over to retrieve a fresh pen from her large tote, she heard someone approaching. "Have a seat. I'll be right with you."

They didn't say a word, but she sensed their presence. She straightened, clipped the paper to the board and then glanced around it. She struggled not to gape when she found the prince sitting on the stool. Again.

Heat swirled in her chest. "Your Highness, you're back."

She noticed this time he was wearing a white T-shirt with the race logo on it. She felt an instant pang of disappointment at not getting another glimpse of his muscled chest. She swallowed hard.

When her gaze rose to meet his, she asked, "What can I do for you?"

"I would like to have another sketch done. I'm more than willing to compensate you."

"Another?" No one ever came back to her and requested a second sketch. "Did something happen to the first one?"

"No. Actually, I need another for a charity auction."

Charity? The prince? Really?

Nothing about the man sitting in front of her was like her father had warned her about the royal family. Istvan was not cold. He was not harsh. And he was not mean.

What was she supposed to make of this prince with his generous heart and dazzling smile that made her stomach dip? The only thing she knew was that the more time she spent with him, the more confused she became. It was best to keep her distance.

"Can't you use the sketch I already drew for you?"

"It can't be that one."

"Why? Was it too silly?" She'd been waiting for him to show his true colors.

He shook his head. "No. It was perfect. That's why I'm keeping it. I need another one for the auction."

"Something more serious?"

"Not at all. I enjoy your sense of humor. So have at it. I don't want any special treatment. You can do the same thing or something different. I don't care."

She inwardly groaned. What was it with this guy? He was making it impossible for her to dislike him. In fact, if she spent more time with him, she might fall for his azure-blue eyes and his sexy accent.

It was best to get this over with as quickly as possible. Indigo was certain that once she completed the sketch she wouldn't see the prince again.

In truth, she didn't need him to sit for her again. She had every detail of his handsome face memorized. She groaned inwardly.

The artist in her demanded she do something different than the first sketch. She never did duplicates of anything. Life was too short for repeats.

This time she decided to portray the prince in his royal world. She told herself it would be fun, but there was another reason— she needed a visual reminder that this man wasn't just another handsome face.

Her father had been obsessed with the royal family toward the end of his life. At the time, she couldn't understand why he went on and on about them. But as she grew older, she realized her father had considered his position as the king's secretary as much more than an occupation. To him, it was his life's calling—the position that had been handed down to him through the generations of his family's service to the royal family.

Not only had he been stripped of his calling, but he was then kicked out of the country like a traitor. It broke something in her father—something time and even love couldn't fix.

Indigo shoved the troubling thoughts to the back of her mind. Instead she focused on her work. She looked at the prince as little as possible, trying to work from memory. But she found herself questioning her memory time and again. Because it just wasn't possible for someone to look as good as him, from his high cheekbones to his strong chin to his perfectly straight nose.

And then there were his eyes. Oh, those eyes! She felt as though she were being drawn in every time their gazes connected. This time the prince wasn't distracted by his phone. This time his attention was solely on her. His unwavering gaze sent a current of awareness zipping through her veins.

She struggled to keep her hand from tremoring. That had never been a problem for her in the past. Why was she letting him get to her? He was just another guy. *Yeah, right.* He was anything but just another guy. And her traitorous body was well aware of it.

Her brush pen moved rapidly over the page. She forced herself not to go too fast. After all, this was her art, and it deserved to be her best.

When at last she finished, she removed the page from the easel and handed it over. She wasn't sure what he'd think of her image. This sketch had him wearing a serious expression with his exaggerated chin slightly upturned as he wore his crooked crown and a royal cape, while holding a scepter in his hand.

He was quiet for a moment as he took in the image. "Is that how you really see me? Looking down on the world?"

He didn't sound pleased. It seemed her image had struck a nerve. She wasn't sure if it was a good thing—that he cared how the world saw him—or a bad thing, because he had the power to get her fired. She hadn't considered that dire consequence when she'd indulged her imagination.

It was best she try and smooth things out. She swallowed hard. "It's not how I see you. I don't even know you. I was just having some fun. If you give it back, I'll try again."

He stood, quietly staring at the image. "No. I will keep it."

"But if you don't like it—"

"Your art has a way of making one look at themselves in a totally different light." At last he smiled. "I like it." He paused and stared at the sketch a little longer. "I really like it."

"Are you sure?" It was in her best interest to make the prince happy, even if it was the last thing she wanted to do. She could imagine her father scolding her for placating the heir to the throne.

"I am positive. I will find a special spot for this."

Perhaps in the wastebasket? She kept the thought to herself. She'd already pushed her luck as far as she imagined it would go that day.

His gaze lifted and met hers. "Is this the only thing you do?"

"Excuse me?"

"Do you do other forms of artwork besides the sketches?"

She nodded. "I do. This is just a side job that I've picked up."

"You have more than one job?" He looked impressed.

"You have no idea."

In addition to her work at the resort, she was constantly adding to her collection of portraits. In her neighborhood, many of the residents were willing to pose for her. She was busy preparing for her first-ever gallery showing in Athens. It was a huge milestone. Plus, she helped care for her mother.

"I'd love to see some of your other work. Would that be possible? Do you have a website or something?"

She shook her head. "No website." But then she realized she'd taken a few photos of her latest pieces to show her agent. She pulled out her phone and pulled up the photos. "These are some recent pieces."

She wasn't sure why she was sharing any of this with him. It wasn't like they were friends—far from it. But it wasn't often she met someone who was interested in her work. And it felt good to be able to share it with him.

Her pieces were done in modern realism. There were paintings of her neighbors' daughters as they played, an older gentleman she'd met at the park and one of her mother. She painted what she saw and then gave the images her own interpretation.

Istvan paused on each photo. He was quiet as he studied them. She couldn't help but wonder what he was thinking. She wanted to ask, but she didn't dare. What if he hated them? As much as she tried to wear a tough outer shell, criticism still had a way of working past her well-laid defenses and planting a seed of doubt about her abilities.

But there was no way she was going to let him think his opinion mattered to her. Nothing could be further from the truth. She knew she was good at what she did. It wasn't her being conceited. It's what she'd been told by her agent, by clients and gallery owners. They were the people in the know.

She shifted her weight from one foot to the other. What was taking him so long? There were three photos for him to see. Unless he'd moved beyond those photos. Her chest tightened. Was he looking at her personal photos?

She moved slightly and craned her neck to get a glimpse of her phone. He was staring intently at the painting of her mother. Did he recognize her?

Indigo immediately scolded herself for overthinking things. There was no way he would recognize her. Her family had moved away from Rydiania when she was very little, so he couldn't have been much older. If he didn't recognize her mother, what was it about the painting that held his attention?

She glanced off to the side and noticed a rather lengthy line of customers had formed. She'd never had this much interest in her sketches since she'd arrived on the island. And then she realized what all the attention was about—the prince.

It was time to draw this conversation to an end. She cleared her throat. "Is there something else you need?"

He held her phone out to her. "These are good. No, they're great. You're very talented. So, then, why are you here doing caricatures?"

Because she needed the extra money to secure her mother a spot at the assisted living facility. But she wasn't about to reveal her struggles to the prince, who had no idea what it was to struggle for the things he wanted or needed.

"Work is work," she said.

He nodded as though he understood. "Thank you for sharing these with me. I see amazing things in your future." He turned as though to walk away, but then he turned back to her. "I was wondering if you'll be watching the race."

His inquiry caught her off guard. Why would he be interested in whether she'd be attending or not? Was he merely trying to make casual conversation? Or was it something more?

Was he flirting with her?

Laughter bubbled up inside her. She quickly stifled it. There was no way this handsome, eligible prince would be interested in her. Not a chance.

"I won't be able to attend. I have to work." She gestured to all the people lined up. The line kept growing. She really would have to work all day to get that many sketches completed.

"Surely they'll give you some time off to watch the race, since most every guest at the resort will probably be in attendance."

What she heard him say was that, being the prince, he was the center of the universe, so everyone would want to see what he was doing. Her back teeth ground together. It took all her willpower to subdue her frustration with him. "I'm sorry. I really do have to work."

"I know your boss—the new owners of the resort. I could get you some time off." There was a gleam in his eyes. Was it a hopeful look?

She shook her head. "I need to get back to work."

It was only then that she noticed him turning his head and taking in the view of the long line, waiting to have their sketches done. "I understand."

And yet he continued to stand there. Why was he being so obstinate? Had he never been turned down before? And then it came to her that no one would turn him down. Well, that was, no one except her.

Secretly, she was tempted to learn more about this prince. If she had met Istvan under different circumstances—if she hadn't known his true identity—she would have liked him. And that right there worried her. She couldn't fall for the enemy, because her father had trusted the royal family and look where that had gotten him—dead in what should have been the prime of his life.

He should go.

And yet his feet didn't move.

Istvan was utterly intrigued by Indigo. The more time he

spent with her, the more he realized she was unlike any other woman he had ever known. And he had known quite a few during his globetrotting years.

There were times when Indigo looked at him and he thought she might be interested in him. And then there were other times when their gazes met and he could see the hostility lurking in their depths. How could she dislike him? She didn't know him yet. Or was it that she held his lineage against him? She wouldn't be the first person.

Whatever it was that was going on behind her beautiful eyes, he wanted to know the answers. He wanted to walk with her on the beach, and as the water washed over their bare feet, he wanted to learn what made her tick. And then he wanted to talk some more.

Okay, maybe he wanted to do more than talk. His gaze lowered. After all, her lush lips had beckoned to him more than once. *Oh, yes.* He definitely wanted to explore them and see if her kisses were as sweet as the berries he'd had for breakfast that morning.

It wasn't that he lacked for female companionship, but none could compare to Indigo, who insisted on speaking to him as she did everyone else. That was it. He never did like being treated specially—making him stand out from the others. He didn't feel special. Not at all.

And maybe part of that had to do with his uncle. When Georgios had abdicated the throne, it had had a huge impact on Istvan. He didn't want to think about that now. It always put him in a foul mood.

He shoved aside the troubling thoughts as his gaze met hers once more. He had something much more pleasant in mind. He planned to ask Indigo to dinner.

Buzz. Buzz.

He wanted to ignore the phone, but as it continued to vibrate in his pocket, it was impossible to ignore. He knew he wasn't going to like it, whoever it was. He'd bet his crown that it was the palace with some other task that required his attention.

"You should get that," she said, as though relieved to have an excuse to brush him off.

A dinner invitation teetered on the tip of his tongue. But he had a feeling if he were to ask her to dinner right now, she would turn him down, and he didn't want that to happen. Maybe another time would be better—a time when there wasn't a line of people waiting for her attention.

He withdrew his phone and saw that it was indeed the palace. He pressed Decline. But when he glanced up and saw the irritation radiating from Indigo's eyes, he realized it was time for him to move on.

"I'll get out of your way." His gaze lingered on her beautiful face for a moment longer than necessary. And then with reluctance, he walked away.

Buzz. Buzz.

When he checked his phone's caller ID, he found it was the palace...again. Whatever they wanted must be important.

With a resigned sign, he pressed the phone to his ear. "Prince Istvan."

"This is the queen's secretary," the older woman said in a measured tone. "The queen would like to remind you that this weekend we are hosting a formal dinner for Spain's dignitaries."

And yet another reminder of the responsibilities awaiting him at home. But this royal regatta was his responsibility, too. It was being held in memory of his uncle. And since he seemed to be the only family member who wanted to remember his uncle, there wasn't a chance he was leaving Ludus Island before the festivities were concluded.

"You may tell the queen that I'll be unavailable this weekend."

"Yes, Your Highness. And the queen would like to remind you that Monday afternoon you have an appointment to sit for your portrait."

The thought of sitting there for the royal artist, who didn't know how to smile, much less make light conversation, sounded like a punishment Istvan hadn't earned. He didn't see why the man couldn't work from a photo. But Istvan had been informed that a photo just wouldn't do.

Who would want to sit in an uncomfortable chair for hours while their mind went numb from boredom? But he hadn't felt that way when he'd sat for Indigo to sketch him. Now, granted the caricature didn't take nearly as long, but she intrigued him. And he had a feeling she could carry her end of a conversation if they'd had a bit more time together.

Suddenly his whimsical thought of commissioning Indigo to do his portrait was taking on more substance, especially after viewing some of her formal work. He wondered if she would be up for a trip. He would definitely make it worth her time.

"Tell my mother I'll make time for the portrait, but I plan to do it on my terms."

"Your Highness?" There was a note of a question to the secretary's tone.

Istvan chose to ignore her inquiry. "I must go." And with that the call was concluded.

He had been butting heads with his parents for years now. They wanted things done their way—the way they'd always been done. He wanted change. He wanted the monarchy to act with compassion.

Once his father had let it slip that Istvan was just like his uncle—thinking the dynasty should change according to the people's whims. But as soon as the king said it, he'd retracted the words. He told Istvan that he would never be like Georgios— he would never walk away from his responsibilities—because he'd raised him different. He'd raised him to be a true king.

CHAPTER FOUR

At last, her shift was over.

Indigo stifled a yawn. Thanks to the prince's insistence on a second sketch, she'd had an endless line of excited subjects. And they'd all had questions about Istvan—questions Indigo did her best to discourage.

She flexed her fingers. Her entire hand ached. She repeatedly stretched her fingers wide apart, trying to ease the ache in them. It only helped to a certain extent. If she had known her sketches were going to be in such great demand, she might have negotiated for a per-sketch fee on top of her base pay.

She folded the easel, grabbed her supply caddy and started toward the resort. With evening closing in, the beach area had quieted down. Everyone must be inside getting cleaned up for dinner. Indigo's stomach rumbled at the thought of food. She hadn't had time for lunch today. She couldn't keep up this pace. If it continued, she might have to mention to Hermione about hiring another artist.

"Indigo." Hermione, the resort's manager, waved as she rushed to catch up with her. "How did the day go?"

Indigo wasn't sure how honest to be with her boss about the overwhelming line of people. On the other hand, it was job security. "There were people lined up all day."

Hermione smiled. "I've been hearing lots of good things about your work. We'll have to discuss extending your time at the resort."

"Thank you." Indigo wasn't sure how that would work out going forward. She had a lot of hopes and dreams relying on her upcoming gallery show. Still, it was like her father used to tell her—*don't take for granted what is in hopes of what may be.* "That sounds good."

"So the prince has taken a liking to your work." Hermione sent her a reassuring smile. "That is huge praise. He's very particular about what he likes."

Indigo should be pleased with this compliment, but it just made her feel more uncomfortable. And she didn't want her new friend to think she was tripping over herself for the prince. "I... I didn't do anything for him that I haven't done for the other guests."

"And that's what makes it even more special."

Ding.

Hermione pulled her phone from her pocket. She read the message on the screen and then sighed.

Indigo hoped it wasn't bad news. Hermione had been kind to her. Indigo liked to think they were becoming fast friends. She appreciated how Hermione had taken a chance on hiring her when neither of them had known if the idea of caricatures would be a hit or a miss with the resort guests. Lucky for Indigo, her fun sketches had been met with great enthusiasm. And now she wished she could think of a way to pay Hermione back for believing in her.

"Is there something I can help with?" Indigo asked.

Hermione glanced up from her phone. Her fine brows were drawn together as though she were in deep thought. "Um...no. Thanks. I've got it."

Indigo didn't believe her. "I'd like to help if I can. After all, my shift is over."

Hermione sent her a hesitant look. "If you're sure." When

Indigo nodded, Hermione said, "I wouldn't ask, but there's a snafu with a shipment at the dock, and on my way out of the building, I forgot to drop off some papers at the gallery."

"Okay. Let me take the paperwork to the gallery. It's on my way out."

Hermione withdrew a clipped stack of papers from her black leather portfolio. "Here you go. Everything is there that they'll need for the shipment." She then gave Indigo specific instructions on where to take the papers and whom to hand them to. It all seemed very straightforward and easy enough to handle.

"You're getting rid of an exhibit?" Indigo had been to the gallery many times. She loved to admire the various artworks. She hoped someday to have one of her paintings displayed in such a prestigious gallery.

Hermione shook her head. "We have agreements with other galleries. We exchange various pieces. This time we're loaning out *Clash of Hearts*."

Indigo remembered the piece because of its vibrant colors from hot pink to silver. It had been created of conjoined hearts of varying sizes that were repeated over the entire canvas. "It's a beautiful piece."

"Thank you. I was the one to acquire it." Hermione smiled brightly. When her phone dinged again, she said, "I better get going. Are you sure you don't mind doing this?"

"Not at all. I'll see you tomorrow." She gave a little wave before turning toward the resort.

Once inside the resort, the plush carpeting in the wide hallways smothered the sound of her footsteps. The resort was quiet. It was a lot like walking through a museum with its many art pieces, not only in the gallery but also displayed on the many hallways.

She found herself referring to it as a commoner's palace. But then again, why shouldn't the resort be fashioned after a palace, since its founder was once a king—a king who stepped aside to let his brother take over. In the process, King Georgios not only gave up his crown but he also lost his country and his family.

And though the Ludus Resort had every amenity imaginable and looked magnificent, it still wasn't a home. Both the former king and Indigo's father had died without ever being able to re-claim what they had loved and lost—their homeland. And for that she felt so sorry for both of them.

She approached the entrance of the Ludus Gallery. The large glass door silently swung open without much effort. The gal-lery was divided between the large front section with its tall white walls that gave the space a wide-open, airy feel and the back section that was the opposite, with black walls and spot-lights used to highlight the gallery's headliner.

In this case, it was the Ruby Heart that was the shining star. Indigo had seen it once before, but it had been in passing be-cause the gallery had been so busy. But today the gallery was quiet. It would give her a chance to admire the precious stone for as long as she wanted.

She approached the glass case. The stone was quite large. It was much too big to ever be worn as a piece of jewelry. The many cuts looked to have been very carefully planned, and each picked up the light, making it sparkle as though it were actu-ally alive and full of energy.

She noticed a sign that displayed background information about the stone. Just as she was about to lean in closer to read the words, she heard someone behind her.

"It's beautiful," the smooth, deep voice said.

Indigo didn't have to turn around to know who was behind her—Prince Istvan. Not sure what to do, she continued to stare at the magnificent jewel. "Yes, it is."

"And yet it pales in beauty compared to you." His voice was so soft that it was as if the words had caressed her.

Heat gathered in her chest before rushing up her neck and set-ting her cheeks ablaze. Thank goodness she wasn't facing him.

She swallowed hard. And then hoped when she spoke her voice didn't betray her. "I've never seen a gem so large."

He moved next to her. "Did you read the legend attached to it?"

Her heart pounded. Her mouth grew dry. "Um, no. I was just about to do that."

"Let me." He leaned toward her as he focused on the display. "'The legend of the Ruby Heart. If destined lovers gaze upon the Ruby Heart at the same time, their lives will be forever entwined.'"

Lovers? Suddenly a very hot and enticing image of her and Istvan entwined in each other's arms filled her mind. She gave herself a mental shake, chasing away the temptation. Why, oh, why had she stopped here? She should have just dropped off the papers and left. Then she could have avoided this awkward moment.

"Hmm…" The sound rumbled in his throat for a moment, almost as though he were a Cheshire cat eyeing up his prey—in this case, that would be her. "I wonder if they might be referring to us."

It felt as though the air-conditioning had been turned off and a blowtorch had been lit in her face. Her mouth went even drier as she struggled to swallow. "I'm quite certain they are mistaken in this case." How she got those words out and did not melt into a puddle on the floor was utterly beyond her. "I should be going."

The only problem was that he was standing between her and the hallway she needed to access to reach the business office, where she was to drop off the papers.

"Having second thoughts?" he asked.

When she glanced at him, she saw the amusement dancing in his eyes. "Not at all. You just happen to be standing in my way."

With an amused smile plastered on his undeniably handsome face, he stepped out of the way. "I look forward to our next meeting."

His words made her heart flutter. She tried to tell herself that it was just casual flirtation, but there was this look in his eyes. Other men had looked at her that way, so she recognized it. It was a look of attraction—a look that said he was interested in taking their relationship to the next level. Her heart went *thump-thump* in her chest.

The prince is interested in me?

She moved quickly toward the privacy of the little hallway. The distance from the prince didn't stop the heat from gathering in her chest and rushing to her face. She resisted the urge to fan herself.

She came to a stop in front of an open door. The sign on the door read Museum Curator. This was the right place. She rapped her knuckles on the doorjamb.

"Come in."

She stepped inside and noticed a messy desk off to the side. A middle-aged man with reading glasses perched on the end of his nose glanced up from a computer monitor. "Can I help you?"

"Yes. Hermione asked me to drop these off." She held out the clipped papers.

"Oh, yes. I was waiting for them." He accepted the papers. "Thank you."

"You're welcome."

It was time to leave, but she hesitated. Was the prince still in the gallery waiting for her? The thought sent her heart racing. She told herself it was the anxiety of dealing with his incorrigible flirting again. Nothing more.

"Was there something else?" the man asked.

"Um…" She quickly weighed her options. "Is there another exit?"

The man arched a brow in puzzlement. "There's the back exit. In the hallway, go to the right. And then make another right. It will take you to the loading area."

"Thank you."

She just wasn't ready to face the prince again. Not yet. She turned right just as the man had instructed.

Her steps were quick as she moved through the hallway. When her hands touched the metal door handle, she pushed it open. She breathed a sigh of relief. She'd escaped. But escaped what?

She wasn't prepared to answer that question. She shouldn't have let Istvan get to her. If she let her guard down with the handsome prince, it would lead to nothing but more heartache. She'd already had enough of that to last her an entire lifetime.

CHAPTER FIVE

THE GRAND RACE was about to begin.

It was the following afternoon, and Indigo couldn't deny that she was a bit curious about the regatta. She'd never been to a boat race before. And just as the prince had predicted, her line of guests had dissipated as the magical hour neared. Even Adara, the resort's concierge, had stopped by to let her know it would be all right for her to take in the race.

What would it hurt? After all, it wasn't like she was going there with the intent to see the prince. She was going because it was the biggest event on the island and everyone was going to watch the boat race, leaving her nothing else to do.

With her art supplies secured in a locker at the resort, she made her way to the area of the beach where the race was to start. However, she stood at the back of a sea of people. There was no way she'd make it to the front. And from back here she wouldn't be able to see a thing.

She glanced around, looking for a better vantage point. Just south of where she stood were cliffs. She didn't know if she could make it up there, but she'd give it a try. And so she started walking at a rapid pace.

When she found a trail that appeared to lead to higher ground, she followed it. It was a bit rugged and steep at times.

Her sandals were not ideal for this trek, but that didn't deter her. And when the trail finally leveled off, she noticed a small clearing, and in the distance was a cliff.

She wasn't the only one to have this idea. Other people were gathered there. Some of the people she recognized as employees of the resort. She wondered if they were supposed to be working, like her. Still, if there were no people at the resort needing anything, why not indulge?

She made it to an open spot along the stone wall. At last, she could see the boats. In fact, they weren't that far away. And Prince Istvan's boat was easy to spot, with its host of flags. The top flag was a deep purple with a gold crown, signaling that there was a member of the royal family aboard.

A loud horn blew. Was this to signal the start of the race? Indigo was curious to see if Istvan would win. His boat was the same length as the others. She wondered if there were limitations on the boat size.

The boats started their engines and then moved into position. Since there were too many to line up in a single line, she assumed each boat had some sort of tracking device to keep track of its time.

And then she spotted Istvan standing behind the wheel of his boat. He was shirtless—again. If she were to paint him— not that she had any plans of doing such a thing—she'd be inclined to included his impressive chest and those six-pack abs. She subdued a laugh when she thought of the horrid looks such a painting would receive from the royal family.

As she continued to stare down at Istvan, he turned. His gaze scanned the crowd, and then it was as though he'd singled her out. His gaze paused. And then he waved. Surely he couldn't be waving at her. As everyone around her raised their hand to wave back, she resisted. It was a small resistance, but she had to prove—even if only to herself—that she was strong enough to resist his charms.

The horn blew again. The prince took his seat. Her gaze

strayed across a digital clock at the end of the dock. Red numbers counted down from ten. And then with a third and final blow of the horn, the boats took off with a roar and a spray of water.

She watched as the prince guided his boat into the lead. Something told her it was where Istvan was most comfortable. And then the boats moved out of sight. From what she'd heard from the people she'd sketched, the race encircled the island. And until they returned, there was nothing here to see.

She followed the trail back down to the resort, where she nearly bumped into one of Prince Istvan's security detail. The man was quite tall. She had to crane her neck to look at his face. And then there were the dark sunglasses that kept his eyes hidden from the world.

"Sorry," she said. "I didn't see you there."

"Ms. Castellanos?"

"Yes." What did he want with her?

"This is for you." He handed her a small envelope before walking away.

She stared at the sealed envelope. It took her a moment to figure out what must be inside…the prince was insisting on paying her for the sketches, even after she'd told him it went against resort policy. Although the extra money would help her mother, she just couldn't keep it. She didn't want to lose her job at the resort.

But she was curious to see how much the prince valued her work. That couldn't be against the rules, right? She slipped her finger in the opening of the envelope and then carefully released the flap.

She reached inside and pulled out a folded slip of paper. This certainly wasn't a check. Disappointment assailed her. So if the prince wasn't attempting to pay her, what did he want?

She unfolded the paper and began to read.

Meet me at the Whale-of-a-Time Suite. 6 p.m.

That was it?

She turned the paper over to see if he'd written more. He hadn't. What in the world was this about? Was this his attempt to ask her to dinner—or something more intimate? Either way, it wasn't working for her. Besides if he knew who she was, he wouldn't want anything to do with her. And then she realized what she intended to do—stand up a prince. Who did such a thing?

The answer was easy…someone who knew the truth about the royal family of Rydiania. They were cold and ruthless. How many times had her father told her so while he drowned his sorrows in scotch?

And so on her way back to retrieve her art supplies, she passed a wastebasket. She paused. Was she really going to do this?

And then she heard the echo of her father's words: *Don't trust a royal.*

I won't, Dad. I remember.

She dropped the note into the trash and kept going. Prince Istvan would soon realize that he couldn't have everything he desired—and that included having her.

He sat alone.

Istvan checked the time. Again.

She was late. He had no patience for tardiness. It had been drilled into him since he was a young boy that you should be early for occasions. Apparently Indigo didn't believe in that bit of logic. As of that moment, she was thirteen and a half minutes late.

This did not bode well for hiring her to do his formal portrait. The painting had to be completed on a specific deadline as stipulated in the contract he'd had drawn up. The Treasury Department ran by a strict timeline. If he were smart, he'd give up on the idea of having Indigo paint his portrait.

Still, he hesitated. Maybe something had had happened to

her. Maybe she had been unavoidably detained. The thought that something might have happened to her bothered him.

He signaled for Elek, his most trusted guard. When the man approached him, Istvan asked, "Did you personally hand Indigo the note?"

The man clasped his hands together as he leaned down. "Yes, Your Highness."

"And did she read it?"

"I do not know, sir. I was called away before she had a chance to open the envelope."

"Well, something must have happened or she would be here." He stood, sending the chair legs scraping over the floor. He was no longer Interested in eating. "We must check on her."

"Your Highness?" Elek looked confused.

"We'll go to her room. Find out what room she's in."

"Yes, sir." Elek pulled out his phone and placed a call.

Istvan began to pace. Something must be terribly wrong or she'd be here. The thought of anything happening to the pretty artist bothered him more than he was expecting.

Elek returned. "She's not staying at the resort."

Istvan sighed. "Of course she's not. She's an employee. I should have thought of that. Do you have her home address?"

Elek nodded. "They didn't want to give it to me, so I had to mention your name."

"It's fine." He would do what it took to make sure Indigo was all right. "Let's go."

Elek didn't immediately move.

"What?" Istvan was anxious to get to the bottom of what had delayed Indigo.

"Are you sure about this?" Elek didn't speak up unless he felt it was in the prince's best interest. "You could try calling her instead."

"Did you get her number?" When Elek nodded, Istvan said, "Well, let's have it."

He reached for his phone and quickly dialed the number. It rang and rang. And then it switched to voice mail.

"Hi. I can't answer the phone right now. I'm probably working on my next masterpiece. Just leave your name, number and a brief message, and I'll get back to you as soon as I can." *Beep.*

Istvan disconnected the call. He wasn't interested in leaving a message. He wanted to know why she'd stood him up. The thought pricked his ego. He'd never been stood up. There had to be a serious reason. And he wasn't going to rest until he knew what it was.

Because the more he thought of Indigo—and he found himself thinking of her quite a lot lately—the more certain he was that he wanted to know more about her.

She didn't appear to be easy to win over. She certainly wasn't swayed by titles. And that's what he admired about her.

If she were to paint his portrait, she would breathe some freshness into his image, just as he wanted to breathe freshness into the monarchy. He recalled the long talks he'd had with Uncle Georgios about the state of the monarchy. Though they didn't agree on everything, there was one area where they both were in agreement—the monarchy needed to change.

And Indigo was his first step in showing the world that when it was his turn to step up to the throne, he would do things differently. So he had to find out what was keeping her.

CHAPTER SIX

SHE COULDN'T STOP thinking of him.

Why would a prince ask her to dinner?

Indigo had absolutely no answer for that—at least none that she was willing to accept. Because there was no way someone like him would be interested in someone like her. No way at all.

And if he thought they were going to have a quick island romp before he flew off to his palace, he could think again. Even if his family hadn't destroyed hers, she was never one for a quick fling. It just wasn't her thing.

"Indi, do you know where I left my book?" her mother called out from the living room.

"Give me a second and I'll look for it."

Indigo had arrived home from work a little while ago. She'd grabbed a shower and switched into a summer dress. Her little two-bedroom apartment didn't have air-conditioning, and the dress was light and airy.

This summer was unusually hot. The first thing she'd done upon arriving home was to open all the windows. The fan in the living room was already on for her mother.

Indigo glanced in the bedroom mirror. Her hair was still damp from her shower, but it wouldn't stay that way for long.

She twisted the long strands and pinned them to the back of her head.

And then she headed for her mother's bedroom. Her mother had been reading a historical series about Scottish highlanders. Her mother read a lot of different things, from romances to cozy mysteries to biographies. Now that her mother's health was failing and she couldn't get around the way she wanted, she said she liked to escape the walls of their apartment through the words in a book.

Indigo glanced around her mother's small bedroom. There were stacks of books everywhere. Some new, a lot old and there were magazines added in. "What did you say the title was?"

Her mother called it out and then added that it should have been on the side of the bed. It was then that Indigo was able to spot it.

She carried it to the living room. "Here you go. Do you need anything else?"

"I don't think so. Why, are you going somewhere?"

"We need groceries." And there was no way she could unwind right now. Every time she closed her eyes, the image of the prince was there. A walk might help. "Is there anything special you want?"

"I have a list on the counter. There's not much. Just a few things." Her mother frowned.

"What's wrong? Are you in pain?"

Her mother shook her head. "I'm fine." She smiled, but it didn't reach her eyes. "I just feel horrible that I've become such a burden to you."

"Mama, don't ever think like that. I love having you around." And she meant it. She would be lost without her mother in her life.

Her mother's eyes filled with unshed tears. "How did I get so lucky to have such a wonderful daughter?"

Indigo shook her head. "I'm not special."

"Of course you are. And as soon as I have a place to move

where I can get by on my own, you'll be able to have your life back. You should be out dating, not staying home, looking after me."

"Mama, I love you. I know you want your independence back, but until that happens, I love having you here."

A tear splashed onto her mother's pale cheek. "I love you, too."

Indigo knew how important it was to her mother to live on her own once more. It's part of the reason she'd taken the job at the resort. Between that income and hopefully the money she would make at her very first gallery showing, she'd have enough money to get her mother into an assisted living center.

The problem was that this was her first gallery showing. She had absolutely no idea how well her paintings would sell. But she wouldn't give up. She'd do whatever it took to make sure her mother was happy.

Knock-knock.

She wondered who that could be. Perhaps her aunt was stopping by to visit. The sisters were really close. In fact, they were best friends.

"Are you expecting Aunt Aggie?"

"No. But you know she drops by whenever she gets a chance. And she did mention that she had a new book to loan me as soon as she finished reading it. Maybe she finished it sooner than she expected." Her mother's face lit up.

Indigo stepped into the small foyer and opened the door. For a moment, the world stood still. There, standing before her, was Prince Istvan. Her heart lodged in her throat. *What in the world?*

She blinked. She had to be seeing things. Her pulse raced. There was no way he was on her doorstep. But after she blinked twice, he was still standing before her.

"Indigo, we need to talk." His voice was deep, with a heavy accent.

"Indi, send your aunt in," her mother called from the other room.

Indigo didn't want her mother to see the prince and get upset.

So she closed the door in the prince's face. "It's not Aunt Aggie." She struggled to sound normal. "Just someone who knocked on the wrong door."

"I hope you helped them."

"I did." She reached for her purse. "Now I'm off. I'll be home a little later."

"Okay. I'm going to read some more."

When Indigo opened the door again, the prince's brows were drawn into a formidable line, while irritation showed in his eyes. Obviously he wasn't used to people closing the door in his face. But to be fair, she wasn't used to people tracking her down at home.

She raised her finger to her lips to silence him until the door was shut and they were a few steps away. Then she paused and turned to him. "How did you find me?"

He paused as though he hadn't been expecting that question. "I had someone ask at the resort for your address."

"And they just gave it to you?" She would have to speak with Hermione.

His lack of a response meant he was accustomed to getting any information he needed. She should have known. If you were royalty, the rules didn't apply to you.

She huffed and crossed her arms. "Why are you here?"

"I want to know why you missed dinner. Did you have an emergency?"

"No." Why would he think that? In the next breath, she realized he wasn't used to being turned down. "Now, I need to be going."

"We need to talk."

She shook her head. "If this is about dinner, I can't."

His dark brows rose high on his forehead. "It doesn't have to be dinner. I would just like a moment of your time."

She tilted her chin upward until their gazes met. "And if I say no, you'll just go away."

Frustration shimmered in his eyes. He wordlessly stared back at her, letting her know he wasn't going anywhere until he had his say.

Tired of the staring game, she said, "I'm going to the market. If you want to walk with me, you can have your say."

"You want me to go grocery shopping?" His voice held a surprised tone.

"It's up to you." She turned and began walking.

For a moment, she heard no footsteps behind her. Was it possible he'd finally given up? She ignored the sense of disappointment that came over her.

And then she mentally admonished herself for having any sort of feelings where the prince was concerned. Because even if he was drop-dead gorgeous and persistent, in the end, he was a royal. And even though she was a Rydianian by birth, she'd promised herself as a child that she would never claim her heritage as a Rydianian citizen. As an adult, she'd never traveled to her birthplace. She preferred to focus her energy on the here and now versus what had once been.

"Wait up." She heard rapid footsteps behind her.

She didn't slow down. What was so important to him? She couldn't deny that she was curious. But she wasn't curious enough to turn back.

He fell in step with her. "How far away is this market?"

"Afraid of a little exercise?"

"Not at all. But these shoes aren't the best for walking long distances."

She glanced down to see he wore a pair of sand-colored loafers. "You don't have to walk with me."

"I want to." He settled a ball cap on his head and obscured his eyes with dark sunglasses. "Listen I'm sorry for overstepping."

The fact he realized that even a prince could overstep impressed her, but she still wasn't ready to let down her guard with him. *Don't trust a royal.* Her father's words echoed in her mind. He'd repeated them countless times over the years. It left an indelible impression.

"The market is only a couple of blocks away." She wasn't sure if it was her attempt at making peace or her way of dissuading him from following her.

The thing about Prince Istvan that worried her the most was his way of confusing her. She knew she should see him as the enemy. And yet there was a part of her that was curious about Istvan. Why was he going out of his way to speak to her? It wasn't like she was rich or famous. And she certainly wasn't a royal descendant. In royal terms, that would make her a nobody. So what was his interest in her?

"Are you this hard on all the men who try to ask you to dinner?" The prince's voice interrupted her thoughts.

"Only the princes." She couldn't believe she'd made that little quip until the words passed her lips.

"I see. So if I was someone else, you would have consented to dinner?"

She turned her head so that their gazes would meet. "You can never be anyone but who you are—heir to the throne."

"Ouch. You make that sound akin to a deadly disease."

His choice of words made her think of her father. In his case being close to the royals had been exactly like a deadly disease that in the end took his life. It might not have been at their hands, but they couldn't deny the role they'd played in his untimely demise.

They continued walking in silence because she had nothing nice to say to him. When she thought of her father and how he'd been treated after a lifetime of duty and devotion, it made her furious.

When she reached her destination, she turned to him. "The walk is over."

She pulled open the door and stepped inside the small market that she knew like the back of her hand. She visited the Samaras Market numerous times a week because she liked to cook with fresh vegetables. Since her mother had been diagnosed with heart failure along with some other health conditions, Indigo had made it her mission to help her mother in every way she knew how, including a vegetarian diet filled with fruits and vegetables. In the end, they both felt better.

She grabbed a basket and moved toward the fresh produce to see what they'd gotten in that week. All the while, she could feel Istvan's gaze on her—following her. He certainly was persistent.

When she picked up some tomatoes, he said, "Those don't look ripe. You might want to try the ones up higher." He pointed to some other tomatoes. "They look like they'll be more flavorful."

She couldn't help but smile at the prince offering her shopping advice. "Istvan, do you really expect me to believe you do your own shopping?"

"Who's this Istvan, you speak of? My name's Joe. And I shop here all the time." He grabbed some tomatoes and placed them in his own basket.

He had a basket? He was shopping, too? Her gaze jerked around to meet his. She couldn't believe he was working this hard to get her attention.

Perhaps it wouldn't hurt to play along for a little bit. "So, Joe, how do you feel about zucchini?"

He shrugged. "I'm neutral on the subject."

"I see. And how about olives? Do you prefer black or green?"

"Green, for sure."

She couldn't resist the smile that pulled at her lips. "Are you planning to follow me through the whole market?"

"Who, me?" His voice held an innocent tone. "I'm just here to do a little shopping."

She honestly didn't know what to make of him. One minute he was infuriating, with the way he took advantage of his royal status, and the next minute he was acting like he was a normal person who was just trying to create some sort of bridge between them.

Secretly she was swooning just a little. After all, what woman didn't want a prince tripping over himself to impress her? Not that she was going to let on to him that his actions were starting to work on her.

As they made their way through the market, making small talk about various items, she noticed the puzzled looks the other patrons were giving them. Maybe because he was wearing sunglasses inside. Between the glasses and the dark ball cap, it was harder to make out his identity.

Or maybe it was his security team that had given him way. But when she glanced back, she noticed his entourage was nowhere to be seen. Was it possible he'd told them to remain outside?

"Why are you doing this?" she asked.

"Just like you, I need a few things." He scanned the pasta before adding his selection to his almost-full basket.

"And what exactly are you going to do with all that food once you buy it?"

"Eat it, of course." His tone was serious as he moved onto some jarred sauce.

She rolled her eyes. Was he always so obstinate? She couldn't help but wonder what it'd be like to spend the evening with the prince. Not that she was planning to do it or anything else. But it didn't mean she couldn't wonder about these things.

He was certainly going through a lot of bother to speak with her. And the funny thing was he never said a word about what he had on his mind. As the minutes passed and their baskets grew full, her curiosity was getting the best of her.

But by then they were at the checkout with a fresh loaf of bread topping each of their baskets. The bread was still warm from the oven. As she inhaled the aroma, her mouth watered. They were definitely having it for dinner. Her mother loved fresh-baked bread dipped in seasoned olive oil.

He let her check out first. When the checker told her the total, Istvan said, "I've got it."

She frowned at him. "No, you don't."

He looked at the checker. "You can just add it to my order."

Her gaze swung around to the checker. "Don't you dare." Then she reached in her wallet and produced the appropriate amount of money. She held it out to the checker. "Here you go."

The young man shrugged his shoulders before taking the money. He quickly counted out her change. And then Indigo turned a challenging look to Istvan.

He was wearing a smile. "You are unlike anyone I've ever known."

She didn't think she was that unusual. "Because I like to pay for my own groceries?"

His gaze held hers. And when he spoke, his rich voice dropped down a tone. "No. Because you are fiercely independent, very stubborn and utterly enchanting."

Her stomach dipped. Why exactly was she resisting spending more time with him? In that moment, the answer totally eluded her.

CHAPTER SEVEN

THIS WAS BETTER than a dinner date.

Wait. Had that outrageous thought really crossed his mind? Istvan gave himself a mental shake.

He had never been grocery shopping before, but if it was this entertaining every time, he wouldn't mind doing it more often. But something told him it wouldn't have been half as much fun without Indigo.

She was as stubborn as she was beautiful. And the more he was around her, the greater the challenge became to work his way past her cool exterior. He'd seen the way she'd looked at him at the beach, and he knew the attraction went both ways. But for whatever reason, she was fighting it.

Once he paid for his groceries and they stepped outside, he offered to carry her groceries. To his surprise, she let him. It was the first thing she'd let him do for her. It was to the point where he almost thanked her for letting him carry her groceries. Then he realized how ridiculous that sounded and instead said nothing.

"This has been an interesting trip to the market," she said. "But I must know what brought you to my door."

So she was curious. Good. That was a step in the right direction. He was pleased to know his banter had actually produced the results he wanted.

"I tried to call, but you didn't answer."

"That was you?" When he nodded, she said, "When it said the caller ID was blocked, I figured it was a spam call."

"Spam? I've been referred to a lot of ways. Some good, some not so good. But I've never been called that."

An awkward silence ensued before she asked, "And what was so important that you had to see me?"

"I have a proposal for you."

She glanced over at him. Suspicion blazed in her eyes. "Dare I ask what sort of proposal?"

"I think you'll like it."

"I won't know until you tell me."

He cleared his throat. Surely even she wouldn't turn down this proposition. Then again, he was finding that he wasn't able to predict Indigo's reactions. It's part of what he liked so much about her. "I would like to hire you."

Her fine brows rose. "Hire me to do what? Cook for you?"

"Hmm... Now that you mention it, that's not a bad idea. Maybe we'll have to negotiate that later." He sent her a teasing smile. "Right now, I'd like to commission you to do my formal portrait."

She stopped walking. She was quiet, as though she were digesting his words. "You want me to paint you?"

"Yes."

She stared at him like he'd suddenly sprouted a third eye. Then, in a calm voice, she said, "No."

She'd turned him down? Really? Suddenly his amusement over her stubbornness turned to agitation. Fun and games were fine for a bit, but this was serious business for him. Did she have any idea how many artists had vied for the honor of painting his formal portrait?

He had to try again. "Don't you realize this would make

your career? You could name your price after this. You could take on any project."

"I do. And the answer is still no."

He knew Indigo was different and did things in her own way. The other thing he knew about her was that her art was very important to her. So then, why would she turn down this prime opportunity?

Perhaps he hadn't explained it well enough. "This portrait I'd like to hire you to do would be high-profile. It will be my official portrait. It will be used for postage stamps, currency and who knows what else."

"That's nice for you, but the answer is still no."

Was it his imagination or had her pace picked up? Was she trying to get away from him? But why? The more he was around her, the more the questions came to him. "Why are you so ready to turn down such a great opportunity?"

She stopped and turned to him. She leveled her shoulders and lifted her chin ever so slightly. "I know you aren't used to being told no, but I have other obligations."

"Move them." It wasn't until the words were out of his mouth that he realized how much he sounded like his father. And that wasn't a good thing.

"No." She glared at him.

This conversation had most definitely taken a wrong turn. He swallowed hard. "My apologies. That didn't come out right. I meant to say that if there's anything I can do to make this an option for you, all you have to do is say the word. I think your work is exceptional, and it has a freshness to it that I'm looking for."

A myriad of expressions filtered over her face. She could say more with her eyes than with her lips, which were currently pursed together.

As the strained silence lingered, he grew impatient. "Will you do it?"

"No." She resumed walking.

At this point he should turn and walk away. With anyone else, that's exactly what he would do, but there was something special about Indigo—*erm, about her work.*

He'd give it one last try and then he was done. If fame and worldwide recognition wouldn't do it, perhaps money would work. "I can pay you." And then he mentioned a large sum of money. "Imagine what you could do with that money."

Her steps slowed. She was still moving—still not saying anything—but he knew he had her attention. She stopped and turned to him. "You can't be serious."

"Of course I am."

She didn't say no this time. In fact, she didn't say anything as she resumed walking, presumably to give his offer serious consideration.

She suddenly stopped. Then slowly she turned to him. "Why me?"

"Because I like your style. It's original, and it has depth to it."

"I'm sure your family already has an artist chosen to do your portrait."

"Don't worry about my family. I'll take care of them." He was certain his mother would fight him about this, but in the end, he would win. After all, he was heir to the throne. His parents would have to get used to the idea that he didn't plan to do things the way they wanted them done. "So you'll take on the project?"

She hesitated. Her gaze moved down the sidewalk as though she were weighing her options. But what was there to consider? He didn't know anyone who would pass up this opportunity, not to mention the small fortune he was willing to pay.

They began walking again. He was starting to think there was more to Indigo's aversion to him than just playing hard to get, but how could that be? It wasn't like they'd ever met before. Maybe she had something against rich people. But if that was the case, she wouldn't work at the Ludus Resort. He was overthinking this. Maybe it was as simple as her being nervous around a crown prince. But she sure didn't act nervous—at least not since their first meeting.

Indigo was a puzzle, and he longed to figure out how all the pieces fit together. And this trip to his kingdom would provide him with that opportunity. So long as she agreed to go with him.

When they came to a stop in front of her apartment building, he asked, "What do you say?"

"I can't just take time off from my new job at the resort." She worried her bottom lip.

"Don't worry about the resort. I'll take care of it. Your job will be safe."

Her eyes momentarily widened. Then she said, "That's right. You're friends with Hermione." Her gaze studied his. "I'll need twenty-five percent up-front."

She wasn't afraid to negotiate for what she wanted. Good for her. "Done."

"And the remainder upon completion of the portrait."

"Done." Then he held his hand out to her. "Shall we shake on it?"

Her gaze moved to his hand. She hesitantly placed her hand in his. He immediately noticed the smoothness of her skin. As her fingertips slid over the sensitive skin of his palm, sparks of attraction flew between them. A current of anticipation zinged up his arm and set his heart pounding. Oh, yes, this was going to be the most amazing adventure.

She withdrew her hand far too quickly, breaking the connection. He instinctively rubbed his fingertips over his palm as the sensation of her touch faded away.

And then recalling the contract, he retrieved it from Elek and then held it out to Indigo. "Here's a formal agreement. Read it over, sign it and bring it with you. My car will pick you up first thing Monday. Six a.m. sharp."

She accepted the papers. "To take me where?"

"To my private jet. Don't worry. We won't start working

Monday. You'll have time to settle into your suite of rooms at the palace."

"The palace?" Confusion showed in her eyes.

"You surely didn't think we'd be completing the portrait here, did you?"

"I, uh, hadn't considered that this would include travel." She frowned.

"If you haven't been to Rydiania, I can promise you that it's beautiful. And while you're at the palace, you'll have access to its amenities."

She shook her head. "I can't."

"Can't what?" Maybe it was him, but he was having a difficult time understanding her today. "Enjoy the amenities?"

"All of it. I'll do the portrait, but it has to be here."

He breathed out a frustrated sigh. He was tired of all the barriers she kept putting up. He'd tried being congenial and generous, but his patience was now razor-thin. They made a verbal agreement, now he expected her to hold up her end of it.

Maybe it was time he be frank with her. Nothing else seemed to be working. "I don't know what is going on with you, but we have an agreement. I expect you to fulfill it. Be ready to go Monday at 6:00 a.m." When she opened her mouth to argue, he said, "I have witnesses to our verbal contract." He gestured to his security team. "Don't push me on this."

Her eyes narrowed. "Now your true colors come out."

He wasn't sure what that meant, but he was beyond caring at this point. He handed over her groceries, plus his own. "Here you go. I will see you tomorrow."

She glanced down at the bags. "But these are your groceries."

"I've lost my appetite. Good evening."

Then he turned to find his car waiting for him. He climbed inside and closed the door. All the while he asked himself why he bothered. If she was that opposed to working for him, why push the subject? Was it his ego? Or was it something more?

In that moment, he didn't want to dissect his emotions. It

was enough that she seemed to have finally resigned herself to the fact that they were leaving on Monday. He had a feeling sitting for this portrait wasn't going to be boring. Far from it.

Had that really happened?

She'd agreed to work for the prince?

Indigo replayed the events in her mind as she let herself into the apartment. As she passed the living room, she found her mother had dozed off with her reading glasses on and an open book now resting on her chest.

The money the prince was willing to pay her for the portrait would be enough to get her mother moved into the assisted living center that her mother had chosen. It would make a world of difference to both of them. Her mother would no longer feel like such a burden to her, which wasn't the truth as far as Indigo was concerned. But it was what her mother thought and felt that was important.

With her mother having round-the-clock help, it would give Indigo the freedom to do what she needed to do to expand her career. Her first step in that direction was the gallery showing coming up in two weeks.

That meant she had two weeks to do the preliminary work for the portrait of the prince. It should be enough time. She just hoped he knew that an oil painting would take much longer. It was necessary to allow the paint to dry between layers. It could take her four to six weeks to complete the project. And that would be pushing it, because she had other obligations.

Indigo put away the groceries, including those the prince had given her. Though she opposed handouts, in this case she didn't believe in things going to waste. Then she prepared a selection of vegetables in a light marinara and served it over pasta.

She shared dinner with her mother, who regaled her with what she'd read in her book. Her mother loved books more than anything, but she wasn't opposed to bingeing on a good television series. It was whatever struck her mother at the moment.

"Mama, I need to talk you." She hoped what she had to say wouldn't upset her.

Her mother leaned back in her chair, having finished her meal. Her oxygen cannula helped her breathe. These days it was her constant companion. "You look so serious."

"It's nothing for you to worry about," Indigo said. "It's just that I had this amazing opportunity come up, and I was hoping to take advantage of it."

"It sounds exciting. I'm assuming this has something to do with your gallery show."

She shrugged. "I don't know. We'll see."

Suddenly her mother gave her an idea or two. She could make this trip work for her in more than one way. Though it was too late to put together any more pieces for the showing, it wasn't too late to start on new pieces for the next show. And from what she'd heard from her father and now the prince, Rydiania was one of the most beautiful countries in all of Europe. She might be able to get some photos and sketches that she could work from later. She tucked the thought away for future use.

"What is the opportunity?"

There was no way she was telling her mother the truth. She didn't want to upset her. "I'm going to be traveling around a bit—doing some research for some future paintings."

"When are you leaving?"

"I need to leave Monday. Will that be a problem?"

Her mother frowned. "Sweetie, I don't want to hold you back. That's why I would like to live on my own again."

"And I have good news there. I think we'll be able to get you moved into assisted living when I get back."

Her mother's eyes filled with hope. "What? But how?"

"I've been working with the finances, and between what you have and what I have or will have very soon, we can afford to get you into the place you chose."

Instead of the excitement she expected to see on her mother's face, she frowned. "This isn't what I wanted."

"You don't want to move?" For months, it was all her mother had been talking about.

Her mother shook her head. "It's not that. I just hate having to rely on you. I hate that you have to pay for me to move. It's just not right."

Indigo got to her feet and moved to her mother's side. She knelt down next to her. "You aren't asking me to do this. I'm doing this because I want you to be happy. And I know living here isn't the same as you having your own place. I love you, Mama. Please let me help you with this."

Tears shimmered in her mother's eyes. "How did I get so lucky to have a daughter like you?"

"I'm the one who is lucky to have you." She gave her mother a hug.

When Indigo pulled back, her mother asked. "How long will you be gone?"

"No longer than two weeks, because I have the gallery showing."

Her mother nodded and smiled. "I can't wait to go. I'm so proud of you."

"Thanks, Mama."

It never ever got old hearing that her mother was proud of her—though there were times when Indigo didn't think there was much for her mother to feel proud about. If her mother knew what Indigo was about to do in order to come up with the money for her mother's new living arrangements, she was quite certain her mother would be disappointed in her.

"Did you speak to your aunt yet about stopping by while you're gone?" her mama asked.

"I wanted to speak to you first." And then she remembered all the food in the fridge. "I already stocked the kitchen. It should keep you for a little while. And there are leftovers from tonight."

"I'm not an invalid," her mother insisted.

Her mother was right, but Indigo also knew it didn't take a

lot to tire her mother. "I just don't want you overdoing things, is all."

"I won't."

"Famous last words." Indigo sent her mother a smile. "Now what can I do for you before I go?"

"Well, you took care of the shopping, and I just got a new shipment of books and I'll take care of calling your aunt. It'll give her a chance to tell me what's been going on in her life. I think she might be dating someone, but she hasn't told me his name."

"Maybe she's not ready to talk about him yet."

"But she's my sister. She's supposed to tell me everything. I live vicariously through her."

Indigo had known for a long time that her mother had no intentions of finding love again. Even if she wasn't dealing with heart issues, she said that she'd had her one great love and that was enough for her. Indigo wondered what it would be like to have a love like her parents had shared.

Indigo was beginning to wonder if there was a love out there for her. Not that she was looking, because right now she didn't have time for romance. She had too many other responsibilities.

Her mother carried her dishes to the kitchen. Her steps were slow and small, but she didn't let that stop her.

Indigo hated seeing her mother being just a shadow of the strong woman who had buried her husband and raised her teenage daughter alone while working as a reporter. Her mother had been such an amazing role model until her health made her slow down.

And now it was Indigo's turn to do everything she could to make her mother's life as comfortable as possible. Part of that included giving her mother back a semblance of independence—even if it meant going back on a promise to her father to never step foot in Rydiania.

CHAPTER EIGHT

SHE COULDN'T BELIEVE she'd agreed to this.

At exactly six o'clock that morning, a black sedan had pulled up in front of her apartment building. There were no flags to reveal that its passenger was a foreign dignitary. And the windows were tinted, hiding the occupants from her aunt's curious view as she'd passed by on her way into the apartment.

Aunt Aggie paused on the doorstep next to Indigo. "Is the fancy car waiting for you?"

Indigo attempted to act casual. "Yes. I'm off to the airport." Her fingers tightened on the handle of her suitcase. "Thanks for helping out Mama."

"You don't have to thank me. I'm more than happy to help out. Good luck with your project." Aunt Aggie sent her a bright smile, as though she knew what Indigo was up to.

But that wasn't possible. Her gaze moved to the dark sedan to make sure Prince Istvan was still inside. She breathed easier knowing he was hidden from sight behind those dark tinted windows.

"Thank you. I should be going." After a quick hug, Indigo made her way to the waiting car.

The driver got out and opened the door for her as well as took her luggage to stow in the rear. To Indigo's surprise, Istvan wasn't waiting for her inside the sedan. According to his driver, the prince had other matters to attend to and would meet them at the private airport.

Istvan was indeed waiting for her outside the hangar. The crew was ready to go and in no time, they were in the air.

A few hours later, Indigo lounged in a leather seat of the private royal jet, where she'd been staring out at the blue sky. In the rear, the prince's security detail was seated. They were so quiet it was easy to forget they were there.

She glanced over to the side to find Istvan sitting across the aisle with his laptop resting on a table in front of him. He had an earpiece, and he talked in a fast, low voice. His fingers moved rapidly over the keyboard. She couldn't help but wonder what had him so preoccupied. Was it royal business? Or something else?

Whatever kept him so busy had given her time to come to grips with the reality of the situation. She stared out the window at the blue sky dotted with a few puffy white clouds. The earth looked so far away as they grew nearer to her birthplace.

Her palms grew damp as she envisioned coming face-to-face with the king and queen. The idea didn't appeal to her. Not at all. There had to be a way to avoid them. She just needed to give it some more thought.

Ding.

Indigo glanced toward the front of the cabin. She noticed a small seat-belt sign was lit up. This must mean they'd already arrived in Rydiania. She glanced over at Istvan to see if he'd noticed the alert.

"I don't care. I've got other obligations. We'll discuss this later." He withdrew the earpiece and placed it in his pocket. Then he glanced in her direction. "I'm sorry about that."

"No problem." And she meant that sincerely. She wasn't sure what they would have discussed during the four-plus hours they'd been in the air.

"The palace isn't happy that I was away. There's a lot to catch up on."

"I can't even imagine." Which was quite true. When she was a young child, back before her father had been exiled, he had come home late at night after she'd gone to sleep. On the rare times he was home early, he'd tell her tales of the royals. She'd been so young at the time that she'd thought they were fairy tales, but as she grew older, she realized many of the bedtime stories her father had told her had been grounded in reality.

"I take it this is your first visit to Rydiania." His voice interrupted her trip into the past. "I'll see that you have a tour. After all, we can't have you locked away painting the whole time you're here."

"I don't mind working the whole time." The faster she finished her preliminary work, the sooner she'd get back to Greece. And even though her aunt was keeping a close eye on her mother, Indigo didn't want to be gone too long. Since the death of her father, she and her mother had grown even closer than before.

"I insist," Istvan said in a firm tone. "All work and no play, makes Indigo a dull girl."

The fact he knew that saying totally caught her off guard. It sure didn't seem like something a royal would know. It seemed... Well, it seemed so normal. Kind of the way it'd felt when they'd visited the market together.

But Istvan wasn't normal. He was a royal. And not just any royal—a Rydiania prince. And no matter how handsome he was or how kind he could be, she couldn't forget that he was one of them. Only she wasn't like her father—she wasn't going into this blind. She knew how cutthroat the royals could be. And armed with this knowledge, she was protected from being hurt by them.

"Buckle up." His voice drew her from her thoughts.

"Um...what did you say?"

"We're about to land. You'll need to fasten your seat belt."

"Oh. Right." Heat rushed to her cheeks, as he'd once more distracted her. She couldn't let that happen again. She had to stay focused.

After fastening her seat belt, she turned her head to the lush landscape. The green was periodically dotted with towns. She really wouldn't mind exploring the area. The last time she'd been outside Greece had been to paint in Italy. Her portfolio had needed some diversity, and the trip to Venice had been quite successful.

A smile tugged at her lips. For so long, she'd struggled to get her art career off the ground. Her father had told her to be more practical. Her aunt had tried to hire her at her hair salon. The only one who had believed in her becoming a success had been her mother. She had told Indigo numerous times that she could become anything she set her mind on.

And now, after this assignment, she'd be able to request high fees for her portraits. And her art would go for large enough figures that she'd be able to maintain her mother's care indefinitely. The thought reaffirmed her determination to make the most of this trip.

As the plane began its descent, Indigo gripped the arms of her seat. The plane shook as it hit turbulence. Her body tensed as her fingers dug into the armrests. *We'll be fine. We'll be fine.*

All of the sudden, a warm hand covered hers. She glanced over to find Istvan gazing at her.

He sent her a reassuring smile. "We're almost on the ground."

She nodded, not trusting her voice. And then her gaze darted back toward the window. The fact she'd flown at all was a bit of a miracle. But she'd learned from her father, who had let the world get the best of him, that she couldn't follow his lead. She had to be strong and face life's challenges if she wanted to make it in this world.

"Are you okay?" he asked.

She nodded.

"Was it bad?"

Her gaze swung back around to him. "What?"

"The plane incident—was it bad?"

How did he know? It wasn't like she ever talked about it. In fact, she didn't really want to get into it. But part of overcoming her fear was talking about it.

"It could have been worse." It never escaped her that her life had been spared that day. "I... I was in a near crash a few years back."

He gave her hand a reassuring squeeze. "That would unnerve anyone."

"At first I didn't want to fly ever again, but I realized if I wanted to follow my dreams, flying would be a part of it."

"That was very brave of you."

She shrugged. She didn't feel brave. She felt silly for being afraid to fly, even if she overcame the fear little by little each time she stepped onto a plane.

"I was on a flight home from London." In her mind's eye she was back on that plane. "It had been the usual flight, with the inevitable delay taking off, but then everything settled down. The plane wasn't full, so I had no one beside me and I could relax. I was so anxious to get home. I wanted to tell my mother all about my art classes." It was right when her art career had started to take off.

"That's a long way to go for art lessons." His voice was gentle and not judgmental. It was though he had said enough to prod her to keep telling her story.

"It isn't far to go when you have a rare opportunity to learn from one of the best artists in the world." And then she dropped the name of a well-respected painter and glanced at Istvan to see if he recognized the name.

His eyes widened. "I understand the reason for your trip. Obviously, like me, he saw the true magnificence of your work."

His compliment made her heart beat faster as heat rushed to her cheeks. Was Istvan serious? As she gazed deeply into his blue eyes, she forgot what she'd been thinking. When she realized she'd been staring into his eyes too long, she lowered her gaze. His hand was still covering hers. It made her heart *tap-tap* even faster.

She needed to focus on something besides the prince. She swallowed hard as she prepared to finish her story. "I was gazing out the window, enjoying the sunshine and blue skies. The next thing I knew, there was a strange sound that I later learned was a bird strike, and the engine went out."

The memory of the fire and smoke was so vivid in her mind—just as it had been in her nightmares for a long time after the event. Maybe other people wouldn't have been affected by the event, but she'd felt like she'd been given another chance at life, and she'd promised herself she wouldn't squander it.

She could feel his gaze upon her. "I… I didn't think we were going to make it out alive. Suddenly the plane started to descend quickly. Too quickly."

"No wonder you aren't comfortable on a plane."

"In the end, our amazing pilot made an emergency landing. It was a rough landing, but I was never so happy to step on solid ground in my life."

"And yet you didn't let it stop you."

"I know what happens when you let setbacks and events stop you from living your life." Now why had she gone and said that? She wasn't going to share the tragedy that had befallen her father.

Just then the plane shuddered once more. She turned her head to the window and found they were on the ground. She could at last breathe a bit easier.

The prince withdrew his hand from hers, leaving a noticeably cool spot. "We have arrived."

While the plane taxied to a private hangar, Istvan gathered his things and placed them in his attaché. All Indigo had to grab was her sketch pad that still held nothing but blank pages. Usually she spent her downtime sketching ideas for a new painting, but she'd been utterly distracted on the flight. She told herself it was the flying and not her company that had her distracted.

As the plane rolled to a stop, she glanced out the window to find a dark sedan waiting for them. This time the sedan was larger, and the country's flags adorned the front of the vehicle. A gold crest of the royal family was emblazed on the door. This vehicle was here to whisk them off to the palace.

Her stomach sank down to her heels. "I don't have to stay at the palace," Indigo said. "I'd be fine staying in the village."

Istvan arched a brow. "You are refusing to stay at the palace?"

"I'm just saying that I would be more comfortable staying in the village. I… I'd get a chance to take in the community and the sights."

He studied her for a moment. "If I didn't know better, I'd think you were trying to get away from me."

She was busted. "If that's not acceptable, just say so."

He shrugged. "I'm not going to make you stay at the palace. You just need to be available to work on the portrait starting tomorrow."

"I will."

They moved to the now-open doorway. A man wearing a dark suit and a serious expression stood at the bottom of the steps, waiting to greet the prince. "Your Highness, did you have a good trip?"

"Yes, I did." Istvan glanced over at Indigo as she joined them. "Jozsef, this is Indigo. She's going to be painting my portrait. Indigo, this is Jozsef, my private secretary, who keeps my calendar manageable."

Jozsef's brows ever so briefly lifted before he resumed his neutral expression. "Your Highness, you should know the queen has hired her own artist."

"I'll deal with the queen later. Right now, Ms. Castellanos would like to have accommodations in the village. Could you find her something appropriate?"

"Yes, sir." Jozsef stepped away and made a phone call.

"You didn't have to make him do that." Indigo didn't want to be an imposition. In fact, she was hoping to make her presence less known by staying the village.

"It's no problem. It's Jozsef's job to handle these matters." When they approached the car, the driver opened the door for him. The prince stood back and gestured for her to get in first.

She did as he requested. The interior of the sedan was done up in black, just like the outside of the car. But on the seat in gold thread was the royal family's crest. And the leg space was more generous than in a normal car. There was even a small bar in the back of the front seats and a dividing window to give them some privacy.

When the prince climbed in the back seat and settled next to her, the space seemed to shrink considerably. His arm brushed hers and sent a cascade of goose bumps racing down her arm.

She moved over. The door armrest dug into her side. When she glanced over at Istvan, she found amusement dancing in his eyes.

"You don't have to press yourself against the door." He closed his door. "There's plenty of room for both of us."

The problem was that sitting back here with him was cozy. Too cozy. And she was increasingly aware of how attractive he was, with his broad shoulders, muscular chest and long legs. Her heart pitter-pattered. She swallowed hard.

She needed to remain professional. She laced her fingers together in her lap. "You do understand that I can't complete the painting in the two weeks I'll be here."

He nodded. "I understand. Do you want me to sit for you tomorrow and you can sketch me or something?"

She shook her head. "I'd like to observe you going about your normal day, if that would be possible."

His brows rose high on his forehead. "You want to watch me work?"

She nodded. "If possible."

"It's certainly possible, but it sounds boring." He sent her a smile.

She noticed the way his lips parted, revealing his straight white teeth. There was a dimple in his cheek that made him even cuter. And when the smile reached his blue eyes, they twinkled.

She subdued a sigh. No one had a right to be that handsome. And try as she might not to like him, she was failing miserably. She'd found absolutely nothing to dislike about him. Was it possible he was nothing at all like his parents? Hope swelled in her chest.

"So why did you hire me if the queen already has someone to do your portrait?"

"Because it's my portrait, and I want to pick who paints it. My country needs a fresh approach. I'm hoping with your help they will see me in a new light and not part of the same old regime that has been running the country in the exact same manner for much too long."

Wow! She really had misjudged him, hadn't she? Her hope was so great that it surprised her.

It wasn't like she was going to let herself fall for him. Not a chance. But she hoped he was different for, um, his country. Yes, that was it. His country could use new leadership. Because it didn't really matter to her personally if he was the same or different. Not at all.

CHAPTER NINE

PERHAPS THIS HAD been a miscalculation.

Istvan had noticed how Indigo made sure to leave a lot of space between them, whether it was on the jet or now in the back seat of the car. What had made her so jumpy around him?

He wanted to ask her, but he didn't dare. As it was, their conversation was finally getting her to relax a bit. And he didn't want to stop talking because the more she relaxed, the more he saw the part of her that had first attracted him to her. Not that he was expecting or even wanting anything to come of this arrangement—other than an impressive portrait that would put his unique stamp on his upcoming reign.

"You just need to tell me what you'll need while you're here," he said.

"Need?"

"Yes. What art supplies will you need?"

"Oh. Okay." She reached in her purse and pulled out a slip of paper. She held it out to him. "Here you go."

He was duly impressed that she was this organized. He glanced down at the list. "I'll see that these items are brought to you."

"Thank you."

Tap-tap.

Istvan opened the window. Jozsef stood there. He leaned down and spoke softly into Istvan's ear. There was no room available in the village. It would seem Indigo would be staying at the palace after all.

He put up the window and turned to Indigo. "It would appear there's a wedding celebration in the village and all the rooms are taken."

"Oh." Disappointment showed in her eyes.

Just then the car engine started, and they began to move. Istvan leaned back in his seat. "Don't worry. You'll like the palace. It's a cross between a home and a museum."

She smiled at him.

"What did I say that was so amusing?"

"I've just never heard anyone describe their home as a museum."

He shrugged. "It has a collection of art from the past and some from the present. Every time a foreign dignitary visits the palace, they feel obligated to bring a gift. So there's quite a collection. Except in my wing."

"You have your own wing of the palace?"

He nodded. "It's one of the benefits of being the crown prince. My siblings all share a wing. And then my parents have their own wing. And that leaves one wing for visiting guests."

"And here all I have is a two-bedroom apartment. It could probably fit in just one room in the palace."

When she sent him a playful smile, he let out a laugh. The more she relaxed, the more he liked her. She reminded him of his younger sister Cecilia. They were both free spirits and full of energy. He had a feeling if they had a chance, they would be fast friends. And then maybe he'd have an excuse to see Indigo again.

She wanted to hate Rydiania.

She wanted it to be the ugliest place on the earth. But instead, she found it to be one of the most beautiful places she'd ever been.

Indigo stared out the window at the tall green trees lining each side of the smooth roadway. When the trees parted, there was a lush meadow with a large pond. Upon the placid water were ducks—a mama and seven ducklings. Inwardly she sighed. If she didn't know better, she'd swear Istvan had created this scene to impress her—not that he had any reason to want to do such a thing.

And yet Indigo felt as though they were driving through a watercolor painting. This wasn't fair. There had to be something about this place that she hated.

Her gaze hungrily took it all in. The roadway wove through the country, and for a moment she felt like she was on holiday and had just landed in paradise. Then she decided that the problem with this place was that it was too rural, with its endless green grass, its abundance of wildlife and array of wildflowers. After all, that stuff was nice if you were an outdoorsy person, but she preferred the hubbub of neighborhoods and shops.

And still she kept her face turned toward the window, memorizing all she saw. She told herself that she kept staring because the alternative would be facing Istvan. She wasn't ready for that. Sketching his striking image with his kissable mouth was one thing, but dealing with him on a personal level was quite another.

"What do you think?" he asked.

Did he know her thoughts had drifted back to him? Totally impossible. She just had to keep her wits about her. She couldn't let him know how easily he distracted her.

She gave a small, nonchalant shrug. "It's great if you're a nature fanatic."

He let out a laugh. "I take it you're not into nature."

Why did he insist on making conversation? It wasn't like they were going to become friends. This was a business arrangement. Period. At the end of these two weeks, they'd never see each other again. She'd return to Greece to complete the portrait and then ship it to him. And yet she found herself wanting to talk to him, because he made it so easy to carry on a conversation.

She shrugged. "Honestly, it's beautiful. I'm just used to spending time in a more urban setting."

He nodded. "I understand."

She felt as though she'd said something wrong. She hadn't meant to. "But if I loved a more rustic life, this would definitely be a lovely place to live."

"Have you always lived in Athens?"

She turned her head toward him. "You don't know? I mean, I figured you ran a background check before hiring me."

"Of course. It's a matter of practice for all hires, but that doesn't mean I actually reviewed the entire report. I just made sure you weren't a criminal. And my private secretary rang your employer. Was there something you were expecting me to see?"

She shook her head. She wasn't ready to dredge up the past. "As far back as I can remember, I've lived in Athens."

"That's a long time."

"Hey, did you just call me old?"

His brows rose. "What?" Worry reflected in his eyes. "No. Of course not."

She sent him a playful smile. Who knew it was so easy to undo the prince's calm, cool exterior? "Uh-huh."

"Do you have a lot of family?"

"I have my mother. My father, well, he died when I was a teenager." Why had she gone and brought up her father? She never discussed him with anyone but her mother. And even then it was about his life, never his death.

"I'm so sorry."

She shrugged off his sympathy, refusing to acknowledge the pain she felt when she thought of the life that had been cut much too short. "It was a long time ago."

"Do you have any siblings?"

She shook her head. Tired of talking about herself, she decided to turn the tables. "And how about you? Any siblings?"

"I have three sisters."

She tried to imagine him as a child with three younger sisters chasing after him. "Your childhood must have been interesting."

He sighed. "You have no idea. My sisters can be a handful. You'll get to meet them while you're here."

"I look forward to it." Did she? Or had she just uttered those words out of habit? She wasn't sure—she wasn't sure about a lot of things lately.

She turned back toward the window. The car wound through the lush valley. Indigo found herself captivated by the majestic scenery. Her fingers twitched with the need to reach for her pencils and sketch pad. But there wasn't time. All of nature's beauty passed by the window far too quickly. Instead she reached for her phone to snap some photos.

Istvan cleared his throat. "I like to think that Rydiania is one of the most beautiful places on the planet. I hope you'll get a chance to do some exploring while you're here."

The idea appealed to her, but she needed to remain focused on her work. "We don't have much time together. I really need to do the groundwork for your portrait."

He nodded. "I understand."

The car slowed as it approached a more urban area. She gazed forward, finding high-rises and a sea of concrete buildings. *A city? Here? Really?*

But then the car turned to the left and completely diverted around the city. "We're not going to visit the city?"

"You sound disappointed."

She shrugged. "I'm just curious to see what a city in Rydiania looks like, especially one that is surrounded by a forest."

"I'll make sure we plan an excursion so you can explore. There's an arts section to the city that I'm sure you'll be interested in. But right now, I'm expected at a meeting at the palace."

"Of course." It was far too easy to forget that he was a prince and not just a commoner, like herself. She would have to be more careful going forward.

A peaceful silence settled over the car as it carried them closer to the palace. She had to admit that she was curious to see it in person. The pictures she'd seen online were striking. She wondered if it was really that impressive or if the pictures had received some touch-ups.

More houses came into view. They were separated by expansive property. Most yards were meticulously cared for with short grass, trimmed bushes and brightly colored flowers from yellow to pinks and reds.

They slowed to a stop and then merged into a single roadway that wound its way into a small village. It was filled with what she imagined were tourists. Some had brochures in their hands. Others had their phones out and were snapping pictures of the rustic storefronts.

This place, with its many unique shops and amazing aromas, from buttery cinnamon to herbs and vegetables, permeated the car. Indigo found herself inhaling deeply. "Something sure smells good."

Istvan smiled. "Oh, yes, there are many wonderful places to eat in the village."

Her stomach rumbled in agreement. "I'll definitely keep that in mind. Is the palace far from here?"

"Not at all. In fact it's just on the other side of the village."

Her stomach knotted. Even though she had agreed to come here to help her mother, she felt as though she were betraying her father. Would he understand her decision? She hoped so.

The car slowed, drawing Indigo's attention. She focused on the very tall wrought iron gate in front of the car. Guards in deep purple uniforms with black hats stood in front of the gate. To either side of the gate were black guard shacks that were much more than shacks, because no shack looked that nice.

With precise movements that must have been practiced for many, many hours, they moved in unison and swung the giant gates open. As the car proceeded along the smoothly paved roadway, Indigo's heart raced and she clutched her hands together.

And there before them stood a gigantic palace. It was built out of a light gray stone. Impressive turrets stood at the corners. Atop the palace fluttered a purple-and-white flag. The car swung around and pulled to a stop beneath a portico. The doors were swung open by gentlemen dressed formally in black-and-white suits.

"Welcome to my home." Istvan sent her a reassuring smile.

She opened her mouth, but no words would come out. What was she supposed to say? *It's beautiful?* Because, well, it was the most magnificent *home* she'd ever seen. Or was she supposed to be unimpressed, as this was the home of the people who had hurt her father so deeply? She pressed her lips back together. Nothing felt quite right.

And so she was quietly led up the few steps to the red runner that led them inside the palace. No matter how much she wanted to hate this place, she couldn't deny the flutter in her chest as she took in its magnificence. *Just... Wow!*

If she hadn't seen all this for herself, she never would have believed it. Because the pictures online didn't come close to doing the palace justice—not one little bit.

It was like stepping into the pages of a storybook—the kind her mother read to her when she was a child. Sunlight streamed into the round foyer through a giant glass dome three stories up from where they stood. The sun's rays lit up the room and gave it a glow. It was though she were standing in a very special place.

"Indi, are you coming?" Istvan called from where he stood on the grand steps that were lined with a deep purple carpet that led to the second floor.

"Indi?" It was the first time he'd called her that, and she wasn't sure how she felt about him using the nickname.

He smiled. "Has no one ever called you that?"

"Um...yes. My friends do."

"Good. It suits you. I'll show you to your room."

As she made her way up the steps, she couldn't help but wonder what had just happened. Was the prince saying he wanted to be friends with her? If so, how did she feel about him taking such liberties? But was it worth her getting worked up over a nickname? Probably not.

Istvan didn't have airs about him like she'd imagined a member of a royal family having. He was down-to-earth. And dare she admit it...if he were anyone else, she would be totally into him.

Still, he was the crown prince of the country that had played a role in the loss of her father. She couldn't ever let herself forget that, no matter how sexy she found his smile or how she could let herself get lost in his dreamy eyes.

When she smiled, she stole the breath from his lungs.

He hadn't felt this alive and invigorated in a long time.

Istvan was certain he'd made the right decision to bring Indi here. She was like a breath of fresh air in this stodgy old palace. He needed someone like her around to remind him of how things could be in the kingdom if the harsh traditions that had been carried on generation after generation were to be replaced with a gentler and more modern way of doing things.

He was going to be the change for his family. He knew his radical ideas would be met with resistance. He just hoped he had the strength to see change brought to this country that was stuck in the ways of the past.

And his first way of showing his country that his reign would be different—that *he* was different—was in his formal portrait. Indi would take his idea of change and make it a visual statement.

They climbed the many steps and paused at the top. He wanted to give Indi a chance to look around and gain her bearings. Not everyone was used to living in a palace. Even though he had grown up within these massive walls, he realized it didn't hold the warmth and coziness that other homes did. He supposed there were trade-offs for everything in life.

His three sisters strode toward them. What were the three of them doing together? On second thought, he didn't want to know. Their eyes lit up when they noticed Indi at his side. In fact, they hardly paid him any attention. He groaned inwardly. His sisters could be quite overbearing when they thought he was interested in someone. Not that he was interested in Indi in a romantic way. At this point in his life, he didn't have time for a relationship.

The three princesses came to a stop in front of him. Gisella and Beatrix were dressed in blouses, pants and heels, while his youngest sister, Cecilia, wore a light blue skirt that barely made it to her midthigh and a pale-yellow halter top.

"Who's your friend?" his eldest sister, Princess Gisella, asked.

He glanced at Indi, who looked curious to meet the princesses. "Indigo, these are my sisters." He gestured to the left. "This is Princess Gisella. She is the oldest. Next to her is my youngest sister, Princess Cecilia. And next to her is Princess Beatrix."

"It's nice to meet you all," Indigo said.

His sisters all wore their well-practiced smiles. They could be so friendly and welcoming when they wanted to be, but they could also become defensive and freeze out people. He had absolutely no idea how they were going to react to Indi. He hoped they would give her a chance.

And then his sisters all spoke at once. Each fired off questions at Indigo, who looked surprised and overwhelmed. His sisters could be like a force of nature when you had to deal with all of them at once—at least that's what his father often said. And Istvan had to agree with him.

"Stop!" His firm tone drew his sisters' attention. "Let Indigo get situated before you bombard her with questions."

Gisella narrowed her gaze on him. "Does Mother know about this?"

"No." He chose not to add any further explanation.

Gisella crossed her arms and frowned at him. "She's not going to like you bringing home an unexpected guest."

His other sisters nodded in agreement.

"She's not a guest. Not like you're thinking. Indigo is an artist. She's here to paint my portrait."

Surprised looks filtered across all the princesses' faces. So they really thought he was bringing home a girlfriend for his family to meet? That would be the last thing he would do with someone he was romantically interested in. His family could be intimidating on a good day, and on a bad day, well… He didn't want to think about it.

"Is that true about you being an artist?" Cecilia asked.

Indigo nodded. "It is. We met when I did a sketch of your brother."

"That sounds interesting," Beatrix said. "Where was this?"

"Stop," Istvan said. "Indigo is tired from traveling."

"Istvan, is that you?" the queen's voice trailed up the staircase.

He turned to the stairs, expecting to see his mother, but she was still downstairs. "Yes. I'm home."

The click of heels on the foyer's marble floor could be heard approaching the stairs. He turned back to his sisters. All he saw was their backs as they all headed in different directions. So much for them helping him manage his mother so she didn't frighten Indigo away.

He leaned over to Indigo and said softly, "Don't worry."

"I'm not." Her tone was firm as she straightened her shoulders.

Most people were intimidated when they first met the king or queen. That didn't appear to be the case with Indigo. Interesting.

"Istvan, there you are." The queen stepped onto the landing. He turned his attention to his mother as she headed toward them. She wore a conservative navy dress with white trim, and near the neckline was her diamond-and-amethyst royal brooch in the shape of a crown. Both of his parents wore their pins daily. He was supposed to wear a similar one since he was heir to the throne, but he found it pretentious. He picked and chose the days he wore his royal pin.

"Hello, Mother." He stepped forward and gave her a feathery kiss upon the cheek.

"It's about time you returned."

He noticed how her gaze moved to Indi, and instead of a surprised look, she assumed her well-rehearsed smile. He knew that smile. It was one of duty that never reached his mother's eyes. She used it as a shield to hide what she was really feeling.

And since he had not advised his mother that he would be bringing home a visitor, he was certain she had been caught off guard—something she hated. His mother liked to know about everything before it happened.

"Mother, I'd like to introduce you to Indigo Castellanos of Athens, Greece. Indigo, I'd like to introduce you to Queen Della."

He noticed how Indi froze. She didn't smile. She didn't do the customary curtsy to the queen. She didn't move. It reminded him of their first meeting. Maybe he should have given her a heads-up on what was expected when first meeting the king or queen. But he'd been distracted by Indi's presence and his excitement to spend the next couple of weeks with her.

An awkward moment passed before the queen said, "Welcome."

He noticed the muscles of Indi's throat work. "Thank you for having me in your...home."

The queen continued to study Indi.

"Mother, I've hired Indi...um, Indigo to paint my formal portrait."

This time his mother couldn't hide her surprise. Her penciled brows rose. "We already have an artist. He's done other royal paintings."

"Not this one." His voice held a firmness. He wasn't going to change his plans. If he backed down now, his mother would always walk over him and his plans. He couldn't be an effective ruler that way.

The queen's eyes grew dark, but when she spoke, her agitation was veiled. "The king is looking for you."

"Is he in the blue room?" It was his father's favorite room in the palace. Though it wasn't the king's formal office, it was the room he used most to conduct his business.

"Yes. He's expecting you to meet with him immediately."

He was not going to abandon Indigo, whose face had gone distinctly pale. "I will see Father shortly." And with that he turned to Indigo. "Shall we?"

Indigo continued to stare at the queen, but he wasn't able to read her thoughts. To say their first meeting hadn't gone well would be a total understatement. The queen turned and made her way down the steps. Indigo watched until she was out of sight.

He gently took ahold of her arm. "Shall we?"

She blinked and looked at him. "What?"

He grew concerned about her. "Are you all right?"

She nodded. "I'm sorry. I...uh, was lost in thought for a moment."

He wasn't sure he believed her. By her pale complexion and the gaze of her eyes, it was almost as though she'd seen a ghost.

Indie walked beside him. Maybe he was just overthinking things. After all, they'd had a busy day of travel, and then meeting the queen without any forewarning or guidance on their customs must have caught her a little off guard. He would have to do better in the future.

CHAPTER TEN

THAT HADN'T GONE quite as she'd thought.

Many times over the years, Indigo had imagined one day facing the king and queen of Rydiania. In none of her fantasies had she stood there silently. That was the second time she'd been rendered silent upon meeting a member of the royal family. What was wrong with her?

She wasn't one to keep quiet when something bothered her. So then why had she been so quiet upon meeting the queen?

Maybe it was the fact that she had hoped the queen would recognize her—that she'd apologize for banishing her father, for ruining his life. Not that Indigo ever really thought any of that would happen.

There was a bit of satisfaction in the fact that the daughter of the man who'd been banished from the kingdom was now an invited guest of the palace. Yes, indeed, it felt good. Although it didn't come close to offsetting the pain and destruction that the royal family had caused hers. And for what? So they could eliminate any threat to them claiming the throne for themselves?

She'd felt a rush of so many emotions on her first night in the palace that she'd begged off on joining the royal family for dinner. She pleaded a headache, which wasn't far from the truth. A tray of food had been sent to her room.

The following morning, Istvan had given her the grand tour of the palace. Her favorite rooms had been the library, with its many bookcases and comfy couches, and the conservatory, with its walls of windows and dozens of plants.

Others would probably have been awed by the throne room or the flag room, but they did nothing for her. She was actually curious about the kitchen, but the tour didn't include that room. She wondered, if a royal got hungry in the middle of the night, did they slip down to the kitchen to get a snack? Or did they have someone to do it for them? She decided it was probably the latter.

As evening settled on her second day in the palace, she was alone in her room. She turned around, taking in the spacious room that could easily fit her apartment. Right now, her home seemed a million miles away. She'd just spoken to her mother, who was enjoying Aunt Aggie's company. Indigo missed them both.

It was time to dress for dinner. She decided to shower. It had been a long day, and a shower would make her feel refreshed. Istvan had said he would be by to pick her up at seven.

She wasn't exactly sure how to dress. Obviously jeans and a T-shirt were out. And so she picked a peach-pink maxi dress. She blew her long hair dry and then pulled it up into a ponytail, pulling loose curls to soften her face.

As for makeup, she didn't usually wear much, which was probably odd considering she was an artist. But she very rarely wore heavy eye makeup or bold lipsticks. Tonight she would do what she normally did. The more she stuck with her usual routine, the more relaxed she'd be.

She applied foundation, followed by powder. She indulged in some glittery sand-tone eyeshadow and mascara. And on her lips, she applied a frosted beige gloss. Okay, so maybe it was more than her normal, but it wasn't too much. She wondered what Istvan would think.

As soon as she realized that she cared at all what he thought of her, she banished the thought. She was here for work, nothing more.

Knock-knock.

Her heart started to race. She sensed Istvan standing on the other side of the door. And suddenly this evening was feeling much more like a date than a business dinner. Perhaps she should have opted for the jeans, but even she knew that would be utterly unacceptable for dinner with the royal family.

"Coming." She glanced in the mirror one last time.

Considering she was having dinner in the palace, she realized her outfit was a bit on the casual side. Perhaps she should have brought something more formal, but then again, she didn't really own anything fit for palace living.

She moved to the door and opened it. Standing on the other side of the door was Prince Istvan. She could tell he had recently showered, as his dark hair was still a bit damp.

Wow! She swallowed hard. His collared shirt had the first few buttons undone, giving the slightest glimpse of his tanned, muscular chest. Her gaze skimmed down to his dark jeans. Jeans? So the royals did wear jeans around the palace, just like normal people. *Interesting.*

"Are you ready to go?" He smiled at her.

So she'd been busted checking him out. Her mouth grew dry, and she struggled to swallow. She had to keep it together. She didn't want him to know how much his presence got to her. That wouldn't be good. Not good at all.

"Yes, I am. I hope I'm dressed all right for dinner." Now, why had she gone and said that? It wasn't like she was looking for approval from anyone.

His smile broadened. "You look beautiful."

His compliment made her heart flutter in her chest. "Thank you."

He presented his arm to her. "Shall we?"

She considered ignoring the gesture, but she didn't want to be rude. So far on this trip Istvan had been nothing but kind and generous. He was making it impossible to dislike him. In fact, she was starting to wonder if she had been wrong about him. The thought startled her.

Instead of guiding her to the front stairs that they'd used when they'd first arrived, he turned and headed in the opposite direction. It must be the back way to the dining room.

Her stomach shivered with nerves. Perhaps she should have pleaded another headache in order to get out of this dinner, too. Yes, that would have been a good idea. Would they believe she had a headache for her entire visit? Probably not.

They descended a more modest set of steps. Her stomach was full of butterflies. There was no way she was going to be able to eat. Not a chance.

When they reached the landing, instead of heading into the center of the palace, Istvan led her to an exterior door, where a guard bid them a good evening.

"I don't understand," she said. "Aren't we having dinner in the palace?"

He pushed the door open to a warm summer evening. He paused to look at her. "Is that what you want?"

"No." The word popped out before she realized it.

He smiled at her. "I didn't think so. I have something else in mind."

She should probably ask about the alternate plan, but she decided it didn't really matter to her. If it meant not having to sit across from the king and queen, she was fine with whatever he planned.

The late-summer sun hung low in the sky, sending splashes of pink and purple through the clear sky. Rydiania certainly had the most beautiful sunsets. Just as she was about to mention it, Istvan came to a stop next to a low-slung cherry-red convertible.

He opened the door for her. "I thought you'd like a ride to dinner rather than trying to walk into the village in those."

She glanced down at her heeled sandals. When she'd chosen them, she'd thought she would be walking down the stairs to the palace's dining room. Her gaze lifted to meet his. "You're right. They aren't good to walk long distances in."

"No problem. I haven't had this car out for a spin in a while. So it'll help us both."

She lowered herself to the buttery-soft leather seat. Istvan closed her door, and then he circled around to the driver's seat. It was then that she noticed just how compact the interior was, because when Istvan settled in his seat, his broad shoulders brushed up against hers. Just the casual touch set her stomach aflutter. She slid closer to the door. It was best to keep her distance—at least whatever distance the car allowed them.

He didn't seem to notice their contact or the fact that she'd moved away from him. If he did notice, he certainly didn't let on. Well, if he wasn't going to be affected by their closeness, neither was she.

She focused her gaze straight ahead as he started the car. The engine purred like a fine-tuned machine. Then the tires rolled silently over the paved drive. There was nothing about the palace that wasn't pure perfection, from the manicured green lawn to the impeccably trimmed bushes to the stunning flower gardens with purple, red and white blooms. Quite honestly, no matter what she thought of the royal family, she couldn't deny that she felt as though she were driving through a painting.

"You seemed really interested in the village when we passed through it," he said. "I thought we would dine there. But if you would rather, we could drive into the city. It isn't that much farther."

She would like to explore the city, but that would mean more time alone with Istvan in this impossibly small car. And if she were to lean her head to the side and inhale deeply—not that she had any intention of doing such a thing—but if she were to do it, she knew she would smell his unique masculine scent mingled with soap. Her pulse started to race. It was quite an intoxicating combination. Again, she wasn't going there. Not at all.

"The village is fine." Did her voice sound funny? A little deep and throaty? She swallowed hard. "It...it's beautiful here."

"I agree but then again, I might be a bit biased."

When she glanced over at him, she noticed the smile that hinted at his perfectly white, straight teeth. It was just one more thing that was perfect about him. Not that she was keeping track.

"I'm surprised you spend so much time away from here." She needed to keep the conversation going in order to keep her thoughts from straying.

She could feel his gaze briefly flick to her. "You've been checking up on me?"

"Uh, no. I mean, I just wanted to know a little more about you before I took the assignment. And the internet showed that you travel quite a bit."

He was quiet for a moment, and she started to wonder if he was going to respond. It was obviously no secret that he traveled all of Europe regularly. The press covered his every move—and every single woman he dined with. She ignored the uneasiness she'd felt at glancing at the picture of him with all those beautiful, glamorous women. It also made her wonder why there wasn't press surrounding the palace or lining the street as they made their way into the village.

"I do like to travel." He didn't expand on his reason for being out of the country so much.

The car slowed as they entered the village. The roads were narrow, with vehicles parked on either side. They stopped numerous times to allow people to cross the road. Indigo couldn't help but wonder if the people recognized the prince's car. After all, there were no royal flags on the hood or gold coat of arms on the doors as there were on other royal vehicles.

If the villagers did recognize the car or him behind the wheel, they didn't let on. Sure some smiled and waved, but it wasn't any different than if an ordinary citizen such as herself had stopped for them. Interesting. Even more interesting was that

Istvan didn't expect any royal treatment. He was definitely different than she'd imagined. But how different? That was still to be determined.

A relaxing dinner.

And a chance to spend some one-on-one time with Indigo.

Istvan was quite pleased with himself for coming up with a legitimate excuse to avoid a stuffy, strained meal with his parents and siblings. He was certain to hear more about hiring a "nobody" to do his formal portrait.

He'd already been given disapproving looks, not only from the queen but also from the king when he'd met with him before picking up Indigo for dinner. His father wasn't happy with him. Not all. And then his sister Gisella had sighed at him and asked the same question she always asked him: *Why can't you just do your part?*

His sister made it sound like he should just go along with whatever his parents expected of him. That was never going to happen. He was not a yes man. Never had been. Never would be.

His intent was to bring about a more modern Rydiania. Though the more he strove to move in that direction, the more resistance he encountered. Was he the only one that realized if they didn't loosen the reins, their position as leaders of the kingdom would be in great jeopardy?

He slowed for a car just pulling out and then proceeded into the now-vacant parking spot. "Anything you are particularly hungry for?"

Indigo shook her head. "I'm curious to try some of the local cuisine."

"Then you've come to the right place. No other place cooks Rydianian cuisine quite the way they do here."

"It sounds like you come here often."

"I do." He noticed how her warm brown eyes briefly widened. "I try to spend as much time in the village as possible."

"Isn't that difficult? You know, with you being the prince

and everything. Don't people constantly want pictures and autographs?"

He shook his head. "It's a small village, and the locals all know me. There's no need for them to treat me different. I don't expect it, and they know it. But when the tourists spot me, it can get a bit lively. Thankfully, the village usually quiets down in the evening, when most tourists return to the city."

"Interesting."

"You sound surprised."

"I am. I just—I don't know—thought you spent all your time in the palace."

"My parents do—for the most part. But I don't see how you can govern a country appropriately when you aren't out among the people finding out what's important to them. Come on." He climbed out of the car.

By the time he rounded the front of the car to open the door for Indi, she already had it open and was standing on the sidewalk. He couldn't help but smile. He loved her independent spirit. She didn't stand on traditions or formalities. He needed someone like her in his life—someone to remind him that he wasn't all that different from the people of Rydiania.

Not that he was planning to keep Indi in his life. He knew her life was back in Greece. And his future was all about the next steps for him to step up as king. Even though he'd been groomed for the position ever since his uncle had abdicated the throne, it was still a daunting challenge.

As they strolled along the sidewalk, villagers smiled and said hello in passing. Most of the people were familiar faces to him.

"They're all so nice," Indi said.

"They definitely are." He felt lucky to be a part of this village. It wasn't the same for him in the big city. He only traveled there with heightened security. Here in the village, his security hung back a bit.

Indi gazed at the quaint shops lining both sides of the street.

"This village is so cute. I want to grab my pad and pencil to sketch out the scenes."

Her enjoyment of the village pleased him. He pointed to a shop on the street corner. "See that place? They bake the most amazing cinnamon rolls with a buttery frosting. It practically melts in your mouth." He moved his finger to the left. "And over there is a bookstore with every genre imaginable. There are so many bookshelves that it's like making your way through a maze." He continued to provide details about the many store-fronts.

"I'm already falling in love with this place." She glanced around the village with big eyes, like those of a child who was set loose in a great big toy store.

They turned a corner. Right across the street was something he knew would spark Indi's interest—an art gallery. He waited for her to spot it.

Indi gasped as she came to a stop. "You have an art gallery, too?"

"We do. Would you like to have a look?"

"I definitely would." She hesitated. "But we have plans for dinner."

"Plans are made to be changed." He wasn't in any hurry to see the evening end—even if his father wanted to have a meeting about new responsibilities that were being transferred to him. All that could wait. Right now, he was more interested in getting to know Indi. He wanted to know everything about her.

She turned to him. "You'd really do that?"

"I would. Let's go."

"As tempting as that is, I'm afraid that if I go in there, we'll miss dinner completely."

"No problem. I'll just have them prepare some takeaway meals."

Surprise lit up in her eyes. "Are you always this accommodating to your portrait artists?"

He let out a laugh. "No. Definitely not."

She smiled at him. It was a smile that started on her glossy lips and lifted her cheeks until it reached her eyes and made them sparkle like fine gems. It swept his breath away. And for a moment, his gaze dipped back down to her mouth. He wondered what she would do if he were to lean over and press his lips to hers.

He had gone into this arrangement intent on keeping things businesslike, but now he was wondering if that had been an error on his part. It had been so long since he'd enjoyed someone's company this much. Perhaps they could mix a little business with a whole lot of pleasure. Oh, yes, that sounded perfect.

He started to lean toward her.

"Istvan, look at that!" Her excitement drew him from his thoughts.

He immediately straightened and gave himself a mental shake. What was he doing? Indi didn't strike him as the casual-relationship type. If she were, it would have happened by now. And he didn't want to do anything that would end up hurting Indi. She was too kind, and in her eyes he saw pain. Someone had hurt her in the past, and he didn't want to do anything to add to that.

He looked to the left and spotted what had gotten Indi so excited. Moving slowly up the road was a horse and wagon. It wasn't an uncommon sight.

"Some of the local farmers believe in doing things the old way." Much like his father believed change had no place in Rydiania. "They bring their goods into the village in their wagons."

"I love it." She retrieved her phone and snapped some photos.

While she watched the chestnut mare, Istvan watched her. He had a feeling his life was going to be a lot emptier when she left next week.

"Istvan?" Indi sent him a puzzled look. "Did you hear me?"

"Sorry. I was just thinking about—" he hastily grabbed the first excuse that came to him "—a meeting I'm supposed to have later this evening."

Her brows drew together. "We don't have to go to dinner if you have someplace else to be."

"Don't you worry. I'm exactly where I want to be." He sent her a reassuring smile. And then he presented his arm to her. "Shall we go have a bite to eat? It's just a little farther."

She hesitated, and then she placed her hand in the crook of his arm. "Let's do it."

"Maybe tomorrow we can come back so you can explore the gallery to your heart's content." And then he recalled that his calendar was busy the rest of the week. "On second thought, we'll have to do it next week. I just recalled that we'll be hosting some important guests the rest of the week."

"Oh. I understand. I could return to Greece if this isn't a good time to work on the portrait?"

"No. Stay. We'll make it work. I just won't be able to make any excursions until after our guests have departed. But then I promise a trip to the gallery."

She turned her head and lifted her chin until their gazes met. "I'd like that."

There was this funny feeling in his chest—something he'd never experienced before. It was a warm sensation that radiated from the center outward. And when she turned away, he wanted to draw her attention back to him. Yet he resisted the urge.

He had to stay focused on the preparation for the transition of power—on establishing his own working relationships with influential businesspeople in Rydiania. His father's health wasn't the best, and they wanted to transfer power while he was still in physically decent shape. To wait until he was frail would put the kingdom in peril. No one wanted that.

But Istvan wasn't anxious for the transition to happen. He had a lot of mixed feelings about it. First, he hated that his father was ill and had to step down. Second, he wasn't sure how he felt about his parents looking over his shoulder while he was on the throne. He knew they wouldn't approve of the changes he wanted to bring to the kingdom—the changes the kingdom needed to see it through another century and beyond.

He halted his thoughts as the restaurant came into sight. A carved red-and-black sign hung above the door.

"L'Artiste Bistro." Her voice held a note of awe. She turned to him. "What's it like?"

He pulled the door open for her. "See for yourself."

She rushed inside to have a look around. Her eyes lit up as she took in all the art, from the mixed-media wall hangings to the busts on pedestals to the plants that were also works of art.

"This place is like a museum." She continued to glance around.

"I thought you would like it. The owner is the sister of the man who owns the art gallery. They decided to combine their talents, and L'Artiste Bistro was born."

"I love it." She smiled brightly.

At that moment, the maître d' spotted them and rushed over to seat them. Instead of requesting his usual table in the back corner of the restaurant, where he was less likely to be spotted by tourists, Istvan decided to sit in the center of the restaurant, where Indi would have a better view of all the art.

After they were seated, she continued to take in the vast amount of artwork. "I feel like I should get up and tour the restaurant."

"Feel free, to but you might want to order first."

She shook her head. "I don't think so."

"Why not?"

"Because…" She glanced around at the other tables. "I don't want to make a scene."

"It's okay. You won't be the first or last to admire the fine artwork."

"Maybe I will after dinner."

As they were handed menus, he realized he was no longer hungry—at least not for food. His gaze strayed over the top of the menu to Indi, who was busy reviewing all the wonderful dishes being offered.

The only thing he desired in that moment was to learn more about the intriguing woman sitting across from him. She was like a real-life work of art, from her silky hair that made his fingers tingle to reach out and comb through her loose curls to her delicate face that he longed to caress. And then there were her lips—*oh, that mouth*. It begged to be kissed. And if there wasn't a table sitting between them, he might have done exactly that.

CHAPTER ELEVEN

THE FOOD WAS DIVINE.

The decor was amazing.

But the company was sublime.

Indigo couldn't believe she admitted that about Istvan. He was supposed to be the enemy, but the more time she spent with him, the more she found herself enjoying their time together.

He was fun. He was thoughtful. And he was compassionate.

How was it possible Istvan was part of a family that could so coldly and meanly disown their own family member, as well as the staff? It baffled her. There was a lot more to Istvan than she'd ever imagined possible.

And there was the fact that he'd brought her here to do his portrait. In his world, she was an unknown artist—an untested talent. And yet he was willing to stand up to his parents and insist on using her services over those of an established artist. It was the biggest compliment anyone had ever paid her.

The evening had gone by far too quickly, and now they were driving back to the palace. She glanced over at Istvan. In the glow of the dash lights, she watched as he skillfully worked the manual transmission as though it were an extension of his body. He maneuvered the sports car easily over the winding road. With great effort, she forced her gaze straight ahead. She didn't want to be caught staring at him.

And then they were pulling into the palace drive. She suppressed a sigh that the evening was over. She wanted to hear more about him, about his travels. Throughout dinner she had been busy answering his questions about her career and how she'd ended up at the Ludus Resort.

At first, she'd been hesitant to tell him too much about herself. She'd thought it would make her feel vulnerable. But Istvan was very laid-back, yet appropriately engaging. He didn't make her feel awkward. Talking to him, well, it was like talking to an old friend.

As the car slowed and they moved toward the back of the palace, she chanced another glance at him. He was a complex man. He was more than a prince, a brother, a dutiful son and an heir to a throne. He was caring and funny. He could even make jokes about himself. Somehow she couldn't imagine his mother laughing at herself—not a chance. She wondered if the king was more like Istvan.

The car pulled to a stop beneath a big tree. "And we're home."

She let out a small laugh.

"What's so funny?"

"You describing this grand palace as a home."

He arched a brow. "Is it not my home?"

"I suppose. But when I think of a home, I think of someplace not so grand and definitely not so large. I mean, you could fit four, no, maybe eight or more of my apartment buildings inside the palace walls."

He shrugged. "I had nothing to do with its construction."

"But you don't mind living there—even though it's more like a museum than a home?"

He was quiet for a moment, as though giving her question due consideration. "I guess it's just what you are used to. I was born and raised here. For a long time, it was all I knew."

"And now that you've been out in the world, if you could

choose something different for yourself, would you?" She knew it was a bold question to ask the crown prince, and maybe she should have refrained from asking it, but she was really curious about his answer.

"I don't know." His voice was so soft that she almost thought she'd dreamed it. But then he shifted in his seat and his gaze met hers. "I don't have the luxury of imagining a different life. My destiny was determined before I was born."

In that moment, she felt sorry for him, which was totally ridiculous. Why should she feel sorry for someone who had every imaginable luxury at his fingertips?

But there was this look in his eyes that tugged at her heartstrings. Before she could decipher its origins, he blinked and the look was gone.

In a soft tone, she said, "It's not fair. You should be able to choose your future."

He took her hand in his own. His thumb stroked the back of her hand, which did the craziest thing to her now-rapid pulse. "You're the first one to say something like that to me."

In that moment, she saw the man behind the title. He seemed so relatable. Because he wasn't the only one living a destiny that had been thrust upon him. She too was fulfilling the destiny left to her by her father—she was taking care of her mother by coming to this country, by facing the very people who had put her family on this painful course in life. But she didn't want to think of that now. It had no place in this magical evening.

As she gazed into Istvan's blue eyes, she was drawn to him. Neither of them had wanted these responsibilities, and yet neither of them could turn their backs on their families. In essence, they were trapped in their roles in life—his preparing to rule a kingdom, and her doing whatever it took to care for her mother.

His gaze dipped to her lips. Her heart *thump-thumped*. His hold on her hand tightened. And then she felt her body leaning toward him.

Between the erratic heartbeats, reality got lost. The reasons that kissing him was a terribly bad idea were lost to her. The only thing she needed to know was what it was like to be in Istvan's embrace—to feel his lips upon hers. The breath lodged in her lungs as anticipation thrummed in her veins.

It felt as though time had slowed down and sped up all at once. One moment she was lounged back in her seat, and the next she was leaning over the center console into his strong, capable arms.

His warm lips pressed to hers. He didn't hesitate to deepen the kiss. His tongue traced her lips before delving past them. A moan emanated from him. It was though he needed this kiss as much as she did.

Her hand landed on his chest. She immediately appreciated the firm muscles beneath her fingertips. *Mighty fine. Mighty fine indeed.*

With the stars twinkling overhead, it was as though they were in their own little world. She didn't want this moment to end. When it did, she knew it would never happen again. And that made her all the more eager to make it last as long as possible. In fact, she wished this kiss would never end.

Her body tingled from head to foot. It'd been a long time since she'd made out in a car. But it wasn't like this could happen in the palace, with so many people around from the staff to the queen hovering about. And definitely no one could know of this very special moment.

This stolen kiss would be both the beginning and the ending. Her heart squeezed with the bittersweetness of the situation. As the kiss deepened, she noticed that he tasted sweet, like the berries and champagne of their dessert. Her hand moved from his chest and wrapped around the back of his neck. Her fingertips combed through his thick hair, and a moan of delight swelled in the back of her throat.

They came from different worlds. He might not have directly banished her father, but assuming the role of crown prince meant he was willing to go along with his family's ruthless behavior.

She pulled back. *What am I doing? Being a traitor to Papa's memory.*

He blinked and looked at her. Confusion reflected in his eyes.

"That shouldn't have happened." She didn't wait for him to say anything as she yanked open the car door. She jumped out. She wasn't even sure she closed the door as she rushed across the parking lot.

"Indi, wait!"

She kept moving. She couldn't face him now. She had no idea what she'd say to him. The kiss had been mind-blowing, but it was so very wrong. As much fun as they undoubtedly could have together, it would lead to nothing but heartache when it was over.

She headed for the back of the palace. She just wanted to go home—her home. Her modest Greek apartment with her comfy bed and pillow, where she could hide away from the world, at least for the night.

But she wasn't afforded that luxury, as she had signed a contract to do this portrait.

She was let into the palace by one of the uniformed guards. Thankfully he recognized her. The last thing she wanted to do was have to explain her reason for being there—or worse, wait for Istvan to get her past security.

She rushed up the back stairway and prayed she wouldn't run into anyone. As luck would have it, when she reached the top of the stairs, she practically ran straight into the queen.

Indigo's heart launched into her throat. With effort, she swallowed. "Excuse me, ma'am. I didn't see you."

The queen's gaze narrowed. "Obviously. Do they not teach you manners where you come from?"

Indigo's shoulders straightened into a firm line. A smart retort teetered on the tip of her tongue. And then an image of her mother in her new apartment came to mind, and she swallowed down her indignation. Her mother had taught her that if she didn't have anything nice to say, sometimes it was best to say nothing at all. Though Indigo didn't necessarily subscribe to that way of thought, in this particular moment it was probably sage advice.

With gritted teeth, she did the slightest of curtsies. "Your Majesty."

The queen studied her as though making her mind up about her. "You know it won't work."

Indigo's heart rate accelerated. Did she know about them kissing? Impossible. They'd been hidden in the shadows of a tree. And somehow she didn't see the queen spending her time spying out windows. But that didn't stop the heat of embarrassment from blooming in her cheeks.

Not sure what the queen was referring to, she said, "Excuse me?"

"Trying to win over my son. You are a nobody—a wannabe. While he is royalty. He is the crown prince, and when he marries, it will be to someone of the finest upbringing with a grand lineage. He will not marry some commoner—some foreigner."

Indigo opened her mouth to protest the part about her being a foreigner. She was very much a Rydianian. But what good would that slight clarification do? And worse, it might make it seem like she was truly interested in Istvan, when nothing could be further from the truth. She pressed her lips together firmly.

Still, Indigo inwardly stewed about being called a foreigner. Both sides of her family had lived in Rydiania for many generations until the queen and king had abruptly forced her family from their home. The thought left a sour taste in the back of her mouth.

"Heed my warning. It's best you leave here. The sooner, the better." Then the queen snorted before lifting her chin and making her way in the opposite direction from Indigo's room.

Indigo's steps were quick and heavy as she made it to her room. How dare that woman look down her nose at her? At least she hadn't abandoned her family or forced them from the only home they'd known, like the royals had done to Istvan's uncle, King Georgios.

When she reached her room, Indigo stepped inside and let the door swing shut with a little more force than normal. In that moment, she didn't care if she made a scene. She was so over dealing with the royals.

If only she was over Istvan, too. The problem was the kiss had awakened a part of her that she hadn't known existed. It was the passionate part of her that was willing to suspend her rational thought in order to appease her desires—and she desired Istvan. A lot.

She flopped down on the huge four-poster bed with a wine-colored comforter and about a hundred different-shaped pillows. Okay, maybe there weren't that many, but there were a lot.

Tap-tap.

"Indi, can we talk?"

Her heart thumped. Her initial instinct was to rush to the door and throw it open. She desperately wanted to see him again. But then what?

Would she throw herself into his arms? Or would she do the queen's bidding and warn him away? She was torn.

Tap-tap.

"Indi, please."

She needed time alone. And so, with great regret, she said, "Go away."

Her breath caught in her throat as she waited and listened. A moment of silence passed, and then the sound of his retreating footsteps could be heard.

What was she going to do? At this particular moment, she had no idea. She'd never expected to feel anything for the prince. And now that his kiss had awakened a bunch of emotions in her, she didn't know how to react.

* * *

What had he been thinking?

The truth was that he hadn't been thinking. Not at all.

He'd been acting out his desires. Ever since he'd spotted Indi at the Ludus Resort, he couldn't help but wonder what it'd be like to hold her in his arms and kiss her. And then once he'd gotten to know her better, his desire only grew.

Istvan sighed. Now that he'd given in to that driving desire, he'd royally messed things up. He clearly recalled the wide-eyed stare she'd given him after she'd pulled away from him. The memory tore at his gut. And then the way she'd fled from the car. She hadn't even stopped to close the door, that's how much she'd wanted to get away from him.

But why? That's the question he could not answer. No other woman had ever reacted that way after he'd kissed her. So what was so different about Indi?

His phone buzzed. He withdrew it from his pocket and found a testy message from the king's private secretary. Istvan was late for his meeting with the king, and his father was not happy.

With a groan of frustration, he made his way downstairs. Thoughts of Indi would have to wait until later. And then he would come up with a plan of how to fix things between them. Because surely there had to be a way to repair the damage that had been done. He just couldn't contemplate losing her friendship. She had brought a light to his life that he hadn't known he was missing. And without her, he feared being plunged back into the darkness.

He came to a stop outside his father's office. He straightened his shirt, leaving the collar unbuttoned. Then he opened the door and stepped into the outer office of the king's secretary, who worked ridiculously long hours, just as his predecessors had done and those before them. The bald gentleman with gold wire-frame glasses glanced up from his computer monitor. The relief immediately showed in his eyes.

He briefly bowed his head. "The king is expecting you."

He scurried to his feet. "Wait here." He disappeared inside the king's inner sanctum only to return a minute later. "The king will see you now."

Istvan was escorted into the king's office. "Your Majesty," the secretary said. "Prince Istvan has arrived."

The king nodded and then with his hand gestured for them to be left alone. The secretary backed out, never turning his back to the royals. And then the door softly snicked shut. They were alone.

"Your Majesty." Istvan bowed to his father as he'd been taught when he wasn't much more than a toddler.

His father was seated behind his desk. There was a mountain of papers on his desk. The king hadn't migrated to computers with the rest of the world and still preferred paper.

"Sit." The king's tone was terse.

Istvan moved to one of the two chairs in front of the large oak desk. He knew he was in trouble, but that didn't bother him nearly as much as having Indi run away from him. He wondered what she was doing right now. So long as she wasn't packing to leave, he had a chance of fixing things. He hoped.

"You seem distracted," his father said. "I take it you've been spending your time with that woman."

"You mean Indigo. And yes, I took her to dinner in the village."

The king's brows rose. "Since when do we entertain the help?"

"She's not the help." The words came out faster than he'd intended. "Indigo is an artist that I've commissioned to do my formal portrait."

The king leaned back in his chair and steepled his fingers. "You've been away from the palace a lot lately. That needs to stop."

Istvan settled back in his chair. He refused to let his father think his disapproving tone or frown bothered him. In truth, Istvan didn't like being at odds with his parents, but they always assumed they were right and their decisions should be followed without question. The older Istvan got, the more their self-righteousness and immediate dismissal of his opinions grated on his nerves.

"I've been very busy on those trips." Istvan struggled to keep his rising temper at bay. "It's not like I was on vacation. I've been drumming up support for the We Care Foundation."

"That needs to stop."

Istvan couldn't believe his ears. "What must stop?"

"You will no longer work on that foundation."

"But I'm the one that founded it." He'd started it after little Jacques, a child from the village, came down with rare disease and his parents struggled to keep their jobs and spend time at the hospital. Istvan had felt the need to do something to help families in similar circumstances.

"Give it to one of your aides. Or better yet, let the staff of the foundation handle it."

Istvan's fingers tightened on the arms of the chair. "That won't be happening."

The king's brows knitted together, creating a formidable line. "You're refusing?"

Istvan sat up straight. "This project is personal to me, and I intend to continue overseeing it. Now, if there's nothing else—"

"There is one other matter. The woman you brought here. She needs to go."

Istvan's anger bubbled to the surface. "The woman has a name. It's Indigo. And she's not leaving until she's fulfilled her contract."

"Istvan, I don't know what's gotten into you, but this is unacceptable. When your king gives you an order, you are to follow it without question."

"When my king's requests are more reasonable, I will take them into consideration." And with that he got to his feet. He gave a brief bow of his head, and then he turned. With his shoulders ramrod straight, he strode to the door.

He couldn't get out of the office fast enough. He was afraid if he stayed he would say something he would regret. And that wouldn't have done his foundation a bit of good. Because whether Istvan liked it or not, the king had the power to shut it down. That thought didn't sit well with Istvan.

When he was young, he'd believed everything he was told—that the king and queen always knew what was best, that the king and queen had been placed at the head of the kingdom by God, and that everyone should follow the direction of the king and queen without question.

But then his beloved uncle, who had been king, stepped down from the throne. Istvan had never understood his uncle's choice to give up the crown. After all, if you were chosen by God for such a mighty position, how could you possibly walk away from it?

And then there were the actions of his father after he'd become the new king. He'd banished his own flesh-and-blood brother from the kingdom. By royal decree, Istvan's uncle could never step foot on Rydianian soil again. And it was not only his uncle but his uncle's Immediate staff. They were all cast out of the realm.

For a six-year-old, it was a lot to take in. Istvan hadn't seen the crown quite the same way after losing his favorite uncle. And when he was forbidden to make contact with Uncle Georgios, Istvan had promised himself that he would track down his uncle as soon as he was old enough to travel alone.

It hadn't been until he was eighteen that he was able to escape his security team and travel to the Ludus Resort, where he was reunited with his uncle and he met his uncle's wife. It had been awkward at first as he'd had many questions for his uncle about the past—a past that his uncle hadn't been so willing to discuss.

The closer Istvan got to assuming the crown, the more he wanted to make changes. He knew his parents would be horrified. In fact, if the king and queen knew he envisioned more of a democracy for the kingdom, they wouldn't step aside and let him take over. Of that he was certain.

And the other thing he was certain of was that Indigo wasn't going anywhere until his portrait was completed. She had a contract, and if it came to it, he intended to enforce it. He just hoped it didn't come to that.

CHAPTER TWELVE

OH, WHAT A KISS.

Indigo yawned again. And again. She'd tossed and turned for a large portion of the night. Even her morning shower hadn't wakened her the way it normally did.

Countless times she'd replayed the kiss with Istvan. And though she wanted to put all the blame on him, she couldn't do it. She'd wanted to kiss him, too. She'd tried to remember who'd made the first move. Or had they moved at the same time?

She supposed it didn't matter now. The kiss was an undeniable thing between them. And she had no idea how to deal with it. Did they talk it out? Did she explain why it couldn't happen again? Or did she pretend it had never happened? Like that was possible.

During the wee hours of the morning, she'd recalled the Ruby Heart and the folklore about how lovers viewing it together would be forever linked or some such thing. Last night, she'd let herself believe some sort of spell had been cast over them and that's why they'd given in to their desires. But in the light of day, she realized how ridiculous it sounded and reminded herself that she didn't believe in folklore or legends.

Showered and dressed, she glanced in the mirror. She'd put on a little more makeup today than she normally would have in order to hide the shadows under her eyes. And there was her hair...should she wear it up? Or down?

This was her third day in Rydiania. It was time to get to work. She glanced at the antique clock. It was seven-thirty. She had to hurry. She wanted to arrive early for the prince's first sitting so she could set up for the portrait. And then she'd have a private word with Istvan about why they needed to pretend the kiss had never happened.

She grabbed her supplies and headed for the door. The problem was that she had no idea where she was headed. She had to stop and ask someone, who had to make an inquiry of someone else, before she was directed to a vast room. The only piece of furniture in the entire room was a single wing-back chair. She couldn't tell if the room was always devoid of furniture or if it had been cleared for the portrait.

The room was too small for a ballroom and yet too large to be a sitting room. But the exterior wall was nothing but big windows. The other three walls were done with white wainscoting on the bottom, while the upper walls were done in a cool brown tone. Sconces were spaced throughout, with various framed nature photos showing the seasons from winter to autumn.

And then she realized where she was—the conservatory. She hadn't immediately recognized it with it being devoid of furnishings. It was such a beautiful room. If this was her home, she'd turn this room into her studio, as it was filled with natural light.

She positioned the chair closer to the windows. She wanted to be able to pick up every nuance of Istvan's handsome face. She knew no matter how long she lived that she would never forget him or the kiss they'd shared. But she couldn't let it distract her. She was here to do a job—a job that would secure her mother's care and independence.

And that was the reason she'd decided to act as though the kiss hadn't happened. It was the only way they were going to move beyond it. She could do this. She could act like that kiss hadn't rocked her world.

"Good morning."

She immediately recognized Istvan's deep voice. She swallowed hard, straightened her shoulders and turned. She forced a smile to her lips. "Morning."

"I stopped by your room and was surprised to find that you were gone already."

"I wanted to get here early and set up. I know you don't have much time, with your guests arriving today. This is a wonderful room to work in. The large windows are perfect. And I hope you don't mind that I moved the chair. I mean, I could put it back, but I thought the lighting was better over here." She pressed her lips together to stop her rambling.

Istvan stepped up to her. "It's fine. Whatever setup you want works for me. But is that really what you have on your mind?"

Her gaze moved to his. Her heart pounded in her chest. *Just pretend the kiss didn't happen.* "I… I think it would be best if we focus on the portrait and nothing else."

Istvan didn't say anything for a moment. "So you just want to act like last night never happened?"

"Yes." She kept her arms at her sides, resisting the urge to wring her hands.

"Are you sure you can resist the temptation?" He arched a dark brow.

What was he trying to say? Did that kiss mean more to him than a passing flirtation? Of course not. After all, he was a prince. And she was, what? An artist. She certainly wasn't fit to be his…what? Girlfriend? Nervous laughter bubbled up inside her. She quickly stifled it.

"I can resist." Two could play at this game. "But can you?"

"I'm not making any promises."

She narrowed her gaze. "If you want me to complete this portrait, you can't be distracting me."

He planted his hands on his trim waist. "Did you just call me a distraction?"

"You know what they say…if the shoe fits."

She couldn't tell if he was flirting with her or just having fun. Perhaps it was a bit of both. Whichever, it was still better than the tension of last night. The flirting she could handle. It was the kissing that totally tripped her up.

He smiled and shook his head. "Are you ready to get started?"

She glanced around at the armchair and her easel. Suddenly this setting just didn't feel right, at least not to get started. "How about I just follow you around today? You know, while you're working or whatever."

"Who am I to argue? I've got a lot to catch up on from when I was on Ludus Island."

"Then lead the way and I shall follow."

He arched a brow. "You're sure about this? Because I have to warn you that it'll get boring."

"Don't worry about me. Just act like I'm not there."

"That would be impossible." He sent her a warm smile that caused a flutter in her chest. "But I shall do my best."

She grabbed her bag with her supplies and slung it over her shoulder. On their way out the door, they passed an older gentleman with white hair. He was dressed in a dark suit, and he had an easel in one hand. Another artist?

Her gaze moved between the two men. They seemed to know each other. Her curiosity was piqued. Was this man her replacement? She hadn't even done her first sketch and she was already being let go.

She recalled the queen's insistence that the palace's artist would do the prince's portrait. Indigo had thought Istvan would stand up to his mother and tell her what he wanted, but it appeared that once more the crown had won out.

Inside, Indigo was totally crushed. She hadn't known until that moment how much she'd been looking forward to completing such an important project. She could hang her entire artistic future on this one assignment. And now it was about to end before it even began.

"Your Highness." The man bowed. When he straightened, he said, "I am here to work on your portrait."

She caught the older man staring at her. Disapproval showed in his eyes as he took in her white-and-yellow summer top paired with jeans. Then he lifted his nose ever so slightly and turned his attention back to the prince.

What was it with this man to turn up his nose to her? Her body stiffened as angry words clogged her throat. She'd had just about enough of everyone in this palace thinking they were better than her. Not even the prince had treated her so disrespectfully.

Although the prince had apparently caved in to his mother's wishes, and now she was out of a job. Her jaw tightened as she resisted throwing accusations at the prince in front of an audience. Why would he continue to string her along?

"I won't be sitting for the portrait today." Istvan's voice drew her attention. "I have business that requires my attention."

The older man momentarily frowned but quickly hid his reaction. "Yes, Your Highness."

After they'd moved some distance down the hallway for some privacy, she stopped walking. "What's going on?"

Istvan paused and turned to her. He wore a sheepish expression. "I may have forgotten to mention that I am having two portraits done."

She frowned at him. "If you no longer wanted my services, all you had to do was say so."

He shook his head. "It isn't that. I still want you to do my portrait."

She crossed her arms. "Why, when you already have the palace's artist doing one?"

He stepped closer to her. She took a step back. He sighed as he raked his fingers through his hair. "You don't understand what it's like with my parents. When they want something, they don't stop until they get it."

"Why keep me here when you know you'll end up using the other portrait?"

"That's not my intention. But in the meantime, it's easier to appease my mother."

Indigo didn't like what she was hearing. Istvan was giving in to his parents. And to her way of thinking, that meant he condoned their decisions. The thought left a bitter taste in the back of her mouth.

If she'd had any second thoughts about abruptly ending their kiss, she no longer did. She couldn't trust Istvan. He was one of them—no matter how much she wished he was different. He was the prince of Rydiania, now and always.

CHAPTER THIRTEEN

A WEEK HAD passed since she'd arrived at the palace. The last several days, the royal family had hosted the country's business leaders, leaving very little time for Indigo to observe the prince.

She'd resorted to taking photos of him. She promised herself that she would delete them as soon as the portrait was complete. She would not keep them and stare at them, wondering what might have been had they met under different circumstances.

And now the moment she'd been dreading had arrived. Dinner with the family.

When Istvan had mentioned it, he'd made it sound so normal. Indigo knew having a meal with his family was anything but normal. Her stomach shivered with nerves.

She wished they could slip away to dine in the village again. The small town was so laid-back and the people so welcoming. It was everything the palace wasn't—warm and inviting. But then again, their dinner in the village had ended with them kissing, so maybe that wasn't such a good idea.

She felt as though she were going to dine with the enemies. How could two people who were so cold as to cast out their own relative, not to mention his loyal staff, have a son who was so friendly and seemingly caring for others?

Indigo sighed as she stared at her selection of dresses. She didn't know which to choose. Istvan had said not to worry, that it was going to be a casual family dinner. She glanced down at her jeans and cotton top. Definitely too casual.

Knock-knock.

"Come in." She expected it to be Istvan checking in on her.

When the door opened, a young maid appeared. Indigo had met her before, but for the life of her, she couldn't remember her name. "Hi."

The young woman smiled. "I am here to see if I can help you prepare for dinner."

"Help me?" she mumbled to herself. Suddenly she worried that she'd totally misunderstood this dinner. Perhaps she needed a few more details. "Uh, come in and close the door."

The young woman did so. "How may I help you?"

It was best to get the awkward part over with first. "I'm so sorry, but I can't recall your name."

"It's Alice, ma'am."

"Please, call me Indigo."

"Yes, ma'am… I mean Indigo. How can I help you?"

"I'm not sure what to wear to dinner. The prince said it will be casual, but I'm not sure which dress to wear." She held out her top two choices from the wardrobe. One was a white summer dress and the other was a little black dress that could be accessorized to make it fancier.

The maid eyed both choices. Her expression was devoid of emotion, leaving Indigo at a loss as to what Alice was thinking.

"May I suggest something else?" Alice asked.

Indigo could use all the help she could get so she didn't embarrass herself in front of the royal family. Not that she was trying to impress them, because what they thought didn't mean a thing to her. But what Istvan thought was starting to matter to her. She didn't want to do anything to ruin this evening for him.

"Yes, please." She couldn't help but wonder what Alice had in mind.

"I'll be right back." Alice disappeared out the door.

Indigo hung up the dresses. She felt so out of place here, where casual wasn't even casual. She wondered if it was too late to plead a headache again. At this rate, it wouldn't be a lie.

This was not going to go well.

Istvan had had a sinking feeling in his gut ever since his mother had insisted on a family dinner that evening—including Indi. He'd warned his mother to be on her best behavior where Indi was concerned. His mother didn't take well to warnings, but he wasn't about to have her drive Indi away.

When the king had overheard the conversation, he'd told Istvan that he was overreacting. After all, it was a family dinner, not an inquisition. Istvan wished he had a normal family and not one that was constantly worried about protecting their public image.

Istvan stepped in front of the mirror to check his tie. He adjusted it just a little. Then he buttoned the top button on his suit jacket and headed for the door. He hoped Indigo was ready. Being late to dinner wouldn't go over well with his very punctual parents. Though his youngest sister was notorious for being late.

He wanted this first meal with his family and Indigo to go well. As much as he didn't want to admit that his parents' opinions mattered to him, they still did. And if they just gave Indigo a chance, he was certain they would see there was something special about her.

He made his way to Indi's door and knocked.

"Come in."

He opened the door and stepped inside. When he caught sight of Indi, her back was to him. It appeared she was struggling with the zipper on her dress.

He paused to take in her beauty—some of her hair was pulled up and held with sparkly pins while the rest fell past her shoulders in long, elegant curls.

"You're just in time. I need help with this zipper."

His gaze lowered to the smooth skin of her back. His pulse picked up. He moved across the room. He reached for the zipper and gave it a tug. It didn't move.

"I think it's caught on some material."

Before he could work on loosening the zipper, she spun around. Her eyes were wide with surprise. "I thought you were Alice."

"Sorry to surprise you." He waited, wondering if she would send him away.

Her gaze moved to the closed doorway and then back to him. "I don't want to be late for dinner." She turned back around. "Do you think you can fix the zipper?"

"I can try." He had to admit that most of his experience was with lowering zippers, not pulling them up.

When his fingertips brushed over her smooth skin, it sent his heart racing. He tugged at the zipper. It refused to move.

His gaze strayed to the nape of her neck. If he were to lean forward and press his lips to that one particular spot, he wondered what sort of response it would elicit from her. The idea was so tempting that he couldn't resist. He leaned closer.

"Is it broken?" Indigo spun around.

His face was only a couple of centimeters from hers. The breath hitched in his throat. His gaze caught and held hers. He noticed how she didn't back away. In fact, she didn't move as she continued to stare at him with desire evident in her eyes.

His gaze dipped to her glossy lips. They were oh, so tempting. And then his vision lowered to the place on her neck that pulsated. That was where he would start. *Oh, yes.*

His hands reached out, gripping her rounded hips. He lowered his head slowly. She didn't move. He inhaled the sweet scent of primrose that reminded him of a cool spring evening with a bit of tangy, fruity sort of twist that was mingled with the hint of vanilla. Mmm...what a heady combination.

When his lips touched her smooth skin, he heard a distinct

hiss as she sucked in air. Her pulse beat wildly under his lips. Her heart wasn't the only one beating wildly.

He began kissing his way up her neck to her jaw. It was slow and deliciously agonizing. He couldn't wait to pull her close and claim her lips beneath his. And if that little moan he heard in Indi's throat was any indication, she was enjoying this moment as much as he was.

Knock-knock.

He heard the click of the doorknob and the slight squeak of the door hinge. A gasp sounded behind him.

With the greatest regret, Istvan pulled away from Indi. As he drew in a deep, calming breath, his gaze strayed across her mouth. Frustration knotted up his gut.

With great restraint, he placed a pleasant look on his face and turned to find the maid with pink-stained cheeks.

"I'm so sorry," Alice said. "I should go."

"No. Please stay," Indigo said. All the while she avoided looking at Istvan. "The zipper on my dress is stuck and, um... the prince was trying to free it, but it won't budge."

So that's what he was doing? He smiled. Just then Indigo's gaze met his, and he let out a laugh. She might be ready to deny the chemistry sizzling between them, but he knew the truth. And this wasn't the end. It was merely a pause—to be continued later.

Had that really happened?

Had she been kissed by the prince? Again?

Indigo's heart raced every time she recalled his hot breath on her neck and the delicious sensations he'd sent cascading throughout her body. If they hadn't been interrupted, she wondered just how far things would have gone.

When his lips had pressed to her skin, reality had spiraled out of reach. All she could think about was how amazing he'd made her feel and how much she wanted more—so much more.

But that couldn't happen. His future was here in Rydiania,

and she shouldn't be here. The truth was they were never, ever supposed to mean anything to each other.

Going forward, she couldn't let her guard down around him. The prince didn't seem to mind playing with fire, but she for one didn't intend to get burned. She'd already lost enough in this lifetime. She wasn't about to lose any more—including her heart.

With her zipper fixed, she was ready for dinner. She stepped out into the hallway, where Istvan was waiting for her. This was the first time she was able to take in his appearance, in a navy-blue suit and white dress shirt with a boring blue tie. Her imagination stripped away the proper shirt and tie to reveal his tanned chest. As soon as the thought came to her, she halted it.

Her mouth grew dry, and she swallowed hard. "I'm ready... I think."

He sent her a slow smile that lifted his mouth ever so slightly at the corners. "Don't worry. This is just a casual family dinner. And if you need further assistance with your zipper, I'm available."

"Istvan, stop." Heat flamed in her cheeks.

"I'm just offering to help."

"Thanks, but no. You've helped quite enough. The whole palace staff is going to think we're having some wild affair."

He gazed into her eyes. "And would that be so bad?"

"No. I mean, yes." She exhaled a frustrated sigh. It was best to change the subject. "You said this dinner was to be casual, but my understanding of casual doesn't include formal attire."

"Ah...but see, that's where you're wrong. This is formal casual. Formal attire would be a tux and a gown."

"Sorry. I'm not up on my royal fashion trends."

"Then stick with me. I'll show you how it's done." He presented his arm to her.

She hesitated, but at the moment her legs felt a bit wobbly. The last thing she needed to do was to take a tumble down that long flight of stairs. And after all, it was just a hand in the crook of his arm. It wasn't like having his lips pressed to the sensitive part of her neck.

In that moment, her gaze dipped to his mouth—oh, that amazing mouth. She wondered at all the wonderful things he could do with it. Not that she would ever know, but it didn't keep her from wondering.

"That will have to wait until later." His voice drew her from her errant thoughts.

She lifted her gaze to meet his. She'd been busted daydreaming. Heat rushed to her cheeks and made them burn. She should glance away, but she didn't.

She leveled her shoulders and tilted her chin upward ever so slightly. "That will never happen again."

"You said that before, and yet look at what just happened." He led them toward the grand staircase.

"That was your fault."

"I didn't hear any complaints. I wonder what would happen if I were to kiss you right here and now."

She stopped and yanked her hand free. "Don't you dare."

"Oh, but I would dare." His eyes twinkled with mischief.

"If you think I can't resist you just because you're a handsome prince, think again." *Wait.* Did she just admit that she thought he was handsome? Inwardly she cringed, but outwardly she refused to acknowledge her faux pas.

"As much as I'd like to continue this debate with you, we can't be late for dinner."

She was relieved to put an end to this awkward conversation. "Agreed."

"Shall we?" He once more held his arm out to her.

This time she accepted his gesture. She refused to acknowledge the way being so close to him made her heart beat out of control. *Nope. Not going there.*

She couldn't remember where the private dining room was in the palace. There were just so many rooms that it could easily be converted into a high-end hotel. Not that Istvan would ever consider it. Still, it was so big just to be a private residence. She couldn't imagine ever calling this place her home.

As they made their way down the grand staircase, she imagined the foyer filled with formally dressed partygoers. Okay. So living here might have its benefits. The parties must be out of this world. Not that she would ever get to attend one with Istvan.

Her gaze moved to him. Her heart pitter-pattered. He was certainly the sexiest date—*erm, escort*—she'd ever had. And there was a part of her that was really curious to know how far things would have gone if they hadn't been interrupted. She quelled a sigh.

Once on the main floor, he guided her to a hallway that led toward the back of the palace. Their footsteps were muffled by a long red runner. The halls were so wide that it felt strange for her to refer to them as hallways. They were like huge, long rooms with a lot of closed doors to each side. And in between were couches—the kind you'd be afraid to sit on, because they looked like pieces of art. In addition, there were ornate pieces of furniture as well as priceless statues and large ceramic vases.

"Something catch your interest?" he asked.

She shook her head. "I'm just taking it all in."

"There's a lot to take in." That was an understatement.

He stopped in front of a set of double doors and turned to her. "Are you ready for this?"

Her heart started to pound. Her palms grew damp. And her mouth grew dry. This would be her first time meeting the king—the man ultimately responsible for the demise of her father. That thought ignited an old flame of anger. She would not let him intimidate her.

Every muscle in her body tensed as she turned to Istvan. "Let's do this."

He sent her a reassuring smile. "Let's."

Istvan grabbed both of the gold door handles. He swung both of the doors wide-open. Her heart leaped into her throat. She felt as though she were walking into the lion's den.

On wooden legs, she passed by Istvan and entered the room. She was pretty certain she was supposed to follow him, with him being a prince, but, ever the gentleman, he let her go first. Although she wasn't sure he'd done her any favors as every head turned in her direction.

Silence fell over the room. Her fingernails dug into her palms. *You can do this. You can do this.* She continued to repeat the mantra.

The king looked like an older version of Istvan, with gray temples and a close-trimmed beard that was peppered with gray. The man didn't smile. His gaze seemed to study her. All the while her insides shivered with nerves. What was he thinking? Did he see a resemblance to her father? Impossible. Everyone said she favored her mother.

"Father," Istvan said, "this is Indigo. She's a remarkable artist, and I've invited her to the palace to do my portrait."

The king's intense gaze never moved from her, though when he spoke it was in reply to his son. "I'm not used to you bringing the hired help to the dinner table."

"Indigo isn't hired help. She's a talented artist and my friend."

Indigo's back teeth ground together. Would it be wrong to tell the king what she thought of him? Probably. And it would definitely have her out of a job. The thought of what this job meant to her mother's quality of life was the only thing that kept her quiet.

She continued to hold the king's gaze. If he thought she was going to glance away or bow, he had another thought coming. There was only so far she would go to keep this job.

"Welcome." The king's voice lacked any warmth.

She couldn't tell if he was always cold or if it was just her presence that brought out his frosty side. "Your Majesty."

"Let's get you seated," Istvan said.

When her gaze surveyed the table, she found two available seats. They were not side by side, like she'd been hoping. Instead they were at opposite ends of the table. One was by the king. The other was next to the queen. Indigo groaned inwardly. Why exactly had she agreed to this dinner?

"She can sit down here," the queen said.

And so the decision was taken out of her hands. All the while the three princesses watched the scene unfold. Whatever their thoughts about the situation, they weren't revealed on their faces. Indigo wondered if that blank stare was something taught or if it was inherited.

Her stomach was tied in a knot as she took a seat to the queen's left while Istvan took a seat to the king's left. At least she could glance in Istvan's direction now and then. But the table was so long that trying to make any conversation with him was nearly impossible unless she wanted to yell.

The meal was slow, and the timings appeared to depend on when the king finished each course. When he was done, the table was cleared, whether others were done or not. Indigo didn't figure this out until the third course. Needless to say, she didn't finish the first two courses.

Conversation was sparse around the table. She wondered if the silence was due to her presence or if it was always this quiet.

At last, the queen asked, "So how exactly did you present yourself to my son?"

Was the queen even speaking normal English? "I didn't *present* myself to him." Was it so beyond the queen's thinking to imagine her son might seek out female company all on his own? "He stopped by my umbrella for a sketch."

Twin lines formed between the queen's brows. "An umbrella?"

Indigo went on to explain her position at the Ludus Resort. The queen listened, as did the princesses, but the men were involved in their own conversation. Each time she glanced in Istvan's direction, he appeared absorbed in his discussion with his father.

"My son wanted you to draw a cartoon of him?" Disapproval rang out in the queen's tone.

"It's a caricature. And it's not exactly a cartoon. It's an exaggerated drawing."

"I don't understand why he'd want you to do his portrait. This portrait is very important. It can't be a cartoon. Thank goodness I've had the forethought to schedule the palace's portrait artist."

Indigo's pride bristled at the queen's disdain over her artistic skills—skills the woman hadn't even witnessed. "I've studied art my whole life. I grew up with a paintbrush in my hand. I am capable of much more than caricatures."

"So your family is in Greece?" the queen asked, dismissing what Indigo had just said.

"Yes. My mother is there."

"It's just the two of you?" When Indigo nodded, the queen said, "Then you must be anxious to return."

"Actually, I am. I have…" She hesitated. She didn't want to share her gallery showing with the queen just to have her make a snide comment about it. "…a job to return to."

"I understand. That sounds important. I'll see that you are on the next flight back to Greece."

Wow! Talk about a bold brush-off. But the queen wasn't the first difficult person she'd had to deal with. And she wasn't going to be rushed off. Not a chance.

"Thank you, but my job here isn't complete yet." She placed her fork on the table. Her appetite was long gone. "Please excuse me. I have some phone calls to make."

There was a gasp from one of the princesses as Indigo got to her feet. With her head held high, she moved toward the door, skirting around the waitstaff as they carried in the main course. She didn't dare look at Istvan. She didn't want to see the disapproval on his face. He should just be happy that she hadn't said what she was really thinking.

She kept putting one foot in front of the other. This assignment wouldn't be over soon enough. She couldn't wait to get out of this kingdom—away from these people.

She was almost to the stairs when she heard her name being

called out. It was Istvan's voice. She didn't slow down. She didn't want to talk to him right now.

He must have jogged to catch up with her, because the next thing she knew, his hand was on her arm. "Indi, wait."

She stopped at the bottom of the steps and turned to him. "I know you want me to apologize, but I'm not sorry. Your mother... She's..." She groaned in frustration.

"I know. And I'm the one who's sorry. I thought my parents would act better than that." He rubbed his neck. "I didn't mean to make you so uncomfortable. Let me make it up to you."

She shook her head. "I'm just going to call it a night."

"But you haven't had much to eat."

"I'm not hungry. Good night."

She continued up the steps. She could feel Istvan's gaze upon her, but he let her go. She wasn't good company tonight. She needed to call home and remind herself why she was staying here when all she wanted to do was leave.

CHAPTER FOURTEEN

THINGS WERE NOT going well.

Sure, his meetings that morning had been productive. And he was starting to catch up on the work that had piled up while he'd been away on Ludus Island, but it was Indi that had him worried.

Ever since she'd found out that he was having two portraits done, she had been unusually quiet and her sunny smile was missing. It was though a big, dark cloud was hovering over them. And last night's disaster of a dinner hadn't helped matters.

He was quickly finding that he never quite knew where he stood with Indi. One moment everything was fine. They would be laughing and talking. The next moment she was looking at him like he was the enemy. He just wanted to find some common ground where they could begin to trust each other.

As his meeting with his secretary about next month's calendar concluded, he could see that Indi was utterly bored. He'd even caught her hiding a yawn not once but twice. It was time for a new plan.

"I'm sorry that took so long," he said.

She waved off his comment. "No problem. I got a lot done."

He'd seen her pencil move over her sketch pad throughout

his meetings. He was very curious to see what she'd been up to. "May I see?"

She clutched her sketch pad to her chest. "No one sees a work in progress."

"But that isn't even the portrait."

"It's the groundwork. You'll have to use some patience."

Throughout his meetings, he'd been distracted by Indi's presence. He'd worked hard to hide his interest in her, but he couldn't hide it from himself. He became quite impatient—to make her smile, to hear her laughter, to feel her lips pressed to his. He jerked his errant thoughts to a complete halt.

What was he doing? There had never been anyone in his life who could utterly distract him. And yet somehow Indi had gotten past his carefully laid defenses to make him care about her. The revelation stilled the air in his lungs.

That wasn't possible. He was just overthinking things. He had to be careful, because with him being the crown prince, he didn't have the liberty to get involved with just anyone. When he got serious about a woman, she had to be the right woman. How many times had his parents told him that?

His future queen had to come with the right background. She had to be perfectly cultured, beautiful and submissive to the authority of the crown.

Though Indi was the most beautiful woman he'd ever known, she was most definitely not submissive—far from it. She had a mind of her own, and she wasn't afraid to speak her opinion— though she did pick and choose the times she shared what she was thinking.

Enough. He needed a distraction. In fact, perhaps it was time for them to go to lunch. He was thinking of heading into the village and perhaps taking time for a visit to the art gallery. He was certain that would return the smile to her face. He grabbed his phone and texted his secretary to arrange a showing at the gallery that afternoon.

Even if they couldn't have anything more between them

than what they had today, it didn't mean they couldn't be good friends—genuine friends. He had enough people in his life that told him what they thought he wanted to hear. Indi didn't do that. She told him the truth whether he liked it or not. He needed her in his life. She grounded him.

With the meeting concluded, he checked his phone and found the answer he wanted from the gallery. He got to his feet and rounded the desk. "I have to meet someone in the village. Would you care to join me?"

Her eyes lit up for the first time that day. "I would like that. Would you mind if I made a detour to the art gallery?"

"Not at all. I actually had that in mind, too." He smiled at her.

She didn't smile back. "Let me just grab my purse from my room."

"I'll meet you out on the drive."

And then she was gone. She might not have smiled yet, but he was certain she wouldn't be able to refrain when they got to the gallery. He grabbed his phone and made a call to confirm that they were on their way. Hopefully it'd get him back on Indi's good side.

Excitement flooded her veins.

This village was where she was born—where her father and mother were born. She never thought she would see this place in person. And now she was here walking through her past—a past she'd been too young to remember.

Still, she felt as though she were at last at home. She knew that wasn't the case, but it just felt like...well, like she belonged. And she would have if it hadn't been for Istvan's family. She'd still have her father, and perhaps her mother's health wouldn't have failed.

She gave herself a mental shake. Instead she focused on her memories. After they'd moved to Greece, her father used to tell her about the village. She strove to recall those stories.

Her father would talk about a fountain in a small square.

She wondered if she could find it. "I love the village. Are there any piazzas?"

"There's a town square not far from here."

Excitement pumped through her veins. "Does it by chance have a fountain?"

"It does. Would you like to see it?"

She nodded. "I would. I love exploring old towns."

In a few minutes they were in the old town square. There were a few two-story buildings on each side. They were all colorfully painted. And the second stories had small balconies. She couldn't help but wonder if these were the original colors. If so, she might be able to find the exact building where she was born.

"I just love the colors. Were they always this color?" She tried to sound casual as her gaze took in the older buildings that held so much character.

"I think so. At least as far back as I can remember."

This made it easy for her. She moved to stand next to the fountain. Her gaze took in the sidewalk café, the bakery whose buttery scent made her mouth water and the florist with bright, colorful blooms filling the big picture window. And then her gaze landed on an indigo-blue building.

Her gaze lifted to the small white balcony and the windows of the second floor. That had been her parents' home. It was the place where she'd taken her first breath.

A rush of emotion came over her. She blinked repeatedly. She had to keep it together in front of Istvan. She didn't want him to know that this place—this country—meant anything to her. She wouldn't give him or his family that power over her.

"Indi, did you hear me?"

She blinked and turned to him. "What did you say?"

"I asked if you want to have lunch here?"

"Yes. I'd like that."

And so they made their way to the cute outdoor café. She remained quiet as she was overcome by so many emotions from seeing her home to standing next to the sexiest man that she'd ever known. When he looked at her, it was like he could see straight through her. And then there was the way her heart pitter-pattered every time he smiled at her.

As they waited for their meals, she said, "I love it here."

"I do, too. I learn a lot from the villagers."

"What sorts of things do you learn?"

"That the village needs a children's after-school program."

"And is that something you're interested in starting?"

"It is." He toyed with a red swizzle stick resting on the white tablecloth. "I've already set up a children's foundation. It provides free accommodations for the parents of sick children and also provides a modest allowance to help with lost wages while their child is sick."

She was stunned into silence. *Wow!* There really was another side to him. And she was mighty impressed. "Your parents must be so proud of you."

"Not exactly. My parents and I have different views of what my responsibilities should be as the crown prince. They want me to do things the way they've always been done."

"And what do you want to do?"

"I want to change things. I think change is vital to the survival of the royal family. And more importantly, I think change is vital to Rydiania. Without keeping up with the changing times and investing in technology, we will fall very far behind the other European countries."

"And while you are worrying about all that, you're running a foundation to help sick children and their parents?"

He nodded. "A three-year-old from the village became very sick. Treatment was in the city. With the parents being there for their son, they weren't able to keep up with their jobs, and they eventually lost everything. I didn't know about it until after they'd lost their jobs and home."

"Talk about making a tough time even worse."

"Agreed. So the foundation is also promoting job protection while caring for a sick family member, but the king won't make it law, because it will change the way things have always been done. When I am king, it's one of the first things I plan to do, whether my parents agree or not. I guess I'm more like my uncle than anyone ever realized."

And then their food was delivered to the table, which was a shame, because she wanted to know what his last comment meant. She suspected he was referring to the uncle who had abdicated the throne. Was Istvan thinking of abdicating, too?

Just as quick as the ridiculous thought came to her, she dismissed it. First of all, he didn't have a throne to abdicate. He was still the crown prince. And he had all these wonderful plans for the country. A person who was thinking of walking away from the crown wouldn't be making plans.

Still, the more she learned about the prince, the more intrigued she became. Something told her if it was up to him, his uncle wouldn't have been cast out of kingdom, along with his most trusted staff and their families.

CHAPTER FIFTEEN

Lunch for two at an outdoor café.

The delicious meal had done the trick.

When Indigo smiled, Istvan relaxed. At last things between them were good once more. And he wanted it to stay that way. They only had four days left together. It didn't seem nearly long enough.

With the bill paid, they headed on their way. He made a quick stop by the bank to discuss some foundation business. Indigo opted to wait outside. She seemed to have fallen in love with the village. He had to admit that it was quaint but held its own unique charms.

His business didn't take long. When he exited the bank, he found Indigo sitting on a nearby bench. She had a book in her hands and was so captivated by the words on the page that she didn't hear him approach.

He cleared his throat. When she glanced up at him, she had a distant look in her eyes. He smiled. "Did you find something interesting?"

"I did." She gathered her things and stood. She turned the cover of the book so he could read it. "I've been reading about the history of this village. It has quite an illustrious history, from wars to royalty."

"So you like it here?"

"If you mean this village, I love it."

"Me, too."

He'd never felt such a closeness with anyone—even when Indi was miffed with him. But he had a surprise for her that he was hoping would make up for the earlier upset.

"Are you ready for your gallery tour?" he asked as they began to walk.

"I am." She smiled brightly at him.

They walked in a peaceful silence. Each of them was lost in their own thoughts. He was thinking about how much it had bothered him when Indigo believed he'd broken his word to her. He'd felt horrible about the misunderstanding.

And if he had been that bothered by her being upset with him, how was he going to cope when she flew back to Greece on Friday? He wanted to ask her to stay longer, but how long would be enough?

His thoughts halted when they reached the big white building that was home to the Belle Galleria. "We have arrived."

"I can't wait." A bright smile lit up her face. Then her gaze moved to the glass door, and the smile slipped from her face.

"What's wrong?"

"The gallery's closed today."

"Don't worry. We're having a private showing."

Her eyes widened. "You arranged this?"

He nodded. "I did. I know how important it is to you."

"Thank you. But you shouldn't have." Her gaze lowered. "I feel awful that people had to come in on their day off."

He could tell she wasn't used to people making a fuss over her. "It's all right. I made sure they were adequately compensated."

Just then someone approached the doors. They unlocked them and pushed them open. As Indi stepped inside, he thought of the other surprise he had in store for her.

The gallery was painted white with a slate-gray floor. The

walls were covered in canvases, while vitrines were strategically placed throughout the large room. Within the lighted glass
cases were smaller artistic pieces. Some were pieces of jewelry,
and others were delicate structures constructed of wire or wood.

Istvan had visited the gallery many times. He found it peaceful and relaxing. And so he followed Indi around, letting her
set the pace. She was unusually quiet as she took time to study
each piece of work. He wanted to know what she was thinking,
but he didn't want to interrupt her process. He was content just
to watch her quietly.

Every now and then she'd make a comment. He listened and
observed. By touring the gallery with Indi, he was able to see
the art with a totally new appreciation.

And then she came to a stop. He almost ran into her.

She gasped. "It's mine."

He didn't have to look to know what she'd stumbled across.
This was his other surprise. "I wanted to share your caricature
with others."

Her eyes were filled with confusion. "I thought you wanted
to auction it off."

"Ah…yes. I still plan to do that with the second sketch. But
this is the first sketch you did for me. After I had it framed, I
decided to loan it to the gallery."

"So it's not for sale?"

He shook his head. "Definitely not."

"Oh."

"Not everything in the gallery is for sale."

"How do you know the difference?"

He motioned for her to follow him back to the prior room.
He approached a portrait of a lush, colorful garden with a dog
hiding in a bush. Then he pointed to the bottom right corner of
the frame. "See this red tag?" When she nodded, he said, "This
means the piece is still available for sale."

"I understand."

"For the most part, they have the sale items together and the nonsale items in a different room."

"You seem to know a lot about the gallery."

He nodded. "I've known the owners for years. They're the reason I started the We Care Foundation."

"I don't understand."

And so he told her of Jacques and his health problems. "He was the three-year-old I mentioned earlier. His parents lost their jobs because they were caring for their son. I'd known them previously from the village and wanted to help. When they said they wanted to start their own business, I was all for it."

"So you started this art gallery for them."

He shook his head. "Definitely not. I wouldn't have had a clue of how to go about it. I just made start-up funds available to them so they could make their dreams come true. They've since paid back the loan. And now my foundation makes similar loans to other struggling families."

"That's fascinating. You're doing such amazing work that helps so many people."

"My family thinks my sole focus should be on preparations for becoming king one day."

"But you're doing that by caring for the citizens. I would think that's what a good king would want to do."

He shrugged. "When my uncle abdicated the throne, the whole country experienced unrest, from riots to staging a plot to steal the throne. I was very young then, but I remember the fear that rippled through the palace. I'd never seen my parents so scared before. At one point, we were driven from the palace in the dead of night because of security issues. We went into hiding in the countryside. My mother changed after that. She became a lot more serious, and her thoughts are always about protecting the crown."

"I didn't know that."

"Why would you?"

She was quiet for a moment. And he sensed there was something she was keeping from him.

When she didn't answer, he asked again, "Why would you know that? You're from Greece."

"I didn't see any reference to the unrest in the history book I just bought," she improvised.

He nodded in understanding. "I'm sure it's in there. You just haven't gotten to it yet."

"Your Highness, I was hoping to catch you before you left." An older woman with short dark hair and a smile that warmed her face approached them. She bowed to the prince.

"Esme, it's so good to see you." Istvan stepped forward and gave the woman a quick embrace. When he stepped back, he asked, "How is Georges?"

"He is doing good. He's at home today. He's remodeling the house. He keeps telling me it's almost done, and then he finds something else to work on." She shook her head. "As long as he's happy, I suppose I can put up with the mess. At least for a little longer."

"And how is Jacques?"

Her smile broadened. "He got a clean bill of health at his last appointment. He's growing up so quickly. He'll be sorry he didn't get to see you today, but he is helping his papa." Esme's attention turned to Indigo. "And who do we have here?"

"Esme, I'd like you to meet Indigo." His attention turned to Indi, who was wearing a friendly smile. "Indigo, I'd like you to meet the owner of this gallery, Esme Durand."

The two women greeted each other, and when Indi stuck out her hand for a handshake, Esme did what she always did—she pulled her into a hug.

When Esme pulled back, she said, "I knew when Istvan brought that sketch to the gallery that there was more to it than liking the piece of art, which, by the way, is excellent. You wouldn't believe how many offers I've had to buy it."

Color flooded Indi's cheeks. "Thank you."

Istvan nodded in agreement. "I am so impressed with her work that I've hired her to do my formal portrait."

Esme's brows rose. "That's quite an honor." Her gaze moved between the two of them. "You make such a cute couple."

"Oh, but we're not," Indi said.

"You're not a couple?" Esme looked confused.

"We're friends," Istvan offered. Though he couldn't help but think of the legend of the Ruby Heart. Were they destined to be together?

As soon as the outlandish thought came to him, he dismissed it. There wasn't a chance. Indi didn't even want to admit that the kiss they'd shared was more than a spur-of-the-moment action. But he remembered how her body had trembled with desire when he'd kissed her neck.

Ding.

His phone interrupted his errant thoughts. "I need to check this." He withdrew his phone from his pocket and read the screen. "I have a meeting at three. I'm sorry, but we need to be going."

Indi nodded. "Of course." She turned back to Esme. "Thank you for opening the gallery for us. I really enjoyed getting to stroll through it. Your pieces are beautiful."

"I hope you'll come back and bring some of your own artwork. I'd love to display it for you." Esme hugged Indi again.

As they walked away, he said, "I hope you're not upset with me for lending them my sketch."

She shook her head. "Not at all. I'm just surprised you think it's good enough to display for the public."

As they walked toward the exit, he said, "I think you are wildly talented and you are about to impress the art world with your talent."

Pink stained her cheeks. "You don't have to say that."

"I know. I said it because I meant it."

Once out on the sidewalk, he turned toward the palace, and she said, "We're walking back?"

"Is that a problem?"

"No. Uh… I just thought you were in a hurry."

"Why waste a summer afternoon? There's time to walk. And between you and me, if I'm a few minutes late for the meeting, they'll wait."

"I suppose you're right. After all, you are the crown prince." She didn't smile.

He felt as though that had come out all wrong. "I didn't mean it the way it sounded. I don't throw my position around. I just meant that I won't be more than a couple of minutes late and they would wait."

He hadn't explained that sufficiently. They continued to walk in silence. There was something about Indi that made him feel a little off-kilter. And it felt like there was something she wanted to say, but she was holding back.

They were passing by a small park on the edge of the village. Trees and bushes were strategically placed on the walkways. Sunshine poked through the leafy canopy as a gentle breeze swept past them.

He wanted to make sure things were all right between them before they reached the palace. "Let's stop here."

She glanced over at the quiet park before turning her gaze back to him. "What about your meeting?"

"This is more important."

Worry showed in her eyes. "What is it?"

He guided her to a park bench. They sat down and he turned to her. "What's wrong?"

She shrugged. "Nothing."

"That's not true. I've had the feeling something was bothering you all day. What is it?"

"I… I just didn't know that you'd decided to go with the palace's artist."

"And I explained that it's just to pacify my mother. When the formal portrait is decided, it will be yours that I choose."

"You can't say that. You haven't even seen it yet."

"No, I haven't. But I know what you're capable of, and I know you'll breathe life into the painting. You'll give my image a different perspective, and that's what I want people to see—I want them to know that when I'm king, I'll bring about change."

Whimper.

He paused and glanced around. "Did you hear that?"

"Hear what?"

"Shh… Listen."

Whimper. Whimper.

Istvan stood and glanced all around. He didn't see an animal anywhere. Could he have imagined it?

Indi stood next to him. She too glanced around.

Not sure if he'd really heard anything, he asked, "You did hear that, didn't you?"

She nodded. "What do you think it is? Are there wild animals around here?"

"There are, but I don't think you have anything to worry about. Whatever it is sounds hurt."

Ding.

When he didn't make any move to grab his phone, Indi asked, "Don't you need to check that?"

He shook his head. "It's just another reminder about the meeting."

She nodded in understanding. "You should get going. You don't want to be late."

He didn't hear any sounds now. And he had no idea where the sound had come from, so he should return to the palace. When he turned to leave, he noticed Indi wasn't beside him. He glanced back. "You're not coming with me?"

She continued to look around. "I think I'll stay here and look for the animal."

"But what if it's a great big bear?" He raised his hands like claws and bared his teeth.

She elbowed him. "You just told me I have nothing to worry about."

Whimper. Whimper.

"There it is again," Indi said. "Can you tell where it came from?"

Istvan was already moving in the direction of the sound. He was headed straight for an overgrown bush near a tree. The closer he got, the louder the whimper became.

He honestly wasn't sure what to expect. He sure didn't want to find a bear cub, as he knew the mama wouldn't be far away. Wildlife abounded around the village and palace with the mountains in the background. But no matter what lay in the bushes, he had to attempt to help it.

Indi moved up beside him.

"What are you doing?" he asked.

"Helping."

"Get back. We don't know what we'll find."

"I'm not going anywhere. You check this side and I'll check the other side."

He watched as she moved around the bush. And then he did the same thing on his side. He stared intently into the shadows between the little leaves, but he couldn't make anything out.

"It's okay," he said in a soft voice. "I'm just going to help you."

"Istvan, over here."

He moved as fast as he could, not knowing if Indi was in trouble or not. When he rounded the giant bush, he found her down on her hands and knees, flashing the light on her phone Into a hole.

"What is it?" he asked.

"A puppy. It's trapped in the hole. Every time it tries to climb out, it falls. We have to help him."

Istvan dropped to his knees. He leaned forward and placed his hand down the hole, but he couldn't reach the puppy, who continued to whimper.

Istvan lay flat on the ground. He gently inserted his arm in the hole. His fingers moved, hoping to feel fur. Still nothing. And then there it was.

He moved his upper body, trying to lower his hand just a little farther. Just enough to wrap his fingers around the puppy's chest. *Just...a...little...farther.*

With a great big sigh, he pulled his arm back. "I can't quite reach him. I was so close."

Frustration knotted up his gut. He rolled over onto his back, expecting to see Indi, but she wasn't there. He sat up and looked around. He spotted her off in the distance.

"What are you doing?" he called out to her.

She rushed back to him with a large, flat rock in her hand. She used it to start dragging the soil away from what must be a rabbit hole, if the bits of fur surrounding the opening were any indication.

He searched around for another rock. With a rock in hand, he joined her. Together they dug at the ground, widening the opening.

He had no idea how much time had passed before he once again lay on his stomach and lowered his arm into the hole. There was no longer any whimpering. He hoped they weren't too late.

He lowered his hand into the hole. He moved slowly, not wanting to hurt the puppy or send it farther down the hole.

And then his fingers once more touched the soft fur. He gently wrapped his fingers around the pup. Very slowly he began to lift.

When the black-and-white puppy was freed, it blinked its blue eyes and stared at him with a sad look. Istvan smiled at him.

Indi ran her fingers over its back. "It's okay, little one. You're safe now." She glanced at Istvan. "What should we do with him?"

"We'll take him home. He needs water, food and a bath."

"Home? As in the palace?" She looked at him with surprise written all over her face.

"Sure. Why not? Let's go. I'll have my secretary notify someone in the village of the hole. It'll need filled in so no other animal falls in it. And I'll have them get out the news about the puppy so the owner will know where to find him."

He was so relieved to have been able to rescue the puppy. He didn't even want to think about what would have happened if he hadn't suggested they stop in the park to talk. And then he realized they hadn't quite finished their conversation.

As they walked quickly toward the palace, he asked, "Are we okay?"

Her gaze met his. "We're good."

"You're sure?"

She smiled at him. "Positive."

He expelled a small sigh of relief. One problem solved—and now another one to contend with. The puppy was docile in his arm. He hoped that wasn't a bad sign.

CHAPTER SIXTEEN

HE'D NEVER HAD a pet in his life.

And suddenly this orphaned puppy was so important to Istvan. Maybe it was because he knew how it felt to lose part of your family. His thoughts briefly strayed to his uncle—the man he'd had a closer bond with than his own father.

Maybe in part it was the fact that he could help the puppy. He could do it himself. He wanted to save the puppy and nurse it back to health. He wanted to feel needed instead of merely being a showpiece of the palace.

They entered the palace through the front door. He wasn't going to waste time walking to the side entrance, which was normal protocol unless they were welcoming guests.

Once in the foyer, Indi asked, "Have you ever had a puppy before?"

"No. But I'm sure I can figure it out." He noticed her lack of agreement. "Maybe you could help me."

She nodded. "I used to have a dog. His name was Charlie. He was big and friendly."

He was relieved to hear that at least one of them would know what they were doing. He took the stairs two at a time until he realized Indi was having problems keeping up with him. He slowed down for her. When he stopped in front of his suite,

Indi rushed to open the door for him. Once they were inside, she pushed the door shut.

"He needs water." Indi turned in a circle, searching the spacious room for something to use as a water bowl.

Istvan moved to the seating area and grabbed a dish from the end table. He handed it to her. "This should do."

Indi gaped at him and then looked at the dish. "But this is an antique."

"It's a bowl." He didn't care how old the dish was as long as it held water. "You can get water in the bathroom."

She moved toward the bathroom and soon returned with a bowl of water. She set the bowl on the floor as he placed the puppy near it. When the creature didn't move to drink, Indi dipped her finger in the water and then dabbed his nose. His pink tongue came out and licked his nose. She did it again. And soon the puppy was drinking out of the bowl—in between dribbling water everywhere.

"I'll start the bath." She started toward the bathroom. At the doorway, she paused and turned back to him. "Do you think there's some baby shampoo in the palace?"

"I don't know, but I can find out."

"What about food?"

"I'll have someone get us some puppy basics from the village."

Indi nodded in agreement before slipping into the bathroom. He placed a call to his secretary, requesting baby shampoo as well as other puppy supplies.

A couple of minutes after ending the call, there was a knock at the door. *That was really fast.*

"Come in." Istvan really didn't want to deal with another visitor. He had more important things to do. He picked up the puppy and held it close to his chest, oblivious to the dirt on its coat.

The door opened, and Gisella stepped into the room. Upon spotting the puppy, her eyes widened. "So it's true."

"If you're referring to this—" he gestured toward the dog "—then yes, I have a puppy."

His sister crossed her arms as she stared across the room. "You know Mother won't approve."

"I know." And that wasn't going to change his mind. The only way he was giving up the little guy was if his owner was located. But he didn't want to think about that now.

"What are you going to do?"

"Keep him."

His sister, being a rule follower, frowned at him. "Why do you always have to cause trouble?"

He was confused. "How is having a dog causing trouble?"

"Isn't it enough that you're the crown prince? You always seem to want more. How much is enough for you?" And with that she spun around and stormed out of the room, almost running into his other sisters.

It appeared news of the puppy had quickly made it around the palace. Beatrix and Cecilia rushed into the room, ignoring him in their excitement to fuss over the puppy, who didn't seem to mind their attention.

"Can I hold him?" Cecilia pleaded with her eyes. "Please."

Istvan shook his head. "He's too dirty."

"I don't mind." She held out her hands for the pup.

He gently handed over the puppy. "Be careful with him."

Cecilia frowned at him. "Of course."

"What are you going to name him?" Beatrix asked.

He kept his attention on the puppy. "I don't know. We haven't discussed it."

"We?" There was a singsong tone to Cecilia's voice.

He ignored his sister's insinuation. "Indi—erm, Indigo was with me when we found him in the park."

"You just happened to be in the park together?" Beatrix looked at him expectantly, like he was going to confide some great love affair.

"It isn't like that," he said.

"Isn't it?" Cecilia asked. "We've all seen the way you look at her."

"Especially Mother and Father," Beatrix interjected. "You have them really worried."

Indi stepped back in the room. "Did I hear someone?" Her gaze landed on his sisters. "Oh, hi."

His sisters greeted her. He didn't want them to say anything further and upset Indi, so he said, "They were just leaving," and gave them a pointed look.

Once they were alone again, Indi said, "The bathtub is ready."

Knock-knock.

This time it was one of the household staff with the requested shampoo.

Istvan lifted the puppy until they were eye to eye. The puppy's blue eyes stared at him, and Istvan felt a protective feeling that he'd never experienced before. "It's okay, little fellow. We're just going to clean you up a bit. And then we'll get you fed."

He lowered the puppy to his chest as he followed Indigo into the bathroom. There were a couple of inches of warm water in the tub, and when he placed the puppy in the water, the puppy wasn't quite sure how to react.

Indi put some baby shampoo on her hands and rubbed them together to suds it up. Then she set to work washing the puppy. "You know, if you plan to keep him around, he's going to need a name."

He definitely wanted to keep the puppy, but he also had to slow down and realize that he might have a home. He might have a family that was frantically searching for him.

"Maybe we should wait on that until we post some notices in the village and see if he has owners that are searching for him."

"But we can't just keep calling him 'the puppy.'"

"Okay, what do you have in mind?"

She studied the puppy for a moment. "It should be something proper, if he's going to be a prince's dog." She paused as though sorting through names in her mind. And then her eyes widened. "I know. You could call him Duke."

Istvan's gaze moved from her to the dog and back again. His parents would have a fit over the name, but that didn't deter him. "I like it." He glanced at the pup. "What do you think, Duke? Do you like your name?"

The puppy just gave him a wide-eyed stare before he stood up and shook, showering them with soap suds. They glanced at each other and laughed.

Since Indi had come into his life, things had been changing. She was showing him that it was all right to go after what he wanted. And as he looked at her, he realized that he wanted her. But he knew it could never work—not with him here in Rydiania and her back in Greece, where her mother lived.

Where were they going?

The following evening as darkness fell over the kingdom, Indigo settled back against the leather seat of Istvan's sport utility vehicle with Duke in her lap. The puppy was in surprisingly good health. Even the veterinarian in the village had been surprised by his appetite and energy. And so far no one had claimed him. They made sure Duke was always with one or both of them, as he wasn't housebroken and they'd already had to clean up a few accidents. And then there was the fact he liked to chew on things—most especially Istvan's shoes. He definitely kept them busy.

But earlier in the day, when Istvan sat for his portrait, Duke had fallen asleep on his lap. While the other artist fussed about the dog's presence being most inappropriate, Indigo thought the scene was precious. And if the portrait hadn't needed to be proper, she would have included Duke. The puppy gave Istvan an authentic quality. And she felt herself falling for both man and dog.

Now all three of them were off on an adventure. She had been surprised when Istvan hadn't opted to take his sports car.

But she supposed if she had an entire fleet of vehicles to choose from, she would mix things up every now and then, too. Though she couldn't imagine having one sports car, much less a selection of top-of-the-line vehicles.

As Duke slept on her lap, her gaze moved to Istvan. She noticed how his long fingers wrapped around the steering wheel. Her gaze followed his muscled arms up to his broad shoulders—shoulders that she longed to lean into as his arms wrapped around her. A dreamy sigh escaped her lips.

"Did you say something?" Istvan's voice interrupted her daydream.

"Um...no." Heat swirled in her chest and rushed to her cheeks. Needing to divert the conversation, she said, "It's a beautiful sunset. With all the oranges, pinks and purples, it makes me long to pull out my paints and put it on canvas."

"Not tonight. I have something else in mind."

"But we already passed the village. Where are we going?" And then she thought about her arrival here and their drive from the airport. "Wait. Are we going into the city?"

"Perhaps. Would you like that?"

She sat up a little straighter. "I would. I mean, while I'm here, I might as well see as much as I can. Where are we having dinner?"

"It's a surprise."

Her thoughts slipped back to her dinner with the royal family. It had been so stressful that she wasn't sure if she'd even eaten, and if she had, she couldn't remember what it tasted like. She could definitely do without a surprise like that one.

Her hand moved over the puppy's soft fur. "Will any of your family be at this dinner?"

"No. Definitely not."

She breathed easier. "That's good."

It wasn't until the words were out of her mouth that she realized her thoughts had translated to her lips. The breath caught in her lungs as she waited for Istvan to respond. She hoped her slip hadn't ruined the whole evening.

"I agree. I'm really sorry about the other night. It won't happen again."

Her pent-up breath whooshed from her lungs. "It's not your fault."

"But they are my family. And if I had known my mother was going to be that way, I never would have agreed to the dinner."

The SUV slowed as it entered the city. Duke stood up on her lap and put his tiny paws on the door so he could peer out the window. The streets were busy, but the prince's escort stayed with them. One vehicle was in front and one in back. Even if they had to run a red light, the caravan stayed together.

"I noticed you're able to move about the village without your escort, but not so much in the city."

"Don't let them fool you. I always have protection. The risk in the city is a lot higher. I can't move about here without bodyguards next to me."

"That must be rough. I can't even imagine what it's like having people watching my every move."

He shrugged. "You'd be surprised what you can get used to. But where we're going, we'll have some privacy."

"That's good, because I doubt many restaurants are going to be happy when we walk in with Duke."

Istvan reached over and petted the puppy. "You never know. He might win them all over."

"You mean like he did with us?"

Istvan smiled. "Exactly."

Woof-woof.

They both laughed at Duke's agreement.

They made their way into the heart of the city. She couldn't help but wonder where the art district might be. She'd love to visit it. But then again, she didn't even know what Istvan had planned for this evening. She just hoped her dress would be appropriate.

She'd chosen one of the dresses that had been delivered to her room the evening before. This time she'd selected a midnight-blue lace minidress. Its stretchy material fit snugly against her hips and waist. Her arms and shoulders were bared by the halter neckline. She'd matched it with her heeled sandals.

"Are you sure you won't tell me what you have planned?" she asked, not that there was anything she could do about her outfit now.

"No. But we're almost there."

The vehicle slowed as the lead car put on its turn signal. They were turning into an underground garage. Interesting.

They parked, and then they stepped into an elevator with two of his security detail. A key-card swipe and a button push had them heading for the top floor. Since she didn't know what kind of building this was, she didn't know what would be up there. She could only assume it was a restaurant with a beautiful view.

The doors whooshed open. They stepped out into a nondescript hallway, and as she glanced around, she noticed there were four doors, numbered one through four. Istvan started for the door with a gold number one on it.

Istvan opened the door and then turned back to her. "Come in."

With Duke in her arms, she passed by him. She got the slightest whiff of his spicy cologne, and for the briefest moment, she considered stopping and leaning in close to him to breathe in that most intoxicating scent, but as quickly as the thought came to her, she dismissed it. She had to keep her wits about her. Letting herself fall for the prince would lead to nothing but heartache.

She didn't know what she expected to find when she stepped through the door. Instead of a sparse modern apartment, she found skylights and greenery. There were plants throughout the large, open room.

She turned back to him as he stood near the now-closed door. "Where are we?"

"This is my new penthouse. I had it completely remodeled."

"It's amazing." Her gaze moved back to the two large couches and handful of comfortable-looking chairs. "It's nothing like the palace."

"No. It's not. And that's the way I like it."

"I didn't know you liked plants this much." Duke began to squirm in her arms.

"I like being outdoors. So I thought I'd bring the outdoors inside."

"Do you mind if I put Duke down to explore?"

"Not at all. I had them stock the apartment with puppy supplies. Where I go, he will go."

She released Duke's leash and then put him on the floor. While the puppy explored, she walked around the room taking in all the details, from the hanging plants to the marble animal statues. Even with so many plants in the room, it still didn't feel crowded. There was plenty of room for a party or just for Istvan to kick back on the couch and enjoy his gigantic television. And off to the side was a modern kitchen that looked as though it had never been used.

In the corner of the kitchen were silver bowls with Duke's name on them. And next to the couch was a box of puppy toys. Indigo smiled. Even when she was gone, she knew Duke would be well cared for and loved. Istvan would see to it.

"How long have you had this place?" She moved toward the wall of windows.

"The remodel was just completed. I've never actually stayed here. In fact, you are my first guest."

She ignored the way her heart fluttered in her chest. She turned to him and found him approaching her. "Thank you for sharing this with me."

"I'm happy to have you here. Please, sit down."

She sat on the couch and found that not only was it nice-looking but it was also comfortable. When Istvan sat in one of the chairs, there was an air of relaxation about him. The worry lines smoothed from his face, and he looked so at home.

She reached into her oversize purse and withdrew a small sketch pad and pencil. She couldn't resist capturing this moment. And though she knew she could easily snap a photo of him on her phone, it just wouldn't be the same.

"What are you doing?" he asked.

She flipped open the sketchbook, and soon she was moving the pencil over the paper in rapid movements. "I just want to capture this moment."

"Wouldn't you rather eat? I have dinner planned for us out on the balcony."

"In just a moment." Luckily, she was quite skilled with sketches, so this wouldn't take long.

She couldn't pass up the peacefulness written all over his face. He never looked like this when they were within the palace walls. This place was good for him. She was glad he'd found a home away from home.

And this sketch was for herself. With only three more days in Rydiania, their time together was drawing to a close. She wanted something to remember him by—the real Istvan, the man who wasn't bothered by getting dirty to save a puppy, who didn't yell when his dress shoes had tiny bite marks.

That wasn't the man she'd expected to find within the palace walls. He also wasn't the man she'd expected to break through the wall around her heart. He was a man of many surprises.

CHAPTER SEVENTEEN

DINNER WAS DELICIOUS.

The company was divine.

And Duke had worn himself out exploring the penthouse and had fallen asleep in his new bed, giving them some alone time.

The meal had been served out on the balcony. Istvan smiled across the candlelit table at Indi. She seemed to enjoy the food, though he noticed she didn't eat it all.

"Was everything to your expectations?" he asked.

"The meal was delicious. There was just so much of it."

She got to her feet, reached for her wineglass and then moved to the edge of the balcony. He joined her there. Quietly they watched as the last lingering rays of the sun sank below the horizon.

She turned to him. "You have such a beautiful view."

He gazed deep into her eyes. "I couldn't agree more." But it wasn't the sunset he had on his mind. He reached out to her. The backs of his fingers brushed over her cheek. "Indi, I—"

"We should go inside." She jumped back as though his touch had shocked her. "It's getting cool out."

Really? Because he thought it was rather warm. But he didn't argue the point as he followed her inside.

Once inside, Indi moved to the sectional sofa with deep

red cushions while he checked on Duke, who lifted his head, yawned and then went back to sleep. Istvan joined Indi on the couch. He still felt as though the disastrous meal with his parents was standing between them, like a wall that he wasn't able to scale.

But he refused to give up the idea of bridging the gap. There had to be something he could say, something he could do, something that would recreate the closeness they'd once shared.

He turned to her. "Indigo, talk to me."

Her gaze met his, but her thoughts were hidden behind a blank stare. "What do you want to talk about?"

He realized that it was up to him to start this conversation. "I'm sorry things haven't gone well with my family."

"Stop apologizing. I don't hold it against you. And, by the way, I really like your sisters."

"You do?" When she nodded, he said, "Gisella can be a little intense."

"That's just because she cares about you."

"So if it's not my family, why do I feel like you keep putting walls between us?"

She turned her head and gazed into his eyes. "Are you happy?"

She was avoiding his questions. He shrugged. "I don't know."

"That's not a very positive response."

He suddenly felt uncomfortable with the direction of this conversation. No one had ever asked him that. "I've never allowed myself to consider the question. My future was mapped out for me even before I was born."

"You don't have to do it. You don't have to become the king— not if it won't make you happy."

He sat up straighter and stared at her. "Are you telling me to walk away from the crown?"

"Of course not. I'm telling you not to make yourself miserable. Find a way to be happy, whether it's here at your penthouse or inside the palace walls. If you aren't happy with your choices, you won't be of any help to those around you."

He'd never thought of it that way. But he did know one thing that made him happy. He gazed at Indi. His gaze dipped to her lips before moving back to her eyes, which reflected her own desire.

"Kissing you would make me happy." He leaned in close to her and claimed her lips with his own. Her kiss was sweet, like the wine they'd been drinking. And it was so much more intoxicating.

He knew this moment—this night—wouldn't be enough time with Indigo. He didn't know how he'd do it, but he wanted to see her after this week. There had to be a way to get her to stay here in Rydiania.

When his arms wrapped around her to draw her close, her hands pressed on his chest. And then, to his great disappointment, she pulled away from him.

"This..." She gestured between the two of them. "It can't happen."

He expelled a frustrated sigh. "There you go again putting up a wall between us. Why do you keep fighting the inevitable?"

"Because your family has a habit of getting rid of the people that don't fall in line with their expectations." She said it so matter-of-factly that it caught him off guard.

"What?" And then he realized what she was referring to. "You mean the way they treated my uncle."

A frown pulled at her face. "It wasn't just your uncle. There were a lot of other people that got hurt when your parents threw them out of the country—expelled them from the only homes they'd ever known."

He was surprised by her level of emotion about something that had happened when they were nothing more than kids. "You must have learned a lot about my uncle while reading that book you bought in the village."

"I didn't learn any of this from a book." Her voice was soft and held a note of...what was it? Was that pain he detected?

As the darkness closed in around them, he longed to be able to look into her eyes. "Indi, tell me what's going on." He reached out, taking her hand in his. "What don't I know?"

Her gaze searched his. "You really don't know, do you?"

"No. Or I wouldn't have asked."

She paused as though gathering her thoughts. "I'm Rydian-ian."

He was confused. "But you're from Greece."

"We moved to Greece when I was very young. But I was born in the village that you love so much."

And suddenly the pieces fell into place. "That's why you wanted to find the village square."

She nodded. "Our home was in the square overlooking the fountain."

"Why didn't you tell me before now?"

"At first I thought you knew exactly who I was from the background check. By the time I realized that you didn't know, we were already here, and I couldn't afford to lose the contract. I'd already spent the money to get my mother into an assisted living unit."

"Whoa! Slow down." He had the feeling he was still missing something big. "Why would I have fired you if I knew you were born here?"

Her gaze lowered. "Because of who my father was."

A cold chill came over him. "Who was your father?"

Her gaze rose to meet his. Unshed tears shimmered in her eyes. "He was King Georgios's private secretary. When your uncle was banished from the kingdom, so was my father. He lost everything."

Istvan got to his feet and moved to the window. He combed his fingers through his hair as he digested this news. Never again would he read just the highlights of a background check.

He suddenly felt like he understood Indi so much better and why she kept putting up barriers between them.

"I'm sorry I didn't tell you sooner." The soft lilt of her voice came from right behind him.

A rush of emotions plowed into him. Anger at her for keeping this from him, anger at himself for not pushing harder when he sensed she was keeping something from him, anger at his parents for wrecking more lives in order to preserve the crown. And then there was sympathy, because he, too, had had his young life turned upside down when his favorite uncle was gone with no explanation and he was forbidden to speak of him.

And then he realized how hard it must have been for Indi to come to Rydiania and then to face the king and queen. He couldn't imagine what that must have been like for her, but he knew what strength it took. He admired her more than he ever had before.

He turned to her. "I'm sorry for what you and your family endured."

The apology was small in light of the magnitude of the damage that had been done. He longed to reach out to her and pull her close, but he hesitated, not wanting her to pull away again.

Her pain-filled gaze met his. "You don't have to apologize. You did nothing wrong. You were just a child at the time."

"Your family moved to Greece?"

Indi nodded. "My mother had some distant relatives there. My father, well, he never liked it there. He was never the same after we left Rydiania. He started to drink. And then one day when I was a teenager..." Her voice trailed away as tears slipped down her cheeks. "I..."

He heard the pain in her voice from dredging up these memories. "It's okay. We don't have to talk about this."

This time he did pull her into his embrace. He wanted to absorb all her pain and agony. In that moment, he would have done anything to make her feel better, but there was nothing he could do but stand there and hold her. He'd never felt so helpless.

Indi pulled back and swiped at her damp cheeks. "I came home and found he'd killed himself." Fresh tears splashed onto her cheeks. When she spoke her voice was rough with emotion. "When he was banished from the palace, from the life of service that had been passed down to him from his parents and grandparents, he lost a piece of himself. He…he was never whole again. It broke my mother to watch the man she loved disintegrate before her eyes, and there was nothing she could do. I can't imagine loving someone that much and then feeling so helpless."

"I'm so sorry."

She gazed at him with bloodshot eyes and tearstained cheeks that tore at his heart. "You lost someone you loved, too."

Even in her moment of great pain, she was able to offer compassion. He was in awe of her. She was the kind of queen Rydiania needed, but now he knew there was absolutely no chance of that ever happening.

He wrapped his arms around her, wanting to protect her from the pain, the horrific memories and even from his parents. They could never find out about Indi's past, because if they did, they'd banish her—the same thing they'd done to her father—in order to keep them apart.

When Indi lifted her head to look at him, he dipped his head to reclaim her lips. Her arms snaked their way around his neck, pulling him closer.

He'd never felt so close to a person. Now that the wall was gone between them, he didn't want to let her go. He wanted to make the most of this night.

This time he was the one to pull back. "Indi, stay here with me."

"You still want me after everything I told you?"

"I do. More than ever. But do you want me?"

She immediately nodded, and desire flared in her eyes. "I do."

He swung her up in his arms and carried her down the hallway to his room. He moved to the king-size bed.

He gazed down at her—wanting her so very much. "Are you sure?"

"I am." She reached out, hooking her fingers through the belt loops on his pants, and pulled him toward her.

Once he was next to her, she pressed her lips to his. This was going to be a night neither of them would ever forget.

CHAPTER EIGHTEEN

THIS PROJECT WAS going better than she'd imagined.

In fact, she was enjoying herself a lot.

Since last night, she couldn't stop smiling. She couldn't prevent what was going to happen in the future, but she could savor each moment she had left with Istvan. Even though it was already Wednesday and her plane was to take off on Friday evening, she intended to make the most of the time they had left.

Istvan had been so sweet and caring after she told him about her past. She had finally decided that he was nothing like his parents, or at least he hadn't given in to those unsavory traits.

When he'd held her and kissed her, he'd revealed to her the vulnerable side of himself. She was glad he had the penthouse, where he could escape and just be himself.

She lifted her gaze from the portrait, where she'd begun to paint his image. She intended to give him an approachable expression—one that hinted at his vulnerabilities but also showed his strength. It would be her greatest piece of work.

Indigo sat on a stool in front of the canvas. She glanced past the easel to Istvan, who sat casually in the armchair next to the window with the sunshine streaming in. He was her favorite subject ever.

Woof-woof.

Duke had decided he'd been held quite enough. He was busy chewing and chasing his toys about the big open floor.

Every time the puppy made a noise, the artist next to her would let out a disgusted sigh. How could anyone dislike a puppy? Especially when one was as cute and loving as Duke.

When they'd arrived at the palace that morning, Istvan's secretary had told him that Duke's owners had been located. The family was honored that their dog's puppy had become part of the royal family. She'd seen the relief in Istvan's eyes when he learned that Duke was officially his, and she'd been happy for both of them.

She continued to work, excited to see the final product, because try as she might, the finished portrait was never exactly how she initially envisioned it. Sometimes it was better, sometimes not. Then her gaze moved to the older man, who frowned as his hand moved rapidly over his canvas. He was very focused. Yet when he found her staring at him, he glanced over at her with a scowl. *Yikes.* Talk about a man feeling insecure about his abilities. If he was comfortable with his skills, he wouldn't care that she was there.

"I need a break." Istvan stood and stretched. "We'll pick this back up this afternoon."

The other artist continued to work while she put down her pencil. She lowered the cloth over the canvas to keep Istvan from sneaking a look. There was nothing about this piece that she was ready to share with anyone.

She glanced over the canvas to see Istvan gesturing to her to join him. She was more than happy to spend some more one-on-one time with him. After their night at his penthouse, she felt closer to him than she had any other man in her life.

"I was thinking we should take Duke for a walk in the garden," he said. "What do you think?"

"I think that would be lovely." Then she lowered her voice. "But what about him?" She gestured over her shoulder to the other artist.

Istvan whispered in her ear, "I think he has plenty to work with."

"Perhaps you're right." As they made their way into the hallway, she asked, "How about we have a picnic lunch in the garden? We can soak up some sunshine while Duke runs around."

"I think it's a great idea. I'll have the kitchen pack up a lunch." He reached for his phone and placed a quick call. When he put his phone in his pocket, he said, "It's all been arranged."

"Thank you." She was tempted to kiss him, but she refrained, as they'd both agreed to avoid any public displays of affection around the palace. Why did life have to be so complicated?

It was a perfect summer afternoon.

But Indigo was what made the day all bright and shiny.

Istvan wasn't ready for this picnic lunch to end. Even Duke had run around and barked so much that he'd worn himself out. He was now stretched out against Istvan's legs taking a puppy nap.

Everything had changed between him and Indi last night. And it was so much more than their lovemaking. They'd learned to trust each other with everything. He'd even dare to say she was the closest friend he'd ever had, but he knew that wasn't a fair assessment, because they were so much more than friends... though he wasn't ready to put a label on it. He just wanted to enjoy it as long as he could.

Ding.

He sighed. "I'm beginning to hate that sound."

"Just change the ringtone." Indi gathered the leftovers.

"No. I mean, I hate that it reminds me that I have obligations when all I want to do is stay here with you." He glanced around to see if anyone was watching. When he didn't see anyone, he gently grabbed her wrist and slowly drew her to him.

"Istvan, what are you doing?" There was a playful smile on her lips. "We agreed on no public displays of affection."

"But there's no one around." He pressed his lips to hers. This was what he would think of on future summer afternoons. Because in this moment with Indi and Duke, life was perfect. He was fulfilled.

Ding.

He groaned as Indi pulled away. She let out a sweet and melodious laugh.

"How can you laugh?" he asked with a frown. "It's not fair that I'm being drawn away from this to go sit in some tedious meeting."

"It's not that bad." She smiled at him as he continued to frown.

"Yes, it is. And it's your fault."

"My fault?" She pressed a hand to her chest.

"Yes. You showed me what I could be doing, and now my business pales in comparison."

She let out another laugh. Her eyes twinkled with happiness. "Well, I'm sorry if I did all that."

"You should be." And then he leaned forward and stole another quick kiss. When he pulled away, he said, "I needed something to tide me over until this evening."

She arched a brow. "Who says you are going to get more of that later?"

He sent her a pouting look. "You wouldn't deny me such pleasure, would you?"

She pursed her lips as though considering his plea. "I suppose not, but we have to go. Now."

With great regret that their leisurely lunch had to end, he helped her collect the remaining things. Then the three of them headed back into the palace. He hoped he didn't have to make any important decisions that afternoon, because his mind would be elsewhere as he counted down the minutes until he could see Indi again. In the meantime, Duke would keep her company.

CHAPTER NINETEEN

HER FEET WEREN'T even touching the floor.

Indigo smiled brightly as they entered the palace. It seemed so dark inside compared to the sunny gardens with their radiant blooms. She'd previously done some sketches and snapped photos of the garden so she could do some paintings when she got home.

Duke wiggled in her arms. Now that he was well-fed, he was a ball of energy. But they'd agreed it was best to carry him through the main parts of the palace where they would likely run into the king or queen.

They'd almost reached the stairs when the queen called out to them. "Can I see you both in the library?"

It wasn't so much a question as an order. Indigo inwardly groaned. The very last thing she wanted to do now was to make nice with the queen. But as Istvan sighed and turned, she did the same.

Once they were inside the library, the queen turned to one of the house staff that had just brought her a cup of tea and said, "Would you leave us? And close the door on the way out."

The older woman quietly nodded and did as she was bidden.

The queen was unusually quiet, and that worried Indigo. She was probably going to complain about Duke running through her flower gardens and trampling a few low-lying stems. As though he sensed he was in trouble, the dog settled in her arms.

The queen looked pointedly at Istvan. "Do you know who this would-be painter is?"

"I know everything I need to know about Indi."

The queen's eyes momentarily widened at his use of the nickname. "I don't think you do, or you wouldn't be rolling around in the garden with her."

Indigo gasped. They had been spied upon. She felt invaded that someone would try to ruin a private moment between her and Istvan.

"We weren't rolling around." Istvan's voice took on an angry tone.

"Regardless, she's been lying about who she is."

"I know who she is," Istvan said calmly.

"No, you don't. Her father was banished from the kingdom."

"I know." Istvan's body tensed as though he were in a struggle with himself to hold back his anger.

This time it was the queen who gasped. "But how could you spend the night with her? You are putting the crown at risk by getting involved with her. You are a prince. She is no one."

Indigo now knew what it felt like to be invisible. But she had something to say. She stepped forward.

"The prince isn't putting anything at risk," Indigo said in a steady voice, though she felt anything but steady on the inside. "We are friends. Your son never led me to believe it would be anything more. And I would never make trouble for him."

The queen gave her a stony look. "If you came here hoping for some sort of revenge—"

"Mother, stop. You are insulting Indigo and making yourself look petty in the process."

Della's eyes narrowed. "Istvan, I suggest you remember that you are speaking to the queen."

The two stared at each other as though waiting for the other to blink. Indigo felt bad that she was responsible for creating this turmoil between Istvan and his mother. She needed to do something to help him.

"I am going back to Greece," she uttered. "Today."

This ended the stare-off between the two as they both looked in her direction. There was a gleam of victory in the queen's eyes while there was sadness in Istvan's.

"I'll make the private jet available," the queen said.

It was on the tip of Indigo's tongue to thank her, because her parents had raised her to have manners, but she decided the queen wasn't worthy of manners, not when she was so willing to hurt her son.

"Don't do this," Istvan said.

Knock-knock.

"Come," the queen said.

It was Istvan's private secretary. He bowed. "Pardon, ma'am. The king has sent me. The prince is late for a meeting."

This was Indigo's cue to make her exit. She headed for the hallway. Istvan rushed to catch up to her. He fell in step with her.

"Don't you have a meeting to attend?" she asked.

"I can't go to it until I'm sure you aren't leaving."

"It's for the best."

He didn't say another word until they reached his suite, where Duke's belongings were, including his kennel. She placed the puppy inside, and he moved to his puffy blue bed. Once Duke was secure, she straightened.

She sensed Istvan standing beside her. She wished he'd just go to his meeting and not make this more difficult. Because she had absolutely no idea how she was going to say goodbye to him. Especially now that she'd fallen head over heels in love with him.

Ding.

Ding.

Ding.

Istvan sighed. "This is important business or I wouldn't leave. Just wait for me and we can discuss it."

And then he leaned in and kissed her. Her heart lodged in her throat, as she knew this would be their final kiss. Because every fairy tale had an ending, and this was theirs.

The meeting took forever.

But in the end, an agreement was reached with the local farmers. And life would continue in the kingdom as it always had.

Istvan rushed to his suite, hoping to find Indi there playing with Duke, but the puppy was still in his crate playing with a stuffed fish. He immediately dropped it upon spotting Istvan. He barked to be let out.

Istvan paused long enough to fuss over the pup quickly and put on his leash. It was time for him to be walked. They moved down the hallway to get Indi for the walk.

Knock-knock.

"Indi?"

He knocked again, with no response. As an uneasy feeling settled in his gut, he opened the door. The dresser was devoid of Indi's sketch pads.

No. No. No.

His whole body tensed as he rushed over to the wardrobe and swung the doors open. The only clothes inside were the dresses he'd bought her. Everything else was gone. Indi was gone.

It felt as though the air had been sucked out of the room. He stumbled over to the bed and sank down.

Why didn't she wait? Why?

"Istvan?" It was Gisella's voice.

He scrubbed his palms across his eyes and drew in a deep breath, hoping when he spoke that his voice wouldn't betray him.

"What do you need?" He kept his back to her as he bent over and picked up Duke.

"I heard about Indigo." He waited for her to agree with their mother about Indigo being trouble, but instead his sister said, "I'm sorry. But you know it has to be this way."

He turned to her. "Does it have to be this way?" He shook his head. "I don't think so."

"What are you saying?" Concern laced her voice.

"Would you be happy if the only thing you had in your life was the crown?"

"Of course." There was sincerity in her words.

He lacked that conviction. He'd always believed there were more important things in life than being crowned king. Indi was one of those things.

"How can it be enough for you?" He felt he was missing something.

"How can it not be enough?" She studied him as though she were concerned about him.

"Maybe the problem is that you should be the heir."

"I wish." And then she glanced down at the envelope in her hand. She held it out to him. "Indigo left this for you."

On wooden legs, he approached his sister. He wasn't sure he wanted to know what the note said, but he couldn't help himself.

He accepted the envelope, and his sister moved on. He slipped his finger under the flap and yanked, withdrawing the slip of paper.

I'm sorry I couldn't wait. I knew if I saw you again that you would talk me out of leaving. Your mother was right about one thing—you are the crown prince. You have to focus on the future. You will be the best king ever. The people of Rydiania need you. I will never forget our time together, but we both must move on. Me with my gallery showing and you with your need to help others. I wish you all the best.

Indi XOX

PS Kiss Duke for me

PSS I'll send you money for the dress.

After reading her letter, he was certain of one thing—his future was with Indi. He didn't care what it cost him. They would be together again. Because he loved her. He'd loved her since the first time she'd sketched him. He couldn't imagine his life without her.

CHAPTER TWENTY

LIFE HAD CHANGED.

She had changed.

Indigo had been home for a few days, and nothing felt the same. Her mother had just moved into the assisted care facility, and she was happy that her mother was finally where she wanted to be. And when her mother inquired about Indigo's melancholy mood, she blamed it on jet lag and the fact that she was going to miss her mother. Neither was a lie.

She hadn't had the heart to work on the portrait of Istvan since she'd been home. She knew she couldn't put it off forever, though. Istvan had wired the remainder of her fee the day after she left Rydiania. Was that his way of cutting ties with her?

She wasn't sure. But she'd kind of been hoping for a phone call from him, and none had come. It was really over. The thought weighed heavy on her mind.

But not tonight.

Tonight was her long-awaited gallery showing. She was so excited.

She'd opted to wear the blue dress from her night in the city with Istvan. It was the only dress she'd taken that he'd given her. And she'd already sent him the money for it, but without a price tag, she'd had to guess at the value.

"Are you enjoying yourself?" her agent, Franco, asked her.

She nodded. "It's great. How did you get the press to show up?"

"I didn't. I thought you arranged it."

She shook her head. "It wasn't me."

"Well, however they found out, it's a good thing. By tomorrow, everyone in Athens will know your name. And it's only up from there."

Franco got a little overexcited at times, but she appreciated his enthusiasm. She wouldn't be a household name like Jackson Pollock or Georgia O'Keeffe, but if her name became known in the art world, her dreams would be achieved.

Suddenly there was a commotion near the front of the gallery. Flashes lit up, and excitement moved over the crowd.

"What's going on?" she asked Franco.

"It seems a celebrity has shown up."

"Who?"

"I don't know. I sent out some invites but didn't hear anything back."

And then the crowd parted and Istvan was there, larger than life in a dark suit with a white dress shirt sans the tie, but he was accessorized by the sweetest puppy in his arms. Her heart pounded. What were they doing here?

"Duke!" Indigo rushed forward and fussed over the pup, who licked her face in return.

"Don't I rate a greeting?" Istvan asked.

A hush fell over the room as cell phones were pulled out to film the moment. Inwardly Indigo groaned. Why was he here in public with her when he knew it would stir up trouble for him?

She forced a nervous smile and then did something she'd never done before. She bowed. "Welcome, Your Highness."

"Indi, you don't need to do that," he said softly.

"I do," she whispered. And she straightened. "May I show you around?"

He nodded. "I'd like that."

And so she walked with him through the gallery. All the while she wondered what he was doing in Greece. She knew what she wanted him to say to her, but she also realized it was an impossibility. As they moved agonizingly slowly through the gallery, all she could think about was getting him alone so they could speak frankly.

When they neared the office, she signaled for him to follow her. Her heart pitter-pattered. He was so close and yet so far away.

When the door closed, she asked, "Can I hold Duke?"

He handed the puppy over.

With the dog in her arms, it kept her from reaching out to him like she longed to do. She ached to feel his kiss again, but she knew that was all in the past.

"You shouldn't be here," she said as the puppy wiggled.

"There's no other place I'd rather be." He stepped closer to her and took Duke from her. Once the puppy was on the floor, Istvan stared deep into her eyes. "I've missed you."

Her heart thumped so loudly it echoed in her ears. "I… I missed you, too. But you shouldn't be here. The press is going to make a big deal of this."

"Let them. I don't care."

He was talking nonsense. "Of course you care. You have to care. You're a prince. And not just any prince, but the crown prince. You can't just walk away from that."

He stepped closer, wrapping his hands around her waist. "I can and I did."

She shook her head, unable to accept the gravity of the words he spoke. Maybe she'd misheard him over the pounding of her heart. "Istvan, this—" she gestured between them "—isn't going to work out. You have your life, and I have mine."

"That's where you are wrong. Because where you go, I will go."

"You can't." How was he not hearing her?

"Can you look into my eyes and tell me that you don't love me?"

Really? This was what it was going to take to make him see reason—to realize that their future wasn't together. But when she stared into his bottomless eyes, she saw the future—their future.

No. No. No. She couldn't let this happen. She couldn't let him give up his future, his destiny, his family. He couldn't sacrifice all that for her.

"You can't do this." Her voice wavered.

"Yes, I can. Don't you understand that without you, I am nothing?"

"Without me, you're a prince—the future ruler of Rydiania."

"I'd much rather be the prince of your heart."

She swooned just a bit. He was saying all the right things. How was she supposed to reason with him when he was being impossibly sweet?

"Istvan, please, be reasonable. What are you going to do if you aren't a prince?" The thought of him being anything but a royal totally escaped her.

He frowned at her. "Do you think I have no other skills?"

"I, uh…" Heat engulfed her cheeks. "Of course you do. I didn't mean it that way. I'm just, well… I'm caught off guard."

The smile returned to his perfectly kissable lips. "Indigo, it is done."

"What is?" Her voice was barely more than a whisper.

"I have stepped down as heir to the throne. Gisella is going to be the future queen. She always should have been the heir. She believes the crown comes first—above all else."

Indigo couldn't believe what she was hearing. She went to step back and ended up stumbling over her own feet. Her entire body was in shock.

Why was he saying all this? What did it all mean? Why

would he do this? The questions swirled in her mind at a dizzying pace.

Istvan wordlessly helped her over to the desk. When she turned to look at him, she noticed a calm serenity in his eyes. He was at peace with this decision.

"You can't do this," she begged. "Go back. Tell them you had a moment of delusion and you didn't mean any of it."

He shook his head. "I can't do that."

"Why not?"

"Because I meant every single word I said before I departed that palace."

Her mouth gaped. This couldn't be happening. She had to be imagining the entire conversation. Yes, that was it. This was nothing more than a dream. When she woke up, all would be back the way it should be—with Istvan at the palace and her at her apartment.

"Indigo, did you hear me?"

She pressed her lips together and nodded. "But you can't give up your family for me. You'll regret it, and I couldn't live with the guilt."

"Indi, relax. I'm still a part of the family."

"You are?" She was relieved but confused.

He nodded. "Because I wasn't crowned, there was no need to banish me. By royal decree, I was removed from the line of succession."

"But you're still a prince?"

"I am."

"Thank goodness. I didn't want you to end up like my father or your uncle."

"Not a chance, with you in my life."

"But why would you do this?"

"Because I love you—I love the person you are, and I like the person I am when I'm around you. So unless you can tell me that you don't love me, I plan to be wherever you go."

Happy tears blurred her vision. She blinked them away. "And if I tell you that I don't love you?"

"Then I will take my broken heart and go live like a hermit in a hut on the top of a mountain."

She smiled and shook her head. "I can't see that happening."

"Neither can I, because I love you, Indigo, and I know you love me, too."

The happy tears returned and splashed onto her cheeks. "I do love you."

As he drew nearer to her, she knew in her heart that this union was right for them. Because she was a better person with him in her life. And now that she'd had a glimpse of the love and happiness they could have together, she couldn't imagine her life without him in it. He was the prince of her heart, now and always.

EPILOGUE

Ludus Island, September

THE LAST FEW months must have been a dream.

There was no way reality could be this good.

Indigo felt as though she was walking on clouds. After her gallery showing, her artwork had been selling as fast as she could produce it. And the amount the pieces were selling for was more than she'd ever imagined. It was enough to guarantee her mother would be able to stay in her assisted living apartment indefinitely.

With Istvan's portrait complete and hanging in the palace, Indigo was working on pieces for a new gallery showing. This time, with the help of her agent, she'd been able to land a spot in Paris. Every time she thought of how far her career had come, butterflies fluttered in her stomach.

Then there was the fact that she had her very own Prince Charming. How lucky could a girl get?

Ever since Istvan had removed himself from the line of succession, the king and queen had started changing their ways. Not only was Istvan still part of the family, but they'd welcomed Indigo as well. It wasn't a warm, fuzzy relationship, but the hostility was gone, and now she could visit the village where she'd been born without worrying that it would cause problems for Istvan.

These days Istvan split his time between Ludus Island, where he had a long-term suite at the resort, and his penthouse back in Rydiania. She was hoping that soon they could spend more time together, because she missed him when he was gone, but she had her mother here in Greece and she wanted to be close to her.

Istvan had texted her earlier that day and asked her to meet him at the resort, yet when she arrived at his suite, he wasn't there. When she texted him, he asked her to meet him out on the patio. She wondered what he was doing out there at this hour.

When she reached the doors that led outside, Istvan was standing on the patio waiting for her. "Hello, beautiful."

"Hello yourself." She rushed to him, lifted up on her tiptoes and pressed her lips to his. She'd never grow tired of his kisses. Much too soon, she pulled away. "So what are we doing here?"

"I have something to show you."

"You want to show me something out there? In the dark?"

He smiled at her, making her heart flutter in her chest. He took her hand in his as they started to walk. "Have I told you how much I've missed you?"

She gazed into his eyes. "Not as much as I've missed you."

The still-warm sea breeze brushed softly over her skin. There were a few couples lingering and enjoying the sunset. She had to admit that the sky was worthy of a painting.

She glanced at him. "Did you want to watch the sunset?"

"Yes. But not here. I have something else in mind." He continued walking across the patio and down the steps to the lit walkway that led to the beach.

He was acting very mysterious tonight. And she was dying to know what he was up to. She didn't have to wonder for long, because soon the beach came into view. With a vibrant orange, pink and purple sunset in the background, there were votives on the beach. Their flickering lights spelled out Marry Me.

Indigo gasped as happy tears blurred her vision.

When she turned to Istvan, he dropped down on one knee. "Indigo, I knew there was something special about you from the first day we met."

"But I don't even remember speaking to you. I was so caught off guard by your presence."

"You didn't have to say a word. It was just your presence that made me curious to know more about you."

She smiled at him. "So it wasn't just coincidence that you ended up at my umbrella for a sketch?"

"Definitely not. I made sure to inquire about you."

She smiled. "You did, huh?"

"Oh, yeah. I wasn't letting you get away."

"I think you're rewriting history. All you wanted from me was my artistic skills."

"That's what I wanted you to believe. And for a while, I tried to tell myself that, too. But there was no denying the way you made me feel. You gave me the courage to go after what I wanted—the life I wanted. And I want to share that life with you."

He withdrew a ring box from his pocket and held it out to her. "Indigo, you have shown me that love is accepting and tolerant. You've helped me find the courage to step out of the destiny I was born into to create the destiny I desire. I love you, and I can't imagine my life without you in it. Will you be my princess?"

She blinked repeatedly, but it was too late. The happy tears cascaded down her cheeks. "Yes. Yes, I will."

He straightened and then slipped the diamond solitaire ring adorned with heart-shaped red rubies on her finger. As soon as she saw the ring, she realized what he'd done.

"So you believe in the legend of the Ruby Heart, huh?" she asked.

He shrugged. "Seemed to work for us. And from what I heard, it worked for Hermione and Atlas."

As she admired the ring, she said, "I wonder who will fall under the spell of the Ruby Heart next."

"I don't know, but if they are as happy as we are, they'll be the lucky ones." He wrapped his arms around her waist and pulled her close.

"How happy are you?"

"Let me show you." He lowered his head, claiming her lips.

Fairy tales really did come true.

* * * * *

Second Chance With The Bridesmaid

Dear Reader,

Taking chances can be scary. It's why people often keep doing the same thing over and over again. This is the case for both Adara and Krystof, and boy, do they have things to work through.

Adara Galanis is comfortable in her position as the concierge at the Ludus Resort. She's been doing it for years and the guests love her. But when Krystof Mikos enters her life, he offers her adventure and excitement but without the commitment of a serious relationship. Despite not being the casual type, she tells herself that she's up for it...until she's confronted with the consequences of her decision.

Krystof Mikos is best man at his friend's wedding on Ludus Island. He worries his friend is making a mistake because Krystof doesn't believe in forever. But this wedding is the perfect time for him to fix things with Adara.

Adara doesn't want anything to do with Krystof, but when their friends' wedding starts to turn into a disaster, it just might take both of them to piece it back together. In the process, will they find their own happily-ever-after?

Happy reading,

Jennifer

Praise for
Jennifer Faye

"A fantastic romantic read that is a joy to read from start to finish, *The CEO, the Puppy and Me* is another winner by the immensely talented Jennifer Faye."

—*Goodreads*

PROLOGUE

July, Paris, France

PITTER-PATTER. PITTER-PATTER.

Adara Galinis's heartbeat accelerated as the elevator slowly rose in one of the poshest hotels in Paris. That wasn't what was making her nervous. As the concierge of an elite island resort that hosted celebrities and millionaires, she was used to the finest surroundings.

Her racing heart had to do with the fact that she had traveled from Greece to Paris on the spur of the moment. She wasn't normally spontaneous. She liked things neat and orderly. Her job provided all the spontaneity she needed in life.

But she had a long weekend off, and in order to spend time with Krystof, she needed to come to him. Ever since they'd met at Valentine's on Ludus Island, they'd been casually see-ing each other.

Krystof was best friends with the island's owner, Atlas Otho-nos. Earlier that year, when Atlas had briefly considered sell-ing the island, he'd contacted Krystof in hopes that he'd want to buy the place. The sale didn't work out, but Adara had caught Krystof's attention. He'd pursued her in a charming sort of way—requesting concierge service and explaining that he wanted to dance with the most beautiful woman at the resort that evening. She was all prepared to extend an invitation on his behalf to whichever woman he'd chosen when he'd announced that the woman he was interested in was her.

She'd hesitated at first. After all, she made it a rule not to fraternize with the guests, but his warm smile and his enchanting way with words had won her over. They'd danced the night away at the Valentine's ball. It had been a magical evening that didn't end until the sun came up the next morning.

Now whenever Krystof stayed at the Ludus Resort, they made sure to spend as much time together as possible. At the end of each visit, he always asked her to fly away with him to some far-flung country. And though the idea tempted her, she'd always turned him down. She just couldn't imagine picking up and leaving without any planning. How was her assistant supposed to know what needed to be done? What if one of her regular clients arrived and she wasn't there? Part of her success was knowing the regulars and anticipating their wants before they had to ask her. She kept extensive files on their regular guests, from their favorite foods and colors to the names of their children and pets.

However, this weekend Hermione, her boss and best friend, had insisted she use some of her accumulated vacation time. Adara had been so focused on her job recently that she'd let her social life slide, and as for hobbies, well, she didn't have any unless you counted shopping.

So when she heard Krystof would be visiting Paris, the shopping mecca of the world, she took it as a sign. She couldn't wait to see him again. Their visits were so infrequent that it was always a rush to be with him. At least that's what she told herself was the reason for her heart racing every time she laid eyes on him.

She ran her hand down over the short, snug black dress. Her effort was a waste, because there was nowhere for the dress to go. It clung to her body like a second skin. It was a far more daring dress than she was accustomed to wearing. She'd bought it specifically for Krystof. She hoped he'd like her surprise.

As the elevator rose, her gaze focused on the increasing numbers. With each floor she passed, her heart beat faster. All too quickly, the elevator quietly came to a stop on the ninth floor. The door whooshed open.

Adara drew in a deep breath and then exhaled. With her fingers wrapped around the handle of her weekender bag, she stepped out. The door closed behind her.

This plush hotel felt so far away from the privately owned island of Ludus. Of course, it wasn't a fair comparison, as the Ludus Resort had been founded by a former king—King Georgios, an amazing man who'd abdicated the throne of Rydiania. She didn't know all the details of why he'd stepped away from the crown, but once he had, his family had promptly disowned him. He'd moved to Greece and bought Ludus Island, where he would live out his days. It was both a sad and an amazing tale.

As she looked around the spacious foyer, she realized her initial assessment had been misguided. Though the wine-colored carpet was plush, and the fixtures were brass on cream-colored walls, that was where it ended. There was no precious artwork on the walls or greenery throughout the hallway. Whereas the Ludus was always looking to make the resort stand out in both big and small ways, it appeared this hotel excelled at a minimalist approach. Interesting.

There was no one about in the foyer. The only sound as she walked was the soft rumble from the wheels of her case. She couldn't wait to see Krystof. She was so excited. She hoped he'd be just as thrilled to see her.

The gold plaque on the wall showed that his room was to the right. She turned that way. Her footsteps were muffled by the thick carpeting. What would he think about her spontaneity? This presumed he was even in his hotel room. What if he was out at a card game or some other such thing?

She would have to phone him, then, to tell him she was here, and the surprise would be ruined, but she was jumping too far ahead. She lifted her head and noticed a stylishly dressed woman at the end of the hallway. The woman knocked on a door. Was the young woman doing the same as her and being spontaneous? She hoped the woman had as good a weekend as she was about to have with Krystof.

Just then, the door in front of the woman swung open. The woman stood off to the side, giving Adara full view of the person inside the hotel room. She stopped walking. The breath caught in Adara's lungs. Krystof stood there. *Oh, my!* Her heart lodged in her throat at the sight of him.

His dark hair was spiky and going every which way, as though he'd just stepped out of the shower. His broad shoulders led to his bare chest. She was too far away to see if there were beads of water on his tanned skin. As her gaze lowered, her mouth grew dry. No man had a right to look as good as him.

He wore nothing more than a white towel draped around his trim waist. She swallowed hard. The only thing wrong with this picture was that she was supposed to be the one standing at his doorway.

His gaze lingered on the other woman. A smile lit up his face. The woman practically threw herself at him. They hugged as though they knew each other very well.

Adara blinked, willing away the image. But when she focused again, he was still holding the woman. So this was what he did when they were apart. Her heart plummeted down to her new black heels.

She turned away before she was spotted. The only thing that could have made this moment worse was if Krystof were to spot her. Her utter humiliation would then be complete.

Her steps were rapid as she retreated to the elevator. She wanted to disappear as quickly as possible. And lucky for her, one of the two sets of elevator doors swung open immediately. An older couple stepped off.

"Could you hold that for me?" Adara asked.

The gentleman held the door for her until she stepped inside. She thanked him. As the door closed, she recalled the image of a smiling, practically naked Krystof drawing that woman into his arms. Tears stung the backs of her eyes. She blinked them away. She wasn't going to fall apart in the elevator. All the while fury churned within her. Why had she let herself believe they shared something special?

It was quite obvious she was just someone to warm his bed whenever one of his other girlfriends wasn't available. How could she have been so blind? Sure, they had said this arrangement was casual, but that was in the beginning—months ago, on Valentine's. She'd thought they were getting closer—starting something more serious. Obviously she was the only one to think this.

She had been so wrong—about him, about herself, about them. She was done with him. Because his idea of casual and hers were two different things. In the end, she wasn't cut out to do casual—not if it meant him seeing other women while he was still involved with her. But it didn't matter now, because they were over.

CHAPTER ONE

September, Ludus Island, Greece

SHE WAS LATE. Very late...

Adara checked the calendar on her phone again. Her gaze scanned back through the days, one by one. She searched for the X that usually marked the first day of her period.

Day by day her gaze scanned down over her digital tablet. This wasn't the first time she'd been through this exercise, but it didn't keep her from wishing that she'd missed the little mark. *Please be there.* And once again, it was nowhere to be found.

Maybe she'd accidentally deleted it. Yes, that sounded like a legitimate explanation. Right now, she'd agree to any logical explanation—any reason except for her being late. Maybe she should have a backup plan. She would think that over for the future, but it wouldn't help her right now.

How was any of this possible? She hadn't been in Krystof's bed in months. After the episode in Paris, he'd messaged her to arrange for them to spend more time together, and she'd replied, telling him point-blank that it was over. They were finished. And then she'd promptly blocked his number.

Since her fling with Krystof, there had been no one else. Like it or not, she wasn't ready to move on. And she was certain she'd had her monthly since she'd been with Krystof. So what was going on?

She didn't feel any different. Just a little tired, but she credited her busy work schedule for her lack of energy. Not only was the resort hopping, but she had been training a new assistant for the past six months—an assistant who was now almost as good as her.

One pregnancy test later, and it was negative. Just as she'd suspected.

Two and three negative pregnancy tests later, and she was certain something was wrong. Hopefully it was just too little sleep or too much stress—something simple and easily remedied. Yes, that must be it. Ever since she'd seen Krystof with another woman, she'd thrown herself into her work even more so than she normally did.

She had known from the first time she'd met him that he wasn't traditional by any stretch. She was so drawn in by his outgoing personality and the way he could make her laugh that she'd talked herself into stepping outside her norm and taking a risk on him. Maybe deep inside she'd thought she could change him.

In the end, she'd been so wrong about herself. She was a one-man woman not suited to casual dating. She'd also been wrong about trying to change him. Krystof had no intention of changing his ways for anyone. Looking back, she realized that she'd let infatuation sway her decision as she'd agreed to his terms.

And now she was the one paying the price. She'd let herself get too caught up in what might have been. The reality of him with another woman in his arms flashed in her mind. It was immediately followed by the ache in her chest. She refused to acknowledge just how much he'd come to mean to her.

Her missing monthly was the wake-up call she needed. She was in her thirties now. If she wanted a husband and a couple of kids, she couldn't waste her time on guys who didn't share her life goals. And Krystof definitely didn't want the same things that she did. He couldn't even commit to having an apartment. He lived out of his jet and a suitcase as he globetrotted around the world. Who did such a thing?

Her head started to throb. She shoved aside the troubling thoughts. It was so much easier to be distracted by her work than to deal with the gaping crack in her heart and now her missing period. Could things get any worse?

But first she had to get settled into her room at the resort. She was going to be the maid-of-honor for her best friend, Hermione. The wedding was going to be here at the resort in ten days' time. Both Hermione, the resort's manager, and Atlas had offered her accommodations until the wedding to make it more convenient for her. She had the bachelorette party to host and the final details to oversee for the big wedding on top of her usual duties. She planned to make Hermione and Atlas's wedding the most amazing event the island had ever seen.

This was the first time since she'd been hired straight out of the university that she was a guest here. Adara wheeled her suitcase into her temporary room. She couldn't believe she was going to be staying at one of the world's most prestigious resorts! As the lights came on, she stood in place, taking it all in. She wasn't used to living in such extravagance.

She'd grown up in a modest home in a small village north of Athens with her loving parents. They'd raised her to be responsible and sensible. They'd also encouraged her to take the position at the Ludus, even if it meant moving away from home. That's why when they'd suddenly died in a car accident while on a long-awaited vacation in Ireland, it had turned Adara's life upside down.

For the past two years, she'd struggled to come to terms with a life without her parents in it. Their deaths had left a gigantic void in her heart. She'd clung to her familiar life at the Ludus. Her good friends at the resort had filled her days with their warmth and companionship. She didn't know what she'd do without Hermione and Indigo, as well as the other employees at the resort.

As her gaze took in her room, she couldn't help but notice it was so unlike her modest little apartment on the outskirts of Athens. This living room contained two white couches that faced each other with a long glass coffee table in the center. Decorations consisting of a crystal X and a matching ball sat on either side of an arrangement of fresh-cut blush peonies. The room's outer wall consisted of floor-to-ceiling windows with sheers that could be opened or closed remotely. At the moment, they were open, letting in the sunshine from the skylights overlooking the indoor pool area.

Ding.

The sound of an incoming message reminded her that she wasn't truly a guest of the resort but rather an employee with a very important job—the concierge. Her job was to make sure the guests' wishes were met and when possible exceeded.

Adara withdrew her phone from her pocket. She glanced at the screen. There was a message from Hermione.

Can we meet to talk?

It wasn't like Hermione to request an unscheduled meeting first thing in the morning. Something was wrong. Was it something to do with the resort? Or the wedding?

Sure. When and where?

Hermione responded, telling her to meet up in the penthouse apartment as soon as possible.

Adara left her still-packed suitcase sitting in the middle of the room. She would deal with it later. She headed out the door and made her way to the private elevator. You had to either have a key card or press the button to have someone in the penthouse buzz you up. As soon as Adara pressed the button, the elevator door opened. It was though Hermione had been standing there awaiting her appearance. Whatever was going on must be serious.

At the top of the resort sat the owner's apartment. It was huge and had the most amazing panoramic views. It was originally built by King Georgios. Seeing as it had all been designed by royalty, it was no wonder the resort loosely resembled a palace.

As Adara stepped out into the small foyer with a white marble floor and artwork adorning the walls, she had to admit the entire floor was truly suited to housing a king.

Hermione was standing at the open doorway to the suite wearing a frown. "I'm so glad you're here. Come in."

Adara followed Hermione inside to the spacious living room that was now a bit chaotic with wedding stuff all over the place, from favors for the guests to bridal magazines and decorations. But it was the two suitcases in the middle of the room that caught and held her attention.

Adara's gaze moved to her friend. "Are you packing for your honeymoon already?"

"No. We're getting ready to visit Atlas's father."

"Oh." Adara wasn't sure what to say, because the last she knew, Atlas and his father had a very strained relationship—to the point where she didn't think they even spoke anymore.

"His father is in the hospital, and I've finally convinced Atlas that we need to go to him."

"Oh, no. I'm sorry. What can I do?"

Hermione's gaze moved about the room. "Can you stay on top of the wedding? I mean, everything is planned. I know this room looks like a mess, but most of it's under control. I promise."

Adara's gaze moved about the room. Every surface was covered with boxes of stuff. Some decorations were complete. Other decorations still needed put together, not to mention the favors. "No problem. And if you need to push back the wedding until things calm down, I can help you with that, too."

Hermione shook her head. "I mentioned it to Atlas, and he

staunchly refused. You know that there's bad history between him and his father." When Adara nodded, Hermione continued. "So he said he wasn't going to let his father ruin his wedding. I'm hoping with all of the time that has passed since they last saw each other that there's a possibility of forgiveness. I know it's a lot to hope for, but I'm worried that if it's not attempted now, Atlas won't get another chance for reconciliation."

Okay. "What else do you need?"

"Just keep everything for the wedding on track. There shouldn't be much to do. But if any questions come up, can you take care of them?"

"Sure. No problem." They really had nailed down all the details already. What could possibly go wrong? "When will you be back?"

"I'm not sure." Hermione grabbed her purse from the couch. She glanced inside, as though making sure everything she wanted was in there, and then she zipped it. "They were light on details about his father's condition at the hospital. All we know is that it's serious."

Adara could see her friend was worked up. She went to her and placed a hand on her shoulder. "It's going to be okay. Everything will be all right."

Hermione nodded before glancing around, as though worried she was forgetting something. "I guess we have everything." She turned back to Adara. "I'm sorry to just up and leave you with everything. Indigo said she would be around sometime today. She just got back from Rydiania. She can help you if you need anything."

Hermione rolled the suitcases to the elevator. As she stood in front of the open doors, she reached into her pocket and pulled out a key card. "If I'm gone for a while, you might need this to get to the wedding stuff. Make yourself comfortable. Like I said, we don't know how long we'll be away. Atlas thinks it'll just be overnight, but I'm hoping he'll change his mind once we get there."

"It's okay. I'll take care of everything. Don't worry about this place." Adara took one of the suitcases and rolled it onto the elevator for her.

"What would I do without you? You're the best friend I could have ever asked for." Hermione moved to give her a hug.

Adara hugged her back. "You're the best, too."

And then they rode the elevator down to the main floor. All the while, Adara went over the wedding to-do list in her mind. It all seemed doable, even if Hermione didn't make it back right away. No worries. She had this wedding stuff under control.

CHAPTER TWO

HE'D RETURNED TO Ludus Island.

Krystof Mikos had been avoiding the island ever since things had abruptly ended with Adara. No woman had ever treated him in such a dismissive fashion. The memory of her brush-off and subsequent blocking of his number still burned him.

But now that he was the best man in Atlas and Hermione's wedding, he didn't have a choice but to return. Though the wedding was still a couple of weeks away, he'd arrived early to steal away the groom for a long and extravagant bachelor weekend. It was his hope that he'd be gone again before he ran into Adara.

He had nothing to say to her after the way she'd ghosted him. He didn't even understand what had prompted her to act in such an outrageous manner. He could understand it better if they'd argued, but that hadn't happened. The last time he'd seen her on the island, their weekend had ended with a lingering kiss. And their final phone conversation had ended with him pleading with her to fly away with him. The destination could be her decision. She'd promised to think about it. So where had it all gone so wrong?

He longed to know the answer, but there was no way he was going to beg her to come back to him—even if he missed spending time with her. He was better off alone—just as he'd been most of his life.

He shoved aside the troubling thoughts of Adara. Right now, he had a bachelor party to focus on. He couldn't believe the man he considered a brother was tying the knot. He'd always thought they'd both grow old as bachelors, seeing as both of them had had rough childhoods and neither wanted a repeat of family life. But ever since Atlas had laid eyes on Hermione, his tune had changed.

Krystof couldn't help thinking that his friend was making a mistake. Sure, spend time with Hermione, have a great time together, but to pledge forever to each other—why?

There was no such thing as forever. Relationships didn't last. All you had to do was to look at the statistics, which would prove his point.

In Krystof's case, he didn't even have to see the numbers. The story of his childhood in northern Greece was proof enough. He never knew his birth parents. His earliest memories consisted of being shuttled from one foster family to the next. His high IQ had gotten him into lots of trouble, and he'd quickly been labeled a problem child.

His life was littered with short-lived relationships. He'd learned not to let people get too close to him—but there were two exceptions, Atlas and Krystof's foster sister, who had refused to let him disappear from her life.

Atlas had surprised him when he'd proclaimed he was about to be married. When he'd asked Krystof to be his best man, what was Krystof to do—turn down his best friend and tell him he didn't believe in marriage? Even he wasn't that heartless. And so he'd agreed to stand up for Atlas—even if he firmly believed it was a mistake.

And now it was time for them to jet off for a long bachelor weekend in Ibiza, which was one of the Balearic Islands, an archipelago off Spain in the Mediterranean Sea. It was known for its nightlife. They were going to have the most amazing time.

He didn't exactly have a plan, because he liked to live life on a whim. However they decided to entertain themselves, it would be memorable.

He'd invited Prince Istvan of Rydiania, who'd said he'd meet them in Ibiza. Krystof had also contacted some of his and Atlas's old classmates from school. It'd be good to catch up with people and find out what had happened with everyone.

Krystof had just flown into Athens on his private jet to pick up Atlas. His hired car whisked him south of the city and onto a ferry that would deliver him to Ludus Island. When the car pulled to a stop beneath the portico of the resort hotel, Krystof made his way inside the lavish lobby with a white marble floor and a large crystal chandelier in the center of the spacious room.

He practically ran straight into Atlas. "Wow. Didn't expect you to be this anxious to leave. I thought we'd head off in the morning, but now works, too." He glanced around. "Where's your suitcase?"

Atlas frowned. "There's been a change of plans."

"Oh." This was news to him. But, hey, he was flexible. "Did you want to go somewhere else? I can call the guys and let them know the new location."

Atlas shook his head. "It's not that. I can't go."

"What?" Surely he couldn't be serious. "Of course you have to go. If this has something to do with Hermione, you can assure her that the partying won't get too out of hand." He sent him a big grin. Of course the partying would get out of hand. It was Atlas's last chance to have a good time before he was married.

Atlas arched an incredulous brow, and then he shook his head. "Do you really think Hermione's going to believe you would ever behave?"

"Why shouldn't she?" He wasn't that wild. He'd gotten most of that out of his system when he was a kid. "I'm a great guy." He planted his hands on his trim waist and straightened his broad shoulders. "Just ask anyone." His thoughts immediately strayed to Adara. "Maybe not quite anyone. But most people who know me love me."

Atlas rolled his eyes. "You definitely don't have an ego problem at all."

"Hey, I might resemble that comment."

Atlas let out a short laugh. "You're making this hard on me, but I can't do the trip to Ibiza. Something happened with my father, and we're heading there now."

That was the last thing Krystof had expected to hear. "Dude, are you sure you want to see him?"

Atlas shrugged. "Hermione thinks it's for the best."

"She doesn't understand. How could she? She wasn't around for all of the bad stuff."

His friend shrugged. "I don't know. It all happened a lot of years ago." He raked his fingers through his hair. "I didn't want to come to the island when my mother willed me this place. I was so angry with her, but while I was here, I found out that what I believed about her wasn't correct."

"But this is different. This is your father. He didn't just walk away. He made every day of your life hell."

"I know. I know."

But still, he was going. Krystof was worried about his friend. Nobody needed to go through that pain again. But it didn't appear anything he said was going to change Atlas's mind about this trip. All he could do was be there for him.

"What can I do?" Krystof asked.

"Hermione suggested delaying the wedding, but I don't want to. My father took a lot of things from me while growing up. I won't let him take this away from me, too." He shifted his weight from one foot to the other. "Would you mind staying here and helping Adara with the wedding details? I know something happened between the two of you, so if it's too much, I understand."

He would be alone with Adara? He wasn't so sure that was a good idea. In fact, he was quite certain it was a very bad idea.

Then an intriguing thought came to him. There would be hundreds of guests for Adara to deal with, but he just might be able to pull her away from all that so they could talk privately for a moment—just long enough to appease his curiosity about why she'd brushed him off.

He could accomplish two things by staying: helping out Atlas and perhaps fixing things with Adara. "I'll do it."

Atlas arched a brow. "Are you sure? Did I mention there would be wedding details involved?"

"I heard." He was certain Adara would handle all those. She liked to be in charge and do things her way.

"And what about the problem between you and Adara?"

"I'll talk to her, fix things with her."

Atlas looked taken aback. "Are you sure about that?"

Krystof nodded. "Don't worry about a thing. I've got this."

"Really?" Atlas's dark brows gathered. "Where's the Krystof I know? What have you done with him? The last I knew you didn't do anything complicated."

"Maybe I'm changing." Had those words really come out of his mouth? The surprise showed on Atlas's face, too. Not wanting to dissect what he'd just said, Krystof rushed on. "I know a thing or two about weddings. Honestly, I can handle this."

"Tell me the last one you attended."

Krystof paused to think. He really gave it serious thought. There were frequent invitations, but he routinely declined them with the excuse that he'd be out of the country, because he was always on the go.

"See. I told you. There's something not right about you agreeing to stay here and help. And I bet I know why—or should I say *who* has you agreeing."

"Atlas, there you are. Did you get the car?" Hermione approached them.

Krystof breathed a sigh of relief that Hermione had interrupted the beginning of Atlas's interrogation. With a smile on his face, he turned to the bride-to-be.

"I was just about to when I ran into Krystof." Atlas moved to Hermione's side and gave her a brief kiss. "I didn't have a chance to call him about the change of plans, so I was just filling him in."

"Hi, Krystof." Hermione hugged him before quickly pulling back. "I'm so sorry that this messes up your bachelor party plans."

"No worries. I understand. I'll message all the guys and explain. I hope your trip goes well. And feel free to take my car. The driver is waiting right out front."

They thanked him and promised to be back as soon as possible. He walked them out so he could retrieve his luggage. He wasn't looking forward to seeing Adara again—at least that's what he told himself.

And yet there was part of him that badly wanted to know where things had gone wrong. Since they'd been apart, he hadn't met anyone else who could garner his attention quite the way she had done. She'd grounded him. She'd actually made staying in one place feel all right for him—at least for a time.

Sometimes she was quiet, and other times she was talkative. She liked to share some of the fascinating details of her work— like the time she'd had to make preparations for a wealthy and influential guest to arrive at the resort via parachute—talk about going out of your way to avoid a traffic delay! She was very gifted in her ability to make people's wishes come true.

He wondered if a guest had turned her head. Did she have another man in her life now? Was that why she'd dumped him without explanation? The thought of her with someone else had his lips settling into a firm line as his gut twisted into a knot.

CHAPTER THREE

EVERYTHING WOULD BE fine.

Adara should be smiling. After all, she was the maid of honor. And the wedding was going to be the biggest, splashiest affair this island had ever seen. She would make sure of it.

If only she didn't have this cloud of worry hanging over her. She regretted doing an internet search to find a reason for her missing period. Instead of it making her feel better, it made her feel worse. She didn't like the possibilities: hormonal imbalances or serious health conditions. What exactly was wrong with her?

She reached for her phone. She'd put this off long enough. She had to call the doctor. But when she got ahold of them, she found out she'd have to wait to get in. The earliest they could squeeze her in was the following Monday. It seemed so far off, even though it was only five days away. Five very long days of worry.

At least she would see the doctor and get her answer before she had to deal with the next stressful thing in her life—seeing Krystof again. Since he was Atlas's best friend, he was the best man for the wedding. She inwardly groaned.

She hadn't spoken to him for over two months. She was still angry with him for being nothing more than a playboy and upset with herself for reading too much into their relationship. She wouldn't make that mistake again. Krystof was a part of her past—a painful lesson learned.

Thankfully, he wouldn't be here until next week, just before the ceremony. Krystof never spent too much time in one place, and without Atlas being on the island, there would be no reason for him to be here. He would most likely swing in at the last minute and then leave immediately after the reception. She could deal with that brief encounter. At least that's what she kept telling herself.

Lunch had come and gone in a flurry of special requests from guests. With her work under control, it was time to meet up with her friend Indigo, who was still doing a few special requests for drawings and portraits for guests of the resort. But Indigo's life was now quite busy, as she split her time between Athens and jetting off to Rydiania with her handsome prince—soon to be her husband. It just went to prove that happily-ever-afters did exist...for some people.

Adara made her way to her guest room. It was going to be her headquarters for all things pertaining to the wedding. As soon as she reached the room, she picked up her digital tablet. Her fingers moved over the screen, and then her gaze scanned down over the list of things to do.

They had worked hard to put things in order ahead of time. The to-do list was in pretty good shape. A smile pulled at her lips. This wedding was going to go off without a hitch. Then the image of Krystof with that other woman in his arms flashed in her mind. Okay, maybe one small hitch. And then a worrisome thought came to her. Would he bring the other woman to the wedding?

Her stomach soured at the thought. But in the next breath, she realized that bringing a date to the wedding would be tantamount to being in a relationship in Krystof's mind. It was something he would go out of his way to avoid. With that thought in mind, she breathed easier.

Knock-knock.

That must be Indigo. Adara closed her tablet and moved to the door. She swung it open. "Indigo, you're just in time."

The breath hitched in the back of her throat. It was Krystof. She blinked, but he was still there. "What are you doing here?"

His dark eyes stared at her while his expression gave nothing away about what he was thinking. "Aren't you even going to invite me in?"

A refusal teetered on the tip of her tongue. A glance over his shoulder revealed a number of guests in the hallway. She didn't need to create a scene. She opened the door wide. "Come in, if you must."

"Such a warm welcome. I feel like you really missed me." Sarcasm dripped from his voice.

She pushed the door closed. "What are you doing here? The wedding isn't until the end of next week."

He walked farther into the room and glanced around. Then he turned to her. "I want to know what I did for you to refuse to speak to me." His gaze narrowed in on her. The heat of his anger had her resisting the urge to fan herself. "You even went so far as to block my number." His voice vibrated with agitation. "You ghosted me. And I did nothing to deserve it."

Her mouth gaped before she forced it closed. Did he really think she didn't know she was just one of a number of women who passed through his life? Did he think she would be okay with that?

She crossed her arms. This wasn't the time for this conversation, not with Indigo about to arrive at any moment. "We're not having this conversation."

"You can't ghost me now. I'm not going anywhere until you explain yourself."

"I don't know why you're making a big deal of this." If he wanted to pretend he hadn't been seeing other women, then she could pretend as well. "It was a casual thing, and now it's over."

"It's another man, isn't it?" He studied her as though he could read the answer on her face.

She refused to glance away. He wouldn't intimidate her into confessing that she'd gone to Paris to surprise him and instead she was the one to be unpleasantly surprised. "If there was another man, would that put an end to this conversation?"

"No."

"Too bad. Now I have work to do." She turned to open the door for him.

"Not so fast. Hermione and Atlas sent me."

The mention of her friends' names gave her pause. Her fingers slipped from the door handle as she turned around. "What do you mean, they sent you?"

"They asked me to stick around to help out with the wedding details while they are away."

She couldn't resist a little laugh. "You're going to help with the wedding? You?"

He shrugged. "Sure. Why not?"

His insistence on staying to help made her amusement fizzle out. "Well, Hermione already asked me to stay on top of things. So as you can see, your help is not needed here."

"I'm sure Hermione has everything planned out, down to the table setting for the reception, but with so many details to keep on top of, there are bound to be a few issues that crop up."

"And you feel that you're the best person to deal with those problems?" His unwavering gaze and confident look irritated her. "I don't think so. You don't know the first thing about the wedding plans."

His gaze lowered to her digital notebook on the table next to him. "I bet if I read your notes, I'd get up to speed pretty quickly."

She checked the time on her smart watch. "Well, that will have to wait." She opened the door and gestured for him to leave. "I have another appointment now."

As he walked past her, he said quietly, "You can't avoid me forever."

Maybe not. But it didn't mean she wouldn't try her best. She leveled her shoulders and closed the door firmly behind him. She pulled her phone from her pocket and started running her finger over the screen as she messaged Hermione.

Did you know Krystof is here?

A couple minutes passed with no response. Adara made her way to the other side of the suite. How was she supposed to deal with Krystof without the buffer of Atlas and Hermione?

Ding.

Adara glanced at her phone.

Sorry. I meant to tell you that he arrived early. I hope it's not too awkward.

Her friend had enough on her mind. She didn't need to worry about Adara's dismal love life. It wasn't like she couldn't deal with Krystof. If only there was some way to distract him—like a high-stakes poker game. And yet there were none planned at the resort in the immediate future.

We'll be fine. How are things there?

Adara grabbed her tablet and moved to the couch. She sat down and opened her tablet. She needed to go over the list of things to do again. She didn't want to miss anything, especially with Krystof looking over her shoulder.

Atlas's father had a stroke. No details yet.

Adara closed her tablet. This was far more serious than she'd been imagining.

I'm so sorry.

I'll let you know more after talking to the doctors.

Don't worry about things here. I've got everything under control.

You're the best. Thank you!

Adara set aside her phone. How hard could it be to keep the wedding on track? After all, everything had been ordered and planned. All she had to do was make sure everything was delivered and put together. It would all be fine.

She just wished she could say the same thing about dealing with Krystof.

It shouldn't bother him.

And yet it did.

Krystof sensed that Adara was keeping something from him. It wasn't like her to be secretive, so if she didn't have a new man in her life, what was going on? And why wouldn't she tell him?

Perhaps she felt her reasons for not seeing him anymore were none of his business. He was the one who had insisted on having no strings between them. Now that he'd seen her, he felt as though they still had some unfinished business. And yet Adara had insisted on putting up a wall between them—a wall he kept failing to get around.

He'd been true to her in the months they'd been seeing each other. He hadn't even been tempted to see anyone else, not even in the last two months. Adara made him feel special—like she really cared about what he had to say.

They'd been having such a good time in each other's company that they'd kept it going for months, which was highly unusual for him. He hated to see it end. If he could just figure out the problem, he could fix it and they could keep going with their arrangement. He just had to get her to open up to him. But how?

He rubbed the back of his neck where his muscles had tightened. He was starting to get a headache. However, he wasn't leaving this island until he got some straight answers from her.

Buzz-buzz.

He pulled his phone from his pocket and glanced at the caller ID. It was Atlas. Krystof pressed the phone to his ear. "Hey Atlas, how's it going?"

"We just saw my father. He's not doing great. We stepped out while he was sleeping to get some coffee. While Hermione is placing the order, I thought I'd check in and see how things are going there. Have you straightened out things with Adara?"

Krystof stifled another groan. "About that…ah…we haven't really had much of a chance to talk."

"What are you waiting for? I don't want anything to ruin this wedding. Not my father. And not your messy love life."

"Hey, it's not like that. We aren't a couple. We were just having fun."

"Did Adara know that?"

The question hung heavy in the air. Krystof swallowed hard. "Of course she did. We talked about it in the beginning."

"You mean the whole way back at Valentine's?"

"Yes."

It wasn't like their arrangement had had an expiration date, did it? Was that what Adara thought? Had she grown bored of him? Impossible. She'd enjoyed their time together as much as he had. He was certain of it.

Things had remained the same between them up until he'd texted her a couple of months ago to arrange their next meeting and she'd messaged him back, ending things. He was the one who normally ended an affair. He didn't like being brushed off. He really didn't like it happening with Adara. There was just something special about her, from the way she took great pains to care for those around her to her gentle laugh that warmed a spot in his chest and the way she made him feel like he was the only man in the room.

"Krystof, you do realize that the Valentine's ball was many months ago, don't you? And you've been seeing her pretty regularly ever since then. Maybe she thought there was something growing between the two of you."

He refused to see it Atlas's way. It wasn't like he'd ever said anything to lead her on. He wouldn't do that—he wouldn't intentionally hurt her. "We were becoming better friends."

"Is that all?"

Was it all? As soon as the question crossed his mind, he shoved it away. "Of course that's all. I didn't deserve her ghosting me with no explanation."

"If you say so."

"I do."

"Then keep your distance from her as much as possible."

"What?" Surely his best friend hadn't just warned him away from a woman, had he?

"I'm not messing around, Krystof. You've done something to upset her already. You can't mess up again."

The stubborn part of him countered with, "And what if I don't stay away?"

A tense silence ensued. "Don't make me regret asking you to stand up for me at the wedding. I don't ask you for much. Just don't mess up my wedding."

"I won't." The promise was out of his mouth before he had a chance to think about the implications. Because even now, he was tempted by the memories of pulling Adara into his arms and kissing her long and hard.

"Thank you. I knew I could count on you. I've got to go. Hermione is coming."

The line went dead.

Wow. Atlas had never warned him away from a woman before. It didn't sit well with Krystof, but since Atlas was under so much stress with having to face his father again after so many years and his upcoming wedding, Krystof would abide by his wishes. Once he got some answers from Adara, of course.

CHAPTER FOUR

IT HAD BEEN a crazy, busy day.

Adara finally stopped long enough to take a full breath. Who knew so many people could have so many special requests while on vacation? But her workday was finally over, and the guests had all been taken care of, from needing a rare brand of shampoo and conditioner to providing a sunset helicopter tour of the island. When it came to Ludus guests, no request was denied... well, within reason. She'd been propositioned today—and she'd immediately shot down the advance from an international star who was twice her age.

She had only been propositioned twice in the entire time she'd worked at the resort. It was the first proposition that had been more like an invitation—an alluring invitation that she had been more than willing to accept.

As the memory of that long-ago Valentine's night filtered through her mind, she remembered being swept off her feet. Krystof had been attentive and charming. He'd been everything she'd been looking for in a man—or at least she'd thought so at the time. So when he'd suggested they start something casual, she'd surprised herself when she'd agreed. It was so unlike her, but there was something different about Krystof.

She shoved aside the unwanted memories. She wasn't going

to let her guard down with him again. Fool her once, shame on him. Fool her twice, shame on her.

Her hope was that Krystof would grow bored at the resort without Atlas around and he would leave until the wedding. It wasn't like she couldn't manage things until Hermione and Atlas returned. She did not need him to help her.

Adara had made sure to review the wedding checklist twice. Everything up to and including the two-week mark had been accomplished. They were in great shape. And that's exactly what she'd told Hermione when she'd called not once but twice that day to check in on the resort and the wedding. Hermione really was a bit of a control freak. That's probably why the wedding couple had had the penthouse remodeled so they could live there after the wedding and be close to their business.

Chime.

It was a reminder on Adara's phone letting her know it was time to try on the wedding dresses one last time. They'd been delivered yesterday, but Indigo hadn't been available until now. So they'd decided to wait and try them on together. Even though Hermione was away, they really couldn't delay it any longer.

Adara was anxious to see the dresses again. Hermione had had both Adara and Indigo pick out the style of dress they preferred. They were simple and classic. The bride had chosen an arctic blue for the wedding color.

She texted a reminder to Indigo to meet her in her guest room. With the workday over, they would have a chance to check out their dresses without being rushed. They'd already had their final fittings, but with Adara now being in charge of making sure there were no foul-ups with the wedding, she wanted to try them on one last time before they put the dresses in storage until the big day. Afterward, she was thinking, they could share a glass of wine and catch up on each other's lives— not that she had much to share.

When she reached her room, she found Indigo pacing outside her door. When Indigo lifted her head and spotted Adara, she sent her a big smile. It was the same smile she'd been wearing ever since Prince Istvan had declared his love for her and placed a ruby-and-diamond ring on her finger.

Adara never asked, but she got the distinct feeling the ring was somehow related to the Ruby Heart on display in the gallery. Hermione swore that gemstone had something to do with her and Atlas finding their way together. Adara didn't believe in legends, but just to be safe, she was keeping her distance from the gallery and the Ruby Heart. She wasn't interested in a love match, especially after the way things had ended with Krystof.

"I hope I didn't keep you waiting too long." Adara opened the door to her room.

"Not at all." Indigo followed her inside. "How's Atlas's father doing?"

Adara placed the files and digital tablet she'd brought with her on the table before turning to her friend. "He's not the best. They're going to stay at the hospital until he's stable."

"That's a shame. I wish there was something I could do."

"There is… We have to try on these dresses one last time, and then I'll put them in storage until the big day." She glanced over, catching Indigo admiring her engagement ring. "Have you two set a wedding date yet?"

Indigo shook her head. "When you marry a prince, a lot of the decisions are taken out of your hands."

"Oh, really? I mean, I just thought with him stepping out of the line of succession that, well, you guys would be pretty much on your own."

Indigo shook her head again. "You would think, but because he did step down from inheriting the crown, the king and queen are even more invested in making a big deal out of our wedding. They want to portray a united front to the world."

"So it's going to be a royal wedding?"

Indigo nodded. Her expression was blank, as though she hadn't made up her mind about how she felt about having the royals involved in her wedding.

"That must be so exciting." And then a thought came to her. "Hey, does this mean you'll be a princess?"

Indigo's eyes widened as she nodded her head. "Can you believe it?"

Adara sent her friend a reassuring smile. "You're going to make the best princess ever."

Indigo let out a laugh. "I highly doubt it, since I have absolutely no idea what a princess is supposed to do. And even when I figure it out, I'm sure I'll do it all wrong."

"Not a chance. You have a big, wonderful heart. You're exactly what the palace needs."

"I'm not sure they'd agree with you, since their son stepped away from the crown for me. Though he would tell you there were other reasons for his decision, I still feel some sort of responsibility."

"But didn't you say before that he's at last getting along with his parents?"

Indigo nodded again. "Yes, they're getting along better than ever. At least, that's what he says. I just hope he never regrets his decision to give up the crown."

"He won't. How could he? After all, he's marrying you, and you both have such amazing lives. Him with his charities and you with your art."

Knock-knock.

"Looks like it's time to try on the dresses." Adara moved to the door and opened it. One of the staff rolled in the rack with the dresses. After thanking him, Adara moved to the rack with the white garment bags. She checked the tags. "This one is yours."

Indigo took it and moved to the couch, where she laid out the garment bag. She pulled down the zipper and then uttered a loud gasp.

"What's wrong?" Adara asked, alarmed.

"This dress. It's not mine."

"What?"

Indigo held up the fuchsia dress with its many sequins and ruffles. It definitely wasn't the slim-fitting blue gown they'd picked. And when Indigo held it in front of her, it was clear it was both too wide and too long.

Adara turned to the garment bag that was supposed to hold her gown. She pulled down the zipper to find another fuchsia dress. Her stomach knotted up. Where were their dresses?

"Where are our dresses?" Indigo unconsciously echoed her.

"I don't know," Adara said.

With dread, she moved to the last dress bag. It was supposed to be Hermione's wedding gown. After the final fitting, the seamstress promised to fix a couple of the loose pearls and steam out any wrinkles before delivering it.

Please let this be the right dress.

Adara lowered the zipper. All the while her heart was in her throat. This just had to be the right dress, because if worse came to worst, they could find new bridesmaids' dresses, but a wedding gown...it was special. You couldn't just run out and buy a new one—especially with the bride away dealing with a family emergency and the ceremony next week.

She paused for just a second in pulling down the zipper, not sure she wanted to see the dress. Indigo moved to stand next to her. Adara pushed the garment bag back to find an ivory bridal gown with ruffles. Lots and lots of ruffles. Hermione's beloved snow-white gown didn't have a ruffle anywhere on it.

Both Adara and Indigo gasped in horror.

Oh, no! This is a mess.

She told herself not to panic. This could be easily resolved. She would just call the bridal boutique. She was certain whoever owned these gowns wanted them back as much as Adara and her friends wanted their dresses.

"We should tell Hermione."

"No." Adara shook her head. "We aren't going to bother her with this. She has other, more important things to deal with at the moment. I plan to find out where our dresses are. Just leave these ones with me, and I'll contact the boutique to sort this out."

Indigo sent her a worried look. "Can I do anything to help?"

"Not right now. But closer to the wedding, I'll need your help making the favors and some decorations."

"I can do that. Just let me know when you need me."

Indigo returned the dresses to the rack and then left. Adara checked the bags for the name of the boutique, but there was no logo. She retrieved a stack of paperwork for the wedding. Somewhere in there would be the phone number for the boutique. For some reason she thought it would be right on top, but it wasn't. And to her frustration, she couldn't recall the name. She'd only been there a couple of times and hadn't paid attention.

There was a knock at the door. With the stack of papers in hand, she moved to the door and opened it. There stood Krystof. She inwardly groaned. She didn't have time for him at the moment. If she hurried, she might be able to reach the shop before they closed for the day.

"Unless this is an emergency, it's going to have to wait. I've got something important to deal with right now." She resumed thumbing through the pages.

"What's the matter?" Krystof's deep, rich voice was unmistakable.

She wanted to ignore him until he grew bored and went away, but she knew him too well. Krystof thrived on a challenge. And her ignoring him would strike him as a challenge to try and distract her from whatever she was working on. And she couldn't let that happen.

With great reluctance, she paused and looked at him—really looked at him. That was her first mistake, as her gaze hungrily took in his tanned legs clad in a pair of navy shorts and a white polo shirt that hinted at his muscled chest. When she drew her gaze upward past his broad shoulders, she admired his strong jawline and squared chin. And then there were those kissable lips that could make her forget about everything else but getting lost in his arms.

But none of that mattered now. The fling they'd had was over. She'd thought she could do the casual thing with him, but she'd been wrong. She was a one-man woman, and she wanted a man who was only interested in her. The memory of him holding that other woman in his arms cooled her warmed blood.

When her gaze finally met his brown eyes, she found amusement glittering in them. Her back teeth ground together. He'd caught her checking him out. Why had she done that? She was over him. It didn't matter how great a lover he was, he wasn't her man. And he never would be.

"What do you want, Krystof? Can't you see I'm in the middle of something important?"

"It wouldn't happen to have something to do with the wedding, would it?"

She considered lying to him so he'd leave, but what good would that do her? It was easier just to honest with him and send him on his way. "Promise this just stays between us?"

His dark brows arched. "Of course. How bad is it?"

"Well, considering they delivered the wrong dresses for the wedding, it's definitely not the best news."

"The wrong dresses! How did you miss this?"

"How did *I*?" Was he serious? "I didn't miss anything. This is the first chance we had to look at the dresses. Remember, some of us have to work for a living." She glared at him.

His brown eyes grew stormy, but when he spoke, his tone was level. "How wrong are they? Maybe it's still something you can work with."

"Are you kidding me?" Then she realized he was perfectly serious. "No. We can't just swap them for the originals. These dresses are the wrong color, the wrong style and the wrong sizes."

"That does seem to be a problem."

"You think? Now if you'll leave me be, I'm about to call the boutique." She returned her attention to the pages of wedding receipts and forms.

She could feel Krystof's gaze upon her, but she didn't give him the satisfaction of knowing that she was paying him any attention. Her priority was fixing this snafu with the wedding before Hermione found out.

In this particular moment, she didn't want to talk to him. She'd already wasted enough time on him. Now she just wanted to pretend he didn't exist, but he was making that difficult as he stood there with his arms crossed over his broad chest and a frown on his handsome face. And that irritated her, too. No one that annoying should be so good-looking.

CHAPTER FIVE

HE SHOULD WALK away. This was not his problem.

And yet Krystof could see the worry written all over Adara's beautiful face. Her brown hair with its blond highlights was pulled back in a braid that swept past her shoulders. A fringe framed her perfectly made-up face.

It was the stubborn jut of her chin and the firm line of her glossy lips that let him know she wasn't giving up until the dress situation was properly resolved—with the original dresses located and returned to her as soon as possible.

He honestly didn't see the big deal. After all, these were just dresses, weren't they? Surely they could buy other dresses.

But he wasn't so out of the loop that he didn't know some women invested a lot of effort and dreams into weddings. They had a vision, and it upset them greatly when that vision didn't come to fruition. That appeared to be the case here.

Thankfully he didn't have any intention of getting married. He'd already had enough people let him down in life. He wasn't about to open himself up just to be hurt all over again. All those vows about loving each other until death—he wondered how many people really believed the words when they said them. Did they really believe in forever? He categorically did not.

He took in the lines that now bracketed Adara's blue eyes and kissable mouth as she stood there with the phone pressed to her ear. As the silence dragged on, twin lines formed between her brows. It didn't appear the bridal boutique was going to answer.

When she disconnected the call, his curiosity got the best of him. "When do they open again?"

"I don't know. They were supposed to be open now."

"Maybe they're busy with other customers. Try again."

He expected an argument, but instead she once more dialed the boutique. She held the phone to her ear as she began to pace. Eventually she disconnected the call and shook her head.

"I don't understand," she said. "Between the three of us, we've been to the shop numerous times, when you include picking out the dresses and the fittings. They were always open during business hours."

He reached for his phone. "What's the name of the shop?"

She told him, and he typed it into the search engine. It took him a couple of tries until he spelled it correctly. And then at last the shop's website popped up on the screen.

He checked their hours of operation. "It says they should be open today until six."

Adara checked the time. "It's only four."

"Maybe we should go for a ride."

"Good idea. I'll take the dresses with me. I don't want to have to make a second trip." She reached for her purse and grabbed the dresses.

When she started for the door, he fell into step behind her. He was certain this mix-up could be easily resolved. After all, who would want a dress that didn't fit them?

Adara stopped abruptly in the hallway. He nearly ran into her. When she spun around, he was so close she stumbled. Her hands landed on his chest. He reached out to her. His fingers grasped her waist, and he pulled her close to steady her.

Time seemed to stand still as she leaned into him. He stared deep into her eyes as she stared back at him. His pulse kicked up a notch or two. For weeks and weeks now, he'd envisioned this moment. When he closed his eyes each night, holding her close and claiming her lips with his own was what he envisioned. And now he wanted more than anything to hold on to this moment—to make it last as long as possible.

His gaze dipped to her lips. All he could think about was how much he wanted to kiss her. The months they'd been apart felt like years. He'd really missed her a lot more than he'd been willing to admit to himself. But he couldn't give in to his desires—not with so much still unsettled between them.

His gaze rose to meet hers once more. He'd missed her smile and her laughter. He missed all of it. Still, he wasn't going to beg her to come back to him if she wasn't interested. Not a chance. He didn't beg anyone for anything.

How could she so quickly dismiss their perfect friends-with-benefits arrangement? Maybe Adara simply needed a reminder? Yes, that sounded like a good idea. His gaze lowered to her lips. They were devoid of any lipstick or gloss, as though she'd been caught off guard that morning and forgotten to put it on. Which was strange, because Adara was the most organized, put-together person he knew. He wondered what had distracted her.

He had always loved to be her distraction, but she hadn't given him the time of day since he'd arrived. And as much as he wanted to kiss her, he refused to do that until things were settled between them.

It was with the greatest regret that he released his hold on her and took a step back. It was though that's all it took for Adara to regain her senses.

She frowned fiercely at him. "What are you doing?"

"Keeping you from falling."

"Not that. Why are you following me?"

"Um..." Was this a trick question? "I'm walking with you to the car."

She shook her head. "No, you're not."

"Of course I am. We have to get this dress thing sorted."

"*We* aren't doing anything. I'm going to go take care of this.

You…well, you can go sit on the beach or find a card game to play." She turned and continued to walk away.

Cards didn't mean that much to him, at least not these days. Years ago, they'd been a quick way for him to climb his way out of poverty. With a photogenic memory and a high IQ, which had earned him a scholarship to a top university, he'd found he was good at card games. Very good.

These days playing cards just didn't hold a challenge like they used to. He'd never told anyone this. He simply let everyone assume he traveled from one card game to the next. In truth, he just liked to travel. Sometimes he played, but often he worked on his computer programing. Utilizing computer language was like a puzzle to him, and it challenged him in a way that cards never had.

He'd developed a social media platform called MyPost. At first it had been a way to connect card sharks and arrange large tournaments. Then MyPost had started to grow. Now he had a staff that managed the site for him, allowing him to continue his nomadic ways.

He continued to follow Adara. "I'm going with you."

This time when she stopped, he was ready for her and had left enough room between them. She turned to him with an exasperated sigh. "Are you really going to stick around until the wedding?"

"I am."

Adara dramatically rolled her eyes. "Is there anything I can say to dissuade you?"

"No." He made a point of checking his Rolex. "We're wasting time."

Her gaze narrowed as she was silent for a moment. "Fine. But when we get there, I'll do the talking."

"Be my guest." But he planned to do some talking before they arrived at the boutique.

She glared at him. "Has anyone ever told you that you're stubborn?"

"Yes."

With a deep sigh, she held out the dresses to him. "If you insist on coming with me, you can make yourself useful." When he took the dresses from her, she said, "Hold them higher. They can't touch the ground." When he went to drape them over his arm, she frowned. "They'll get wrinkled that way."

Was she serious? They weren't even her dresses. "Why do you care?"

"Because if I was the person that owned those dresses, I'd hope someone would take good care of them."

He lifted the dresses until she was satisfied. Then she turned and continued walking. She pulled out her phone and made a call. "Demi, an emergency has come up. I need to step out for a bit. Can you handle things here?" Her head bobbed up and down as though she were agreeing with whatever was said on the other end of the phone. "Thank you. I appreciate this."

"Everything okay?" he asked.

"With the resort, yes. As for the wedding, it will be fine as soon as we find the correct dresses."

When they came to the end of the hallway, instead of turning right to head to the lobby, Adara turned to the left. He was confused. "I thought we were leaving."

"We are. My car is parked in the back."

"But why don't we just take one of the resort's sedans?"

"Because those are for guests." She kept walking.

He hurried to keep up with her. "Of which I happen to be one."

"But I'm not."

"Really? Because I'd heard from Atlas that you're staying at the resort until the wedding."

"That's just a matter of convenience. I'm not a true guest." She stopped at the exit and turned to him. "Must we do this?"

"Do what?"

"Talk. It'd be so much easier if I was doing this alone." And then she slipped on her sunglasses and headed outside.

He may have been warned off pursuing Adara by his best friend, but if he could just get her to stop long enough to really listen to him, he was certain he could clear up their misunderstanding. And then they could go back to their friends-with-benefits status. No one would get hurt, because emotions wouldn't be involved.

And this car ride was the perfect opportunity to have a conversation. He refused to let the opportunity slip by him. He was certain that by the time they returned to the resort, he'd know exactly where things had gone wrong between them.

Why was he here?

Not the wedding part. She understood about his best man duties. But why was he in her car? Why was he inserting himself in the preparations when she was fully capable of handling them alone?

Adara had no answers. It certainly wasn't because wedding planning excited him. And it wasn't likely he was still interested in her—not when he could have his pick of so many other women. So was what he said true? He was just looking out for his best friend?

He'd just told her he planned to stick around until the wedding and seemed insistent he should insert himself into the wedding plans. But why? She wanted nothing to do with him. What about that didn't he get?

She needed to tell him point-blank that she didn't want him around. Maybe then he'd move on to his next card game or next beautiful woman. The thought of him with another woman in his arms had her gripping the steering wheel tighter. She refused to let her thoughts go there.

When they reached the ferry to the mainland, he took a phone call. She thought at first it was one of his girlfriends, and once again an uneasy feeling churned in the pit of her stomach. However, when he mentioned assets and liabilities, she breathed easier. A business call. She couldn't deny her curiosity. Was this a new direction in his life? She was dying to ask him questions, but she refused to get drawn into his world again.

With him distracted, she moved to the upper deck and approached the railing. She hoped for a little breathing room. Krystof was starting to feel like her shadow. She couldn't ever remember him being so attentive. In fact, she was quite certain he'd never been this persistent. Was it guilt? Had he spotted her back at the Paris hotel after all?

She'd never know, because she wasn't going to discuss that episode with him. To live through it was enough humiliation for her. She didn't want to rehash the horrible scene.

Was it possible he regretted the other woman? Did he realize what a good thing he'd had with her? It would serve him right if he had regrets. She had her own for thinking he could change.

There had been the briefest moment when she'd first run into him again, when the episode in Paris had vanished from her mind. For a split second, she'd forgotten everything except how good they were together.

When he had gazed into her eyes, her heart had pounded so loud that it'd echoed in her ears. Her body had thoroughly and completely betrayed her. Because there was absolutely no reason she should want him any longer.

She'd been wrong to get involved with him in the first place. He was nothing like her. He acted without thinking. He didn't believe in making plans. He didn't even comprehend the use of a day planner. He liked to live on a whim. She could understand being spontaneous for dinner, but not as a lifestyle choice.

She liked to have everything sorted and arranged on her digital calendar, with its handy reminders. Every minute of her workday was accounted for, and she took comfort in knowing what to expect from her day. She didn't have to worry about where she should be and what needed doing, because it was already organized.

"I wondered where you'd gone." Krystof's voice came from behind her.

She inwardly groaned. So much for her moment alone to gather her thoughts. She grudgingly turned. "What do you need?"

"You."

Her heart leapt into her throat. His bold answer stood between them like a declaration. What was he trying to say? That he wanted her back? *No. No. No.* That wasn't going to happen.

She turned back to stare out at the sea. She concentrated on the swells of the water, trying to calm herself. Then, hoping her voice didn't betray the way his words had unnerved her, she said, "I'm not in the mood to play word games. Just go."

"No. I'm not going to be dismissed like you've been doing for the last two months." There was a resolute tone to his deep voice. "We're going to talk. It's long overdue."

She turned to him, noticing his arms were crossed and his lips were pressed in a firm line. "You have nothing to say that I want to hear."

"Too bad. I'm going to say it anyway."

She noticed how he'd waited until they were stuck on the ferry between Ludus Island and the mainland. There was absolutely nowhere for her to go to avoid him. She should have known his offer to join her today came with an ulterior motive.

She narrowed her gaze on him and jutted out her chin. "Once you have your say, will you give me some space?"

"I can't do that. I'm staying until the wedding whether you want me here or not. This isn't about us. It's about Hermione and Atlas."

"Agreed. But it doesn't mean you have to be everywhere I am."

"I'm just keeping my word to Atlas."

She restrained a sigh. She wondered how much longer he was going to use that excuse. There was another reason he was sticking around. "Is that the only reason?"

"Of course."

"Because if you think you and I are going start up again where we left off, it's never going to happen."

A muscle in his jaw twitched. "You make it sound like you were miserable with me. I happen to know different. I know how to turn you on. I know the spot to kiss on your neck that makes you moan—"

"Stop!"

Just then the whistle blew long and loud, letting everyone know they would soon be pulling into the dock. With her face hot, she rushed back to the car. She'd wanted to tell him that he was wrong about knowing such intimate details about her, but she wasn't going to lie. The truth was that he knew far too much about pleasing her—more than anyone had ever known.

She didn't care if he followed her or not. That wasn't quite true. But she told herself that it didn't matter what he did. She was finished speaking to him, because he was utterly impossible.

CHAPTER SIX

SHE'D REJECTED HIM. AGAIN.

At least that was the way it felt after their conversation on the ferry.

Krystof wasn't used to being cast off once, much less twice. In fact, it had never happened before. He was always the one who did the walking away. And now that it had happened, he wasn't quite sure what to do about it.

His pricked ego told him to cut his losses and leave the island. Because Adara was completely and utterly organized. She didn't need anyone, including, apparently, him. The thought didn't sit well with him, but he refused to evaluate why it bothered him.

As for the wedding, what could go wrong? Okay, other than the mix-up with the dresses. But they were almost to the dress shop, and then the dresses would be sorted. In no time, they'd head back to the island with the correct ones.

With the bachelor party canceled, his services weren't needed on the island until the wedding. Between now and then, he could visit Singapore or perhaps head to Paris to work on his tentative plan to buy a tech company. He'd been putting off exploring the option until after the wedding, but why put it off when he could do it now?

And so he decided that, after things were remedied at the

dress shop, he would go back to the resort to collect his things and then he'd be on his way. Atlas would understand, since he'd warned him not to stir things up with Adara. Yes, that's exactly what he'd do.

Adara slowed the car before gracefully maneuvering into a parallel parking spot. Krystof glanced around at all the colorful shops with their showroom windows painted with the stores' logos and the colorful awnings. If he liked to shop, which he categorically did not, this would be the area he would frequent. It was welcoming, and he appeared not to be the only one who thought so, because the sidewalks were busy with pedestrians carrying lots of shopping bags.

His gaze took in one side of the street before moving to the other. He searched for their destination. It was easy to spot because of the pink-and-white-striped awning with a wooden sign that read Dora's Wedding Heaven. In the big picture windows were mannequins—naked mannequins.

Where are their clothes? Aren't they supposed by wearing wedding dresses?

He wasn't so sure about this shop. It was an odd display, to say the least. And then he noticed the lights were out. That was strange, too. He checked the time. It was only a few minutes after five. The shop was supposed to be open until six.

"It looks like they've closed early," he said. "And they really should consider clothing their mannequins."

"Leave it to you to notice that." She rolled her eyes before gathering her purse. "I'm going to try the door." She got out of the car.

He'd come this far. He might as well go the rest of the way. And so he followed her across the street.

Adara made it to the door and pulled on the handle. The door didn't budge. She tried again. "I don't understand. Why would they be closed?"

He noticed the sign above her head. It read Out of Business. Well, that certainly wasn't good news.

He nudged Adara and pointed. When she saw the sign, there was a loud gasp. She took a couple of steps back on the sidewalk as though she were stunned by this turn of events.

"That can't be right," she said. "I just talked to them the other day to make arrangements to have the dresses delivered."

He noticed the phone number on the door. He tried it, only to find it was disconnected.

"Why didn't you leave a message?" Adara asked.

"The phone has been disconnected."

"That can't be right." She dialed the number and then held the phone to her ear. A low growl let him know she'd gotten the same response. She ended the call and looked at him. "Now what are we going to do?"

He noticed how she'd said *we* this time, but when he went to point it out to her, the worry reflected in her eyes silenced him. "They can't just hold your dresses hostage."

Adara once more stepped up to the glass door. She pulled out her phone and selected the flashlight app. He stepped up beside her. She held the phone to the door, letting the light reflect through the window onto the empty dress racks. The dresses were all gone. The store was completely deserted.

"No. No. No." Her voice filled with frustration. "This can't be happening. They seemed like such nice people."

"You don't know what happened. They might very well be nice people. We'll get this sorted." He hoped. "Let's go."

He turned around to find they weren't the only ones peering in the windows of the shop and asking questions. He cleared his throat. "Does anyone know what happened to the owners?"

The six or so people who had stopped in front of the shop shook their heads. No one seemed to know what had happened. This didn't bode well for them finding the correct dresses.

Once back inside the car, he checked the time. "Do you want to grab something to eat?"

She shook her head. "I have no appetite. What I want is to find the dresses for the wedding. How could this have happened?" She turned her head until their gazes met. "How am I going to tell Hermione that her wedding dress is missing?"

"You're not." His words were quick and firm. "She has enough to worry about."

"But I can't keep this from her forever. When she gets back, she's going to learn the truth."

"Unless we can figure out what happened between now and then."

Turmoil shown in her eyes. "Do you think we can do it?"

"I don't know." He couldn't lie to her. He had absolutely no idea what had happened to the dresses. Were they delivered to the wrong people? Or had the owners taken off with them to offload somewhere else? "All I know is that we can try our best to find them."

She nodded as she started the car. "We'll do everything we can."

"Yes, we will." He fastened his seat belt.

In that moment, he realized his plans to escape the island and the woman who'd rejected him had just been upended. Because somewhere along the way, he'd promised to help her resolve this problem.

And though he'd like to think it would just take a phone call or two to locate the gowns, he had a feeling it wasn't going to be that simple. Just as working with Adara wasn't going to be simple. But he would deal with it all, one way or the other.

This was the worst.

Okay, maybe not quite the worst. But it wasn't good.

Adara tried the phone number for the shop again and again. And then she started a search for the name of the owner. It wasn't as easy to find as she might have thought. Because the owner's name wasn't Dora.

Go figure.

The owner was actually a man. And when she tried to find a phone number for him, she ran into problems. It was a common name, so she had a long list of names and numbers. This was going to take some time, and it was getting late.

Knock-knock.

Krystof stuck his head inside her office. "I thought I'd find you here."

She sighed and leaned back in her chair. "I've been trying to get ahold of anyone involved with the shop."

"And did you find someone?"

"No. And the owner's name isn't Dora. It's Michalis."

"Interesting." He stepped farther into the office.

"I've called a dozen people by that name, and they all say they have nothing to do with the shop." She turned off her computer. She needed a break. "How did things go for you? Were you able to come up with a way to track down the dresses?"

"I'm not sure. I have an idea. I'll let you know if I'm successful."

His words gave her a glimmer of hope when she desperately needed something to cling to. "Don't keep me in suspense. Tell me what you're doing."

"I'd rather not. It might not come to anything."

"Please. I've struck out all evening. I need some hope."

"I'll make you a deal. Come have some dinner with me, and I'll tell you my plan to find the dresses."

She arched a brow. "How can you be sure I haven't already eaten?"

"Because I know you, and you were set on locating the dresses. You wouldn't have stopped to eat. And that's why I'm going to make sure you have something to eat tonight."

"I don't think that's part of your responsibilities. You only promised Atlas that you'd help with the wedding."

"Um, but you're a part of the wedding, so I have to make sure you take care of yourself." This was his chance to dig a little deeper into what had happened between them. "That is, unless you have a date with someone else?"

She shook her head. "No date."

"What about a boyfriend?" He couldn't help himself. He had to know if she'd moved on.

Her eyes widened momentarily. "No boyfriend, either."

"Good." So if it wasn't another man, that meant whatever the problem was between them was likely fixable.

"Good?" She eyed him suspiciously.

That would teach him for letting his thoughts translate into spoken words. "Yes, good, because now you have no excuse not to join me."

She hesitated as though making up her mind, and then she shrugged. "I guess I can't argue about that."

He hadn't expected her to give in so easily. Every now and then she totally surprised him. This was one of those times.

"Then let's go."

She stood and rounded the desk. On her way out the door, she turned off the lights. That was a good sign. He was worried she was going to work all night trying to find the dresses.

"Where are we having dinner?" she asked.

"I thought maybe we'd dine in my suite. I already ordered food. It should be there when we arrive."

She stopped walking. "Krystof, I don't think this is a good idea. I told you we're not going back to the way things used to be."

"I heard you. I just knew that a lot of the resort's restaurants would be booked, and I thought you would be tired and want a chance to kick off your heels and relax. I promise I have no plans beyond that."

She hesitated, as though trying to decide if she should believe him or not. "Okay. Just a quick dinner, and then I'm off. I have an early day tomorrow."

"Sounds like a plan."

As they resumed walking, she asked, "How did you know what to order me?"

"It wasn't hard. We spent quite a few meals together. I know that you prefer fish or vegetarian meals. So I ordered scampi and wild rice with a salad."

Her eyes said what her mouth didn't. She was surprised he knew her so well. "It sounds good. And suddenly I'm hungry."

He liked the idea of them sharing a friendly meal. He held the door of his suite for her. He had been given the gamer-themed suite. There was a super-size flat screen on one wall with all the various gaming consoles, as well as a dedicated internet connection for online role playing. There were a couple of gamer's chairs that were so comfortable he would buy one if he had a place he called home.

The room was painted with graphics from various games. And a 3-D roulette table was on the ceiling. There were vintage pinball tables and early video games. On the other side of the room was a pool table, a Ping-Pong table and a shuffleboard table. And there were more games that he hadn't even gotten to yet, including a dartboard and a basketball hoop.

The best part was that the room had excellent soundproofing, so you could crank up the stereo system and play games the entire night without bothering the other suites. Not that he was into that these days. He found the idea of staying up all night and sleeping all day not as appealing as it had been in his younger years.

He noticed Adara taking in the room, kind of like a kid in a toy store. "I take it you haven't been in this suite."

"This is a large resort. There are a lot of suites that I have yet to visit. And they redecorate them on a regular basis. Nothing about the resort gets stale or, worse, old. Guests like to be constantly surprised. This suite looks like it was created for an overgrown kid."

"Did you just call me a kid?"

She shrugged. "I didn't say that, but if the title fits…"

He'd wondered how long it would be until she started to complain about his transient lifestyle. He'd told her from the beginning that he wasn't going to change, not for her, not for anyone. He'd always been proud of his easy, breezy lifestyle, without any ties to any one place.

But seeing as how she didn't want to resume their friends-with-benefits arrangement, he didn't feel a need to defend his choices. He did as he pleased. He had no one to answer to except himself. And up until that point, it was the way he liked it. But since meeting Adara, he was finding his lifestyle perhaps a little too freeing and, dare he admit it, lonely.

"I'm sorry," she said. "I shouldn't have said that. After all, you're helping me locate the missing dresses. I'm just tired, and there's so much to worry about."

So much to worry about? He was confused. "I thought the only problem was with the dresses."

"Oh, yes. Right. Don't mind me. I guess the hunger is getting to me, too."

She tried to cover for her slip, but he didn't believe her. There was obviously more going on than she was willing to share with him. He wondered what it could be.

"Why don't we play a game while we wait for the food?" she suggested.

She didn't have to ask him twice. "What would you like to play?"

She turned in a circle, taking in the numerous games. "How about pinball? I haven't played that since I was a kid."

"Pinball it is."

And so they took turns playing. He had to give it to her—she was pretty good for not playing since she was a kid. The more they played, the more the worry lines on her face faded and the more she smiled.

Someone knocked at the door.

"That would be our dinner." He moved to the door and opened it. A server stood there with a white linen–covered cart.

"Good evening, sir. Where would you like your dinner set up?"

"I think it would be a nice evening to eat out on the patio."

The young man, in black trousers and a white dress shirt, nodded. "Certainly. Just give me a moment."

"Not a problem. We have a round of pinball to finish." He turned back to Adara.

She pushed the ball-launch button. The screen lit up with flashing lights as the machine *ding-ding-dinged*. Krystof enjoyed watching her play. She was very focused on the game. And when she scored an extra ball, she gave out a little cheer.

For the first time ever, Krystof didn't feel the need to win. He'd already won by being in Adara's presence and feeling her happiness. He just hoped his idea to locate the dresses would work out in order to sustain her good mood.

Dinner was waiting for them by the time Adara's last silver ball slipped down the chute. She'd won the round, and her big smile made Krystof grin, too.

They moved out onto the private patio where a table had been set with a linen tablecloth, candles and a red rose in a bud vase. Beneath silver covers was their meal, still warm, and the aroma was divine. For the most part, dinner was quiet as they each made short work of their food.

As they leaned back to sip their coffee, Adara asked, "What is your idea to get back the dresses?"

This was his moment for a confession. It was something he didn't tell many people. "I have posted it to my social media on MyPost."

"MyPost? You're on there?" Surprise was written all over her face. "I just didn't see you as the type to share things on social media."

"I actually developed the platform."

She sat up straighter. "What?"

For the first time, he felt awkward for allowing everyone to think he was nothing more than a card-playing nomad. He cleared his throat. "I write code."

Her mouth gaped. It took her a moment to gather herself. "Why is tonight the first I'm hearing of this?"

He shrugged and shifted his gaze to the moonlight as it played over the darkened sea. "Because I don't talk much about it. I guess I got used to keeping things to myself when I was growing up. Without ever knowing my parents, I learned the only person I could count on was myself."

"I'm sorry. That must have been so tough for you."

He shrugged. "I never really knew any other way to be."

"So you went to school for programming?" When he nodded, she said, "Wow. That's very impressive. And you own MyPost?"

"I do. I've hired a team to do the day-to-day maintenance. It's gotten a lot bigger than I ever imagined." The site had millions of users that spanned the globe, and it was growing every day.

"So you're no longer involved with it?"

That was the thing. He'd had thoughts about ways he could expand it to make it more vital to a larger group of people. "When I started it, it was just a means to bring together card players. A way to plan and organize card games around the world. But I couldn't leave it alone, so I'd work on it in my spare time. It just grew and grew. And now it's getting so large that I either need to sell it or take a more active role in its processes."

"And what will you do?"

"I'm not sure I'm willing to give up traveling and be locked into one place."

"Oh." The light in her eyes dimmed as she busied herself with reaching for her glass of water. "What does all of this have to do with the dresses?"

"I've put up a post about the dress shop closing and asked if anyone else also received the wrong dress."

She set aside her water glass. "Wait. Are you saying you have that many friends on MyPost that your post would have a chance of reaching the right people?"

He shook his head. "I don't have any friends on the platform. I belong to a private card group. That's it. But I'm the owner. I can make the platform do what I want. And so I constructed a notification that has gone out to each and every user. When they log on, they'll see it. They will have to read it and click through to get to their page."

Adara reached in her pocket and pulled out her phone. Her fingers rapidly moved over the screen, and then there was a gasp. "You really did it."

He smiled. "I did. Now we have to hope it'll be seen by the right people."

She continued staring at her phone as her fingers moved over the touch screen. "And you formed a private group for all of those affected by this issue. There are already people in the group. We aren't the only ones searching for the right dresses."

"Yes, but so far no one has dresses like you're searching for."

Adara's gaze lifted to meet his. "This is wonderful. Thank you."

He shrugged. "It's not a lot. It still hasn't recovered the dresses."

"But it might. This is more than I've been able to do." Then twin lines formed between her brows.

"What's the matter?"

She shook her head. "Nothing."

"It's definitely something, so out with it."

"I was just wondering if Hermione would see it. Maybe I need to call her now and tell her what happened." Her fingers began to move over the phone again.

He reached out and placed his hand over hers, pausing her actions. "Don't phone her. The chances of her being on social media right now would be slim, don't you think?"

Adara paused before nodding.

"And hopefully the dresses will be recovered before she realizes anything happened."

"I hope you're right." She made a point of checking the time on her phone. "It's getting late. I should be going."

He wanted to ask her to stay. He wanted to pull her into his arms once more and kiss her lips. Instead he said, "And I have a card game to get to on the mainland."

A brief frown skittered across her face as she got to her feet. When she faced him, her face was devoid of expression. "I don't want to keep you."

"I'll walk you out." He had to rush to catch up with her quick steps.

She was mad at him *again*. And once more, he didn't understand what he'd done. Was he supposed to work all night trying to recover the dresses? At this point, he didn't know what else he could do.

At the door, she paused and turned to him. "Thank you for the help today."

"You're welcome. I don't know that I did much, but I have a feeling everything will work out." And then he leaned forward. He resisted the urge to place a kiss on her lips and instead pressed his lips to her cheek.

When he pulled back, he noticed that pinkness had bloomed in her cheeks. And as much as he wanted to pull her into his arms and kiss her properly, he knew it wasn't a good idea. She wasn't ready for that.

At least not yet.

CHAPTER SEVEN

HE'D KISSED HER cheek, not her lips.

What did that mean?

Adara had wondered about the kiss the rest of the evening and late into the night. She'd gotten to know Krystof fairly well over the last seven months. He was a man who knew what he wanted and wasn't afraid to go after it.

There was nothing in that kiss that spoke of passion or longing. And she couldn't deny that it disappointed her. She knew she should be fine with it, because they both wanted different things in life.

He'd obviously found what he was looking for in that other woman. She tried to tell herself that it didn't matter—he didn't matter to her. So then why was her stomach knotted?

The following day, she was thankfully busy all morning—too busy to have breakfast with Krystof when he stopped by her office. In fact, she'd come to work early today. It was so easy to be early when she was staying at the resort. Before Atlas and Hermione owned the resort, it would have been impossible for her to stay in a suite. There had been rules about the employees not being able to utilize the resort's amenities, from the rooms to the spa. But the new owners had seen fit to relax those rules—within reason.

She had spent the lunch hour in her office making phone calls to track down the owner of the bridal shop. And so far she hadn't had any luck. It was like the owners had just up and disappeared overnight. How was that possible?

Someone rapped their knuckles on the door.

She glanced up to find Krystof standing in the doorway. He sent her a smile that made her stomach dip. She automatically returned his smile. As soon as she realized what she was doing, she pressed her lips into a firm line.

"Hi. What can I do for you?" she asked in her concierge voice.

"It's a matter of what I can do for you."

"For me?" She had absolutely no idea what he was talking about.

"You know how I told you I set up that message on MyPost?" When she nodded, he said, "I've had a response. Someone has the wrong wedding dress. They think it might be the one we're hunting for."

"Did they include a photo?"

He pulled it up on his phone and then held it out for her to see. "I hope it's the right one."

"Me, too." She took the phone from him and stared at the image. It was the correct shade of white. The quality of the photo wasn't good enough to make out the detail of the bead-work. But the neckline was all wrong. Instead of the sweet-heart neckline that Hermione had loved, this one had a square neckline.

Her heart sank. "This isn't the right dress."

"Are you sure?"

She nodded. "I'm positive."

"Oh. Okay. We'll keep looking. It'll turn up."

"I hope so."

"We should take pictures of the dresses you have and I'll post them to the group. The more eyes we get on the post in MyPost, the more people will talk about it. The more attention the wedding dress mix-up gets, the better chance of finding the correct dresses."

"Good idea. I've had them moved to my room so they were out of the way." She glanced at her calendar. "We can go now. I have a half hour before I'm supposed to meet with the Carringtons about their cocktail party."

As they walked to her room, the awkwardness between them returned. She had no idea how to make small talk with him, nor did she want to. If she hadn't caught on to the fact that he was seeing other women, would he have even told her?

She told herself that it didn't matter now. It was all behind them. She needed to stay focused on the task at hand—the hunt for the wedding dress.

In the end, Krystof was all wrong for her. Maybe it was the fact that something was possibly going wrong with her body. It had her looking toward the future differently. She wanted a real relationship. Something with strings and words of endearment. Was it so wrong to want someone to say *I love you*? Someone who wanted to stick around through the good and the bad? Was that asking too much?

Krystof had made it clear during their time together that he wasn't that kind of man—the kind who settled down. And for a time she'd thought she was perfectly okay with that—that it would be enough. She'd been wrong.

"Adara, isn't that your room we just passed?" Krystof's voice drew her from her thoughts.

She glanced around and realized he was right. She'd been so deep in thought that she'd walked straight past her room. The heat of embarrassment climbed up her neck and settled in her cheeks, and she retraced her steps.

"I... I'm not used to staying here yet." She let herself into the room.

Compared to his suite, her room was very modest. On the opposite side of the room from her white couches and glass coffee table was a king-size bed with an assortment of pillows in shades of aqua and white.

Although with Krystof in the room with her, it suddenly didn't seem so big—and the bed loomed large. She felt his gaze following her. She tried to ignore him but soon found it was an impossibility.

"I have the dresses over here." She'd had them place the cart into the spacious walk-in closet. She rolled it out. "We can just photograph them hanging on the rack."

"Or you could model all the dresses," he teased.

"Not a chance."

"Why not? I thought you wanted to get married."

"I never said that." Not to him, anyway. She thought some day she might get married and have a family of her own—something like her parents once had. But she didn't want to think of any of that now. "I'll just unzip the garment bag and fluff out the wedding gown."

She did that, and he took a photo. And then they did the same with the bridesmaid dresses. But as she was putting the wedding dress carefully in the garment bag, some of the material got caught in the zipper. As she struggled to free the material without damaging the dress, she pulled too hard on the garment bag, and the rack began to fall on her.

Krystof launched into action and caught the rack before it could touch her. When she straightened, she turned too quickly and bumped into him. She got a brief whiff of his spicy cologne. The scent was enough to take her back in time to a place where it would be so natural for her to just lean forward and press her lips to his.

Her heart started to beat quickly. She tilted her chin upward until their gazes caught and held. She should pull away, and yet her feet wouldn't cooperate.

The breath solidified in her throat. She couldn't remember why she was resisting falling into his arms and picking up where they'd left off. She longed to feel the passionate touch of his kiss. Because in that moment, she missed him so very much.

"Adara, where did things go wrong with us?" he asked gruffly.

It all came rushing back to her. His suggestion that they should have a casual relationship. His repeated requests for her to take time off work to visit him in various parts of the world. Her eye-opening surprise, the one time she'd done that, only to find him with another woman.

She shook her head. "Don't go acting like it matters to you."

"I'd really like to know."

Her gaze narrowed as she tried to decide if he was messing with her. Sincerity reflected in his gaze. He really didn't know that she'd seen him in Paris.

She sighed. "Remember how you kept asking me to meet you for a weekend?" When he nodded, she continued. "Well, I finally did. I flew to Paris in July, and I saw you with another woman."

His brows lifted, and then he stared off into space as though he were trying to recall the specific occasion. She started to wonder how many women he had on the side. Was she just one of a multitude?

"I don't recall seeing you."

She noticed how he ignored the mention of another woman. "You're right. You didn't see me. I'd just stepped off the elevator on your floor of the hotel. When I turned the corner, I saw a woman at your door."

His eyes widened. "Adara, you got things wrong in Paris."

"So you're saying I imagined you answering the door smiling, wearing nothing more than a bath towel, and the woman rushing into your arms?"

"No. I'm saying you misunderstood the situation."

There was a part of her that wanted to believe him, and it annoyed her that she could still be drawn in by him. "I think I got the gist of it," she said dryly.

"No, you didn't, because the woman was my sister."

"Your sister?" Surely she hadn't heard him correctly.

He nodded his head. "Yes, my sister."

Thank goodness she had the dress rack to hold her up. It took a moment for this information to sink in.

Krystof had a sister? Since when? From everything he'd told her, he was an only child who'd been abandoned by his parents. Had he done one of those DNA tests and found his sister that way?

Or was this just some sort of story he had concocted to try and fix things between them? She studied him for a moment. Krystof might be unconventional in a lot of ways, but she didn't think he'd outright lie to her just to have his way. With that thought in mind, she decided to hear him out.

"Okay," she said. "I'm listening."

For a moment, he stood silent. Was he surprised that she'd agreed to hear him out? Or was he trying to find a starting point?

He cleared his throat. "When Celeste found out I was going to be in Paris, we made plans to meet up. I had no idea you were going to surprise me with a visit."

And this was exactly why she didn't like to live spontaneously. Sometimes those spur-of-the-moment decisions worked out, but a lot of the time, they didn't. In her case, it most definitely hadn't worked out.

But if that was his sister, did it mean he wasn't seeing anyone else? Her heart leaped with joy, but her mind tamped down the excitement. There was something not quite right with this story.

"I didn't think you had any siblings." She narrowed her gaze on him, hoping to determine the truth of the matter. "I thought you were an orphan who didn't know your parents. Has that changed?"

"Of course it hasn't changed." He raked his fingers through his hair. "Celeste isn't my biological sister. She was another orphan. We shared the same home for years. She was a couple of years younger than me, and I would watch out for her."

The thought of Krystof playing the protective big brother thawed her icy heart toward him. But she wasn't quite ready to forgive and forget. "So you're saying there's nothing between you two?"

His nose immediately scrunched up. "Between me and Celeste? Ooh... No. She's like my sister."

"But she's not your biological sister. And years have passed. Maybe feelings between you two have changed."

Distaste was written all over his face. "Adara, I have no romantic interest in Celeste. She is now and will forever be the closest thing I have to a sister. Don't try to make it out to be something it isn't."

He was right. She was pushing too hard in her earnest attempt to keep the wall up between them. She took a deep breath. "I'm sorry."

"So you see it was all a big misunderstanding." He smiled at her triumphantly, and her heart dipped like she was on a giant roller coaster. He stepped closer to her. "Now can we at last kiss and make up?"

"No." The answer was quick and short.

She knew if she didn't stop this madness right away, he would wear away her resolve and then what? They'd go back to the way things used to be where they only saw each other when he had time to stop by the island. And their phone conversations were intermittent at best. No. She'd already recognized that she needed a more stable relationship.

He reached out to her, his hands caressing her upper arms. "Come on. You know we were good together." He gazed deep into her eyes and lowered his voice. "Adara, I've missed you."

Her heart skipped a beat. It would be so easy to lean into him and claim his lips with her own. There was a part of her that was dying to do exactly that—but there was another part of her that knew a few stolen moments would never be enough for her.

She pulled away from his touch. "Um... I need to get back to work."

"I understand. I'll have these pictures posted online."

"Sounds good. Thank you."

"No problem." And then he let himself out of the room.

Adara stood there watching him walk away. She told herself repeatedly that she couldn't just fall back into his arms—even though that was what every fiber of her body wanted to do.

Still, she couldn't play by his rules. She couldn't do a casual, no-strings-attached relationship. Seeing him with that other woman—even if it had been innocent that time—had taught her that lesson. So why did she feel so disappointed that he seemed to have accepted her refusal so easily?

CHAPTER EIGHT

AT LAST THINGS were getting back on track, Krystof thought with satisfaction as he strode away from Adara's room. She now knew the truth about Celeste.

That was a good thing, because he didn't know how much longer he could resist kissing her.

Krystof knew Adara still wasn't convinced resuming their arrangement was a good thing. He just needed to take a different approach, that was all. One that drew her out of her safe and predictable life—one that showed her she needed to go after what she wanted.

He had no idea how hard it was going to be to resist her, especially when she looked at him with desire burning in her eyes. But he knew to act in those moments would be a mistake, because she was still putting up a wall between them.

If he could just convince her that they were good together, they could go back to the way things used to be. Lots of fun and no strings. After all, she had her career to focus on, and he had...

His thoughts stumbled as he realized he'd handed most of the control over MyPost to his very capable staff. And his interest in playing cards was waning. But there was still the chance to buy that tech firm in Paris. The only thing holding him back from doing just that was the idea of having to set down roots somewhere. There was still a part of him that felt like he needed to be out searching—no, exploring—exploring for the next big adventure and not locked in somewhere. A memory of his childhood being locked in a small room with no windows came rushing back to him. He pushed it away. That was then and this was now.

Later that day, Krystof stood off to the side of Adara's office as she spoke with a mother and daughter who'd brought in a wedding dress for Adara to examine, and in exchange she'd let them see the wedding dress that had been mistakenly delivered for Hermione. It would appear that though the dresses were a fairly close match, neither had the right one. This mix-up was far larger than he'd imagined. And so the search continued.

As the mother and daughter headed off for dinner, Adara turned to him with a worried gaze. "This isn't looking good."

"No worries. We're not giving up. The page I set up for the dresses is just starting to pick up the pace. And now I'll add the pictures of this other wedding dress we've just seen."

"I don't understand how all this happened in the first place. How could they have mixed up so many orders?"

He shrugged. "I have no idea. I don't know if it was intentional, to take the focus off the owners suddenly closing up shop without delivering all of the gowns, because those stories are starting to crop up online, or if someone unintentionally mixed up all of the tickets with the names. I have a feeling we'll never know the answer."

"I feel like I need to tell Hermione now. That way she'll still have time to get another dress."

"A wedding dress? I thought those took months to order."

Adara sighed. "They do. But maybe she could buy one off the rack or find one at a secondhand shop."

"Do you really think that's what she'd want?"

Adara shook her head. "No. She loved that dress. She knew

as soon as she saw it that it was the right one for her. And she didn't bother to look at any others after it."

"Then I think we need to keep looking for it."

Adara's gaze searched his for reassurance. "Do you really think we'll find it?"

"I think we're headed in the right direction." He wanted to promise her that they'd find the dresses, but he honestly didn't know if it was possible, especially in the short amount of time they had left until the wedding. But there was nothing more they could do right now. "Let's go get something to eat."

Adara's gaze moved back to her tidy desk. "I still have a lot of work to do."

He glanced at his Rolex. "And it'll wait. It's time to eat. Come on."

"But…"

"Adara, just leave it."

She expelled a sigh. "Okay." She followed him to the door and switched off the lights. "Dinner at your place? Or mine?"

"Actually, I have something different in mind." He presented his arm to her.

Her gaze moved from his eyes to his arm and then back again. After a brief hesitation, she placed her hand in the crook of his arm. "Where are we going?"

"You'll see."

They quietly walked through the resort. Their footsteps were muffled by the lush carpeting. On the walls were fabulous pieces of art. It was like walking through a museum. It gave Krystof an idea. Perhaps he'd start collecting art—finding the next big artist. Speaking of which, he'd already met a rising artist, Indigo Castellanos. He would have to make sure and purchase one of her works. She could be the start of his collection.

He paused to look at a painting of the ocean. "This is very good."

"I didn't know you were into art."

"It's a new passion of mine."

"Have you checked out the gallery yet?"

He shook his head. "I haven't."

"We could see it after dinner."

"Sounds like a plan." He smiled as he led her outside.

Little by little she was letting down her guard with him. In fact, they were almost friends again. His plan was working. That's good, because he'd missed her smile and the way it was so easy to talk to her about anything and everything.

"Where are we going?"

They continued to the other side of the patio and down the steps. He knew with all she'd been doing for not only her job but also the wedding that she needed to slow down and relax. And he had the perfect idea.

"We're going to eat dinner."

"But where? The restaurants are all behind us back in the resort."

"This is a special dinner. Just trust me."

When they reached the beach, they slipped off their shoes and set them aside. Evening had settled in, and the sun was hovering on the horizon, sending a cascade of pinks and purples over the puffy clouds.

"You want to go for a stroll along the beach?" she asked.

"Not exactly. But now that you mentioned it, it's not a bad idea." He tucked the idea aside for later.

He'd asked the staff to place his surprise for Adara just out of sight from the resort for privacy. So as they moved past a dune, he heard Adara gasp. He watched as she pressed a hand to her chest and gaped.

Candles lined a path of red rose petals to a table with a white linen tablecloth. A few torches surrounded the table, granting some light now that the sun was sinking below the horizon. The staff had done an excellent job.

"Krystof, what have you done?"

"I hope you like it."

"I love it." Her gaze briefly flickered from the table to him.

"But how did you do it? I'm the one that usually sets up these special moments."

A smile played at the corners of his lips. "I may have sworn your assistant to silence as we devised this evening."

"Remind me to give Demi a raise."

"I'm sure she'll appreciate it."

"If I'm not careful, she'll be replacing me."

"Trust me. You're irreplaceable." He'd come to that startling conclusion in the time they were apart. She was very special.

They walked along the rose petal–adorned path. Adara stopped next to the table and turned to him. She tilted her chin upward and stared into his eyes. "This is beautiful. But why did you do it?"

A gentle breeze blew and swiped a few strands of hair into her face. He reached out, tucking those silken strands behind her ear. And then he gazed into her eyes. "I want to show you how sorry I am about the way things ended between us."

"You didn't have to go to all of this trouble."

"I wanted to."

He longed to pull her close and press a kiss to her lips. By the way she was looking into his eyes, she wouldn't have complained. But he knew it was too soon. She might kiss him now, but later she would change her mind. He had to be patient, and eventually she'd see that they were better off with their friends-with-benefits arrangement.

He mustered his resolve and moved past her to pull out a chair for her. Once they were both seated, she said, "If I didn't know better, I'd think you were trying to seduce me."

He smiled. "Is it working?"

"Wouldn't you like to know," she teased.

It was a pleasant dinner. No, it was better than that. He was captivated by her words and spellbound by her beauty in the candlelight. He didn't want the evening to end.

With soft music playing in the background and the lull of the tide, they enjoyed a candlelit meal. She told him about some of the more interesting aspects of her job, and he shared snippets of what he'd been up to in the last few months. Then the conversation shifted to his interest in art. She seemed genuinely enthusiastic about him starting an art collection.

"So if you were to collect art," she asked, "where would you keep it?"

He went to speak but then hesitated. He realized he didn't have an answer for her question. "I guess that would pose a problem."

"Unless you were to buy a place." Her eyes lit up. "You know, somewhere to keep your treasures and perhaps to call home."

"I'll give it some thought." Settling down wasn't really in his plans.

"You're frowning. I see you don't like that idea." Disappointment reflected in her eyes.

He owed her an explanation. Maybe then she would stop pushing for him to be something he wasn't. "I know you want me to stay put and create a home, but that just isn't me."

"But why? Everyone I know has a home, except you."

He sighed as he lounged back in his chair. He didn't like to dig around in his memories. Most of them were not happy ones. And though he knew he had it better than others, it still wasn't the happy, loving family that people witnessed on television sitcoms. In fact, his past was quite the opposite.

"I keep moving around because I was stuck in an unhappy foster home where I never felt I belonged." He toyed with the hem of the discarded cloth napkin on the table. "It was a place that I couldn't escape—no matter how many times I ran away." He stopped himself there.

He'd said more than he ever intended. He refused to say more. The past needed to stay exactly where it was—in the past. He never spoke of it. It was none of anyone's business. When he glanced at Adara, she was studying him. She was probably wondering about all the bits of his life that he hadn't told her. Even she wouldn't guess how bad it truly had been.

But it was better this way. He didn't want anyone to view him with sympathy. He was strong and successful. Maybe he wasn't the traditional version of a success story, but he'd created his own version of it.

CHAPTER NINE

HER HEART ACHED for him.

Adara quietly ate her tiramisu as Krystof drank a cup of coffee and stared out at the sea. He seemed lost in his thoughts. She wondered if he was thinking of his past.

She felt bad that she'd pushed him about his nomadic life after he'd gone to such effort to show her a good time. And the dinner had been fantastic. It was an evening she'd created for clients but never had the opportunity to enjoy herself.

And now it was almost over, and she felt guilty that she'd ruined it for Krystof. She wanted to make it up to him and put the smile back on his face.

As she took a last bite of the most delicious tiramisu, she considered suggesting they take a moonlight stroll along the beach. However, as she observed him, she changed her mind. She didn't think that was such a good idea. He was already lost in his thoughts of the past. She needed to get him to think about something else—perhaps a possibility for the future. And then she had her plan.

She wiped her mouth, set aside her napkin and then got to her feet. She moved over next to him. "Come with me."

He shook his head. "I don't think so. I'm just going to sit here for a few more minutes."

That was the very last thing he needed to do. The past had already robbed him of so much. It didn't need to steal any more of his happiness.

She reached out and took his hand in hers. She gave a tug. "Come on. It'll be worth it."

He arched a brow. "You aren't going to give up, are you?"

She smiled and shook her head. "Not a chance."

"Okay. You win." He stood. "Where are we going?"

"You'll see."

And so they set off for the spot where they'd left their shoes. Once the sand had been brushed off and the shoes put on, hand in hand they headed inside the resort. Along the way they passed numerous guests dressed in their finest clothes for dining at one of the three Michelin-starred restaurants at the resort.

She kept her fingers laced with his. She told herself she only did it because she didn't want him to slip away. But there was a part of her that enjoyed the feel of her skin against his. There was one thing they'd always had: chemistry. Lots and lots of sizzling, fiery chemistry.

The problem was sex was all they'd had. Sure, they'd had good times together outside the bedroom, but there was never any depth to any of it. Tonight had been totally different. Krystof had let down his guard long enough for her to get a glimpse of the man inside—the man with scars and insecurities. She had a feeling there was a lot more to his story, but what he'd told her was a start.

His admission dug at her heart. It was hard to hold him at a distance when he had showed her his vulnerabilities. She'd witnessed just how alone he was in this world—partly from a tragic childhood and partly from him keeping people out so he wouldn't be hurt again.

She wanted to help him—show him that taking a chance on a relationship was worth the risk. But she didn't know if she was the right person to coax him from his safety zone. After all, she was dealing with her own medical issues at the moment. But maybe she could help him with this small step forward.

She approached the large frosted glass doors of the Ludus Gallery. "We're here."

Krystof glanced up. "It's the gallery." He stared at the sign with the hours of operation. "It's already closed."

Adara held up a key card. "I can get us in."

He shook his head. "I don't think it's a good idea."

"Sure it is." She didn't wait for him to argue. She flashed the card in front of a card reader, and then she had to press her palm to a biometric security device. The light on the reader changed from red to green. There was a click of the lock releasing at the same time the lights automatically turned on. "See. Easy."

She reached for the oversize brass handle and then easily pulled open the glass door. She held the door for him. Once he was inside, she closed the door and locked it.

He slowly walked around, taking in the various exhibits. He moved closer to the wall and lifted his chin to admire the gallery's latest acquisition. "These are really nice."

"I'll be sure to let Indigo know you said so."

"Indigo did these?"

"Yes. She has stopped working at the resort in order to pursue her art full-time."

His gaze moved along the wall, taking in the portraits of people in everyday life, from an older woman watering flowers to people at the beach and then one of children playing ball and lastly a baby. It was though each portrait displayed a different stage in life.

"These are quite impressive, but I'm sure she won't have time to work on her art once she marries the prince."

"She says she's not giving up her art, and Istvan doesn't want her to. He says he wants her to do whatever will make her happy." Adara hoped that someday she'd be so lucky. She wanted to meet a man who respected her love of her work that much.

They moved on to some pottery displays before viewing various pieces of antique jewelry. The gallery was expanding to the point where they'd soon need to build an addition. Krystof stopped to take in a series of seascapes. Each was the same scene but displayed at various times of the day. She stood next to him, taking it all in. She never tired of visiting the gallery. There was always a new display.

But tonight it was the man next to her that held her attention. She longed to show him that he didn't always have to be on the go, that he could stop in one place and not be hurt.

"How often do you get new exhibits?" Krystof's voice drew her from her thoughts.

"They've really been stepping up their exchange program. In fact, only about half of the gallery's pieces are here right now. The rest have been loaned out." She pointed to the left. "Do you see that large portrait with the tie-dye design?" When he nodded, she said, "That was borrowed from a gallery in Rome." Then she turned and pointed to another portrait. "See the portrait of the lion? It's made from thousands and thousands of seeds. I forget where it originated, but it's the most recent piece on loan to us."

"It's quite a collection." He moved nearer to the lion to have a closer look. "I can't believe I haven't been in here sooner." He turned and pointed to another set of closed doors. "What's back there?"

"It's where they have special displays."

"That sounds intriguing. Can we have a look?"

Under other circumstances, she would have made an excuse not to go back there. But since Krystof had emerged from his dark thoughts of the past, she was eager to do whatever it took to keep his thoughts in the present. And so she moved toward the back room.

She swiped her key card to open the door. While the front of the gallery was a large area with tall, white walls, the back room was much smaller, with black walls and spotlights that focused on the gallery's headliner.

This time Krystof pulled the door open for her. "After you."

"Thanks." She had to step close to him—so very close.

It would have been incredibly tempting to stop and turn to him. Kissing him definitely would have distracted him—and her. His kisses were so mesmerizing that they would often cause her to forget her common sense and lose herself in the moment.

But those moments were behind them now.

And with great regret, she continued past him and into the back room. She swallowed, hoping when she spoke that her voice didn't betray the fact that his nearness had gotten to her. "And these displays back here are royal jewels."

"Let me guess—they are on loan from Istvan's family."

"Actually, they belong to Istvan himself. He inherited them from his grandmother. And the Ruby Heart is the highlight."

Krystof approached the glass case. "The ruby is really large. Too big for a piece of jewelry."

She stepped up beside him. She couldn't resist getting another glimpse of the precious jewel. It was the most amazing gem she'd ever seen. With its many precise cuts, it was a work of art. The spotlights danced upon the various cuts, making it seem as though the gem had a power all of its own.

"There's a brass plaque with it. I can't quite make out what it says." He moved closer to try to read it.

She had hoped he'd miss that part. "It's really no big deal. There are more pieces to see out front."

As though he hadn't heard a word she'd said, he started to read aloud. "'The legend of the Ruby Heart. If destined lovers gaze upon the Ruby Heart at the same time, their lives will be forever entwined.'"

When Krystof's gaze moved to meet hers, heat rushed from her chest up her neck and filled her cheeks.

"Do you think the legend is talking about us?" His voice was low and deep.

"Krystof…" She meant to set him straight, but when his gaze met hers, the words clogged in the back of her throat.

He turned to her and pulled her close. It was as though she were having an out-of-body experience as she leaned into him. She tilted her chin upward. The breath hitched in her lungs.

And then he lowered his head, capturing her lips with his own. Oh, how she'd missed him. Her hands moved up over his shoulders and wrapped around the back of his neck.

It didn't matter how many times they kissed—it always felt like the first time. As the kiss deepened, a moan swelled in the back of her throat.

She didn't want this moment to end. She met him move for move. She opened her mouth to him. His tongue touched hers, and a moan escaped. He was amazing.

It would be so easy to fall for him. But she refused to let herself do something that foolish, because he'd made it clear he didn't feel the same way about her. What had he called them? Oh, yes, friends with benefits. He thought it was cute. She didn't. She wanted more—a real relationship with strings, complications and the hope for a future together.

His fingertips worked her blouse loose and touched the bare skin of her back, sending goose bumps cascading down her body. Her thoughts scattered as her heart beat so loud that it echoed in her ears.

And that's why she didn't realize they were no longer alone.

"Oh, Ms. Galinis, it's you."

She jumped out of Krystof's arms. Heat once again filled her cheeks. She drew in a deep breath, hoping it would calm her racing heart. Her hands moved to her hair, smoothing it. Then her fingertips traced her still-tingling lips. She straightened her shoulders and lifted her chin ever so slightly as she turned.

She forced a smile onto her face. "Good evening, Christos. Yes, it's just me. I was showing Mr. Mikos around the gallery."

The night guard's forehead wrinkled. "You do know it's closed?"

"Um, yes. And we were just leaving." She quickly glanced at Krystof, who was wearing an amused smile at her awkwardness. "Weren't we, Krystof?"

"Yes. That's exactly what we were doing." He let out a laugh as he made his way past her and headed for the door.

The heat in her face amplified. She resisted the urge to fan herself. She turned to the guard. "Shall I lock up, or would you rather take care of it?"

"I'll handle it." He sent her another confused look, as though he still didn't understand why she would be in the gallery after hours. It was a first for her.

She didn't stick around. She walked quickly to the door. She was so anxious to be out of there. In her rush, she practically ran into Krystof in the hallway. "Oops. Sorry."

"I'm not," he teased. "If you'd like to walk into my arms again, I'm all for it."

She shook her head. "It shouldn't have happened. It was a mistake."

"If that was a mistake, I don't mind being wrong."

She lifted her gaze and frowned at him as he looked at her with amusement dancing in his eyes.

"I can't do casual," she said bluntly.

"I happen to think you do a mighty fine job of it." A smile lifted the corners of his mouth. "Commitments don't last. Forever is just a romantic notion. All we have is the here and now."

The image of him with Celeste in his arms came back to her. The searing jealousy that she'd felt when she'd thought he was interested in someone else meant she was in serious danger of falling for him.

She couldn't let that happen. She refused to set herself up for heartache when Krystof walked away. And he would. She was under no illusions about him ever settling down. Maybe not this week or next week, but soon he'd grow bored with her, and then he'd be gone.

She suddenly regretted bringing Krystof to the gallery. Not

only had they been caught making out by the security guard, but they'd gazed upon the Ruby Heart together. And though she didn't believe in legends, she couldn't deny that Hermione and Atlas, as well as Indigo and Istvan, had gazed upon that ruby, and both couples were now getting married. She suddenly felt nauseous.

"I... I'm going to call it a night." Her gaze didn't quite reach his. "Thank you for dinner. It was lovely."

And then, without waiting for him to say anything, she turned and walked away. She resisted the urge to glance over her shoulder. If she wanted to survive this wedding with her heart still intact, she had to keep him at arm's length.

The kiss only made him miss her more.

Krystof spent that evening in a high-stakes poker game that ran most of the night. He'd played on the edge with over-the-top bets and lots of bluffs, hoping the high stakes would distract him from his thoughts of Adara. It didn't work.

After sleeping late the next day, he was tempted to seek out Adara. He resisted going to her as long as he could, but eventually he gave in to his desire. There was only one problem—he couldn't find her. Was she avoiding him?

It wasn't like he'd set out to kiss her. It was a spur-of-the-moment thing, and she had been just as involved in that kiss as he'd been. His thoughts strayed to the Ruby Heart's legend, and he wondered if it had something to do with it. He quickly dismissed the idea. He didn't believe in legends. And it wasn't like this thing between him and Adara hadn't been going on for months now.

By that afternoon, he was ready to face whatever Adara threw at him. But before he could go in search of her, he had an alert on his phone that someone thought they had the bridesmaid dresses. Now he had the perfect excuse to see her.

Demi informed him that Adara was working in her suite. When he showed Adara the photo of the dresses, she said they looked like the right ones, but she wouldn't know for sure until she saw them in person.

The only problem was they had to drive into Athens to meet the person at their home. The ride was quiet, as neither of them broached the subject of the kiss. He didn't want to do anything to push her farther away. He was starting to wonder if his plan to put things back to the way they'd been before Paris was going to work out. Even though the chemistry between them was still there, as fierce as ever, Adara was fighting it at every turn.

In a surprise turn of events, the person did have the right bridesmaids' dresses, but not the right wedding gown. Now they only had one more dress to locate—and, of course, the dresses in their possession to return to the appropriate owner.

"Don't worry," he said as he navigated her car toward the ferry. "We'll find the wedding dress."

"I hope you're right." Adara's fingers moved rapidly over her phone as she answered messages.

With a mix-up at the resort to sort out, Krystof had offered to drive so that she would be free to deal with the problem. She was reluctant to hand over her car keys, but with a sigh, she did it.

Buzz-buzz.

"That better not be more bad news," Krystof grouched as he navigated her car through traffic.

She frowned at him. "Did you have to say that?"

He chanced a quick glance at her. "Why?"

"You've probably just jinxed us."

"Jinxed us how?"

"Oh, never mind." She focused back on her phone. "It's the booking agent for the band for the ceremony."

She pressed the phone to her ear. The conversation was brief. When it concluded, she sat there quietly for a moment, as though taking in what she'd learned.

He gave her a brief glance. "Well, don't just sit there. Tell me what they said."

"There's been an accident, and two of the band members have been injured."

"That's awful." He slowed to a stop at an intersection.

"I agree. Thankfully everyone lived, but they will need some time to recover. In the meantime, we don't have any music for the wedding."

"Maybe this is a sign," he said.

"A sign?"

"That the wedding shouldn't happen."

She gasped. "Are you serious? You don't think Hermione and Atlas should get married?"

He shrugged. He should have kept his thoughts to himself. When he glanced over at Adara, he found her staring expectantly at him. He focused back on the road. "What? You have to admit that nothing about this wedding is easy. The bride and groom aren't even here."

"They are where they're needed. And the wedding doesn't have to be easy. It just has to be right for Hermione and Atlas."

"If you say so."

"I do."

"So what are you going to do?"

"Me?" Her voice rose an octave. "Why should I fix this problem? I thought you wanted to help with the wedding plans. Wasn't that what you said?"

She surely didn't think he would know what to do about this latest problem. "Yes, but this is different."

"Different how?"

"Because it's an urgent problem. The wedding isn't far off."

"And why should I fix it instead of you?"

He panicked and reached for the first excuse he could think of. "Because you're a woman and this is a wedding."

When he chanced a glance in her direction, she was sitting there with her arms crossed as she glared at him. "Really? Are you saying a man can't plan a wedding?"

He sighed. "I'm certain a man could do just as good of a job planning a wedding."

"You think so?"

"I do."

"Good. Then you can find a replacement musical group."

He tapped the brakes a little too hard, jerking them in their seats. "What?"

"You heard me. Unless you don't think you're up to it."

He briefly turned to her with an arched brow before focusing back on the road. "Is that a challenge?"

A smile tugged at the corners of her lips as she settled back in her seat. "Why, yes, it is."

He refused to back down. How hard could it be? And maybe this would at last get him back in her good graces so they could pick up where they'd left off. The thought definitely appealed to him.

There was a moment of silence as he pulled the car off on the berm of the road, and then he turned to her. "What exactly do I need to do?"

"The booking agent is going to email us a list of available musical groups."

"And then what?"

"Then you go listen to them. She's going to include where they are each playing. All you have to do it stop by and check them out."

"And that's it?" He stared at her, not believing it was that easy.

"Yes. That's it."

"Fine. I'll do it." He put the car in Drive and eased back out into traffic.

He didn't like it, but he'd do it. It really didn't sound hard. Who didn't like to listen to a bit of music? It'd be even better if Adara was listening to it with him. Hmm. He might have to plan something to get her to accompany him.

CHAPTER TEN

WHAT WAS IT with this wedding?

Adara had been involved with a lot of weddings, and she couldn't recall any having this many setbacks. It was getting so bad that for a moment she wondered if Krystof was right about this being a sign that it shouldn't take place. As soon as the thought came to her, she dismissed it.

This wedding was right for both Hermione and Atlas. They truly loved each other. And no amount of wedding dilemmas would change their devotion to one another.

Adara had just finished making arrangements for a guest's twenty-fifth wedding anniversary. A party planned for the next evening on the patio with silver and white balloons, a live band, and endless champagne. Another wonderful example of how love could endure. She refused to let Krystof's negativity get to her.

She was almost to her office when her phone rang. She glanced at the caller ID and then pressed the phone to her ear. "Hey, Hermione. How are you doing?"

"As well as can be expected. How are things there?"

"Uh…" She entered her office and closed the door. "The resort is doing fine. No problems."

"But there is a problem. I can hear it in your voice. It's Krystof, isn't it?"

Adara sank into her chair. "He's fine. And you don't need to hear this. You have enough going on with Atlas and his father."

"I could use the distraction. So Krystof is pushing for you to get back together, isn't he?"

Adara sighed. "He wants things to go back to the way they were before I mistook his foster sister for his girlfriend in Paris."

"You did what? Oh, dear. How do you feel about that?"

Part of her was eager to feel Krystof's strong arms around her as he trailed kisses down her neck. The other part of her knew that she could easily get in too deep with him. With every detail she learned, it was easier to imagine starting a real relationship with him. And in the end, she'd be left with a broken heart.

Adara swallowed hard. "I don't want to go backward. I want a real relationship. I'm not saying we would have to get married or anything like that, but I want a commitment. I want to matter to him enough that he would go out of his way to see me often and not just when it's convenient for his schedule. I want to know that I'm the only woman in his life. Is that asking for too much?"

"No." The answer was quick and firm. "But I take it that's not what he wants."

"He wants all the fun without any strings. And that was all right for a while, but now I want more."

"I'm surprised he's sticking around and not off to a card game."

"He's been helping with the wedding."

"Helping? This is certainly surprising news. How exactly has he been helping?"

This was her chance to tell Hermione about the nightmare with the dresses. She needed to tell her now so she had time to make decisions in case her dress never showed up. It just broke her heart to pile more bad news on her friend.

"There's something I should tell you," Adara said.

"I knew there was something wrong. What is it?"

"The dresses were delivered."

"And?"

"Well, um…they weren't the right dresses."

"What? But how?"

And so Adara told her about the dress mix-up and the closing of the bridal boutique. "Krystof is helping to get the word out online about the dresses. We weren't the only one to get the wrong ones. It appears the last delivery was all mixed up. We've recovered the bridesmaid dresses and we're hoping yours will turn up soon, but I can't promise we'll get your wedding gown back in time for the ceremony."

Hermione was silent for a moment as though digesting all the information. "This is awful, but this week has shown me that in the grand scheme of things, a dress isn't what's important. In the end, it doesn't matter if I have a wedding dress or not. What matters is Atlas and me promising our hearts to each other."

Things must be bad for Hermione to be so Zen over the loss of her wedding dress. Adara's heart went out to her and Atlas. "Aw…that's so sweet. You two make the perfect couple."

They talked a little more before they ended the call. Adara was more determined than ever to make sure this wedding was the best it could be.

She had been serious.

Krystof glanced at the itinerary on his phone. Adara had forwarded a list of the musical groups and the times they would perform that week. Today he had two groups to listen to. One was performing at a school this evening. Did he even want to know how old the members of the group were?

And the other was at a gallery in the city. The gallery one he didn't mind. It was the school one that he didn't want to attend. It would remind him of his childhood. It was something he didn't want to dwell on. But he refused to let Adara down.

He had to be at the school by seven. He hoped their performance was at the beginning of the show if he hoped to make it to the gallery across the city. Even then he'd be pushing it.

He put on a white button-up. He left the top buttons undone, gave the sleeves a tug and then threw on a deep blue blazer. He wore dark jeans with loafers. It was as dressy as he got—at least without a wedding or funeral involved.

He exited the suite and headed toward the lobby. When he turned the corner, he practically ran into Adara. He reached out, grabbing her arm to help her regain her balance.

In that moment, time slowed down as his gaze met hers. He watched as her blue eyes widened in surprise. When her gaze took him in, he noticed how her pupils dilated ever so slightly. If she was anyone else, he'd say she was interested in him. But she'd made it perfectly clear that she was over him.

What was it about this woman that had him wanting her, even after she'd rejected him? He decided it was best not to delve too deeply into that subject.

"Whoa." He regretted having to let her go as his arm lowered to his side. "Where are you off to in such a hurry?"

"I was actually going to see you." She took a step back and gave his attire a quick once-over.

When her gaze once more met his, he asked, "Do you approve?"

She nodded. "You look very handsome."

A smile pulled at the corners of his lips. "Thanks." He thought of telling her that she looked beautiful but refrained. He didn't want to ruin this peaceful moment. "What did you need? I don't have much time. I have to hurry if I'm going to make it to both performances."

"Well, I was going to tell you that I'm done working for today, and if you wanted, I could tag along with you tonight."

Wait. Had he heard her correctly? She was going to spend time with him—voluntarily? He felt a surge of happiness.

And then another thought came to him. She didn't trust him.

She thought he was going to let their friends down without her guidance. Well, that wasn't going to happen. He'd show her.

He decided to turn the situation around. "You can come with me as long as you don't mind a late dinner."

Her eyes widened. "Did you just blackmail me into having dinner with you?"

He let out a laugh. "I wouldn't put it that way. But I was thinking that as long as I was in Athens, I would try one of their newer restaurants."

"Oh. I see." Her gaze lowered as though she were considering whether or not this was worth her time.

"It's okay. I see you're not interested. I'll go alone." He started to walk away.

"No. I'll go."

He paused and turned to her. "Are you sure?"

She hesitated. "I am."

"Then let's be on our way. I don't want to be late and miss the first performance." He didn't wait for her response as he turned and headed for the lobby.

Once they were on the road, he chanced a glance at her with the warm rays of the setting sun lingering on her face. The beauty of the moment stole his breath away. He had to remind himself that they weren't on a date.

The ride into the city was quiet. Adara spent a great deal of that time on her phone. He wondered if something important had happened. Surely it couldn't be another problem with the wedding. Or perhaps she was just using it to avoid him.

When he pulled into a parking space near the school, he asked, "Is everything okay?"

"Um…" She typed a couple more words and pressed Send before she lifted her gaze to meet his. "Yes. Why?"

"Because you've been on your phone since we left the island. I was beginning to think you were avoiding me."

"No. Of course not. It's just with the wedding, my assistant has been filling in a lot for me. And she had some questions about the notes on my calendar."

"You like to plan out every part of your life, don't you?" He couldn't imagine what that must be like. He preferred to live on a whim and a chance.

"Yes. I try to schedule most of it."

"You never do anything spontaneously?"

A frown pulled at her glossy lips. "The last time I did something spontaneous, it didn't work out at all."

He couldn't help but wonder if she was referring to her sudden appearance at his Paris hotel suite. If only she had hung around, he could have cleared things up. He didn't like that she clung to that unfortunate event and used it to reinforce her opinion that spontaneity wasn't for her.

Just like tonight, she wanted him to think that her accompanying him was spontaneous, but he had a feeling she'd had it planned out for some time. He wanted to know what had happened in life to make her so cautious.

"We should go in," she said, drawing him from his thoughts.

"Right." While she gathered her purse, he exited the vehicle and quickly rounded the back end. And then he proceeded to open her door for her. She glanced up at him with a wide-eyed stare.

"What?" he said. "Can't a guy open the door for a lady?"

Her brows furrowed together as she stood. "A lady, huh?"

This was his cue to take things further. He stepped closer. As his gaze held hers, he reached out, gently brushing his thumb down over her cheek. He lowered his voice. "A very beautiful lady."

She didn't say a word, nor did she move away. But there was this place on her neck where her pulse beat rapidly. It matched the rapid thumping of his own heart.

He should turn away. He should focus on why they were standing in that parking lot with the lingering rays of the sun shining down on them. And yet the reason escaped him. All he could think about was kissing her.

His gaze lowered to her mouth. Her plump lower lip shimmered. It beckoned to him, drawing him to her with a force that smothered any sense of logic. Because this kiss...he knew it would change everything.

When he drew her closer, he heard the swift intake of her breath. And then he lowered his head, claiming her lips with his own. Oh, the kiss was so much sweeter than he recalled. And she was so addictive. He couldn't imagine ever getting enough of her. He could hold her in his arms all night long if she'd let him.

She didn't move immediately. In fact, he was pretty certain she was going to slap him or at the very least pull away. He didn't know how she could fight this chemistry burning between them.

As though she suddenly surrendered to the flames of desire, her lips moved beneath his. And when his tongue traced her lips, she opened up to him. A moan swelled in the back of her throat.

Her hands rested on his chest as his wrapped around her waist, pulling her snug to him. Her curves pressed into his hard planes. He wondered if she could feel the pounding of his heart.

No other woman evoked this sort of reaction from him. No other woman had ever been such a challenge. She made him think that for once the catch would be so much better than the chase—especially with those sweet, sweet kisses.

The sound of a loud car pulling into the lot drew his attention, but nothing was going to get him to let Adara go. He worried that once their kiss ended, Adara would put the wall straight back up between them. And this time the wall would be so high he wouldn't be able to scale it.

Honk-honk.

The decision was taken out of his hands when the car wanted the empty parking spot next to his car. With the utmost reluctance, he lifted his head. Adara's eyelids fluttered open. She gazed up at him with a dazed look in her eyes.

Honk.

"We better move," she said.

He nodded and then presented his arm to her. When she glanced down at it and then sent him a questioning look, he said, "Come on. You don't want to keep them waiting."

She huffed but then proceeded to place her hand in the crook of his arm.

They walked in silence across the parking lot. He couldn't help but notice how natural it felt. Sure, he'd had lots of women on his arm, but Adara was different. Not only was she the most beautiful woman he'd ever known, but she was also the greatest challenge. And he did love a challenge. In fact, he thrived on them.

Adara jerked his arm. "Is something wrong?"

"What?" He'd been so lost in his thoughts that he hadn't been following what she'd been saying.

She stopped walking and removed her hand from his arm. "You aren't even listening to me. What's wrong?"

So she'd felt that, huh? Apparently his thoughts had been more jolting than even he had thought. "It's nothing."

"Okay. If you won't answer that question, then answer this one. Why did you kiss me?"

His gaze lowered to her now-rosy lips, thinking how much he wanted to kiss her again. With the greatest of effort, he lifted his gaze to meet hers. "Because I needed to prove something to you."

"And what would that be?"

"That spontaneity isn't a bad thing. In fact, it can be quite enjoyable." He smiled at her. "Would you like me to show you again?"

A slight pause ensued, as though she too were tempted to indulge in another kiss. "No. That can never happen again."

Never again? He was confused. She'd enjoyed it. Of that he

was certain. So why was she continuing to put up a wall between them?

He'd explained the mix-up at his Paris hotel room. Was she expecting something more from him? Adara had known from the beginning that he didn't do commitments. But he'd been utterly and completely faithful to her since they'd met on Valentine's Day. The fact that she had been the only woman in his life all this time shocked even him.

"We're going to be late." Her voice drew him from his thoughts.

She turned and walked away. He was left to follow her. He noticed how she didn't say anything about not enjoying the kiss. In fact, he'd have sworn he heard her moan—or perhaps that had been him. The smile on his face broadened. He just might need help with all these musical auditions.

The more he thought of it, the more he liked the idea. And if he were to prove that he was awful at selecting the right music for the wedding, Adara would have no choice but to accompany him to all the performances. And then they could have some more spontaneous moments.

CHAPTER ELEVEN

HE'D KISSED HER.

That wasn't the part that worried Adara. It was the part where she'd wanted more. More kisses. More touching. More of everything from him.

Her traitorous heart had run amok when his lips had touched hers. And logic had totally abandoned her. She'd clung to a man who didn't believe in commitments or putting down roots. What had she been thinking? He was a nomad and proud of it.

So even if the unfortunate incident in Paris with his sister hadn't happened, eventually their relationship would have run its course. Just like all his other relationships. And she didn't want her heart to end up a casualty of his inability to stay in one place.

She wished the wedding was over already, but it was still several days away. They would be very long days with Krystof on the island. And trying to avoid him was not an option, with them both participating in the wedding.

And that's why when Sunday rolled around and it was time to listen to another musical group, she seriously considered skipping it. But this would mean relying on Krystof's judgment to pick the right music for the wedding. From what she'd seen on Friday evening, he didn't take this task very seriously.

He was ready to pick the first group they'd heard. And though they were good, she wasn't prepared to go with the first group without doing their due diligence. This was too important to make snap decisions.

It was with the greatest hesitation that she once more pushed off what was left of her duties that day to her assistant, who surprisingly didn't complain. And then Adara headed toward her room at the resort to change into a sundress—something more appropriate for a concert in the park.

She was tempted to go to the park in her business clothes. She didn't want Krystof to think she was making an effort to look nice for him. But she had been wearing a long-sleeved blouse due to the resort's air-conditioning. It would be really warm at the park. If she were to switch into a summer dress and sandals, she'd be a lot more comfortable.

She subdued a sigh now that she'd just talked herself into dressing for their date—erm...their outing. Because there was no way she was going to date him again. She wanted more than he would ever offer.

She wasn't getting any younger. And if she wanted to find someone to build a future with, she couldn't waste her time with a man with commitment phobia. Krystof couldn't even commit to having a home. The closest thing he had to a home was a suite at a Paris hotel. Who lived their life out of a suitcase?

It didn't take her long to change clothes, but then she decided to wear her hair down and to touch up her makeup. After all, it was hard to tell who'd they run into at the park.

Knock-knock.

"Coming." She gave her reflection one last check.

Then, with her purse in hand, she started toward the door. She briefly paused to grab the throw blanket from the end of the bed. After all, they would need something to sit on.

She opened the door, and Krystof was there leaning against the doorjamb. He gave her outfit a quick once-over. "You look beautiful."

The heat started in her chest and then worked its way to her cheeks. "Thank you."

She stepped into the hallway, pulling the door closed behind her. "Shall we go?"

"Lead the way."

She needed to get this evening over as quickly as possible— before she did something she'd later regret, like confusing this outing for a date. Her steps came quicker. She could feel Krystof keeping pace with her.

"Is this a race?" he called out from behind her. "Because I get the feeling you're trying to get away from me. If that's the case, you don't have to go this evening. I can handle it on my own."

She turned to him. "I'm fine."

"Or we could just go with the first group we heard on Friday." He arched a brow, waiting for her response.

"Are you serious?"

"Sure. Why does it matter?"

"Because this wedding has to be perfect, or at least as close to perfect as I can make it. Don't you want Atlas to be happy?"

Krystof shrugged. "I don't think Atlas is going to care about the music."

"But he will care if his bride is happy."

"I just don't get it." He resumed walking.

She fell in step with him. "Get what?"

"Why he'd even want to get married. He was doing fine on his own. And we all know that most marriages don't last."

"Wow. I knew you weren't into commitments, but I didn't know how far your dislike for them went."

He didn't look in her direction. "I'm just speaking the truth. You can look up the statistics for yourself."

She didn't know how to counter his total disrespect for marriage and love in general. And so she remained quiet as they made their way into the city and to the park.

As Krystof pulled into a parking spot, he said, "So that's it—

you're not going to speak to me the rest of the evening because I'm not in favor of marriage?"

She shifted in her seat in order to face him, and only then did she realize her mistake. This car was much too small and Krystof's shoulders were far too broad, bringing her into close contact with him. Her heart pounded so loud that it echoed in her ears.

It was only when a smile lifted the corners of his very tempting lips that it jarred her back to her senses. What she needed right now was some fresh air, preferably very far from him. But since that wasn't possible at the moment, she'd take what little bit of breathing room she could get.

And with that she turned away, opened the car door, and with the blanket draped over her arm, she alighted from the vehicle. There was already a crowd of people in the park near the stage. She wanted a spot where they could clearly see the group but far enough back that they would have space to themselves.

She picked a spot straight back from the stage, under a tree where they could spread out the blanket. "What about sitting here?"

He shrugged. "Works for me."

She meant to spread the blanket by herself, but Krystof set down the insulated bag and insisted on helping her. She didn't want him being nice to her. She wanted to wallow in her frustration with him. First, for him being against this wedding. And second, for him being opposed to commitments of any kind.

When the blanket was spread out, they sat down. Krystof pulled the insulated bag over. "Would you like to eat first?"

She really didn't have an appetite at this point, but if they were eating, it would mean they didn't have to converse with each other. "We can eat. What did you pack?"

"Me? Nothing. But the kitchen was more than willing to help with our expedition."

"Yes, the resort does excel at catering to the guests." She was very proud of the people she worked with. They went above and beyond to make the guests' visits the very best.

And so she wasn't surprised when Krystof withdrew arrangements of cheeses, vegetables and fruits. It was a lot of food. And it looked quite delicious.

Just then the music started. As a local jazz group began to play, the sounds of the keyboard filled the air with a melodious tune. Two violinists, a guitar and drums stood ready for their moment to chime in. The upbeat music immediately drew her attention. Their conversation would have to wait until later.

The concert in the park had been a nice distraction.

Now that it was over and they'd returned to the resort, Adara wasn't ready for the evening to end. They still had to get to the bottom of Krystof thinking Hermione and Atlas's wedding shouldn't take place. That had her worried.

Krystof had walked with her to her room. He hesitated at the open doorway as though not sure if he should enter or not.

Adara placed her purse on the table and then turned to him. "Aren't you coming in?"

He stepped inside and closed the door before moving to the couch to sit down. "Do you think we've found a replacement band?"

"I don't know. We have one more band to hear the day after tomorrow."

"So you aren't going to pick a favorite yet?"

She shrugged before she reached inside the fridge. "Would you like something to drink?"

"Some water."

She grabbed two waters and then joined him on the couch. After she handed him the bottle, she kicked off her shoes and curled up next to him.

She was worried about Krystof. Something from his past had damaged him to the point that she worried he'd never be able to truly let someone in to love him. If he couldn't believe love was possible for Atlas and Hermione, when everyone could see how they felt about each other, how was he supposed to believe it was possible for himself?

She twisted off the cap of her bottle and took a long, slow drink, enjoying the cold water. Ever since they'd arrived at the park, she'd wanted to ask him questions, and yet she hadn't wanted to ruin the afternoon. But she couldn't hold back the questions now. She longed to understand him better.

In a gentle voice, hoping not to evoke an argument but rather to learn why he thought the way he did, she asked, "Why do you think Hermione and Atlas don't belong together?"

He lowered the bottle of water to the table. "I didn't say they don't belong together."

Now he wanted to play word games with her, but she wasn't having any part of it. "You said you thought they shouldn't get married. So if you aren't in favor of the wedding, it means you don't think they should be together."

He turned his head, and their gazes met. "Those two things are not the same. I think they make a great couple. For now."

"For now?" She rolled around the implication of his words in her mind. "So you think they're going to break up?"

He shrugged. "Statistics prove that relationships don't make the long haul."

Irritation pumped through her veins as she sat up straighter. "What is it with you and numbers?"

He lounged back and rested his arm over the back of the couch. "Numbers are reliable. Numbers make sense."

At last, they were getting somewhere. She was starting to understand what made him tick. "And is this why you spend so much time playing cards?"

He nodded. "Cards are based on odds. Odds aren't reliable, but they are understandable."

"So you don't like relationships because they revolve around emotions? And you think emotions aren't predictable?"

He glanced away. "I guess."

It wasn't much of an acknowledgment. She wanted to know more. She felt as though they were just scratching the surface. "Why did you agree to be the best man if you don't believe the marriage will work?"

His gaze darted to her. His brows furrowed together. "Like I'm going to turn Atlas down."

"So emotions between friends do matter to you?"

"I… I didn't say anything about emotions. But Atlas is a friend. I've known him since we were in school together. I'm not going to let him down."

His loyalty to his lifelong friend meant a lot to her. It meant that he was capable of commitment. If only he would let himself take a risk on a relationship. A risk on love.

"What are you thinking?" he asked.

Heat warmed her face as she glanced away. "I was just thinking for a man who makes his living by taking risks with cards, you aren't willing to do the same thing with your life. Why is that?"

"Maybe because my whole life has been full of unknowns and risks. Now I prefer to keep my risks at the card table only."

Her heart ached for him. And now it didn't seem like he was willing to rely on anyone. She wanted him to trust her. She wanted to prove to him that not all people walked away.

Her gaze met and held his. "You can trust me. I'm not going anywhere."

CHAPTER TWELVE

HE WANTED TO trust her.

And he did…as a friend.

Krystof found himself staring into Adara's eyes. He knew she was asking him to trust her with so much more than friendship. The thought sent an arrow of fear through his heart.

He had once staked his fortune on a high-stakes card game, and it had unnerved him much less than letting down his guard with Adara. He knew she had a way about her that could get past all his defenses. And it would be so easy to let himself care about her more than was safe.

"Tell me about it." Adara's voice was soft and coaxing. "Tell me who turned you against relationships."

He resisted the temptation to lay open all his harrowing scars. He'd never felt this compulsion before—not before he'd met Adara. His past was something he didn't share with anyone, including Atlas.

She placed her hand on his thigh. "You can talk to me—about anything. You don't have to keep putting up walls between us."

Was that what she thought he was doing? Because what he was really doing was protecting her from how messed up he really was on the inside. If she knew about his past, she would run for the door and not look back. He was nothing but damaged goods.

He lowered his arms to his sides and rubbed his damp palms over his thighs. "You don't want to know this."

"I do. If you'll share it with me."

Maybe that's exactly what he should do. He should lay it all out there for her to see that he was never going to be the traditional loving husband and devoted father she wanted. Even if he could stop moving, he wouldn't know how to be either of those things. Adara deserved someone so much better than him.

If he told her about his past, he also knew any hope of them resuming their friends-with-benefits relationship would be over. She would see through his outward facade of being successful and instead see how truly broken he was on the inside. He would once again be totally alone in this world.

It was one thing to choose this solitary life without knowing what it'd be like to share it with someone loving and caring, like Adara, but to know that sort of kindness and companionship and then to lose it—well, it might be more than he could bear. The thought of that sort of loss scared him.

And nothing scared him. He had no choice. He had to do whatever he could to dissuade Adara from wanting more from him than he could give her.

Before he could change his mind, the long-buried memories came rushing back to him. The feeling of helplessness he'd felt growing up crashed over him. And when he'd finally become a legal adult—when he was on his own—there was an unrelenting sense of determination that he was never going to feel trapped by his memories. He would tell her, and then he'd cram those haunting thoughts back in the box at the back of his mind.

Adara didn't say anything as he struggled to pull his thoughts together. He'd never stopped long enough for anyone to question his nomad lifestyle or his lack of a place to call home. In fact, he'd been doing it for so long that he'd thought of it as normal...until Adara happened into his life. Now how did he explain any of this to her?

He cleared his throat. "I never knew my parents. To this day, I don't know if they are alive or dead. I don't know their names. I don't know why they abandoned me. I don't even know what my birth name was or if I ever had one. My name was given to me by a social worker."

He chanced a glance at Adara as unshed tears gathered in her eyes. His body stiffened. He didn't want anyone's pity, most especially hers.

He refocused on his bottle of water, now sitting on the table. If he continued to take in her emotional response to his story, he didn't think he'd get through it.

But he must tell it. He had to make it clear to her why they didn't belong together—of why he couldn't transform into the man she deserved. He would do it for her. And then, when he'd bared his soul to her, he would move on, just like he'd been doing his whole life.

His mouth grew dry as his mind conjured up the painful memories. He swallowed hard. "My third, no, my fourth set of foster parents had no patience with me. I got into trouble every day of my childhood. I was curious and far too smart for my own good. By the time I was old enough to think for myself, I knew I had to get away. I didn't belong there. I believed my birth parents were out there waiting for me and I just had to find them. I was certain if that happened, everything would be right in the world."

He paused as he gathered his emotions. He could remember the desperation he felt as a little boy, longing for the love of his parents. He'd felt so lost and alone with people who didn't like him, much less love him.

All this time, Adara sat there quietly taking it all in. He wanted to look at her, but he didn't allow himself. It was all he could do to hold it all together and get through this story—his story.

He cleared his throat. "Each time I ran away, I was returned to the home. I would be locked in a small, windowless room for days at a time. There was nothing in there. No bed. No blanket. Not even so much as a pillow. Sometimes I felt like I was going to lose it in there."

In his mind, he could still see the details of those four walls. No one should ever be treated that way. "My foster sister was the only person in that home that I ever felt close to. She would sneak over to my door when the adults were distracted. We'd play word games. I don't know if I'd have made it through that period without Celeste. I will forever be indebted to her. If she had been caught, she would have paid dearly."

Adara placed her hand on his and squeezed. "I didn't realize."

He shook his head. "Of course you wouldn't. Only Celeste knows what I went through, because she lived it with me. To this day, I still have to deal with episodes of claustrophobia." He turned to her. "Do you understand what I'm saying?"

"I'm sorry all of that happened to you. I can't even begin to understand what you lived through." Her eyes shone with sympathy.

"Don't do that. Don't look at me like that. I didn't tell you so you'd feel sorry for me. I told you so you would understand that I can never be the man you deserve."

"The man I deserve? I don't understand."

He pulled his hand away from her and stood. He began to pace. "I can't stop moving around. I can't feel trapped in a house—in a traditional life. I... I just can't do it."

He couldn't believe he'd admitted all this to her. It wasn't that he didn't trust her, because he did. He knew she'd keep the skeletons of his past to herself. But he couldn't help but wonder what she thought of him now. Did she think less of him because he wasn't able to overcome a childhood trauma? Or, worse, did she feel sorry for him?

He moved toward the door. He should leave. He'd told her about his pathetic background. He'd told her how broken he was. And now she knew that they would never be together—not in the way she wanted.

And then he felt her hands on his back. She didn't say anything as her arms wrapped around his sides, and then her cheek pressed to his back. For a moment, she held him, and he let her. He went to remove her hands, but once he touched her, his hands stayed there. For that moment, he let himself take comfort in her touch.

As they stood there quietly, moisture dropped onto his hand. Where had it come from? And then there was another drip. He lifted his head to see if there was a leak in the ceiling. He didn't see anything.

He raised his hand to his cheek and found the moisture had come from him. They were the tears he'd never allowed himself to shed. He'd always told himself he was strong—that he didn't need to cry. But being here with Adara, all his suppressed feelings had come erupting to the surface. He was helpless to hold back the tidal wave of emotions.

When Adara let go of him, he thought she was walking away. Instead she came to stand in front of him. She gazed up at him with warmth in her eyes. She reached out and caressed his cheek, wiping away his tears.

And then she did something most unexpected. She lifted up on her tiptoes and pressed her lips to his. He hadn't known how much he needed her touch until she was kissing him.

He felt like a drowning man—a man drowning in his loneliness and self-isolation. And Adara was a life preserver pulling him back to the land of the caring.

He kissed her with a need and hunger that he'd never known before. He wrapped his arms around her waist, drawing her to him. Her soft curves fit perfectly to his hard planes. Oh, how he'd missed her.

In that moment, he didn't think about the implications of what they were about to do. There were no promises of tomorrow. There was only here and now. Living in the moment, he scooped her up in his arms. Her hands slipped around his neck.

Their kiss never stopped. It was as if she were oxygen and without her he would suffocate. He carried her to the king-size bed and gently laid her down. She wouldn't let go of him and instead pulled him down on top of her.

This was going to be a memorable night. If it was their last time together, he wanted the memories of her to carry with him forever.

CHAPTER THIRTEEN

OH, WHAT A night.

Before her eyes were even open, Adara reached out for Krystof. Her fingers touched nothing but an empty spot. Her hand moved up and down the sheet. The spot was cold.

Her eyes fluttered open. She scanned the room. There was no sign of him. He must have left sometime during the night.

That was something he never would have done before. He was always there in the morning. Granted, he was always the last one up in the morning. He claimed he was a night owl, while she was an early bird. A smile tugged at the corners of her lips at the memory.

But this morning there was no shared coffee in bed or the teasing of how he would groan that it was too early to get out of bed yet. Today he was already gone.

Even though he had slipped away while she was sleeping, she wasn't upset. In fact, she was hopeful. Last night had been a big breakthrough for them. She now understood him in a way she never had before.

People he was supposed to be able to trust the most in the world had let him down in the worst way. First, his birth parents had abandoned him as a toddler. And then his foster parents had abused him. Tears stung her eyes as she took it all in. How could they do such monstrous things to a child?

She was so thankful that Celeste had been there for him. Her feelings toward the woman shifted from jealousy to gratefulness. It's funny sometimes how life worked out. Maybe someday she and Celeste would be friends.

Chime.

She reached for her phone. It was a reminder for her doctor's appointment. She turned it off. Today she would see the doctor about her missing monthly. She was clinging to hope that it was something minor—something that could be fixed with a week's vacation, or at worse with some medicine.

She climbed out of bed, started the coffee machine and headed for the shower. She'd deal with the doctor first, and then she'd find Krystof. She thought he might be feeling vulnerable after his admission last night, and she wanted to assure him that everything was all right between them—in fact, it was so much better than all right.

Forty-five minutes later, showered and dressed, she headed for the door. She had to drive into the city, so she needed to get going. She didn't want to get stuck in Monday-morning traffic and miss her appointment. She opened her door and nearly ran into Krystof. He was pacing outside her door.

She stopped. "How long have you been out here?"

"I... I don't know." There were shadows under his eyes, as though he hadn't slept. "Not that long."

"Why are you pacing out here? You should have come inside."

"I didn't know if you were awake, and I didn't want to bother you. You looked so peaceful when I got out of bed."

When she went to hug him, he stepped back. She tried to tell herself that it was all right. Last night had been big for him. She knew he wasn't going to take it well in the morning light.

She lifted her phone and checked the time. If she wasn't on

the road in five minutes, she was going to be late, and she just couldn't afford to miss this appointment.

"Krystof, we need to talk, but I have an important appointment right now. I can't miss it. Can we talk later?"

His gaze searched hers. And then he nodded.

She lifted up on her tiptoes and pressed a kiss to his unshaven cheek. And then she headed down the hallway. She had no idea what would come of her appointment, but she was hoping for good news. And later they'd talk. Everything was going to work out.

She'd blown him off.

She didn't see him the same way she used to.

Krystof needed something to keep his mind from the ghosts of the past, the mess of the present and the impossibility of the future. His gut reaction was to hop on his plane and jet off to the next big card game. It's what he did when life got too complicated.

And yet he'd promised Adara he'd be here to help her with the wedding. He didn't want to break his word to her, even if staying here and facing the sympathy in her eyes would be one of the hardest things he had ever done.

He had his assistant send over the financials for the tech company he was seriously considering buying. It would give him the ability to expand MyPost into a more varied social media platform—so it could help people the way he'd been using it to help reunite brides with their missing wedding gowns. As of this morning, there were five relieved brides, but there was still no sign of Hermione's wedding dress. But he wasn't giving up hope.

As he pulled up the financial statements and various spreadsheets on his laptop, he started to relax. Numbers were reliable. They never lied. They were always what they appeared. One plus one always equaled two.

Minutes turned to hours as he worked in his suite, closing

out the rest of the world. He shoved thoughts of Adara and all that had happened the previous evening to the back of his mind—even memories of their lovemaking. He wasn't sure if she'd spent the night with him because she'd truly wanted to or if she'd done it out of sympathy. He had the feeling it was the latter, and that made him feel even worse.

Come that evening, there was an alert on his phone. Thinking it was from his assistant, he checked it. To his surprise, there was a response to his posting about the wedding dress on MyPost. Someone had Hermione's wedding dress. It wasn't for certain, but this time the pictures looked like it was the right one. In turn, it was believed that Adara had the missing dresses for their wedding party. They would be at the resort the next morning to exchange the dresses.

Krystof tried to phone Adara, but she didn't answer. He got up to get himself a cup of coffee. And then he tried again. It went to voice mail.

A frown pulled at his face. It felt as though she was avoiding him. He now suspected that she'd spent the night in his arms because she felt sorry for him. He never should have said anything to her. Instead of clarifying things, his revelation had only made everything feel so much more complicated.

He set off for her office, but when he reached it, the door was closed and locked. Next he tried her room, but she didn't answer the door. Finally he tracked down Adara's assistant. Demi checked and told him that Adara was in the penthouse. What was she doing there?

With some instructions, he made his way to the private elevator to the penthouse. He pressed the call button and wondered if Atlas and Hermione had returned. But it was Adara's voice on the intercom.

"Yes?"

He cleared his throat. "I have news."

"Come on up."

Immediately the elevator opened, and he stepped inside. He

wondered what Adara was doing there. The elevator moved swiftly, and soon the door slid open. He stepped out and found Adara standing there. She looked expectantly at him.

"I've been trying to reach you," he said.

"You have?" She pulled her phone from her pocket, glanced at the screen and then frowned. "It died. I forgot to charge it last night."

He was the reason she'd forgotten. "About last night—"

"Why don't you come in? Indigo is here." She turned and headed for the living room of Hermione and Atlas's home.

He followed her. His gaze moved around, taking in all the wedding supplies. And then his attention focused on Indigo, who was sitting at a table near one of the floor-to-ceiling windows that offered the most amazing view of the sea. Greetings were exchanged.

He turned to Adara. "What's going on?"

She sat down at the table. "We're working on the final details. And you're just in time to help."

He shook his head. "I don't think so."

"Oh, come on." Indigo patted the chair next to her.

He hesitated, but he didn't want to be rude, so he finally sat down. "What are you doing?"

"These are *koufeta*." Adara held up a white tulle pouch of sugar-coated almonds.

He watched as she gave the tulle a twist and added white ribbon with a small printed note with the wedding date as well as the bride and groom's names.

"Why are you wrapping nuts?" He could honestly admit that he knew nothing about wedding traditions.

"The almond symbolizes endurance." Indigo added almonds to a piece of tulle and gave it a twist.

"And the sugar coating symbolizes a sweet life." Adara finished tying a bow and adjusting the note before setting the favor aside. "See, it's easy. Now wash up." When he hesitated, Adara said, "Hurry. We have two hundred favors to make."

"Two hundred?" Surely he hadn't heard her clearly.

She nodded. "They wanted to include as many friends and resort employees as they could, since neither of them have much family. Now go."

He reluctantly got up and moved to the kitchen, where he washed his hands. He did notice that Adara wasn't acting any different than normal with him. Was it possible that she'd gotten over whatever had had her rushing off this morning? He hoped so.

When he returned to the table, he noticed a stack of cut tulle at his spot as well as a bowl of almonds. He supposed he could help for a little bit. After all, two hundred was a lot of favors to put together.

Both Adara and Indigo were busy adding almonds to their tulle. He spooned some almonds into his piece of material.

He was just about to give the tulle a twist when Adara asked, "Did you count the number of *koufeta*?"

He shook his head. "I didn't know I was supposed to."

"You have to," Indigo said. "The number of *koufeta* needs to be odd, because an odd number is undividable. It symbolizes the bride and groom will remain undivided."

It made sense, he supposed. He did like the part that relied upon numbers. And so he set to work. Adara made a couple of adjustments to his first favor. By his fifth one, he was on his own.

"So why did you need to see me?" Adara asked.

And then he realized he hadn't told her about the reason for him stopping by. "The wedding dress has been found."

"What?" Adara stopped what she was doing to look at him with her mouth gaping. "Really?"

He nodded and smiled. He was so glad he was able to make her happy again. "They're bringing it to the resort tomorrow."

"That's amazing," Indigo said. "You're a lifesaver. Just wait until Hermione hears the news."

"Hermione." Adara jumped up. "I have to call her." She

reached for her phone but then put it back on the table. "But my phone is dead."

He pulled his out of his back pocket and held it out to her. "Here. Use mine."

"Thanks. Hermione's going to be so relieved." Adara moved to the balcony to place the call.

With some wine, they continued to work. Dinner was delivered to the penthouse. Krystof eventually gave up on trying to slip away. Because not only did they have favors to assemble, but they also had some table decorations to make. By the time they finished, it was close to midnight, and they were all exhausted.

Tired or not, Krystof was relieved. Things were mostly back to normal with Adara. Granted, she was a little more quiet than usual, but he'd told himself that she was tired. And why wouldn't she be? She was always working. Maybe he should do something about that.

CHAPTER FOURTEEN

SHE DIDN'T DO well with waiting.

Instead she threw herself into her work.

Tuesday morning, Adara sat behind her desk. She had just finished setting up a surprise engagement for one of the resort's regular guests. They were planning to have a plane fly over the beach with a banner that read, Will You Marry Me? Adara smiled at the thought. It was certainly a grand gesture.

Krystof stepped through her open doorway. "Are you ready?"

She blinked and looked at him. "Ready for what?"

"Remember, the dress is being dropped off today." He arched a brow. "I can't believe you'd forget something like that."

"Sorry. I've just had a lot on my mind lately." That was the biggest understatement of her life. In that moment she realized she'd been so caught up in her medical drama, she'd never had that talk with Krystof. "I'm sorry I got distracted and we never got to talk."

"No problem." He sent her a smile that didn't quite reach his eyes. "What has you so worried?"

Could he read her so easily? She hoped not. "The...uh...wedding, of course. There's just so many details. And we have to confirm a replacement musical group for the ceremony."

"I was thinking about that, and I already have a favorite."

"But you haven't heard the last one yet."

"I don't need to hear them. I already like this one."

She sighed. Normally she'd insist on hearing the final group, but time was short. "Okay. If we agree on the same musical group, then we'll skip the party tonight. Agreed?"

"Agreed."

"Then what group did you like?"

"I liked the string quartet at the school. They were excellent and classy."

Her mouth gaped. They'd just agreed on something. "I was just thinking the same thing. I'll call the booking agent and set it up. One less thing to worry about."

"Now let's go get those dresses," he said.

She glanced down at her desk and the other things that needed her attention. A busy resort meant there were a lot of guests with a lot of requests.

"Come on," Krystof said. "That can all wait."

"Easy for you to say. You don't have to deal with any of it."

With a sigh, she stood. They went to meet the woman and her daughter. The gowns were exchanged and then Hermione's wedding dress was placed in the penthouse for safekeeping. After so much worry, it was such an easy, painless resolution.

"I'm so relieved," Adara said on the elevator ride down to the main floor.

"Now you can stop worrying so much."

"Not yet—there's still a lot to do before they say 'I do.'"

"What you need is a nice, relaxing lunch."

She glanced at the time on her phone. "It's not even noon yet."

"It will be soon. And I have something special in mind."

"Krystof, you don't understand. I have a meeting at one with Mr. Grant. And I have a meeting at two with the Papadopouloses."

"What I have to show you is more important."

Concern came over her. "What is it? What's wrong? Does it have something to do with the wedding?"

"Just come with me." He gave her outfit a once-over. "Do you have something more casual to wear?"

"Not with me. I didn't anticipate needing anything casual."

"No worries. We'll take care of it." He took her hand in his. "Come with me."

"But my appointments—"

"No worries. May I borrow your phone?"

"No." She tightened her hold on her phone. Without it, she'd be lost. It had her calendar and all her contacts. "Why do you want it?"

"Never mind." He turned to the left and walked toward her assistant, Demi.

What in the world had gotten into him? He'd been acting different ever since he'd told her about his past the other night. And he was certainly intent on showing her something today.

Part of her wanted to run off with him. The other part of her said that she had responsibilities here at the resort. She was torn as to what she should do. Finally the curiosity about what had him so excited won over. What was he up to?

Where was the fun in her life?

She worked all the time.

Krystof knew he might not be serious and responsible—at least by other people's estimations of him—but he had a different outlook on life. If you took it too seriously, it would do you in.

He'd promised himself that he would enjoy his life. He wouldn't get hung up with the normal responsibilities that people sometimes found themselves trapped in. And so when he'd found that he had a knack for cards, he'd used it to his advantage. After all, who could turn down a challenge? Because that's what a poker game came down to—who could outbluff who?

But Adara was so locked into her routine that her life lacked any real moments of fun and spontaneity. Maybe if she were to experience some with him, she would understand him better.

After a stop at the boutique for some casual clothes and swimsuits followed by a visit to the Cabana Café, he took her hand and they set off on their journey. This outing would do them both some good. They'd been too intense about this wedding and other things. They needed to remember how to have fun.

"Where are we going?" she asked. "I thought maybe we were going on a boat ride, but you're leading us away from the water."

The vegetation grew denser. The leafy trees, lush greenery and bright flowers were beautiful, with shades of green and pinks and reds lining the dirt path. He noticed how Adara slowed down to smell the wildflowers.

When the trees grew denser, it provided a canopy. Slices of sunlight made it through here and there, lighting up the ground. He had never been to a more beautiful place. The gentle sea breeze rustled through the trees' leaves and carried with it a light floral scent.

"It's beautiful out here," Adara said.

"You make it sound like you've never been here before."

"I haven't."

"What?" He stopped in front of her. "You mean to tell me you've been working at the resort for years and you never ventured outside?"

She shrugged. "What? Don't look at me like that. It's not like I was a guest. I was hired to work here. And that's what I do."

"And you never wanted to escape your office to go explore the island?"

"I didn't say that. But I can't just run off whenever I feel like it. I have people counting on me to do my job. Not everyone can be like you."

Ouch. Her comment zinged right into his chest with a wallop. Maybe she was right. Maybe he should take on more responsibility. He thought of that tech company in Paris. He'd gone through the financials and didn't see any reason he shouldn't buy it.

"I'm sorry," she said apologetically. "I shouldn't have said that. I know it's the only life you know. The only life you want."

He paused and stared into her eyes. It wasn't the only life he knew. Because of her, he was finding there was more to life than he'd allowed himself to experience. And there were definite benefits to staying in one place.

"Come on. We're almost there." At least he hoped so. He'd heard about this spot from Titus, the front desk clerk.

They continued to walk until the trees grew sparse and the sound of water could be heard in the distance.

Her face lit up. "Is that the waterfall?"

"If my directions are correct, then yes. That's the twin falls."

With her hand still in his, she took off in a rush. They moved quickly over the overgrown path. It didn't appear many of the guests ventured far from the beach to experience this raw beauty.

Adara didn't stop until they had a clear vision of the twin falls—a high waterfall that spilled onto a piece of rock that jutted out and then a much shorter waterfall that ran into a pond down below.

He moved to a clearing, where he spread out a blanket and placed the picnic basket next to it. The bright sunshine rained down on them. This had to be one of the most magnificent places in the world, but its beauty couldn't compare to Adara's.

He watched as she turned around in a circle, taking in the scenery. The smile on her face told him everything he needed to know. His surprise pleased her.

While she looked around, he stepped off to the side and plucked a white orchid. With the bloom held behind his back, he approached Adara. "I take it you've never been here, either?"

"No. Never. It's so peaceful and beautiful."

He stepped closer to her and held out the orchid. "Not nearly as beautiful as you."

Color flooded her cheeks. She accepted the flower. "Thank you."

His gaze met and held hers. His heart started to pound. All he wanted to do in that moment was to draw her into his arms and hold her close, but he resisted the urge.

"I brought you here," he said, "because I wanted to show you that spontaneity can be good, too. Your whole life doesn't have to be planned out. Leave some room for the unexpected."

"I'm starting to think you might have a good point."

A smile pulled at his lips. "I'm glad. Now, let's have some fun."

When he pulled off his polo shirt and tossed it on the ground, her eyes grew round. "Krystof, I like the way you think." She glanced around. "But not here. What if someone saw us?"

He let out a laugh and pulled her to him. He pressed a kiss to her lips. "I like the way *you* think. But you don't have to worry."

Disappointment flickered across her face. "So you didn't bring me out here to seduce me?"

"I didn't say that. But that will have to wait for a moment." He enjoyed the way her cheeks turned pink at the thought of their lovemaking. "I have something else in mind first." He took off his socks and shoes. He glanced over at her. "You might not want to wear all of that."

She arched a brow. "You just want to see me in my new bikini, don't you?"

"Well, of course." He placed his socks in his shoes.

He told himself that he should turn away. If he got distracted, he'd forget the reason he'd brought her out here. But then her gaze met his and she gave him a mischievous grin. She gently placed the orchid on the ground next to her. When she straightened, she pulled out the hem of her blouse from her shorts.

His breathing changed to shallow, rapid breaths. And then she slowly unbuttoned her shirt. His heart beat frantically. This was the sweetest torture he'd even endured. His gaze was glued to her. There was no chance of him turning away. His body simply refused to move.

And then, ever so slowly, the shirt slid off her slim shoulders before fluttering to the ground. The breath caught in his throat. He should do something. Say something. But he continued to stand there as if in a trance.

When she reached for her shorts, he thought his heart was going to beat out of his chest. She undid the button on her waistband. He swallowed hard. She slowly unzipped them. She wiggled her hips, allowing the shorts to slip down, and then she stepped out of them. His mouth went dry as he took in the little yellow bikini from the resort boutique that showed off her curves.

"Do you like what you see?" Her voice was deep and sultry.

His voice didn't work, so he vigorously nodded.

She stepped up to him, lifted up on her tiptoes and pressed her lips to his. He kissed her back. He'd never tire of having her so close. There was something so very special about her—something he needed in his life.

When he went to pull her closer, she quickly backed away. A smile played upon her lips. "You said you brought me all the way out here for something other than kissing, so what did you have in mind?"

He sighed. "Did you have to throw my words back in my face?"

A big smile lit up her eyes, making them twinkle. "Yes, I did."

He took her hand in his. "Okay. Let's go."

He led her toward the lower waterfall. There was a large space between the two layers of rock. He led her to that protected area. While they were shielded from the rushing water, in front of them the waterfall flowed down from above, hitting the layer of rock they stood on, and then the water spilled down into the pond below.

"This is so amazing." Adara practically had to shout to be heard over the waterfall.

He turned to her. "Almost as amazing as you."

When she looked at him like he was the only man in the

world, his resolve crumbled. He drew her into his arms. And as they stood there on the rocks with the water spilling down, he claimed her lips with his own.

He was finding that the more time he spent with her, the more time he wanted to spend with her. And his driving need to keep moving around—to never stay in one place too long—was dissipating.

With the greatest regret, he pulled back. If they were to kiss any longer, his reason for bringing her out here would be lost. He took her hand in his as he made his way to the edge of the rock.

Adara stopped. "What are you doing?"

He turned to her. "Come on."

"Out there?" She pointed to the edge. "I don't think so."

"You can do it."

"And what are we going to do once we get out there?"

"We're going to jump?"

"Jump!" She started shaking her head. "No. Not a chance."

He gave her hand a reassuring squeeze. "It'll be fun."

"You don't even know if it's safe. What if the water down below is too shallow?"

"I'll have you know I asked Titus at the front desk about it. He said this is a popular cliff-jumping spot. Don't you trust me?"

"I... I trust you." Her gaze moved to follow the water down to the pond below.

"Then come on. Do something spontaneous."

"I did. I came here with you."

"Yes, you did." His thumb moved back and forth over the back of her hand. "Now let's go do something daring."

Her skeptical gaze met his. "You're serious, aren't you?"

"Of course I am." He kept a hold on her hand as he continued toward the edge.

She hesitated at first, but then she followed him. "I can't believe you want us to jump off a cliff."

"It's not a very high one."

Her gaze lowered to the water down below. "High enough."

He turned to her. "Will you jump with me?"

"I… I don't know."

She was so close. He just needed to coax her a little more out of her comfort zone. And then he hoped it would be the first of many new experiences for them.

"What will it take to convince you to jump with me?"

She cautiously leaned forward to peer at the water below, and then she pulled back. "I get to pick our next date."

He liked the idea of there being a promise of another date. "I'll do whatever you want."

"Then what are you waiting for?"

Hand in hand, they moved to the edge of the cliff. He turned his head to look at her. She gazed into his eyes. This was a new beginning for them.

Her heart raced as the blood pulsated in her ears. Adara chanced a glance to the side, at the water rushing down to the pond below. He really wanted them to jump? All the way down there?

Krystof squeezed her hand. When she glanced back at him, he said, "You don't have to do this if you really don't want to."

She swallowed hard. "I know."

Part of her wanted to turn and go back to the place where they'd left their picnic lunch. It would be the safe thing to do—the smart thing to do. And yet her feet wouldn't move.

As she stared into his eyes, it calmed her. She instinctively knew he would never do anything to endanger her. All he wanted her to do was to step outside her comfort zone. But could she do it?

It was so far down there. She had never done something like this before. Maybe this wasn't the best way to step out of her comfort zone. Maybe she should find some other thing to do. Yes, that sounded like a good idea.

"Adara, you can do this. You'll be with me." Krystof's voice was deep and soothing.

"Couldn't we go back down and have a picnic lunch?"

"We will, soon. I promise." He held his hand out to her.

She glanced down at the water again. She turned her head back to him. Her attention focused on his outstretched hand. Her heart pounded in her chest as she placed her hand in his. Her fingers laced with his as though it were the most natural thing.

Don't back out. You can do this.

She needed to prove to herself that she could do the daring and unexpected. Maybe since her parents' deaths, she had sought safety and security within her scheduled plans. Maybe now, with so much time having passed, it was finally time to try something different.

Her gaze rose to his. "Let's do this."

He smiled at her and then nodded. "Let's." They both turned to the edge of the cliff. "At the count of three."

By now she was clutching his hand so tight that it must be cutting off his blood flow, but he didn't complain. Had she forgotten to tell him that she didn't like heights?

"One…"

Her heart beat against her ribs.

"Two…"

Why did it look so far down?

"Three…"

The jerk of his hand spurred her into action. And then she felt weightless as she fell.

Splash.

Somewhere along the way, she'd lost hold of Krystof. She sank deep into the water. She felt as though she were never going to stop slipping farther into the dark depths of the pond.

At long last her body stopped dropping. Now she had to get to the surface. She started to kick her legs, hoping she was headed in the right direction. It was hard to tell as the light moved through the water. She hoped she was swimming upward.

She kicked hard. Her lungs began to burn. She kicked harder. Where was the surface? Panic had her swimming with all her might. Was she almost there?

And then she broke the surface. She gulped down oxygen, never so happy to be able to breathe. She coughed, having inhaled a little water.

"Are you okay?" Krystof's voice came from behind her.

She gathered herself and turned in the water to face him. He was smiling at her. "What are you smiling about?"

"You did it. You took a chance and did something out of the ordinary."

And then she realized he was right. She beamed back at him. "I did. Thanks to you."

She swam closer to him and wrapped her arms around his neck. He lowered his head and caught her lips with his own. His skin was chilled from the water, but she didn't mind, because his touch was all she needed to warm her up.

As their kiss intensified, her legs encircled his waist. The temperature of the water was long forgotten. She had other, more urgent matters on her mind now.

With her wrapped in his arms, Krystof swam on his back to the edge of the pond. He released her to heft himself out first, and then he turned back to help her out.

He swept her up into his arms and resumed kissing her. He carried her back to the clearing. He gently laid her down on the blanket. She refused to let him go. She drew him down on top of her. For her, this was the greatest risk of all. Because every time they made love, he made his way deeper into her heart.

CHAPTER FIFTEEN

LIFE COULD CHANGE in the time it took to flip a coin.

Adara should know, since it'd just happened to her.

One moment, she felt as though her feet were floating above the ground. She'd been so proud of herself for cliff jumping. It was something she'd never done before. It showed her that she could accomplish things she hadn't even considered until this point.

Throughout their picnic lunch at the waterfall followed by their dinner in bed, as well as the following two days they'd spent together, she had started to envision her life a bit differently. She'd even considered what she might do if she no longer worked at the Ludus Resort. After all, her assistant, Demi, was a natural. She could take over, and Adara would be free to do something else. The problem was that she liked her work as a concierge. She liked working with people and making their visions come true.

Krystof pushed her to question her life's decisions. Had she settled too soon? Should she have explored the world more to see if there was somewhere else that she fit in? Should she have worried more about her romantic life than her career? If she'd focused on romance, maybe she'd already have a baby and her current medical problem wouldn't feel so enormous.

The doctor's office had called on Friday morning and insisted they couldn't give her the test results over the phone. She had to meet with the doctor. It was at this point that she could no longer pretend this situation wasn't serious. They never called you into the office to give you good news.

It was the worst time, too. Atlas and Hermione had just arrived back on the island. With the wedding taking place tomorrow, they needed to finish up some last-minute wedding details. However, Adara couldn't delay her doctor's visit. She needed to know what was going on with her. She'd quietly slipped away.

The doctor had told her she was having early-onset menopause. She'd replayed his words over and over in her mind. How was this possible? She was only thirty-two. No one she knew went through menopause that early.

When he'd mentioned that sometimes it ran in families, she'd thought of her mother. Adara had been their only child. Whenever she'd asked her mother for a little brother or sister, her mother had said that wasn't going to happen. Maybe now Adara understood why her mother had looked so sad when she'd said those words.

And now Adara's vision for the future was ruined. There would be no happy little family for her. She wouldn't know what it was like to carry a baby in her body. She wouldn't hold her baby in her arms. Each time the thoughts tormented her, the backs of her eyes stung with unshed tears. She blinked them away. They would have to wait. She didn't have time to mourn the future she'd envisioned.

Right now, they'd just finished an elaborate wedding rehearsal dinner. The six members of the wedding party had dined out on the penthouse balcony. She'd love to say the food was delicious, but she hadn't eaten much, and what she had eaten had tasted like cardboard.

While Krystof, Atlas and Istvan were inside getting everyone some more drinks, the women were seated at the table. Hermione was all smiles. She looked like the happiest bride.

"How is Atlas's father doing?" Adara asked her friend.

"He's been moved to physical rehab. I was hoping he could be here for the wedding, but everyone agreed it would be too much for him."

"I'm sorry he couldn't make it," Indigo said. "But we'll take lots of pictures for you to share with him."

"Thank you. I think he'd like that. He's changed a lot since Atlas last saw him," Hermione said. "He's been sober for three years now. He apologized to Atlas. And I think he really meant it."

"How did Atlas feel about that?" Adara asked.

"He's being cautious. And I can't blame him after all he's been through. But I think there's a chance for some sort of relationship going forward. I just don't know what it'll look like. I guess it's just going to be a day-by-day thing." Hermione turned to Adara. "And how are things with you and Krystof? I hear you two have been spending a lot of time together."

Adara hesitated. She wasn't ready to dissect her complicated relationship with Krystof. Yesterday she would have said they were both learning to take risks and they might have a chance at building a lasting relationship. But today, after speaking to the doctor, she felt confused and unsure about what her future would hold.

Hermione didn't need to know any of this at her rehearsal dinner. Adara frantically searched for a more neutral topic of conversation.

Indigo leaned forward. "On Tuesday, they went cliff jumping at the twin falls."

"What?" Hermione's eyes opened wide. "But why?"

Adara shrugged. "Why not?"

Hermione smiled and shook her head. "Looks like Krystof is having an influence on you. If I'm not careful, he'll steal you away from me."

Adara shook her head. "I don't think so. What would I do?

I couldn't just follow him around the world watching him play cards."

"I'm sure you could find something much more entertaining to do with him." Indigo laughed.

As Adara's face grew warm, Hermione let out a giggle.

"What's going on out here?" Atlas handed Hermione a drink.

"We were just catching up on things." Hermione thanked her fiancé and then sipped at her drink.

Krystof placed a hand on Adara's bare shoulder. His touch felt good. She resisted the urge to lean her head against his arm. She refused to allow herself even that small bit of comfort. The news from the doctor had her seeing things differently—had her pulling back from Krystof.

With his other hand, Krystof handed her some ice water. They'd cut off the bubbly a while ago, because no one wanted to party too much with the wedding tomorrow.

He crouched down next to her. "Can I get you anything else?"

She shook her head. "I'm good."

He'd never been this sweet and attentive before. He was changing before her eyes. She didn't know what it meant, but she definitely felt like he was moving in the right direction. The destination was still a bit fuzzy, though.

The wedding day had arrived.

With the sun barely above the horizon, Adara was wide-awake and showered. She was a mixture of excited and relieved. She couldn't believe all the obstacles they'd had to overcome to make it to this point.

Ding.

She reached for her phone resting next to the bed. It was probably Hermione thinking of one last detail for the wedding. But when she read the message, she learned it was the bakery delivering the cake. *This early?*

She texted back that she would be right there. She twisted her hair and clipped it up. Later she would do something more formal for the wedding. Right now, she had to make sure the cake made it safely into the walk-in fridge.

In a pink flowered summer dress and sandals, she rushed to the elevator and down to the main floor. She hurried to the employee entrance and found the catering van. There were two deliverymen.

"Thanks for being here so early," Adara said. "This is one less thing I have to worry about."

"Where do you want these?" The shorter of the two men loaded the cake boxes onto a cart.

She explained the directions to the appropriate kitchen. "You can place the boxes on the large table to the left of the door. I'll make sure they are placed in the fridge."

The shorter man took off for the door. When she went to follow him, the taller man stopped her. "I just need you to sign off on the delivery."

"Oh. Certainly." She wondered if she should get the bride to do this, but she suspected Hermione was still tired from her journey yesterday. It was best to let her sleep as long as she could. Adara held her hand out for the receipt.

When he handed over the clipboard, she glanced at the name. Nikolaou.

Please don't let this be another mix-up.

"Um…this is the wrong bill. This is the Kappas or Othonos wedding."

The man's bushy brows drew together. "I don't understand. This was the receipt I was given. Let me look up front." He strode to the front of the truck and swung open the door.

It took a few minutes for him to come back with a small stack of receipts. "What did you say the name was?"

She repeated the names. It took him a moment to sort through the papers. And then he pulled out a slip. "Here it is." He held it out to her. "Just sign."

She wasn't going to just sign. After the last mix-up, she didn't trust the receipt was correct. "What about the cakes? Are they the right ones?"

The man's brows scrunched together again. "Of course they're right."

She was understandably having a problem taking it for granted that the cake hadn't been mixed up just like the receipt. "Maybe I should go check."

"Lady, I don't have all day. It's the right cake. Just sign the receipt."

She crossed her arms. "How can you be sure? You mixed up the receipts."

He expelled a frustrated sigh. "Because the cakes were double-checked at the bakery and marked one through five. This is the only five-tier cake we're delivering today. Therefore it's the right cake."

His explanation sounded reasonable. While the man grumbled about falling behind in his schedule, she read down line by line. And when she was satisfied that it was correct, she signed off. He pulled off a yellow carbon copy and handed it to her.

On her way to the kitchen, she passed the shorter man with an empty cart. Now all she had to do was put the layers of cake in the fridge until it was time for the wedding, and then the kitchen crew would see to assembling it for the reception.

She smiled as she made her way through the hotel. She approached an older woman pushing her cleaning supply cart. "Good morning, Irene."

The woman sent her a big, friendly smile. "It's a gorgeous day for a wedding."

"Yes, it is. I hope you're ready to dance the evening away."

"I still can't believe they invited the staff."

"I can. Hermione looks on all of us as her family. And Atlas finally has the family he never had growing up."

Irene placed a hand over her heart as she sighed. "It's so good they found each other."

"Agreed. I have to get going and see to the cake."

"I bet it'll be beautiful."

"It will be. Soon, you'll see for yourself."

"Then I better get my work done early. I don't want to miss this wedding."

"See you later."

And then they continued in opposite directions. Irene wasn't the only excited member of staff. In fact, there had been a lottery to see which staff got to attend the wedding and which had to work, because without the lottery, it had been chaos with everyone trying to swap shifts. At last, it was settled. Some employees would be wedding guests, and the others would get a bonus in their next paycheck. It wasn't perfect, but Hermione and Atlas had done their best.

Adara entered the kitchen and looked to the left. The table was empty. Her chest tightened in panic. Where was the cake?

Her gaze swung around the kitchen, searching for the pink bakery boxes. And then she spotted them on the table to the right of the door. She blew out a pent-up breath. It appeared the guy wasn't any better with directions than the driver had been with finding the right receipt.

Adara couldn't believe how much cake there was, but Hermione had fallen in love with this design. There were alternating flavors—the bottom tier was chocolate with a cherry ganache filling, and the next layer was vanilla with a lemon curd filling. Adara's mouth watered just thinking about eating it. She wasn't sure which layer she preferred more.

Now she had to get the cake moved into the large walk-in fridge. The wedding wasn't until that afternoon, but the cooking staff would be there shortly to begin the preparations. Adara hoped to be gone before they showed up.

She walked to the fridge and stepped inside. There were mounds of food everywhere. There was a spare shelf here and there, but no group of shelves. Some rearranging was in order.

Minutes later, she had a spot for the cake boxes. She moved them one by one, starting with the largest. She held the boxes tightly and took slow, measured steps so as not to trip. She had never been so nervous while holding a cake before. But this wasn't just any cake—it was her best friend's wedding cake.

The first four layers were secure in the fridge. This just left the cake top. She couldn't resist taking a peek. She loosened the tape very carefully. She lifted the lid.

Inside was a pale blue cake with an array of pastel flowers. It was beautiful. And it would totally fit the beach theme of the wedding.

She closed the box, resealing the tape. You couldn't even tell that she'd taken a sneak peek. She carefully lifted the box so as not to tip it to one side or the other.

With the box secure in her hands, she started across the kitchen to the fridge. Just as she stepped in front of the kitchen door, it began to open. It was as if time slowed down.

She froze. The door moved. Her voice caught in her throat.

The door hit the box. It jarred her, and she screamed, "Stop!"

CHAPTER SIXTEEN

IT WAS TOO late.

The door struck Adara's fingers.

It pushed her hands back. The box hit her chest. Adara gasped.

The cake box tilted. The lid pressed against her. "Oh, no! No! No! No!"

When the door moved back, she lowered the cake box. Her sole focus was on the cake inside. Was it salvageable? She doubted it.

"What's wrong?" Suddenly Krystof appeared in front of her.

"How could you?" Of all the people to be on the other side of the door, why was she not surprised to find it was Krystof? He was always acting first and thinking later.

His dark brows furrowed together. "What did I do?"

"You ruined everything!" She moved to the closest table and placed the box on it.

"Ruined everything? Don't you think that's a little overdramatic?"

"No. I don't." Her fingers shook with nervous energy as she worked to loosen the tape on the lid. "It just can't be ruined."

"What?" Frustration rang out in his voice.

Her gaze met his as she gestured at the cake box. "What do you think?"

"How am I supposed to know? Someone told me they saw you come down here, and I came to see if you needed any help."

She shook her head. "You have the worst timing ever."

His eyes widened. "Why are you so mad at me?"

All her pent-up emotions came bubbling to the surface. Instead of dealing with her infertility issues, her anger and frustration was focused on the fate of the cake.

"It doesn't matter." She didn't have time to get into this with him. "Just go."

"I'm not leaving." He moved up next to her. "What has you so upset?"

At last she managed to loosen the tape. She lifted the lid. And the cake was even worse than she'd imagined. The frosting was smashed against the lid and the side of the box. The fluffy chocolate cake was split open. Now what was she going to do?

Krystof peered over her shoulder. "Wait. Is that the wedding cake?"

"It was."

"Was?"

"You squashed it against me when you came flying through the door. How could you do that?"

"Wait." He pressed his hand to his chest indignantly. "You're blaming me?"

"Of course I am. You're the one who slammed the door into the cake."

"How was I supposed to know you were standing there? It's not like there's a window in the door or anything!"

She hated that he had a good point. Right now, she needed someplace to focus her frustration. And Krystof was the only one in the vicinity. And it might have had something to do with him trying to win her over when she knew that soon he'd be gone on his next adventure, while she'd still be here on Ludus

Island. But she refused to think about that now. She had a cake disaster to deal with.

"What are you going to do?" Krystof looked at her expectantly.

She was tired of solving problems. "What are *you* going to do? After all, you are the best man. So what's it going to be? And don't take long, because we don't have much time."

His brows furrowed together. "Why should I fix it?"

"Because you ruined the cake." She sighed. There was no time for him to figure out a solution. "Never mind. I've got this." She withdrew her phone from her pocket and pulled the receipt from her pocket. She dialed the number for the bakery.

"What are you doing?"

As the phone rang, she held up her finger for Krystof to wait. After a much-too-brief conversation with the bakery, she disconnected the call.

"What did they say?" Krystof leaned against the table.

She placed her palms on the cold metal of the tabletop and leaned her weight on them as she stared straight ahead. "They can't help us. They said they delivered unblemished cakes and what happened to them after they were delivered is our problem."

"Can't they make us a new cake? I'm willing to pay whatever it'll cost. I'll even throw in a bonus."

She was relieved he was finally comprehending the severity of this situation. "They said they're fully booked today. And even if they wanted to help, there simply isn't enough time to bake a new cake, cool it, decorate it and deliver it."

Krystof raked his fingers through his hair, scattering the loose curls. "Then there won't be a cake top. There will still be a cake. That's all that's needed."

"What?" Surely she hadn't heard him correctly. "You can't be serious." When he nodded, she said, "How many weddings have you been to where there wasn't a beautifully decorated cake? And the cake top is the showpiece."

"I don't go to many weddings."

"You're avoiding the question."

He sighed. "Fine. What are you going to do?"

"I think you mean what are *we* going to do, because this mess is as much your fault as mine." Her mind raced, searching for a solution. Because she wasn't going to let Hermione down. "Let me get the next smallest cake."

"*I'll* get the cake. We know what happened the last time you carried one of the cakes."

"Hey, that's not fair."

"But true."

She inwardly groaned. "Fine. The cakes are in the walk-in. They're on the left side in pink boxes. Make sure you grab the smallest box, and please be careful. We can't afford to lose another layer."

"Trust me. I'm sure on my feet."

She rolled her eyes as he walked away. Lucky for her, she'd taken some cake-decorating classes with her neighbor. And here she'd thought those craft classes would never be useful. Boy, had she been wrong.

She'd also learned a shortcut to making fondant. She just had to find some marshmallows, powdered sugar, shortening, food coloring and water.

"I'll be right back!" She ran out the door.

The best part of working at an exclusive resort was that they had a lot of specialty items. It shouldn't be hard to find the ingredients. And she was right.

Ten minutes later, she was back in the kitchen with the necessary ingredients. Krystof was busy scrolling on his phone. She set the box of items on the table.

"Make yourself useful and find me a mixer." She didn't wait for him to answer. She moved to the sink and washed up.

A few minutes later, she had a batch of fondant. She tried to remember what the topping looked like. It was flowers. Flowers were not easy to make. You had to make each petal, and that took tools that she didn't have.

"What's wrong?" Krystof asked. "Why aren't you doing anything?"

"I am doing something. I'm thinking."

"If you don't hurry, this kitchen is going to fill up with the catering staff."

She glared at him. "You don't think I know that, but I can't recreate the delicate flowers the bakery made for the original cake top."

"Then make something else. Something easier."

"But then Hermione will know."

Krystof smiled and shook his head. "Don't you think she'll know no matter how you decorate the cake? There'll be a layer missing."

Though she hated to admit it, he was right. "Fine. How do you think we should decorate it?"

He shrugged. "How should I know? If it were up to me, there wouldn't be any decorations."

Why had she thought he would be any help? If she couldn't make flowers, what else could she make that would be rather easy and still fit the wedding's beach theme? She stared at the blue cake. And then she realized she'd come up with the answer—beach items.

"I'll make a sand dollar, a starfish and seashells. They can't be that hard, right?"

"I don't know. I guess not," he said dubiously.

And so she set to work dividing the fondant and then coloring it different shades. She left part of it white. She removed a rolling pin from the box as well as the edible markers. Boy, she loved working in this place that had a little bit of everything.

She consulted an image on her phone as she created it. When she'd finished making the sand dollar, she asked, "What do you think?"

Krystof lowered his phone to look at her creation. "Not bad."

She frowned at him. "Not bad? I'd like to see you do better."

"Okay. It's really good. Better?"

"Much." She laid the sand dollar gently on the top of the cake and frowned.

"What's the matter?"

"It just doesn't look right."

They moved it around, and still she was certain they were missing something. She started to make a starfish. It was a lot harder than it looked in the photo. And considering she didn't have the right shaping tools, she had to make do with what she found in the kitchen.

"I've got it." Krystof started for the door.

She paused as she was about to cover the starfish with granulated sugar. "Where are you going?"

"I have an idea. I'll be right back." Without waiting for her to say another word, he dashed out the door.

She had no idea what he found so urgent at this moment. But she didn't have time to worry about him. She had her own issues. Like making the top of the cake look presentable. Her art skills were not the best—at least she didn't think so.

And though she wanted to cry in frustration, she kept working—kept trying to make the best collection of seashells possible from fondant. She'd make as many as she could and then pick the best ones to place on the cake.

She didn't know how long she continued to work while Krystof was off on his errand, but finally he returned. He stepped up next to her at the counter and perused her work. He was very quiet. Was that a bad sign?

With nerves frazzled, she asked, "Are they that bad?"

"Bad? No. I think they're great."

She glanced at him, at the edible seashells and then back at him. He wasn't smiling or laughing. In fact, he looked quite sincere. "Are you being honest?"

His gaze met hers. "Of course I am. You don't agree?"

"I think there's nothing I could create that would replace the beautiful flowers that were on the original cake top, but these will have to do."

"I disagree. This is going to be much better."

"I don't know about that." She stared at the decorations she'd created. "I feel like there's something missing." She was so worried that she was about to mess up her best friend's wedding, and then she'd never forgive herself.

Krystof reached for a bag of brown sugar and the granulated sugar. He mixed them together. And then he carefully sprinkled it on top of the cake.

"What are you doing?" She moved closer to him. "Wait. Is that supposed to be sand?"

He smiled as he turned to her. "You did say it was a beach theme. And what is a beach without sand?"

"You're brilliant." She reached out and hugged him. "It pulls it all together."

The movement had been an automatic response. She turned her head ever so slightly and breathed in the slight scent of soap mixed with his masculine scent. *Mmm...*

CHAPTER SEVENTEEN

THE SENSUOUS TIMBRE of the violins filled the air.

This was it. It was time for the ceremony.

Adara turned to her friend. "Are you ready for this?"

Hermione's face lit up with a brilliant smile. "I definitely am."

"You look beautiful. I hope Atlas knows how lucky he is."

"Almost as lucky as me. Thank you for all you've done."

"You're welcome." She carefully hugged her friend, trying not to mess up her wedding dress or the styled curls that fell down her back.

Hermione pulled back. "Now you and Indigo better get down that aisle, or else I'm going to beat you to the end."

"You wouldn't."

"Don't tempt me. I can't wait to say 'I do.'"

They both laughed. It felt good to lose herself in the moment and not to think about her problems anymore.

"And I think there's a man waiting at the end of the aisle for you, too." Hermione arched a brow. "I've seen the way you two look at each other. It's a lot more than the fling you had going on before. I think Krystof really cares about you."

Heat swirled in Adara's chest and rushed to her face. "This day isn't about me or Krystof. It's all about you and Atlas." At that moment, the music changed. "I think that's our cue to walk down the aisle."

"This is so exciting," Indigo said. "Let's get these two married."

Indigo was the first down the steps to the beach in the artic-blue gown that showed her slim, tanned shoulders and gave a hint of her lower legs and the sandals they'd picked out. Adara waited until her friend turned the corner, and then she started after her.

When she turned the corner, she saw the sea of white chairs and the handsomely dressed guests. Her gaze moved up the center aisle to the flowered arch and then to the right, where the groom stood. Her gaze quickly moved past him to the best man, who was staring back at her. Her heart skipped a beat.

For a second, she let herself imagine what it'd be like if this was their wedding. Would Krystof stare at her like he was doing now? Or would his gaze be warmed with love?

And yet the way he was looking at her now, it made her feel like the most beautiful woman in the world. For a second, she wondered if he'd look at her the same way if he knew she was broken on the inside. And then she pushed aside the bothersome thought. Today was for celebrating her friends' love. Tomorrow she'd deal with her diagnosis.

At the end of the aisle, she felt a gravitational pull in Krystof's direction, but she resisted the urge and instead took her position to the left of the aisle. She turned to watch Hermione approached them. She looked breathtaking. The pure joy on her face was the way every bride should look on their wedding day. In that moment, as Hermione stepped up to Atlas—as they stared lovingly into each other's eyes—Adara realized all the challenges of the past couple of weeks had been totally worth it. Hermione and Atlas got their happily-ever-after.

Hermione turned to her and handed her bouquet over so that she could hold both of Atlas's hands. As Adara took the flowers, her gaze strayed past Hermione and immediately connected with Krystof's. Was he still staring at her?

As they exchanged vows, Adara was utterly distracted by Krystof's presence. Any time her gaze would stray to him, he'd be looking back at her. What was up with him? Why was he being so attentive?

She looked so much like a bride.

He should turn away, but his body refused to cooperate.

Krystof couldn't keep his gaze from Adara. And then her head turned ever so slightly, and their gazes met. His heart started to pound.

She wore the most brilliant smile that filled his chest with warmth. It was as if she were the sun and he a mere planet in her orbit. He could imagine her walking up to him—being there with him.

Whoa! Where had that thought come from?

He reined in his thoughts. Sure, they were having a good time together. But they had a casual thing going. Why ruin it with a bunch of promises that would one day be broken?

After all, when the wedding was over, he would be on to his next adventure. This time it wasn't a card game. This time he was heading back to Paris. He'd made a decision. After his research and speaking with consultants, he'd determined the tech firm would be a worthwhile investment.

He would return to the island regularly to see Adara. And he had hopes of convincing her to go on some adventures with him. They made a good pair. He hoped it would continue after the wedding. But for how long?

As the priest spoke of love and eternity, Krystof knew as sure as he was standing on that white sand with the sea softly lapping at the beach that one day Adara would be standing there in a white dress with flowers in her hair and stars in her eyes. She would be staring into the eyes of the man she loved. She would be staring at him.

Whoa! Where did that come from?

It was this wedding. It had him all out of sorts. When it was over, they could get back to the way things used to be.

And then the ceremony ended. Mr. and Mrs. Othonos started up the aisle. Now it was his turn to walk Adara up the aisle. He stepped forward and presented his arm to her. When she smiled at him, it stirred this unfamiliar sensation in his chest. He assured himself that it was nothing.

With her hand tucked in the crook of his arm, they were headed toward the patio area that had been reserved for the reception. Adara expelled a dreamy sigh. "Wasn't that the most wonderful wedding?"

"All thanks to you." And he meant it. "You worked really hard so that everything was perfect for them."

"Thank you. But this wedding was a team effort. There were a lot of people that helped with the arrangements, especially you."

He shook his head. "I didn't do much at all."

"You did more than you think. You helped me sort out the dresses and pick out the music. And let's not forget how you helped decorate the cake."

"Huh. I did do a lot, didn't I?" He sent her a teasing smile. "What did you do again?"

She rolled her eyes. "Give a guy a compliment and it goes straight to his head."

He loved this side of Adara. That trip to the waterfall had done them both a lot of good. It had been an amazing afternoon—one he wouldn't mind repeating in the very near future.

She elbowed him lightly. "What are you smiling about?"

Should he tell her? He didn't see what it would hurt. "I was thinking about our day at the waterfall."

"You mean the day you had me playing hooky from work?"

"Oh, come on. You know you enjoyed it." There was no way he was going to believe that she hadn't. It was a day he would never forget. "We should do it again."

He expected her to agree, but instead, she said, "Come on. We need to form a receiving line." She grabbed his hand to lead him to the spot where he needed to stand. "They're waiting for us."

As her fingers laced with his, a jolt zipped up his arm and sent his heart racing. It didn't matter how much time he spent with her—she still had this special effect on him. He was so relieved they'd patched things up between them. And he would show her how much he appreciated her presence in his life later that evening.

Just a little longer...

She could keep it together a little longer.

Adara was indeed happy for her friends, but the doctor's diagnosis continued to linger on the edges of her thoughts. It was so much to take in. In an instant, everything about her life had changed.

She glanced around and spotted Krystof talking to a guest. At that moment, he glanced in her direction. When their gazes met, he smiled. It was a balm on her tattered heart.

She knew there was a lot more to her than whether or not she could give birth. But in this particular moment, it's where her mind wanted to dwell.

And yet when Krystof looked at her like he was doing now, she felt complete and whole. He made her feel like anything was possible even when she knew that wasn't the case.

Krystof was now headed in her direction. He stopped in front of her and held his hand out to her. "May I have this dance?"

"I... I don't think so." She had to start putting some distance between them.

"Come on. Please. I'm going to look awfully silly dancing out there all by myself."

"You wouldn't."

He smiled at her, making her stomach dip. "I'd do anything to make you smile."

And then he held one hand over his chest and held his other hand at his side as though he were dancing with an invisible person. He started swaying to the music. She couldn't believe her eyes. He was really going to dance without her.

People were stopping to watch their exchange. If she didn't dance with him, they were just going to draw even more attention. And she had promised herself that she was going to have a good time tonight—even if that good time was found in Krystof's arms.

And so she stepped up to him. He reached out to her, and she walked into his arms. It felt so natural to be with him. It was though at last she was exactly where she belonged.

She corrected her thoughts. She didn't belong with Krystof. And he didn't belong with her. All they were having was a good time together. Nothing more. In the morning, he would leave on his next adventure. And she would be left to pick up the pieces of her life.

CHAPTER EIGHTEEN

THE BRIDE AND groom had departed.

The reception was over.

Krystof had just finished talking to Prince Istvan when he noticed Adara across the room. She was at the buffet speaking with one of the staff, who was clearing the serving dishes. Once she finished her talk, instead of heading toward the lingering guests, she turned toward the kitchen.

He followed her. When he stepped in the kitchen, it was abuzz with staff rushing to clean up so they could head home. There was no sign of Adara. Had she slipped out the back way? Was she trying to avoid him?

He knew she'd been a bit quiet and more reserved than normal during the reception, but he wrote that off to exhaustion. She'd worked so hard to make the wedding the best it could be that she'd worn herself out.

He turned and exited the kitchen. He made his way to Adara's room. He told himself that he needed to make sure she was feeling all right, and then he'd let her get some rest.

He raised his hand and knocked on the door. No response. After a moment, he knocked again. "Adara, it's me. I just came to check on you." He knocked one last time. "Adara, please open the door."

He heard the click of the lock, and then the door swung open. Adara stood there with her hair down and her makeup smudged. Wait. Had she been crying?

"What do you want?" she asked.

He stepped past her into the darkened room, where only the large-screen television cast light. He turned back to her. "What's wrong?"

"Nothing's wrong. The wedding was a success. Hermione and Atlas are happy newlyweds."

She was saying all the right things, but he didn't believe her. He stepped up to her and gazed into her bloodshot eyes. "Adara, what's wrong?"

"Why do you keep asking me that? I answered already."

His gaze searched hers. "But did you? Really? Because I think something has been bothering you all evening. No. Make that since yesterday at dinner. You've been doing your best to cover it up, but there's something wrong. If it's about me leaving tomorrow, I've been giving that some thought."

Her brows gathered. "What are you talking about?"

"I'm talking about me starting to put down roots. I have to fly to Paris briefly but I'll return. Then I could stay here for a while and work on expanding MyPost. It was so helpful with finding the dresses that I think with the right leadership, the site could do a lot of good for so many more people."

"And you're going to—what? Live here at the resort?"

He smiled and nodded. "For a while. And while I'm here, I'm hoping we could spend more time together. We can see where things go with us."

"No." The two-letter word had a big crescendo.

Krystof's eyes widened. "Isn't that what you've wanted all of this time? I thought you wanted a committed relationship. I thought you wanted me staying in one place for more than a week at a time."

"No." She waved him off as though she were frustrated. "I mean, yes, but not now."

If he'd thought there might be a problem before, he was certain of it now. "Adara, talk to me. What's going on?"

Her fine brows drew together as her lips pursed together. For a moment, she stood there silently glaring at him. "Why are you pushing this?"

"Because I care."

Her eyes momentarily widened. "You do?"

He nodded. "You can talk to me."

He'd never let his guard down long enough to admit that he cared about anyone before, but he got the feeling Adara really needed to hear it tonight.

She sighed. Her shoulders drooped as though they were bearing the weight of the world upon them. He couldn't imagine what had her so worked up.

"Why don't we go out on the balcony?" He gestured for her to lead the way.

For once, she didn't put up an argument, but instead she moved to the balcony high above the now-closed pool area. It was a tranquil spot. He filled a glass with water and followed her. She took a seat in one of the cushioned chairs.

He handed her the water. "Thank you." She took a sip before setting it aside. "Maybe I should head back to the kitchen and make sure there are no problems."

"They have everything under control."

"How do you know?"

"Because I went in there looking for you. And they looked like they knew exactly what they were doing. All you need to do is sit here and tell me what's going on with you."

Adara opened her mouth as though to argue the point but then wordlessly pressed her lips together. "I don't know why you brought me out here. There's really nothing to talk about."

"And I think that is the biggest understatement I've ever heard." He wanted to push her for answers, because he was concerned, but he resisted the urge. The more he pushed, the more she'd shut down on him. And so he sat there quietly staring down at the pool.

After several minutes of silence, she sighed. "You aren't going to move until we talk, are you?"

"I'm not leaving until I'm sure you're okay. If that means we talk a bit, I'm good with that. If you want to sit here quietly and drink your water, I'm fine with that, too."

Her gaze narrowed. "Since when are you so Zen?"

A smile pulled at the corners of his lips. "Zen, huh?"

"Don't let it go to your head." She took another sip. "I can't believe you're holding me hostage."

He arched a brow. "A little melodramatic, don't you think?"

She set aside the water. "You just don't understand."

"I would if you talked to me. Don't you think after all we've shared that you can trust me?"

She hesitated as though she had to actually give the answer to that question some serious thought. His pride was pricked. Because no matter what he had or hadn't done, he had never betrayed her. And he never would.

"Adara?" His voice was filled with disbelief.

"Okay. Yes, I trust you."

"Then talk to me. If I can help, you have to know that I'll do it."

She shook her head. "That's just it. No one can help."

Had there been a wave of emotion in her voice? He turned to look into her eyes, and that's when he saw the gloomy look on her face. Whatever was weighing on her mind was serious.

"I care about you," he said. "And I'll support you through whatever this is."

She got to her feet and moved to the railing. "I can't have children."

Had he heard her correctly? Maybe she'd said she *wanted* to have children. The thought had the breath catching in his lungs. Children were not something he'd ever considered in his life.

Still, this wasn't about him. This was about Adara and her

desires. And he needed to keep his promise to be there for her, no matter the subject.

He stood and moved next to her. In a soft voice, he said, "What has you thinking about this?"

Her face grew pale. "Does it matter?"

"Yes. It matters to you, so it matters to me."

"Please stop. Stop being so understanding. So caring." Her voice wavered with emotion.

He reached out to where she had her hand resting on the railing. He placed his hand over hers. "I think life happens, and we have to deal with it as it comes to us."

She struggled to keep her composure.

He was being so nice to her. She didn't know what to think.

Adara didn't dare turn her head to look at Krystof. She knew if she looked into his eyes, she'd lose the little control she had on her emotions. She didn't know he could be so understanding.

"I don't even know where to start," she said.

"At the beginning usually helps."

It felt strange discussing something so distinctively female with a man. And yet she knew that whatever she discussed with Krystof wouldn't go any further. He'd proved that over and over again.

"It started when I missed my monthly."

Krystof remained quiet. Very quiet. But he didn't remove his hand from hers.

"I knew I wasn't pregnant, because you were the only person I'd been with in a really long time. And I'd had it since the last time we were together. But as one month passed without it and then two, I knew something was terribly wrong."

"And I didn't make things easy for you. I'm sorry."

She shook her head. "It wasn't your fault. You had no idea that I had a medical issue."

"Maybe if I had slowed down, I would have realized you were dealing with something."

She glanced at him and saw the serious look on his face. "Don't blame yourself. Even if you had noticed back then, I wouldn't have talked to you about it. Back then I was still in denial about what was happening."

"Which is what?"

"Well, the doctor said it could have been a lot of things. And so they ran a bunch of tests. It took a while for them to all come back. Yesterday, I met with my doctor."

"That's where you went?"

She nodded. "They wouldn't give me the results over the phone. I had to go to the office. I know I probably shouldn't have done it the day before the wedding, but I just couldn't wait any longer."

"Of course you should have gone. I just wish you'd have said something to me. I would have gone with you."

She shook her head. "It was something I needed to do on my own." She drew in a deep brew. "I found out that I have early-onset menopause."

He paused for a moment as though digesting this information. "And this is the reason you can't have children?"

She nodded once more. "I think my mother had it, and now I have it. I… I didn't even know if I wanted to have children." Her voice wavered with emotion. "I mean, I thought maybe someday if I met the right person, I might have a family with them. But now that decision is out of my control." Her vision blurred with unshed tears.

"Can they reverse this menopause?"

She shook her head as the tears spilled onto her cheeks.

Krystof reached out and pulled her into his arms. She didn't want to need his hug, but she longed for the reassurance that everything was going to be all right.

And so she let herself be drawn into his embrace. Her arms wrapped around his trim waist as her cheek landed on his shoulder. Her face nuzzled into the curve of his neck. She inhaled his masculine scent mingled with a whiff of spicy cologne.

In that moment, she was distracted from her sorrow, and instead she lived in the moment. Her heart pitter-pattered quickly. And just as quickly, she remembered that she would never make anyone the perfect partner, because she was only a part of whom she'd once been.

She pulled away. "I'm sorry. I shouldn't have cried on your shoulder."

"My shoulder is there for you any time you need it."

She had to keep her emotions under control. She couldn't let herself fall apart and have him put the pieces back together. He was at last understanding that he had options if he put down roots—he could have a family of his own. Just not with her.

He studied her for a moment. "And now it all makes sense."

"What makes sense?" She had no idea what he was talking about.

"The reason you've been going out of your way to make sure everything was perfect for the wedding."

"And what reason is that?"

He reached up and ever so gently tucked a strand of hair behind her ear. "Your body feels out of control, and so you felt a need to control every aspect of the wedding. I just want you to know that you can relax now, because you've accomplished your goal. This was the best wedding."

She hated how easily he read her. Because if he could figure all that out, he would also know that she felt inadequate and uncertain of what her future would hold. Would she stay at the resort forever because she didn't have any other place she belonged—no other family of her own?

The more the troubling thoughts crowded into her mind, the more her emotions rose. And she couldn't fall apart now. Not when Krystof was prepared to hold her together—to be there like she'd thought she wanted.

But now she couldn't be the person he needed. If they were to stay together, he might one day want a family. She couldn't give it to him. He'd feel compelled to tell her that it didn't matter. But it did matter so much that she felt utterly gutted. And someday it might matter that much to him, too.

"Krystof, you need to go."

"I'm not going anywhere. I'm here for you." He looked at her like he really cared. And it was making this so incredibly hard.

"I don't need you." She stepped back. "We're not a couple. We never really were. This is my problem to deal with. Not yours."

"Adara, why are you doing this?"

She was doing what was best for both of them. "Are you going to leave?"

"No. I'm not going anywhere."

Of all the times for him not to want to leave at the first chance. She knew if she stayed here, he would wear her down and they'd spend the night together. And in the morning, they'd be right back in this same awful position, because they had no future.

She didn't know why he was trying so hard. It wasn't like they were in love or anything. He felt sorry for her—that was it. And she couldn't keep doing this.

"If you aren't going to leave, then I am." She turned and went back inside the room.

"Adara, where are you going?"

"It doesn't matter." She grabbed her purse and keys before heading for the door.

"Adara, wait. Don't go."

She kept walking.

This time Krystof didn't try to stop her. He must have realized there was nothing that could be done for her. She was broken beyond repair.

CHAPTER NINETEEN

HOME AT LAST.

Her apartment didn't feel warm and comforting like she'd thought it would. It felt cold and empty.

Adara hadn't slept much that night. She already missed Krystof, and he hadn't even left the island yet. But he would soon be jetting off to some card game in a far-off location.

She hoped he wouldn't give up on finding someone special in his life. She wanted him to be happy, and she didn't think his nomadic ways would make him happy the rest of his life.

Knock-knock.

No one knew she was home. It had to be Krystof. Was he there to say goodbye on his way out of town?

She scrambled out of bed. She glanced in the mirror. Her day-old makeup was smeared. She had raccoon eyes. She rubbed them. It only smeared her makeup more.

Knock-knock.

Whoever was on the other side of the door wasn't going away. Adara groaned. She didn't want to see anyone.

"Coming!" In her shorts and T-shirt, she headed for the door. She swung it open. "Hermione, what are you doing here?"

"Good morning to you, too."

And then Adara remembered her manners and opened the door wide. "Come in. Shouldn't you be on your honeymoon?"

Hermione moved into the living room and sat down on the couch. "We're leaving today to visit Atlas's father, and if he's doing well, we're going on our honeymoon. But first, I wanted to check on you."

"Why?" Adara sat down, too. "What did Krystof tell you?"

Hermione's brows drew together. Concern reflected in her eyes. "Nothing. I haven't seen him this morning. But now I want to know what's going on with you two."

She couldn't hold it all in any longer. She needed her best friend. And so it all came tumbling out about her diagnosis and how Krystof wanted to stay on at the resort.

"So what did you say?"

"I told him we're not a couple. I… I told him we never really were." Her voice cracked with emotion. "I told him… I told him I didn't need him."

Hermione reached out and gave her hand a quick squeeze. "But you do need him, don't you?"

Adara shrugged. And then she gave in to the truth and nodded. "But he's finally figuring out that he doesn't have to be a nomad. He can make a home, have a family, if he wants. But I can't give him that."

"Did you ask him what he wants?"

Adara shook her head. "He would just say what he thought I'd want him to say."

"Would you want him making decisions for you?"

"No. But this is different."

"Is it?" Hermione arched a brow. "Or are you afraid to let yourself admit that you love him?"

"What? No. Of course not. We weren't a couple. It wasn't ever serious."

"And yet you two made sure that no matter how many miles separated you, that you saw each other regularly for months.

I've seen the way you both look at each other. If that's not love, I don't know what it is."

It was true. She loved Krystof. She couldn't keep hiding from the truth. "But we're so different. I like to have my life planned out, and he doesn't even know what country he'll be in tomorrow."

"Have you ever considered another life—someplace far from Ludus Island?"

"No."

"Maybe you should give it some thought. I'll miss you, but we can video chat and visit often. The resort will always be home to you."

Could she be happy somewhere else? Could she be happy always moving around? She didn't know the answers.

Krystof had taught her that she needed to take chances and reach for the things she wanted. She had been thinking about starting her own event-planning business. Was now the time for her to be her own boss? Was it time to take a leap with Krystof?

It was time to move on.

And yet his bags weren't packed. He didn't want to leave.

Krystof rode the elevator to the penthouse. He wanted to say goodbye to Atlas before they both left. He had no idea when he'd see his friend again. He had a feeling it would be a long time before he set foot on Ludus Island again.

The elevator stopped, and the door opened. Krystof stepped off and found Atlas standing in the doorway to the penthouse. He waved him inside. "Come on in. Hermione isn't here right now."

Krystof stepped forward, coming to a stop right inside the doorway. "I won't take much of your time. I just wanted to wish you the best. And let you know that I'm getting ready to leave."

"Thanks for all you did. We both really appreciate everything you and Adara did for us and the wedding. So where are you off to? The Riviera? The Orient?"

He shrugged. "I don't know."

"You don't know? I know you like to be spontaneous, but don't you need a destination before you get on your jet?"

"I'll figure something out." There was no place he wanted to go. That had never happened to him before. He wasn't even excited about purchasing the tech company in Paris anymore. He just knew he couldn't stay here, not after learning that Adara didn't want a future with him. "I won't be back for a while."

"What happened with you and Adara? I thought you two were getting along really well."

Krystof blew out a breath as he leaned back against the door-jamb. "I thought so, too. And then when I told her that I was planning to stick around the Ludus so we could figure things out, she told me to leave."

"How did you tell her?"

"Tell her what? That I'm leaving?"

"No. How did you tell her that you love her? Did you include flowers and champagne?"

"What? No. I didn't do any of that."

Atlas waved him in the living room, where he went to the bar and poured them each some scotch. "Here." He held out the glass. "Take this. I think you're going to need it."

Krystof took the glass and took a healthy sip. "I don't know what to do."

"You need to tell Adara how you feel about her."

"Even though she already told me that we're over?"

"What do you have to lose? I don't know too many women who are willing to put up with your idiosyncrasies, but Adara has stuck it out this long without you stating your feelings for her. Maybe she's tired of waiting around. Maybe she thinks you don't love her."

"But I do." It struck him how easy it was to make that confession.

"Good. Tell her that. Don't hold back anything. And one more thing—when you tell her, don't forget the flowers."

"But will any of that sway her?"

Atlas looked at him pointedly. "Do you really love her? Are you willing to change for her?"

Krystof had been giving this a lot of thought. In fact, it's all he'd thought about last night. "Yes. Yes, to it all."

"Then why are you standing there wasting time telling me? You need to go tell Adara all of this before it's too late."

Krystof put down his glass. "I will."

"And by the way, she's at her apartment on the mainland."

"Thanks."

Krystof headed out the door. He wasn't good at romance. He had no experience at it. But he could do flowers. He would buy her all the flowers in the world if she would just give him another chance.

She had changed him. She made him want to stay in one place—to have a place to call home. He wanted someplace that could be their home.

CHAPTER TWENTY

HER HEART RACED.

Her stomach was twisted up in knots. And her thoughts were scattered.

Adara continued to pick out an outfit to wear when she talked to Krystof—if he was still on Ludus Island. For all she knew, he'd listened to her and left last night. And then she recalled Hermione mentioning he was still on the island that morning.

But would he hear her out? Would he give her a chance to apologize? She had no idea, and she couldn't blame him if he didn't want anything to do with her.

She chose a summer dress instead of her usual business attire. Instead of putting her hair up, she left it down. Instead of putting on all her makeup for a polished look, she applied foundation, powder, mascara and lip gloss. It was a very casual appearance. And though all this was a diversion from her usual routine, she looked in the mirror and approved.

Change was scary and unnerving, but she could do it. She could move beyond the routine that she'd found comfort in for so many years. She could be something else, or do something else. It was in that moment she knew—with or without Krystof, she was leaving Ludus Island and going on an adventure. She had no idea where she'd end up, but the fun would be in the journey.

She wanted Krystof to join her. Not because she couldn't do it on her own, but rather she wanted to share it with him because somewhere along the way he'd become her best friend. He was the person she confided in, the person who inspired her to be more than she was now. And, most of all, she loved him.

She went to put on her high heels but then reconsidered. She dug a pair of beautiful sandals out of the back of her closet. She'd bought them on a whim and never found the right time to wear them because they didn't go with her business attire. But now was the right time. She slipped them on. They were so comfortable and looked adorable.

She searched the closet for a matching purse, because she liked things to be organized and matching. But she decided that not everything had to be perfect. Sometimes things just had to be good enough. She was good enough as she was.

Knock-knock.

Was Hermione back? Had she forgotten something? On her way to the door, Adara glanced around the living room for something that looked out of place, but she didn't notice anything.

She swung the door open and was greeted with a sea of red roses. Her mouth gaped. She'd never seen so many flowers in an arrangement. There had to be hundreds of them.

And she was certain there was a person behind them, but she couldn't see their face. Was it possible it was Krystof? Her pulse raced. He'd never bought her flowers before. But if not him, who else could it be?

The flowers lowered, and there was Krystof. "These are for you."

She'd have taken them from him, but she wasn't sure she could hold so many flowers. When Krystof did something, he definitely went all in. But what did this mean?

She opened the door wide and backed out of the way. "Come in."

He stepped into the living room. "Adara, we need to talk."

"I was just coming to see you."

His eyes widened. "You were?"

She nodded. "I need to apologize for last night. I shouldn't have said those things to you and then walked out."

He went to approach her, but the flowers stopped him.

"Why don't you put those on the table?" She gestured to the small table in her kitchen.

He did as she asked. They took up the entire table. And then he returned to her. "I'm sorry, too. I pushed last night when I should have let you take all of this at your pace. I should have told you that I'd be there for you, no matter how long it took for you to make sense of your diagnosis."

Her gaze met and held his. "You'd really wait for me?"

He stepped closer and took her hands in his. "My life hasn't been the same since you danced into my heart on Valentine's Day. I thought I could ignore what was happening between us. I thought it would just flame out, but none of that has happened. Adara, I love you and I want a future with you—no matter what the future looks like or where it is."

Tears of joy stung the backs of her eyes. "But I can't even give you the family you deserve."

He gently cupped her face. "That would never change my feelings for you. I love you."

"I love you, too." She lifted up on her tiptoes and pressed her lips to his. Her heart filled with love for him. The warmth spread throughout her body.

And before she was ready, he pulled back. His gaze once more met hers. "Stop worrying about everything. I don't even know if I want a family."

"But you might someday, and I don't want to take that opportunity away from you."

"If we did choose to have a family, I would love to adopt. I was an orphan, and I would like to bring a child into our hearts and share a happy, loving home with them."

Adara hadn't even considered that option. She was so caught

off guard that he had given this some thought. The idea most definitely appealed to her. "I would like that, too. But there's one more thing…"

"What's that?"

"We have to have someplace to call home—someplace we can return to after an adventure. A place to keep all our treasures."

He pressed his hand to his heart. "This is where I keep the greatest treasure—your love."

Her heart swooned as their lips met. Her life would never be boring again, and she didn't mind that at all. As long as Krystof was by her side, she would always be at home.

EPILOGUE

New Year's Eve, Paris, France

IT WAS ALMOST midnight.

Adara sat at the ornate desk in the corner of their spacious living room awaiting Krystof's arrival. The mail was stacked neatly in the center of the desk with a cream-colored envelope from the royal palace of Rydiania on top. Her chest fluttered with anticipation. She knew someone who was royal.

She reached for the silver letter opener. Excitement coursed through her veins. It easily slipped beneath the sealed flap and gently sliced it open. She pulled out the invitation.

She couldn't believe she—well, they'd both, been invited to the palace to witness their friends, Indigo and Prince Istvan, be married. Adara expelled a dreamy sigh. She was so happy that Indigo had found her very own Prince Charming.

And she wasn't alone. Hermione was now happily married. And even Adara had found her own true love. How had they all gotten so lucky?

Since Hermione and Atlas's wedding, there had been a lot of changes. Adara had quit her job at the Ludus Resort. The decision had weighed on her, but if she was going to take chances, most especially with her heart, she also had to take chances with her career. She had to reach for her dreams. Giving up all she'd known, from her comfy apartment to her longtime job, was the scariest thing she'd ever done.

But now she resided in Paris, one of the most beautiful cities in the world. And she'd launched her very own business. She was now an official event planner with her own staff. She planned special events, from conferences to weddings, and the world was her stage. She'd traveled all over the world to some of the most glamorous locations.

Best of all, they'd been able to find a way to make both herself and Krystof happy. She could still have a career that fulfilled her, and Krystof didn't have to curtail his wanderlust, as he traveled with her when his work schedule allowed. And in the end, they had a place to call home—this spacious five-bedroom Paris apartment that was situated along the world's most beautiful avenue, the Champs-Élysées.

Adara had taken great pains to take both of their tastes into consideration when she'd decorated it. There was a touch of classic flair mixed with some modern touches. It had been a tough balancing act, but she'd learned that some of the best things in life were worth the extra effort.

And they'd even brought a bit of Ludus Island to their home. Over the fireplace hung a portrait of the twin falls that Krystof had commissioned Indigo to paint. It had turned out perfectly and was a constant reminder of the magical day they'd spent there.

Their life had settled into a comfortable routine of new adventures. Krystof had bought the tech company he'd been eyeing and merged it with his MyPost social media app. The company was taking off with him at the helm, and best of all Krystof enjoyed the new challenges it presented him.

Speaking of Krystof, the apartment door opened and he stepped inside.

"And how was your day?" He crossed the foyer into the living room.

"It was really good. And you're really late. Problems with your meeting?"

"Actually it was just the opposite. We're expanding, and negotiations ran long."

"That's awesome." She smiled at him. "You're really happy, aren't you?"

He slipped off his coat and laid it over the back of a white couch. "I definitely am, with you in my life."

Her heart skipped a beat. "I was beginning to think I'd have to usher in the new year alone."

"The plane got grounded for a bit in Rome due to bad weather. But I would never let you celebrate alone."

She held up the opened envelope with a royal seal on the back. "Look what we got."

"What's that?"

"An invitation to the royal wedding." She beamed. "Isn't it so exciting? We're going to the palace for a royal wedding."

"It's not as exciting as this." He walked over and placed a leisurely kiss on the nape of her neck. A throbbing sensation spread throughout her body. "I've missed you."

"You were only gone overnight."

"It was still too long."

She reached up and caressed his cheek. "Have I told you lately how much I love you?"

"No." He sent her a serious look as he straightened. "You haven't."

She got to her feet. "Are you sure I haven't?"

"Very sure. The last time you told me was on the phone this afternoon. And that was so long ago." He pursed his lips in a pout.

"My apologies. I love you from the bottom of my heart. Am I forgiven?"

"I suppose. Don't let it happen again."

"I won't. Did you get something to eat?"

"They fed me well on the jet." He glanced down at her work clothes. "I thought you'd be ready for bed by now."

"And miss the fireworks? Not a chance."

Krystof checked the time on his Rolex. "It's almost midnight."

"Let's go out on the balcony."

"I'm right behind you."

As they made it to the railing, they could hear the jubilant voices from the street below.

"Ten—nine—eight—"

She gazed up at her husband. *Her husband.* It sounded so nice.

"Seven—six—five—"

She was the luckiest lady in the world.

"Four—three—two—"

Her heart pounded with love—love she hadn't known was possible.

"One!"

"I love you," he said.

"I love you, too."

And then their lips met as the fireworks popped and sparkled overhead. This was going to be the best year ever.

* * * * *

Keep reading for an excerpt of
Just Give In...
by Kathleen O'Reilly.
Find it in the
All She Wants anthology,
out now!

1

EVERY FAMILY STARTED with a house, a mother, a father and a passel of squabbling siblings. Brooke Hart had no father, two unsociable brothers who seemed deathly afraid of her and a 1987 Chevy Impala.

As far as families went, it wasn't much, but it was a thousand times better than before. Then there was the mysterious message from an estate lawyer in Tin Cup. They needed to "talk" was all that he said, and apparently lawyers in Texas didn't believe in answering machines and voicemail, because every time she tried to call, no one answered. In her head she had created all sorts of exciting possibilities, and journeyed cross country to see the lawyer, bond with her brothers and find a place to call home, all of which was exciting and expensive, which meant that right now, she was in desperate need of a job. Money was not as necessary as say, love, home and a fat, fluffy cat, but there were times when money was required. One, when you needed to eat, and two, when your three-year-old Shearling boots weren't cutting it anymore.

In New York, the boots had been cute and ordinary and seventy-five percent off at a thrift store. In the smoldering September heat of Texas, she looked like a freak. An au courant freak, but a freak nonetheless.

As she peered into the grocery store window, she studied

an older couple who were the stuff of her dreams. In Brooke Hart's completely sentimental opinion, the spry old codger behind the cash register could have been Every Grandpa Man. A woman shuffled back and forth between the front counter and the storeroom in back. Her cottony-gray hair was rolled up in a bun, just like in the movies. The cash register was a relic with clunky keys that Brooke's hands itched to touch. The wooden floor of the grocery was neat, but not neat enough, which was the prime reason she was currently here.

They looked warm, hospitable and in desperate need of young, able-bodied assistance.

The one advantage to living with Brooke's mother, Charlene Hart, was that Brooke knew the three things to absolutely never do when searching for a job.

One. Do not show up drunk, or even a more socially acceptable tipsy. Future employers frowned on blowing .2 in a Breathalyzer.

Two. Do not show up late for an appointment. As Brooke had no appointment, this wasn't a problem.

And the last, but most important rule in job-hunting was to actually show up. Although Brooke believed that deep down her mother was a beautiful spirit with a generous nature and a joyous laugh, Charlene Hart was about as present in life as she was in death, which was to say, not a lot.

Frankly, being family-less sucked, which was why she had been so excited to track down her two brothers. Twenty-six years ago, a then-pregnant Charlene Hart had walked out on Frank Hart and their two young sons, Tyler and Austen. Seven months later, Brooke had been born in a homeless shelter in Oak Brook, Illinois. Charlene never spoke of Frank, or her sons. Charlene had rarely spoken of anything grounded in reality, and it wasn't until after she died that Brooke found an article about Tyler Hart on the internet. After feeling so alone for all her life, she had stared at the picture of her brother, with the same faraway look in his dark eyes, and the world felt a little less gray.

She knew then. Over and over she had repeated her brother's name, and Brooke realized she wasn't family-less after all.

To better appeal to her brothers, she'd concocted the perfect life. Storybook mother, devoted stepfather, idyllic suburban residence, and a rented fiancée (two hundred bucks an hour, not cheap). But her brothers had clearly never read the Handbook on Quality Family Reunions, and although they'd been polite enough, their shields were up the entire time. If they found out the truth of Brooke's less than storybook existence? A disaster of cataclysmic proportions. Relatives never reacted well when poor relations with no place to call home showed up on their doorstep. They weren't inclined to "like you" or "respect you" or even "want to be around you." Oh, certainly, they might act polite and sympathetic, but homelessness was a definite black mark, so right now, she wasn't going to let them find out.

And then, when the time was right, Brooke would spring the truth on the boys, and work her way into her new family's good graces.

Her first step involved getting a job, paying her way, shouldering her own financial burdens. Second, find out what the lawyer wanted.

Slowly she sucked in a breath, bunching her sweater to hide the green patch beneath the right elbow. In New York, the mismatched patch looked artsy, chic-chic, but to two elderly citizens, it might seem—frivolous. Finally satisfied that she looked respectable, Brooke walked through the rickety screen door, catching it before it slammed shut.

The friendly old proprietor gave her a small-town-America smile, and Brooke responded in kind.

"I'm here about the job. I think I'm your girl. I'm energetic, motivated. I have an excellent memory, and my math skills are off the charts."

The man's jovial mouth dwindled. "We didn't advertise for help."

"Maybe not, but when opportunity knocks, I say, open the door and use a doorstop so that it can't close behind you."

Behind her, she heard the door creak open, as if the very fates were on her side. Her spirits rose because she knew that this small grocery story in Tin Cup, Texas, was fate. Emboldened, Brooke pressed on. "When I saw this adorable place, I knew it was my perfect opportunity. Why don't you give me a try?"

The old man yelled to the back: "Gladys! Did you advertise for help? I told you not to do that. I can handle the store." Then he turned his attention to Brooke. "She thinks I can't do a gall-darned thing anymore."

From behind her, an arm reached around, plunking a can of peas on the wooden counter. The proprietor glanced at the peas, avoided Brooke's eyes, and she knew the door of opportunity was slamming on her posterior. She could feel it.

Hastily she placed her own competent hand on the counter. "My brothers will vouch for me. Austen and Tyler. I'm one of the Harts," she announced. It was a line she had clung to like a good luck charm.

At the man's confused look, she chuckled at her own mis-step, hoping he wouldn't notice the shakiness in her voice. "Dr. Tyler Hart and Austen Hart. They were raised here. I believe Austen is now a very respectable member of the community. Tyler is a world-famous surgeon."

She liked knowing her oldest brother was in the medical profession. Everybody loved doctors.

The man scratched at the stubble on his cheek. "Wasn't that older boy locked up for cooking meth?"

Patiently Brooke shook her head. If the man messed up this often, she would be a boon to his establishment. "No, you must have him confused with someone else."

A discreet cough sounded from behind her, and once again the proprietor yelled to the back. "Gladys! Which one of the Hart boys ended up at the State Pen?"

Astounding. The man seemed intent on sullying her family's good reputation. Brooke rushed to correct him, but then Gladys appeared with four cartons of eggs stacked in her arms. "There's no need to yell, Henry. I'm not deaf," she said, and then gave Brooke a neighborly smile. "He thinks I'm ready to be put out to pasture." She noticed the can of peas. "This yours?"

"It's mine," interrupted the customer behind her.

Not wanting to seem pushy, Brooke smiled apologetically. Gladys placed the eggs on the counter and then peered at Brooke over silver spectacles. "What are you here for?"

"The job," Brooke announced.

"We don't need any help," Gladys replied, patting Brooke on the cheek like any grandmother would. Her hands were wrinkled, yet still soft and smelled of vanilla. "Are you looking for work?" she asked. Soft hands, soft heart.

Recognizing this was her chance, Brooke licked dry lips and then broke into her speech. "I'm Brooke Hart. I'm new in town. I don't want to be an imposition on my family. Not a free-loader. Not me. Everybody needs to carry their own weight, and by the way, I can carry a good bit of weight." She patted her own capable biceps. "Whatever you need. Flour. Produce. Milk. And I'm very careful on eggs. People never seem to respect the more fragile merchandise, don't you think?"

Gladys looked her over, the warm eyes cooling. "You look a little thin. You should be eating better."

The hand behind her shoved the peas forward, sliding the eggs close to the edge. Smartly, Brooke moved the carton out of harms way.

"I plan to eat better. It's priority number two on my list—right after I find a job. I'm really excited to be here in Tin Cup, and I want to fit in. I want to help out. Perhaps we could try something on a temporary basis." She flashed her best "I'm your girl" smile. "You won't regret it."

"You're one of the Harts?" asked the old man, still seeming confused.

"Didn't think there was a girl. Old Frank hated girls." From the look on Gladys's face, Gladys was no fan of Frank Hart, either.

"I never actually met my father," Brooke explained, not wanting people to believe she was cut from the same rapscallion cloth. "My mother and I moved when I was in utero."

"Smartest thing she ever did, leaving the rest of them," said Henry.

Brooke blinked, not exactly following all this, but she needed a job, and she sensed that Mr. Green Peas was getting impatient. "I really need a job. My brother Austen will vouch for me."

Gladys's gray brows rose to an astounding height. "Nothing but trouble, that one. Stole from Zeke..." Then she sighed. "He's doing good things now, with the railroad and all, but I don't know."

"That was a long time ago." Henry chimed in, apparently more forgiving.

"It's getting even longer," complained the man behind her.

Gladys shook her kindly head. "We're not looking to hire anybody, and you being a stranger and all. No references, except for your brother..."

"I'm new in town," Brooke repeated in a small voice, feeling the door of opportunity about to hit her in both her posterior and her face, as well. Doors of opportunity could sometimes be painful.

"I'll vouch for her."

At first, Brooke was sure she had misheard. It had happened before. But no, not this time. Brooke turned, profoundly grateful that the goodness of small-town America was not overrated. She'd lived in Atlantic City, Detroit, Chicago, Indianapolis and six freezing weeks in St. Paul. She'd dreamed of a little town with bakeries and cobblestone streets and hand-painted signs and people who smiled at you when you walked past. She'd prayed for a little town, and finally she was about to live in one. "Thank you," she told the man behind her.

He was tall, in his mid-thirties, with chestnut brown hair badly in need of a cut. There wasn't a lot of small-town goodness emanating from the rigid lines of his face. A black patch covered his left eye and he had a thin scar along his left cheek. In fact, he looked anything but friendly, but Brooke didn't believe in judging a book by its cover, so her smile was genuine and warm.

"You know her, Captain?" Gladys asked.

Mr. Green Peas nodded curtly. "It seems like forever."

"It's about time you're making some friends in town. We were worried when you moved out to the old farmstead, not knowing a soul in town and all. I'll tell Sonya, she'll be happy to hear that."

Not sure who Sonya was, but sensing that Captain's opinion counted with these two, Brooke faced the couple. "Please, give me a job," she urged. "You won't regret it."

From somewhere in the tiny grocery, Brooke could hear a relentless pounding. A rapid-fire thump that seemed oddly out of place in the sleepy locale.

Thumpa-thumpa-thumpa.

Gladys and Henry didn't hear the loud noise.

No one did.

Because, duh, it was her own heart.

She told herself it didn't matter if she didn't land this job with this homespun couple. It didn't matter if her brothers didn't welcome her with open arms. It didn't matter if the lawyer had made a mistake.

She told herself that none of it mattered.

All her life Brooke had told herself that none of it mattered, but it always did.

Her hands grasped the counter, locking on the small tin can. "What do you say?"

Gladys patted her cheek for a second time. Soft, warm... and sorrowful.

"I'm sorry, honey. We just can't."

As rejections went, it was very pleasant, but Brooke's heart still crawled somewhere below the floor. They had been so friendly, the store was so cute with its handpainted Hinkle's Grocery sign over the door. She'd been so sure. Realizing that there was nothing left for her in this place, Brooke walked out the door, opportunity slamming her in the butt.

Her first day in Tin Cup. No job, no lawyer, an uneasy brother who didn't know she was here, and—she glanced down at the can of peas still stuck in her hand—she'd just shoplifted a can of peas. Brooke fished in her jeans pocket for some cash, brought out two crumbled dollars, an old Metro Card and a lint-covered peppermint—slightly used.

Two dollars. It was her last two dollars, until she found a job, of course. All she had to do was go back inside, slap the money on the counter and leave as if she didn't care. As if they hadn't shouted down her best "Pick me!" plea.

Brooke turned away from the store with its cute homespun sign and restashed her money. Better to be branded a thief than a reject. It wasn't the most honorable decision, but Brooke had more pride than many would expect from a homeless woman that lived out of her car.

Once she was gainfully employed, she'd pay back Gladys and Henry. They'd understand.

And was that really, truly how she wanted to kick off her new life in her new home? As some light-fingered Lulu, which apparently all the Harts were supposed to be, anyway?

After taking another peek through the window, she sighed. No, she wasn't going to be a light-fingered Lulu, no matter how tempting it might be. And especially not for a can of peas.

In the distance a freckle-faced little girl on a skateboard careened down the sidewalk. Eagerly, Brooke waved her down, hoping to recruit an unwitting accomplice so that Brooke Hart wouldn't be another unflattering mug shot on the Post Office wall.

"Hello," she said, when the little girl skidded to a stop and then Brooke held out her hand. "Can you give this to Gladys? Tell her it's for the peas."

The girl examined the proffered money, then Brooke, innocent eyes alight with purpose. "You going to tip me for the delivery?"

Yes, the entrepreneurial spirit was strong in this one. Who knew that honesty was such a huge pain in the butt? And expensive, too. After jamming her hand in her pocket, Brooke pulled out her last seventeen cents. Reluctantly, she handed it to the kid, who stood there, apparently expecting more.

"Please?" asked Brooke, still wearing her non-stranger-danger smile. At last, the little girl sighed.

"Whatever," she said and kicked a foot at the end of the skateboard, flipping it up into her hand.

"That's pretty cool," Brooke told her, and the girl rolled her eyes, but her mouth curled up a bit and Brooke knew that she'd made her first friend in Tin Cup. Sure, she'd had to pay for the privilege, but still, a friend was a friend, no matter how pricey, no matter how small.

"Whatever," the girl repeated, then pulled open the screen door.

Now that Brooke's fledging reputation was somewhat restored, or about to be, her job here was done. She dashed across the street, leaping into her eyesore of a car before anyone could see. She had big plans before she showed up on Austen's doorstep, and it wasn't going to be without a job, without any money and in a car that should be condemned.

Once safely behind the wheel, she tossed the can of peas onto the backseat, the afternoon sun winking happily on the metal. It fit right in with the hodge-podge of things. A portable cooler, one beat-up gym bag, her collection of real estate magazines, the plastic water jug and now peas.

Peas.

What the heck was she supposed to do with peas?

Don't miss this brand new series by
New York Times bestselling author Lauren Dane!

THE CHASE BROTHERS

Ridiculously hot and notoriously single

One small town.
Four hot brothers.
And enough heat to burn up
anyone who dares to get close.

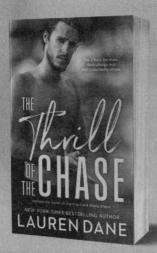 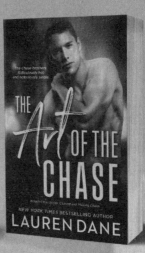

Includes the first two stories
Giving Chase and *Taking Chase*.

Available September 2024.

Includes the next stories
Chased and *Making Chase*.

Available December 2024.

MILLS & BOON

millsandboon.com.au